BAMBOO ROAD

ANN BENNETT

monsoon

monsoonbooks

First published in 2017
by Monsoon Books

No.1 Duke of Windsor Suite, Burrough Court,
Burrough on the Hill, Leics. LE14 2QS, UK
www.monsoonbooks.co.uk

First edition.

ISBN (paperback): 978-981-4625-25-8
ISBN (ebook): 978-981-4625-26-5

Cover design by Cover Kitchen.

MIX
Paper from
responsible sources
FSC® C018072

Printed in Great Britain by Clays Ltd, St Ives plc
19 18 17   1 2 3

For Nick

1

First light in Bangkok. Sirinya stands beside a small suitcase on the platform at Thonburi station, a little way apart from the crowd. She is waiting for the early train. The city is already awake. She can feel its heartbeat, sense its raw energy. The air is filled with the shrill blasts of horns and the hum of a million engines. In the distance, through the shimmering pollution haze, she sees the glow of lights from traffic crawling along a flyover.

She shifts in the heat. Despite the hour, sweat is already running down the inside of her blouse. Twenty-five years in a cold country and she has almost forgotten the sultry climate of her homeland. But now, as the hot air wraps itself around her in a clammy embrace, she remembers, and it feels as natural as breathing. It's as if she's never been away.

Her heart beats a little faster as the old blue and white diesel train creaks into the station. She has never travelled on this railway before, but the horror of its construction still scars her mind. As the train grinds and squeaks to a halt beside the low platform, an image comes to her. A half-dug cutting, deep in the hills, glimpsed between the teak trees from a jungle trail. She remembers how she paused, clutching the tree trunk, astonished to see half-naked white men labouring there. Most of them so thin they were little more than skeletons. In the full glare of the noonday sun they worked with hammers, pickaxes and shovels, chipping away at the granite, passing the waste in bamboo baskets down a line of waiting men, to be tipped over the edge of the precipice by the last man. It was a scene of constant movement as men lifted hammers above their heads, slamming them down on metal spikes, repeating the process again and again. Japanese guards strutted about yelling at the workers, prodding them with sticks, lashing out at them with lengths of bamboo. She had stood there staring, aghast, waves of shock passing through her, but she'd quickly turned and gone on her way, afraid that the guards would notice her. Years later she can still hear those sounds. The ringing of metal on rock, the chipping and the hammering, the brutal shouts of the guards.

Sirinya shudders and passes a hand over her face now, trying to suppress the memory. She follows the other passengers up the wooden steps and into the stifling carriage. A man turns and helps her up with her luggage. She smiles and thanks him in Thai.

'Kop khun kha.'

Speaking her mother tongue feels strange after all these years, but it is already coming back to her. She knows it's always been there, lying dormant like an old engine, rusting and forgotten in a shed. With a little polish it will soon be in perfect working order again.

She heaves her suitcase onto the luggage rack and settles herself on a wooden bench beside the window. The carriage fills up quickly with passengers and their baggage. Then, with a great blast of the horn the train creeps out of the station and starts on its ponderous journey through the western suburbs of the city. Sirinya stares out of the window as they rattle through neighbourhoods of rickety wooden houses, nestled amongst dense vegetation. People preparing breakfast on their verandas look up as the train passes. It rumbles over canals where houses are built on stilts over the water, past golden temples where saffron-clad monks parade in single file for their morning alms. Her heart lifts as she glimpses a giant statue of the Buddha in meditation pose. How long it has been since she went to the temple, lit a candle and knelt before the Buddha, felt the peace and serenity that her faith used to bring.

How different this is, she thinks, from the English countryside where she made her home, with its neat houses and neat people, the muted greens and browns of the landscape. She will not miss it, she knows that much. No matter how long she lived there, she would never feel accepted, would always be an outsider.

The man who'd helped her has sat down beside her. He is middle aged, like herself. He looks educated, smart, dressed in a white cotton shirt and black trousers. The train rattles over another bridge and the canal below is framed momentarily like a still photograph. Below, a group of naked children dive off a floating platform into the murky water.

'It reminds me of my own childhood,' says the man, catching her eye as she smiles at the scene.

'Oh yes, me too ...'

'Are you going all the way to Nam Tok?' he asks.

'No. I'm getting off at Kanchanaburi. What about you?'

'I'm going all the way. Visiting my mother. I go every month.'

She nods and smiles, but doesn't reply.

'Is Kanchanaburi your home?' he asks after a pause.

'It used to be. I was born there. Lived there until I was about twenty.'

'Where do you live now?'

She hesitates. That is a good question. She is returning, but she doesn't yet have a place she can call home. She shrugs.

'I'm not sure yet. I've been away for many years. Living abroad.'

He raises his eyebrows. 'Really? Whereabouts?'

'England. My husband was English. He died a few months ago. After the funeral there was no reason for me to stay.'

'Oh, I'm so sorry,' says the man.

He seems kind and well meaning, but Sirinya is in no mood to talk. She just wants to think, to plan, to brood. She turns and stares out of the window as the train begins to gather speed, flashing past banana groves, patches of untamed jungle, and out into open country. Here, emerald rice paddies stretch far into the distance, dotted with the odd coconut palm. Groups of workers in cone-shaped hats, knee-deep in water, bend to their timeless task. It is all so familiar. The years seem to melt away.

In a couple of hours she will be back there. Back in the place where it all happened; the place that has not been out of her thoughts through all these years of exile. And as she has done a million times, she visualises returning to the familiar street, walking past the house where the Kempeitai had their headquarters during the war. She wonders if the building will still be there, and what it might be used for now. Will it be just another hardware shop again, peddling its dusty wares as if nothing extraordinary has ever happened there? Will she be able to walk past it without breaking down, despite the passage of time? She knows she can do it. She is strong. She will steel herself, hold her head high and walk past that house.

But it is a house further down the same street that she needs to visit first. She has promised herself she will go there before even stopping at her uncle's shophouse, where she knows her cousin will be waiting. She imagines, as she has countless times over the years, knocking on the shabby front door, waiting breathlessly on the step for it to open. Will Ratana still be there? What will the years have done to her? Will she still powder her face and make up her eyes heavily like in the old days? Will her glossy black hair be streaked with grey now, like Sirinya's own?

She shivers, despite the heat, and closes her eyes.

'Are you alright?' her companion's voice breaks through her thoughts. 'You look a little pale.'

'I'm fine, thank you. Just rather tired.'

She turns away and stares out of the window again, not wanting to encourage conversation.

* * *

She remembers the day that everything changed; for her and for everyone else in the sleepy, harmonious little community of Kanchanaburi. It was the day that their peaceful existence came to an abrupt end, when the Japanese occupation of Thailand became more than just headlines in the local newspaper.

She recalls it as clearly as if it were yesterday. She and her cousin, Malee, were wandering beside the river; the broad, fast-flowing Mae Nam Khwae. They had grown up on its banks and had never been far from the gentle sound of its voice. It was the lifeblood of the town.

She can still feel the fierce temperature of that afternoon back in 1942. The sun was high in the sky, the air quivering in the intense heat. She knew the monsoon would soon break, and until then any physical activity, virtually any movement at all, was strength-sapping. The two girls had been helping out since early morning in Malee's father's shop. For the past few days at the end of their shift, they had got into the habit of coming down to the river to relax and to wash the sweat and exhaustion of the day from their bodies.

This stretch of land, on the far side of the river from the town, was owned by Malee's father. It was a long walk upriver from the centre of town to the crossing at Ta Mah Kham, where a boatman ferried them across for a few ticals. They had then walked back downriver, down the Bamboo Road, the dirt track that only the locals knew about, which wound along the riverbank, through towering thickets of bamboo, to reach the patch of grassy land where they knew they would be able to bathe in peace. A few buffalo lazed around, dozing in the heat, dried mud encrusting on their bodies, only moving to twitch the flies away with their tails.

The two girls stopped at a little outcrop of rocks on the riverbank and stripped down to their underwear. Then, leaving their towels and clothes on the rocks, they waded into the shallow water. The pebbles were uneven and slippery underfoot, but they were soon in up to their waists. They stooped to swim. Both gasped and shrieked at the shock of the cold water as they dipped their shoulders under the surface, but once they were in it felt deliciously cool and refreshing. They were both strong swimmers and raced each other up to the place where their favourite casuarina tree leaned out over the water and back again. Then they lay floating on their backs, contemplating the clear blue sky.

When they had cooled off and their skin was beginning to soften and wrinkle, they got out of the water, spread their towels on the grass and lay down, allowing the sun to burn off the droplets of water.

'That was wonderful,' said Malee. 'What would we do without the river in the hot season?'

'It's a lifesaver,' agreed Sirinya.

They lay in companionable silence for a while, staring up at the sky through the motionless branches of a pine tree. Sirinya closed her eyes and dozed, the light behind her eyelids burning red.

'Oh, by the way, I saw Narong yesterday,' said Malee suddenly.

'He was asking after you.'

Sirinya snapped open her eyes and shifted impatiently. She loved Malee, but wondered why her cousin could not leave this particular subject alone. She turned away.

'Aren't you interested?' said Malee, when Sirinya didn't reply.

'You know I'm not. How many times do I have to tell you that?'

'Oh, I know you are really. How could you not be? Every girl in town's a little bit in love with him.'

'Including you?'

'No, not me. Of course not, silly. I only have eyes for Somsak. You know that. But Narong really likes you, Siri. You're being very cruel to him.'

'I don't trust him, Malee. It's as simple as that. He's too smooth, too sure of himself. I'm sure you know what I mean.'

'I think you should give him a chance. Let him take you out at least. What harm could it do?'

'I don't need a man. I like to be independent.'

Malee laughed. 'You will need a man one day. How will you support yourself otherwise?'

'Don't be ridiculous …' Sirinya began, turning back to face her cousin, but then she noticed that Malee's expression had changed. There was sudden fear in her cousin's eyes and her mouth had dropped open. She was staring across the stretch of scrubby grassland towards the gate at the far end of the meadow. Sirinya followed her gaze. Four soldiers dressed in khaki uniform and helmets were marching towards them. Sirinya's heart started beating fast. Her mouth went dry with shock.

She stared at the men, confused. At first she thought they were Thai, but she had never seen a Thai soldier in modern-day khaki uniform. The only ones she had ever seen had been taking part in ceremonial parades at the Grand Palace in Bangkok, dressed in elaborate traditional battledress. Within a few seconds the truth had dawned on her. She remembered the grainy newsreel she had seen at the local cinema a few weeks before. The flickering film had shown Japanese soldiers carrying weapons, advancing stealthily through the jungles and rubber plantations of Malaya. They'd been shown swarming on bicycles down jungle tracks, driving tanks down narrow roads between tall trees, or manning machine guns from behind banks of earth. She recognised the uniforms from that film. They were Japanese soldiers.

She knew about the Japanese pact with the Thai government, how the Japanese had been allowed to enter the country, but she had never seen a Japanese soldier in the flesh before. She knew they were in the south of the country, that Malaya and Singapore had been occupied since February, but she had no idea that they were in this area. What could they possibly want with this little backwater?

There was no time to wonder. Remembering that she was only wearing underwear, she grabbed her clothes and pulled her blouse over her head in a flash, wrapped her sarong style skirt around her waist. Malee was doing the same. To Sirinya's relief, the soldiers were no longer moving towards them. They had stopped a few yards away and seemed to be conferring together. One of them produced what looked like a map from his pack, and the four of them were studying it, pointing at it, gesticulating, deep in discussion.

Sirinya's heart had stopped beating quite so fast.

'Whatever do they want?' Malee whispered.

Sirinya could see from the way Malee bit her lip and was taking quick, shallow breaths that her cousin was afraid. Sirinya was afraid too, but there was also another emotion in her heart struggling against the fear, which was even more powerful. It was anger. Anger fuelled by outrage.

'I've no idea, but I'm going to ask them,' she said. 'This is private land. They can't just barge in here as if they own the place.'

'Siri, be careful … they've got guns,' hissed Malee, but Sirinya was already striding towards the group of soldiers.

They stopped talking and lifted their heads from the map to stare as she approached them.

'What are you doing here?' she demanded.

One of them stepped forward. He stared straight at her. His face was covered in fine sweat. His expression was stern.

'You must leave at once,' he said. 'You go now,' he said pointing towards the gate behind him. His Thai was very poor and heavily accented, but Sirinya could just about make out what he was saying.

'This is private land. It belongs to our family,' she said, aware that her voice was shrill with nerves. Her heart was thumping hard again. She knew she was right to challenge the soldiers, but she couldn't help feeling it was a little foolhardy too. She noticed one of the men move his hands towards a rifle slung over his shoulder.

'Siri, please,' she heard her cousin say under her breath, but she would not be deflected.

'You go!' said the soldier, raising his voice, beginning to move towards the girls.

'Come on, Sirinya!' said Malee, stepping towards her and grabbing her arm. She felt Malee pushing her, trying to propel her forward. But Sirinya stood firm.

'Who own this land?' barked the soldier.

'My father,' said Malee, in a thin voice, addressing them for the first time, lifting her chin and staring the soldier straight in the eye.

'Where is he?'

Malee pursed her lips and carried on staring, remaining silent.

'We will find him anyway. But if you tell us it will save us trouble. Be quicker.'

'We're not telling you,' said Sirinya.

'You will tell us!'

The one next to the speaker suddenly drew his gun and pointed it straight at them. Despite her bravado Sirinya was shaking all over now. She could feel Malee's arm, trembling against her own.

The other two soldiers sprang forward and grabbed the two girls by their arms. Sirinya felt rough hands gripping her, the fingers digging into her flesh. She could smell the strange sweaty odour of the soldier's body and clothes, the tobacco and alcohol on his breath.

The soldier with the rifle came up close and thrust his gun forward, directly at Sirinya, pushing it into her forehead. The cold hard metal dug into her skull. She was beyond fear now. She could hardly breathe. Everything around her became a blur. She could not focus. She wanted to blurt out her uncle's address, but her mouth and throat were paralysed with terror.

'Leave her alone,' said Malee, her voice shaking. 'He lives on Saeng Chuto road in the centre of town. The vegetable shop. Halfway along. Now let us go!'

At a nod from the speaker, the gun was withdrawn. 'We need to see him about this land.'

'He won't talk to you,' said Sirinya.

'Oh, I think he will,' said the soldier with a smile that sent a chill down her spine.

2

With that the soldiers turned and walked quickly away, out through the scrubby bushes towards the gate at the far end of the field. The two girls stared at their retreating forms, stunned. Relief coursed through Sirinya. She thought her knees might give way. She heard the engine of a lorry choke into life, the roar of it revving up and then drawing away down the metalled road, which led towards the nearest river bridge at Tambon Lat Ya, a few kilometres north.

The girls clung to each other, sobbing, in a mixture of relief that the soldiers had gone, and shock at what had happened.

'I wonder what they want with Father. I wish there was a way of warning him,' said Malee.

'I know. If only we could get across the river. We could get into town more quickly. It's almost opposite here.'

'We could try swimming,' said Malee.

Sirinya stared out across the wide, fast-flowing water.

'We'd never make it. We'd get swept away. Remember that poor young boy last rainy season?'

Malee was silent for a moment, then she said, 'Perhaps they only want to talk to Father. They seem to be interested in the land. It would be good to warn him they are coming, though. Tell him what they are like.'

'Yes. We should let him know that they wouldn't hesitate to use their guns. Come on, let's get back as quickly as we can. We can take the Bamboo Road. They'll have to go the long way round. We'll probably beat them to it even if they do have a lorry.'

Sirinya still remembers that frantic run back along the old Bamboo Road beside the river. It seemed to take forever. On and on they ran, retracing their steps between interminable bamboo clumps, which leaned over the little track in places, barring their way, slapping against their faces as they passed. The tall bright green stems seemed to mock their progress, like sentinels. Sirinya's breath came in painful gasps. It was still unbearably hot even though the shadows were now lengthening and the sun was rapidly dipping behind the far-off hills. But she ran on, sweat pouring from her, pushing the bamboo aside, fighting the urge to stop and catch her breath, to rest her aching limbs.

'Come on, Siri,' Malee shouted over her shoulder, racing ahead. She had always been the fitter of the two.

At last the bamboo thinned out, giving way to scrubby grassland beside the river. They had finally reached Tha Maa Kham, where an aged boatman waited during daylight hours to ferry locals across. When they arrived at the crossing, he was on the other side, sitting on the bank, gossiping to a passing farmer, his little boat moored up beside him. Malee cupped her hands together and shouted. At first he didn't hear and carried on with his conversation. Sirinya joined in and they shouted together, bellowing at the tops of their voices. Eventually his companion noticed their shouts, and pointed to where the girls stood on the other bank. The old man shaded his eyes and peered across. Seeing them he waved and hurried into his little boat, casting off from the shore with an oar. It felt like an age before he reached them. They watched him row frantically, battling against the strong current with frail arms. Sirinya held her breath, willing him to make it.

Once they were safely aboard, the journey back to the other

side only took a few minutes. The boatman let the little boat drift downstream so he could drop them nearer the centre of town. The girls thanked him as they got out and handed him five ticals each. He thanked them with a toothless smile, putting his hands together to 'wai' and bowing deeply.

Dusk was fast approaching as they entered the main street where Malee's family shophouse was. Shopkeepers were closing up for the day, taking down stalls from the pavement, carrying goods inside. But still the food sellers worked on the pavement, preparing evening meals, frying in woks over flickering gas flames, the smell of lemongrass and galangal floating on the air. Exhausted now, the two girls half walked, half ran the final few yards. But as they drew closer, Sirinya stopped and grabbed Malee's arm.

'Look! They've got there already,' she said pointing. The army truck was parked directly outside the shophouse. The four soldiers were trooping towards the building, guns slung over their shoulders.

'I hope they won't harm Father,' said Malee, tears welling in her eyes.

'Don't worry. They have no reason to do that.'

'But you know what he's like,' said Malee, twisting her hands in anguish.

Sirinya bit her lip. She did know what he was like. Her uncle was stubborn, idealistic, a man of principles. Even though he was a humble shopkeeper he was also prominent in the local commune or tambon. He was known throughout the community for taking a strong stand against exploitation, corruption, or unfairness of any kind.

Sirinya and Malee approached the shophouse with trepidation. They walked past the empty lorry. Heat radiated from it as if from a stove, its metal chassis ticking as it cooled. A small crowd of onlookers had gathered to stand and wonder at it. Mechanical vehicles were still fairly rare in Kanchanaburi in 1942.

The shop was closed, the shutters down and the outside stalls empty. The girls let themselves in quietly through the front door. As soon as they entered they heard the sound of raised voices coming from the apartment above. They exchanged anguished glances, imagining how Chalong would be reacting to the bullying tactics of the Japanese officers, dreading that any moment they would hear a gunshot.

The door to the apartment opened at the top of the stairs and Malee's mother, Piak, appeared. She was clutching her sabai shawl close to her chest and her face was drawn with anxiety.

'Mother!' said Malee, rushing up the steps to her and throwing her arms around her. 'What's going on?'

'Japanese soldiers are here speaking to your father. They said something about wanting to buy the river meadow from him. Your father asked me to leave them to speak alone.'

'We were swimming down there earlier and the soldiers came into the field. We tried to get back to warn him they were coming.'

'They seem very aggressive,' whispered Piak, twisting her shawl. 'They have guns.'

She looked ashen-faced, her slender frame huddled with anxiety. How different she was from her own mother, Sirinya thought. Bold and stout and full of humour. It was sometimes difficult to imagine that they were sisters.

Malee took her mother's hand and the three of them went upstairs to the apartment above the shop. They stood outside the door of the living room and put their ears to the wooden panel. At first Sirinya could not make out what was being said. There was a lot of rapid conversation in Japanese, then she recognised the translator's stumbling Thai.

'We need that land. You will agree to our price, or things will get very bad for you.'

Chalong laughed. 'It's not the price I care about, can't you see that? I don't want to sell it to you at any price. You shouldn't be in this country at all. If our government had any backbone ...'

There was a shuffling of feet and scraping of chairs. Piak closed her eyes.

'You don't frighten me,' Chalong said. 'I don't want my land to be owned by a foreign power.'

'It is not for you to say! You don't have choice. If you don't sell land we will take it anyway. We come first to offer you money out of courtesy.'

'But why do you need it? What do you want with my land?'

'We need it to land supplies there from river, and build camp for prisoners.'

'Prisoners?'

'From Singapore. We have many British men, Australian, Dutch men in camps there. We bring them here.'

'Why on earth here?'

'They will work for us here. Build railway. Railway into Burma.'

Chalong laughed again. 'Now I *know* you're joking. That is impossible. It's dense jungle and a mountain range of limestone and granite all the way. People have talked about that before. Engineers have done surveys. But it will never happen. Nobody can work in that jungle either. It's full of malarial mosquitoes.'

'It is not impossible! Japanese engineers are the best in the world. They say it can be done. We have manpower. We have determination. It will be done by Imperial Japanese Army.'

There was another hasty conversation in Japanese and then the interpreter's voice cut in once again.

'Here is money. It is good price. We are fair to you. Sign this paper please and the land will be ours.'

'I told you before I don't want your money.'

'You will take, or we take you prisoner. You have no choice. Now please sign paper.'

There was a short silence. Sirinya exchanged anguished glances with Malee and Piak. They held their breath. Was Chalong signing the document?

'You *will* sign the paper. If you do not we take your wife and daughter to prison in Bangkok. They will suffer. We see your wife. She not look well. Prison conditions are harsh. It will not be good for them to be in Japanese prison. We *will* do this ... Now sign the paper.'

'You give me no choice. You ... you ...'

Then, after a pause. 'Thank you, Mr Chalong. Imperial Japanese Army very grateful to you. Now you not go on land any more. Land belong to great Imperial Japanese Army now.'

'Just go now, please. Get out of my house.'

'One more thing before we go. We see you have vegetable and rice store. Do you deal wholesale?'

'I don't see that it's any of your business,' came the muttered reply, 'but yes, I bring in vegetables and rice on the river for distribution.'

'I thought so. You could be very useful to us. When prisoners are brought here to work we will need supplies. We will be back to discuss.'

The three women exchanged anxious looks again. But then they heard movement in the room and footsteps behind the door. Before they had time to move away, the door flew open and the soldiers burst out and clattered down the stairs, pushing them aside. As soon as they had gone, Piak ran inside the room to her husband. Malee and Sirinya stood staring after the soldiers, not knowing what to do or say.

Chalong sat at the table in the centre of the room, his head in his hands. Piak stood behind him, her arms wrapped tightly around him. When the girls entered the room he turned and looked at them. On his face was an expression Sirinya had never seen before. His usual genial smile had vanished. He looked haggard and weary, defeated even. But there was something else in the way he dropped his gaze as they approached. She realised with shock that it was shame.

* * *

Sirinya stares out at the old familiar countryside as she remembers those days. Beyond the wide flat plane covered in rice paddies, the faint shape of blue hills begins to smudge the horizon. It is odd, she reflects, that those years are more vivid and more immediate to her than all the time she spent abroad. Coming back has brought them into sharp focus. Johnny, her husband, had known that would happen. How wise he had been. He had known her better than she knew herself.

'What will you do when I'm gone?' he'd asked her from his hospital bed during his last days. He had already suffered one heart attack and the doctors had warned that his heart was so weak it was quite possible he could have another one. Sirinya had spent those days by his bedside, hardly leaving the room, dozing in the chair beside the bed at night, doing her best to ensure he was as comfortable as possible during the day.

'Please don't talk like that, Johnny,' she'd said.

'I'm just being practical,' he said, with a weak smile. 'Just thinking of you, Siri.'

'Well, please don't,' she repeated, squeezing his hand, such a lump in her throat that she couldn't say more.

'You'll go home, won't you?'

'Home?' she asked, dropping her eyes to the floor.

'You know what I mean. To your real home. Back to your own country. What would there be to keep you here?'

'My home is here now,' she said lifting her eyes and looking at his face, drained of colour and drawn with pain.

'Only because of me. I know you've never really felt settled here although you've never once complained. You've been so wonderful to me, Siri. You've never shown it, but I know that deep down your heart has always been back there. Back there in the jungle, beside that great river. Back in the place you grew up.'

Her eyes filled with tears at the thought that this good, kind man who had given her so much and with whom she had shared more than half her life, might soon be taken from her.

'I know you've never truly loved me, Siri,' he held up his frail hand to stop her as she tried to protest. 'No, let me speak. I've got to say this. It didn't stop you from being the most caring, loyal and devoted wife I could ever have wished for. And far more than I deserve, I know that.'

'Please, Johnny. How can you say that? Of course I love you.'

'Oh, I'm not a fool. You love me like an old friend. We're comfortable together. But I know very well who you still hold a torch for. And I've always known I could never come close to that. But I've never really minded. Just having you with me through the years has been enough for me.'

'Oh, Johnny,' she couldn't say any more, she was so overwhelmed.

He had never spoken like that to her before. Not in all the twenty-five years they had been together. She realised that he was only saying these things now because he knew he was dying.

It was the last conversation they'd had. He had drifted off to sleep still holding her hand. She didn't like to move away or disturb him by taking her hand away, so she sat there beside him, watching the rise and fall of his chest as he slept, too uncomfortable to sleep herself. But she must have dozed off because a few hours later she awoke with a start, his grip on her hand had tightened and he was thrashing about on the bed, his face contorted with pain, his lips blue. The machines around him were all bleeping and buzzing at once. Sirinya pressed the bell and within seconds the bed was surrounded by white-coated medical staff, who brushed her aside in their haste to help him. But one nurse noticed her there, took her hand and guided her out of the room.

She sat in the echoing corridor, with its smells of disinfectant, on a hard plastic chair and waited, numb with shock, knowing that the frenzied efforts of the medics inside the room would not make any difference.

They'd been very kind, the doctors and nurses. Someone brought her a hot, strong cup of tea and, later, someone else called her a taxi. She could not cry, she felt so raw and empty. As soon as she got back to the cold, empty house that she and Johnny had shared throughout their married life, she knew that he'd been right and that she couldn't survive here without him. But it was not until she sat down alone at the kitchen table that the tears came. Tears of gratitude for his love and protection, tears of loss and tears of loneliness.

The train has stopped now at a tiny village station. She stares out at the platform, where locals wait patiently in the sunlight with boxes and bags, caged hens and baskets of vegetables to board the train. A hawker approaches the window. He has a tray hung from a rope around his neck, filled with cups made from thick green bamboo sticks.

'Shall I buy you a drink?' asks her neighbour. 'You look very hot.'

She turns and smiles at him again. He clearly hasn't taken the hint that she wants to be left alone with her own thoughts.

'Yes, please,' she says, relenting, 'that's very kind of you. It is hot in here.'

'The fans never work properly on these old trains,' he says. 'Would you like some sugarcane juice? I think that's what he's got in those makeshift cups.'

'Oh, yes, please. I haven't tasted that for so long.'

The man stands up and pulls down the window. After a brief but heated bargaining session with the hawker, he gives him a few coins and turns back into the carriage holding two short tubes of wide green bamboo. Sirinya takes one from him, puts it to her lips and drinks. The cloying, sugary taste takes her straight back to her childhood. It is the drink that her mother would buy for her from roadside stalls when they were on their way to see her grandmother in the village deep in the Tenasserim hills. The taste reminds her of the dust rising in clouds from the unmade roads, the sun beating down on them as they sat on the back of the songthaew, the open-backed vehicle which took them as far as the road would go, the slight feeling of nausea mounting in her stomach as the vehicle switched back and forth on the mountain bends.

'Do you have family in Kanchanaburi?' asks the man.

'Just my cousin now. The rest of them have passed away. My cousin is about my age. She runs a vegetable shop in the centre of town.'

'Have you kept in touch with her over the years?'

Sirinya shakes her head. 'Not really. We tried at first, but neither of us is a good letter writer. After a few years it was only on birthdays. We were close once though ... very close ...'

3

The train has filled up with passengers from the village. It is crowded now and most of them have to stand in the aisle. It pulls slowly out of the little station with more trumpeting of the horn. Sirinya thinks about her cousin. Why had Malee never thought about marrying after Somsak died? Why instead had she chosen to live the life of a spinster in the house where she had been born and grown up? She had devoted her life to caring for her ageing parents, carrying on the business after they had gone. What will she be like now? Will there be any trace left of the carefree, frivolous girl Malee had once been? Sirinya feels her nerves tingle with excitement at the thought of seeing her cousin again, but more at the anticipation of seeing Ratana once more. How will Ratana react when she opens her door and sees Sirinya standing there? Will she even remember the dreadful wrong she did her all those years ago? The thought of finally confronting Ratana, telling her that she has guessed the truth makes Sirinya's heart beat quickly, her stomach tighten. At last, after all these years of harbouring anger and hatred, there is an end in sight.

The train journey is almost over now. The hills, once a far-off blur on the horizon are now closer and she can make out the limestone rocks and thick jungle covering them. The train is running through the river valley. Sirinya's heart leaps as she glimpses the sun glinting on the Mae Nam Khwae for the first time for two and a half decades. There it runs, wide and majestic, just as it always did. She knows that it has always been part of her soul, and that being separated from it has made her somehow incomplete.

She stands up and smooths down her crumpled clothes. Before she can reach up to the rack to get her suitcase, her ever-vigilant companion is up on his feet and taking it down himself.

'Thank you,' she smiles.

'Well, good luck with your homecoming,' he says. 'I hope it goes well for you.'

'Have a nice stay with your mother,' she responds.

'If you ever need anything, or if you are ever in Bangkok and would like to meet, here is my card.'

He hands her a business card and she glances down at it. It is written in Thai script on one side and on the other side is what looks like Chinese characters.

'Kasem Suttichart, dealer and importer in fine gold and jewellery', followed by a telephone number and an address in Chinatown.

'That's kind. I'll keep it safe. Perhaps I'll need to come to Bangkok one day.'

She does not tell him that being in the city brings back such disturbing memories that she has no desire to spend any time there. She turns towards him and puts her hands together in a wai. He does the same, then she squeezes past the standing passengers to the door. The train is pulling into Kanchanaburi station.

She stands on the platform for a few moments gathering her composure, overwhelmed with a multitude of different thoughts and emotions now she has finally arrived. She is reluctant to make a move, so she watches as other passengers disgorge and disperse, by taxi, samlor, rickshaw or songthaew. The train looks a good deal emptier as it pulls out of the station. Kanchanaburi is the main stop on the line.

She turns and walks through the station entrance onto the

turning area outside. Almost all the vehicles have already gone, just one lone samlor rider waits there. He looks old and weak. Sirinya would like to walk, but it is not practical in the noonday heat with her suitcase.

'Could you drop me in Thanon Saeng Chuto, please. At the far end, near the temple?'

He names a price that she knows is more than she should pay, but she is tired and feels pity for the old man working in this heat, so she agrees without bothering to bargain. She settles herself on the seat of the samlor behind the driver and they set off. At first she doesn't recognise the place. The roads are wider, buildings spaced out in grassy grounds and surrounded by greenery. Many of the houses look newly built.

But when they turn off the main road and into the more densely built old town, she begins to get her bearings again. She recognises many of the old shophouses they pass, the food market, the taxi stand in the centre of the town. They turn into Saeng Chuto road and head towards the far end. Nothing much has changed here, although there is more traffic, more people about, the ugly neon signs above the shops are new. Her heart is beating fast as they approach the house where the Kempeitai had their headquarters during the war. It looks unremarkable, just like its neighbours. There is nothing to alert passers-by to the brutality meted out there during those three long years. She stares at it, trying to comprehend how the passage of time can disguise past events. It is now a hardware shop again, just as it was before the war. Just as she had guessed it would be.

The driver slows and turns to speak to her. 'You want end of the road?'

'Yes. If you drop me near the temple that will be fine,' she doesn't want him to wait. She will find a way of getting back to Malee's house. The samlor put-puts towards the end of the road. She waits, holding her breath. In a moment Ratana's house will come into view. Round the next bend.

'Stop just around the corner please.'

As they round the bend, she stares blankly. The house has disappeared. There is a gap between the buildings, and a piece of waste ground is all that is there, covered in scrubby grass and bamboo. A goat grazes tethered by a chain and a couple of soi dogs root around in the undergrowth.

'You want to get down, madam?'

'I was going to visit this house ... but it's gone,' she says, feeling stupid.

'Big fire there a few years ago. All the family died who lived there. Police never found out what happened.'

She swallows hard, aware that all the blood has drained from her face, willing herself not to faint. Perhaps Ratana has moved away? Perhaps it was a different family who died in the fire? In all the years she has spent mulling over the past she has never once considered that Ratana might be dead. It simply hasn't entered her mind, so focused has she been on what she would say to Ratana when she confronted her with the truth.

The samlor rider is watching her face, waiting for further instructions.

'Do you know the name of the family?' she asks, holding her breath, dreading the answer.

'No. I not know. You knew family who lived here, madam?'

'A long time ago,' she says. He is looking at her with curiosity, waiting for her to go on.

'Could you turn round please?' she says weakly. 'Take me to Chalong's shop at the other end of the road?'

He shrugs and starts the engine.

Sirinya hardly registers the shops and houses they pass for the first few minutes as they retrace their route along the length of Saeng Chuto road. She is reflecting on the shock of what she has just discovered. If Ratana died in that fire, it changes her whole reason for being here. It ruins her plan of confronting Ratana, of setting the record straight, of purging herself of the pain of the past. She feels helpless, thwarted. Now she will never find a way to rid herself of the harm that Ratana inflicted upon her all those years ago.

But after a few minutes, she can't help but notice familiar landmarks again. If she half closes her eyes it is as if nothing has changed since the old days. Still the street vendors fry their aromatic concoctions on woks over stoves on the wide pavements. The broad road is still filled with stalls overflowing with all manner of goods set up in front of the line of three-storey shophouses. But there is more traffic now, more neon signs and advertisement hoardings, more people milling about, and far more noise. A confusion of engines and horns, and modern Thai and western songs blast from transistor radios in every stall and shop, melding into each other in a discordant mess of sound.

As they draw closer to Chalong's shop her nerves start to tingle again. In a few minutes it comes into view. It is just as it looked the last time she saw it: white walls, blue painted doors and window frames, an old-fashioned painted sign in Thai script on the wall above the door proclaiming 'Chalong's Fruit and Vegetables'. The shop is open. Pomelos, mangoes, papaya and citrus fruits are stacked in brightly coloured pyramids on tables on the pavement.

With trepidation, Sirinya pays the samlor driver and stands, twisting her hands, feeling foolish beside her suitcase in front of the shop. She watches an assistant weighing avocados for a customer behind one of the stalls. It is a young man, someone she doesn't recognise. He was probably not even born the last time she was here.

She picks up her suitcase and moves towards the blue door, but before she has gone five paces a figure suddenly emerges from the dark recesses of the shop and comes running towards her.

'Sirinya!'

She catches a glimpse of her cousin's face smiling broadly before she is enveloped in an embrace.

Malee has grown stout over the years and her jet black hair is completely grey now and cut short. But she still has the same smile. A smile that lights up her whole face, and radiates delight.

'I'm so happy to see you!' she says. Her voice sounds just the same, 'Why didn't you let me know which train you were coming on? I would have come to the station to meet you ...'

'Oh, I wasn't sure of the times. It doesn't matter. It was no trouble getting a samlor.'

'You look just the same, Siri,' she says standing back and taking Sirinya in. 'Twenty-five whole years, and you haven't aged a bit.'

'That can't be true, Malee! And you don't look so bad yourself, you know.'

'Oh, me? I'm old, fat and grey now. But you! England must have suited you. Come. Come on upstairs. I'll make us some jasmine tea.'

She takes Sirinya firmly by the arm and guides her into the old familiar house. The smell is just the same. Floor polish and mosquito coils mingled with the smoky exotic aroma of incense. Sirinya stops for a second and breathes deeply. It's good to be back.

'Come on, Siri,' said Malee impatiently pulling her arm. 'Don't waste time down here. Come on upstairs.'

The flat above the shop has a modern feel now. There is not a trace of the heavy teak furniture that Chalong and Piak had favoured. The old table where they had shared countless meals on the oilskin cloth, the dresser where Piak had stored their best china, the wide wooden bench where they used to relax and listen to the radio, are all gone.

'What do you think?' asks Malee, smiling with pride.

Sirinya looks around, taking it all in. It is painted white, and everything is pale. The old brown lino has been removed and the floorboards stripped and varnished. A low pine table stands in the middle of the room, a couple of futons with pale silk cushions lean against the wall. Bowls of lotus blossoms and flickering candles stand on side tables. Traditional Thai prints hang on the wall and a thin muslin curtain covers the window to provide shade.

'It's lovely, Malee. Very tasteful.'

'I like it. Now come and sit down. I will boil the water. I'm so sorry about Johnny, Siri. So sorry. He was a good man. I've been lighting candles for him at the temple.'

'Thank you. Yes, he was a good man. Too good for me,' she lowers her eyes.

'You mustn't say that,' Malee says, going into a small kitchenette and returning with a plate full of satay and pandan-leaf parcels. She sets it on the table and beckons Sirinya to eat. 'He loved you.'

'I didn't deserve his love, Malee. He knew that too. He said some strange things towards the end.'

'Please don't dwell on his last days. It was his whole life that mattered. Remember the life you had together. If he hadn't come to find you in Bangkok when he did, who knows ...'

'Please don't remind me,' Sirinya says with a shudder.

Malee goes back into the small kitchenette and bustles about.

'I won't be a moment. Sit down please, Siri,'

Sirinya sinks down on one of the futons. 'Malee what happened to Ratana's house?' she calls.

Malee comes and stands in the doorway holding a tea tray. Her smile is gone. 'You didn't go down to that end of the road did you?'

'I did. It was a dreadful shock. The samlor man said it had burnt down.'

Malee goes pale. She crosses the room and sets the tray down on the low table. 'It did,' she says slowly, 'About five years ago. Ratana's husband and her mother were killed. It looked like arson. They thought someone had posted a petrol soaked cloth through the letter box.'

'What happened to Ratana?'

'Nobody really knows. She left shortly afterwards. She was in a dreadful state. We all assumed she'd gone to Bangkok.'

'Why didn't you write and tell me?'

'Oh, I don't know. You and I weren't writing that much at the time. And I didn't want to stir up old memories. What happened in the war is dead and buried long ago.'

'But I needed to know. It's part of the reason I came back ...'

Malee is staring at her now, confusion clouding her expression. 'What do you mean?'

'I came back partly to see Ratana. I needed to speak to her. To confront her.'

'Confront her? Oh, Siri, with what? I know she did things during the war that none of us approved of. And she was ... well, she behaved very badly at times. But I don't see the need to confront her. I don't understand you.'

'Never mind.' Sirinya looks down, but now she feels Malee sit down next to her, take her hand.

'Explain it to me,' Malee says gently. 'It must be important to you.'

Sirinya turns to her. How can she give voice to the thoughts that she has never revealed to anyone, not even Johnny? They are thoughts and suspicions that have been festering in the back of her mind for many years. There they grew and multiplied like bacteria on rotten meat. She stares at her cousin for a long time. She knows she can't tell her what she's thinking.

'There are things she did,' she says bitterly, 'things that I can't forgive, Malee.'

There is a long silence. Sirinya watches Malee's face. She looks her age suddenly, all the vibrancy has drained from her eyes. Finally Malee says in whisper: 'What things, Sirinya? And why ever do you think that? What evidence do you have?'

'I can't tell you everything. Not at the moment. But I don't have evidence. I don't need evidence. It is obvious though when you think about it. The truth didn't occur to me for a couple of years. But believe me, Malee, since then I've had plenty of time to think and I have thought about it. I've thought about it for years. Over and over. From every angle. She was close to lots of Japanese during the war, and I know now what she did.'

'No. No, Siri, you're quite wrong. She was a good soul. A bit wayward, maybe, but good underneath all that. But she is long gone now, and what is the use of raking over the past?'

'But she ruined my life.'

'Don't talk like that. Look, it hasn't been good for you living such a long way from your people. I can see that now. Your people and your faith. You must have felt very lonely and bitter, even though you had Johnny. Please, eat some food and let us go to the temple when we have had our tea. We need to speak to the monks. You need to let go of all this hatred and pain.'

Sirinya takes a bite of one of the sticks of satay. She has not tasted authentic Thai food for a long time. The hasty snack she ate at a food stall in Bangkok the previous evening did not come close to this. The tastes of ginger and lemongrass seep through her, comforting her, reminding her of where she belongs. Suddenly she feels all the fight drain from her. She thinks with longing of the temple, the discordant clanging of the prayer bells, the chant of the monks in prayer, the smell of candles and incense and the beautiful statues of Buddha exuding peace and calm. Malee is right, she needs to go there.

4

They walk into the temple compound. It is just as Sirinya remembers. The great temple building, with its steep red and green roof trimmed with gold leaf, rises before them surrounded by neat lawns shaded by angsana trees. To the right, stands the long building that houses the monks' living quarters. As they walk towards the building, a feeling of well-being seeps through Sirinya's veins and into her soul. They reach the front steps. Malee takes off her shoes and places them on a rack. Sirinya does the same and they mount the steps and enter the tranquillity of the temple.

It is dark inside, apart from the flickering of a thousand candles. The air is filled with the sombre chanting of monks, which echoes around the walls. They walk forward towards the altar, and stop to take votive candles from a table to light before they kneel. As soon as she entered, Sirinya had felt the benign presence of the Buddha and now she lifts her face and sees the great gold statue dominating the end of the building. The smile on its lips exudes something indescribable; an all-pervading sense of serenity. It is something she knows she has been lacking for decades. Emotion wells up in her chest. It almost overwhelms her with its power. She kneels beside Malee and places the candle on the steps in front of the statue. She realises her eyes have filled with tears.

They kneel there, heads bowed for a long time. Sirinya tries to remember how to empty her mind, to let peace take over and envelop her, but it has been a long time and her mind will not settle.

After they have meditated, they stand up and bow their heads.

'Let us go and see Phraa Wicharong. He will help you, Siri,' says Malee.

They retrace their steps out into the compound and Sirinya blinks as they emerge into the bright sunlight. They walk around the building to the garden of meditation where a group of saffron-clad monks sit under a tree. One of them sees the two women approach and comes forward to meet them.

'Khun Malee,' he says, putting his hands together in a wai. 'Good afternoon. I hope you are well today. And you have brought a friend.' He smiles a welcome to Sirinya.

'She is my cousin, Phraa. Sirinya Foster. She has been away living abroad for a long time. She needs some guidance. Could you please speak to her?'

'Come child,' he says, beckoning Sirinya towards a bench under another tree. Malee turns to walk away. 'I'll wait inside the temple until you're ready,' she says.

'You look troubled,' says the monk as they sit down. 'I can see that you have a mind that is not at peace. Tell me what is bothering you.'

He is looking straight at her, searching her face with his kindly eyes. She cannot meet his gaze and looks down at her lap.

'Come, the first step to eliminating an unsatisfactory state is right understanding. You remember that from our teachings long ago?'

She nods. 'I have been harbouring some grudges,' she says at last. 'From the war.'

The monk shakes his head slowly. 'That is a long time ago. It must have caused you much pain to be in such a state for so long. You need to let go of those thoughts to get yourself back on the path.

You need to release yourself.'

She looks at him. 'I can only let go of those thoughts by finding out the truth,' she says. 'I came here to confront the woman I think did me wrong, but she is not here and I'm not sure if I'll be able to find her. She might even be dead.'

'It makes no difference if she is here or gone, dead or alive, you need to forget. Forget and release yourself from pain and suffering. You must remember the eightfold path and the four noble truths?'

'Yes ... yes I do remember.'

'Follow them, my child and you will soon find you are able free yourself from your harmful thoughts. If you work hard at this, you will find your karma. You know there is an old saying from the texts: 'If a man speaks or acts with an impure mind, pain pursues him, even as the wheel follows the ox that draws the cart.' You are in pain because you harbour bitterness towards another. Come to the temple every day, my child. Meditate often. Bring offerings to gain merit.'

'Thank you, Phraa, I will do that.'

Later that evening, after she and Malee have shared a meal, exhaustion overtakes her. Malee shows her to a small room on the top floor of the shophouse, under the steep roof. It is the room she and Malee had shared when she used to help out in the shop all those years ago. As she enters, she remembers the shape of the room, the position of the window, high up in the roof, but it is different now, clean and bright with a modern bed and furniture. She slides between cool linen sheets under a mosquito net and looks up at the ceiling fan whirring away above her. A feeling of peace overtakes her and she slides easily into a deep sleep. But her dreams take her back to the time that shaped her life, the time she carries with her and cannot forget. Soon it is as if she is there again, reliving the day when she first saw prisoners arriving in the area in their thousands.

The jungle road stretched ahead of her, a wall of greenery. Sirinya squeezed the accelerator and the motor-rickshaw surged forward along the dirt track, the engine squealing. Giant ferns brushed the windscreen, creepers and leaves encroached onto the track in front of her. The sun was high overhead, bouncing off the windscreen with a blinding glare, making her blink and squint. It was stifling in the cab and sweat stood out on her brow and trickled into her eyes. She glanced behind at Malee, perched on the wooden bench, bouncing around amongst the pile of crates filled with fruit and vegetables. Her uncle always insisted they went together to make deliveries to his customers in outlying villages.

'You alright, Malee?' she shouted above the buzz of the engine.

Her cousin nodded, hanging onto the side-bar. 'It's not far to Whang Khanai now, is it?'

'No, just a couple of kilometres through this last stretch of forest.'

Sirinya turned back and peered at the track ahead. She caught sight of something strange emerging from round a bend a few metres in front.

'What on earth is that?'

Was the sun paying tricks on her? She slowed the vehicle to a crawl, then pulled it onto a patch of grass at the side of the track. On their deliveries they had encountered monkeys, wild elephants, even the odd jungle cat, but Sirinya had never seen a sight such as the one in front of her now. Advancing towards them was a sea of faces. White men. An army of them, drawing closer and closer.

'Who are they?' Malee stared ahead, her eyes widened in alarm. She was trying to edge backwards between the crates.

They had rarely seen westerners before, and the ones they had seen were mostly on the big screen in the picture house; Clark Gable, Cary Grant, Laurence Olivier. But these men looked nothing like matinee idols. Sirinya stared at them, too shocked to feel fear as the men advanced slowly and steadily.

As they moved closer, she could see from their clothes that they were, or had once been, soldiers. They were dressed in ragged khaki. Some simply wore shorts, their bare torsos burnt brown from the sun. Others wore only loin cloths. Some shambled along in shabby boots, but many walked barefoot. As the first few drew closer to the rickshaw she saw that many of them were pitifully thin, their ribs standing out, the shape of their thigh bones visible beneath leathery skin. Beneath their sunburn their faces looked pale and drawn. Many looked sick and were being helped along by their friends, supported on either side by two others, their feet dragging, too limp and weak to support their bodyweight. Others carried two backpacks, obviously helping weaker comrades.

As the first column drew parallel with the rickshaw, some of the men peered inside with a spark of curiosity in their defeated eyes. Their gaze slid over the girls, they appeared more interested in the crates of fruit and vegetables stowed in the back.

Behind the first wave of men marched two Japanese soldiers wielding bayonets. They kept prodding the backs of the unfortunate men immediately in front of them, yelling 'Sousou, Tokkyuu' at them.

Wave after wave of men came. Sirinya peered ahead. There was no end to the column in sight.

An idea struck her and she turned to Malee.

'Let's give them some fruit. They look starving,' she said.

Malee was still trying to conceal herself behind the crates. At this suggestion she opened her eyes wide in fear. 'No, Siri. Let's not go near them. You don't know what might happen.'

'What could happen? We'd only be helping sick men. What could be wrong with that?'

'We need to deliver this load to the customers in Whang Khanai. They are expecting it. What will Father say?'

'Your father is a good man. He'll understand.'

She turned to the boxes stacked behind her and prised open the lid on a crate of bananas with her fingers. She drew out a few bunches, then eased herself out of the driving compartment and stood up. Tentatively she held out the bananas to a passing group of men.

They turned to look at her. The man nearest to her stared. His face was pale and sweaty. He looked exhausted, but after a second he smiled and took the bunch.

'Thank you,' he said, 'Thank you so much.'

From then on she handed bunches to every group that passed. Soon the crate was empty, so she opened another one. This time it was oranges. Malee had reluctantly emerged from her hiding place and was standing beside her, passing fruit out to her from the crates. The men all took them with surprise in their eyes and with heartfelt thanks.

Malee passed Sirinya the last orange and she held it out. The man who took it stopped and looked into her eyes. He was young, about her age, with dark hair and high cheekbones. His eyes were brown with flecks of gold in them. He was very thin and wore only ragged shorts, but despite that he appeared fit and healthy.

'There are two Jap guards behind the next group of men,' he said. 'Don't let them see you doing this. They might punish you. Who knows what they are capable of. Please. Sit back in your van until they have passed. Then make sure you look out for the others. They are spaced out, two to about every hundred men.'

Sirinya understood English from the basics she had learned at school, but mainly from listening to the BBC World Service and going to the movies. She smiled at him gratefully and he took the orange.

'Thank you,' he said, and he held her gaze for a few moments. Then his companion, a taller man, about the same age, with unruly brown hair, took his arm, 'Come on, Charlie,' he said and they both moved on. She stared after him and a chill went through her that she didn't understand. Something had happened when he looked her in the eyes, some connection had been made. She stared at his group as it moved on and she noticed that he was still looking back at her.

'Come on, Sirinya,' said Malee. 'You heard what he said. Let's wait in the cab until the Japanese soldiers have passed.'

She remembers returning to the town that evening, later than usual. They had had to spend time explaining to the bewildered stallholders in the village that some of their cargo had been lost on the way. The girls had promised to return the next day with more supplies.

Dusk was falling as they entered the town and as they turned into Saeng Chuto road, Sirinya sensed immediately there was something wrong. At this hour the road was normally full of activity; the clatter and shouts of stallholders shutting up shop, evening street hawkers frying food over open stoves. But tonight the stalls had already been emptied. The road was silent. No hawkers were out cooking, no queues of hungry customers thronged the pavements.

They moved slowly along the street.

'What's going on down there?' asked Malee, pointing ahead.

Two Japanese army lorries were parked outside a shophouse

across the road from Chalong's. Groups of soldiers were carrying furniture into the building. A small crowd of onlookers had gathered at a safe distance to watch silently.

Sirinya parked the motor-rickshaw outside Chalong's shop and the girls hurried inside. Upstairs they found Chalong and Piak watching the scene from the front window.

'What's happening?' asked Malee.

'It's the Kempeitai,' said Chalong, his face grave. 'Japanese secret police. You can tell by the white armbands they wear on their uniforms. They're moving in. They must have forced the owner and paid him off. He and his family left earlier looking very shaken. So, it looks as though we have new neighbours.'

5

A few days later, Sirinya was walking alone through the town, making for the riverbank. The presence of the Japanese army had cast a dark shadow over the town. Kanchanaburi was no longer the colourful, carefree place it had once been. Her uncle now insisted that she and Malee stayed in the apartment in the evenings, that they did not wander as they had before through the streets or by the river, meeting friends, stopping for a snack or a drink at a food stall. She found these restrictions hard to bear, and resented being a virtual prisoner inside Chalong's home.

She had even thought about returning to her family village to be with her mother and grandmother. It had been weeks since she had been back home and she suddenly longed for the simplicity of the life there in the hills; rising at dawn to feed the pigs and hens, working in the fields by day, eating a simple meal of fried rice and vegetables on the porch of her grandmother's hut by evening, going to bed on the floor of the hut shortly after sunset. She decided to try to persuade Chalong to let her go there on her next days off. But she knew he'd be reluctant, with the Japanese soldiers patrolling the neighbourhood.

This afternoon Malee was working alone in the shop. Chalong had a visitor, a man Sirinya had never seen before, with whom he was deep in discussion in the apartment above the shop. Trade was slow, and before the visitor arrived, Chalong had said that Sirinya could take the rest of the day off. She had wasted no time in rushing up to her room, changing her clothes and slipping out of the back door alone.

Only a few brave street vendors were out touting their wares. There was hardly anyone about, and those who were, hurried about their business, heads down. The presence of the Kempeitai in the house on Saeng Chuto Road had instilled fear into the place. If the soldiers were out on the streets they stopped and searched people at random. They also insisted that everybody had to stop what they were doing and bow to them as they passed.

Now, she wandered on the riverbank, watching the fast-flowing water, hoping that it would exert its timeless power of peace and calm over her. She sat down on a rock, trying to lose herself in the sound of the rushing current, the endless flow of the river. But when she lifted her head and glanced over at the opposite bank, she noticed that the landscape had changed dramatically.

Directly opposite her was the field that Chalong had been forced to sell to the Japanese army. It was no longer the sleepy meadow she had known and loved; it was transformed. It was now alive with movement and activity. She got to her feet and shaded her eyes, peering across the water. Men were busy carrying lengths of bamboo and great bundles of palm leaves. Some were tying the lengths of bamboo together, or hammering stakes into the ground. She realised they were constructing long huts out of these rudimentary materials. Even from this distance Sirinya could tell that the men looked the same as the men that she and Malee had seen on the road to Whang Khanai. Most were very thin and dressed in rags. As they worked, uniformed guards strutted around amongst them with sticks and bayonets, occasionally striking out or prodding someone at will.

She turned away, horrified. How could this be happening here, in this quiet, beautiful place that had always protected and sheltered her? A shudder went through her. She needed to get away from this spot. She turned to retrace her steps up the bank to the path. But sensing she was not alone she stopped and looked up. There, standing at the top of the bank watching her was Narong.

'What are you doing here, Siri?' he asked, moving towards her.

'I just wanted some fresh air, but I've been watching what's going on over there. It's quite shocking, isn't it? Look at the state of those poor men.'

He smiled, 'Yes they do look in a state. They don't look much like soldiers do they?'

'They must have been virtually starved, by the look of them.'

He shrugged. 'Why won't you see me, Siri?' he asked, turning away from the bank. She noticed his car parked on a piece of ground nearby.

'Things haven't been easy lately, what with the Japanese soldiers in town,' she said. 'You know, the secret police have moved into one of the shophouses opposite my uncle's shop.'

'It's not because of the Japanese soldiers though, is it? You've been avoiding me for weeks.'

'What makes you think that?' she dropped her eyes, not wanting to meet his gaze. It was true.

'I've been into Chalong's shop several times. You're never there.'

'Oh, I'm often out,' she said evasively, 'I have lots of deliveries to make.'

He watched her silently for a moment, as if he was assessing whether she was lying. Then he said, 'Would you like a lift home now? I've got my car here.'

'No, thank you. I came down here to get some fresh air. A walk will do me good.'

He shrugged. 'If you say so. How about coming out with me

this evening?'

'I'm sorry, Narong. I have to get up early to work.'

'Well, what about your day off?'

She had run out of excuses. Why did he persist? Perhaps she should just tell him now that she had no desire to continue seeing him. Get it over and done with.

'Look, why don't I come with you now,' she said on a whim, turning back towards him. 'Perhaps we could drive out into the country? I have a little time this afternoon.'

He brightened visibly, walked over to the car and opened the door for her. She slid onto the leather passenger seat. He started the engine and revved it several times making a throaty roar.

As he drove through the streets towards the edge of town, Sirinya thought back to the first time she'd met him. He was a new acquaintance of Somsak's, and apparently had returned to live in Kanchanaburi after a long absence. Malee had introduced them, and the four of them had gone to the cinema together one evening. Before the programme began, they'd gone to the hotel in the centre of town for a drink. Malee and Somsak were soon engrossed in each other's company, deep in conversation. Sirinya felt a little awkward left with this stranger.

'I haven't seen you before,' he said, toying with his beer and appraising her. 'I'm sure I would have remembered you if I had done.'

She smiled politely and sidestepped the compliment.

'I went to school here in the town,' she said. Then I went back to live in my family village in the hills with my mother and grandmother. My grandmother owns some land there. A small farm. But I wasn't back there for very long. My uncle has been expanding his business so he asked me to come back and help out in the shop. What about you?'

'Oh, my parents live in the town, but I've been away for most of my life. School in Bangkok, then university there too.'

'So what brings you back now?'

'I've just started working in my father's paper factory. I'll be taking over from him when he retires, so I have to learn the ropes.'

'Ah, yes,' she said slowly.

Now she understood. The paper factory was the town's biggest employer, established here to exploit the bamboo that grew rampant everywhere around. Hundreds of people were employed there; she had seen crowds of them walking to their shifts early in the morning, even before the monks began their morning rounds. She'd thought there was a pampered look about Narong when she first set eyes on him; his expensive clothes and shoes, manicured hands. There was no denying he was good looking. Liquid brown eyes with long lashes, regular features, perfect skin. But there was something ice-cool about his manner. Something that stopped her warming to him.

At the cinema, while Malee and Somsak held hands and whispered together, he'd shifted restlessly about in his seat throughout the film, *Gone with the Wind*. Although it had been cut ruthlessly for Thai cinema, it was still over three hours long. Sirinya sensed Narong's impatience and boredom.

As they came out into the warm night he said, 'Well thank goodness that is over. That was a real marathon, wasn't it?'

'I thought it was just wonderful,' said Sirinya, half her mind still dreamily occupying the landscape and atmosphere of the deep south of America.

'Would you like to go for a spin in my car,' he asked. She swallowed. 'Car?' she stared at him. She'd never met anyone of her own age who owned a car before.

'Yes, Father bought it for me as a home-coming present. Partly to make up for having to live back in this dump again.'

She eyed him coldly. 'I don't think so, thank you,' she said.

But after that night, he'd been round to the shop many times to see her. She was always cool with him, but he persisted. He often brought her flowers from the market; lotus blossoms or a spray of orchids. One day he brought her a more expensive gift: a close-fitting turquoise dress made of thick, raw silk.

'I thought it would suit you,' he said, and for the first time she noticed an anxiousness in his manner, as if he really cared how she would respond. She couldn't help feeling flattered, and held it up to her cheek to feel the texture of the cloth.

'Thank you. It's very kind of you.' Later when she tried it on, she was amazed to find that it fitted perfectly and complemented her skin colour and her jet black hair.

Finally she'd agreed to go out with him on two or three occasions. He drove her out through the narrow streets of the town. As they roared past, people stopped to stare. Sirinya could not help feeling self-conscious at this shameless display of wealth when most people here had few material possessions. They were soon out in the countryside, speeding along the bumpy valley roads, past villages and temples, rice fields and tapioca plantations. He drove quickly and recklessly. The car was a green sports car, an open-topped Bugatti. Sirinya's hair soon worked its way free from its ribbon and streamed out behind her. Despite her reticence, the feeling of the wind rushing through her hair, the hot air on her face, the countryside flashing past was exhilarating, and she'd found herself laughing with pleasure, turning to him with shining eyes.

Once, he drove her into the hills, to the Erewan waterfalls. They swam in the deep cool rock pools beneath the falls, floating on their backs, letting the river fish nibble at their skin. But she still felt ill at ease with him. As if, despite all his charm, he was hiding something from her. She would often catch him watching her, as if he was silently judging her.

That last time had been a few weeks ago. That day, on the way home, she'd taken the decision not to see him again. She knew that this uneasiness she felt in his presence was never going to be dispelled. And although he'd called at the shop a few times after that, she'd hidden in the storeroom when she saw him approach. She could not explain why, even to herself, but his attentions made her feel uncomfortable. She knew she should find the courage to tell him that she did not want to see him, but for some reason she always made excuses to herself.

Now, as before, Sirinya found herself shrinking from the gaze of people who turned to stare, looked up from their snacks at food stalls, or from sweeping the road to watch the Bugatti roar past. Unconsciously she kept her head low and slipped down in the seat a little.

This time he drove eastwards beside the river, along a road fringed by jungle on one side.

'Where are we going?' she asked.

'I'm not sure. We could drive to Bangkok.'

'Bangkok? But that's over a hundred kilometres.'

'It would only take a few hours. I'd like to take you there. Forget all about this rotten place for a while.'

'No, Narong,' she said, alarmed. 'That's too far. I said I have some time, but I haven't got that long!'

He drove on in silence. Then he said, staring ahead, 'I want you to understand what I am, Sirinya. I know you think I'm some spoiled rich kid. And maybe that's true. But I'm much more than that.' He began to accelerate, to take bends at speed, skidding on the uneven road surface.

Sirinya was thinking quickly. She hadn't intended this turn of events. She'd just thought they would go for a short drive and she would tell him gently that she didn't think there was a future for them.

'Look,' she said, trying to keep her voice steady as the greenery flashed past at an alarming pace, 'why don't you pull over? We can talk properly then.'

He glanced at her bitterly, then swerved the car off the road into a clearing and skidded to a halt.

He sat staring ahead of him, breathing heavily. Sirinya tried to slow her pounding heart. The thought flashed through her mind that he was unstable, that her rejection of him might tip him over the edge. Perhaps he might even try to harm her?

She got out of the car and leaned against the door, taking deep breaths, wondering what to do. Should she take a risk and tell him the truth about how she felt?

Then, as she lifted her head and looked through the trees she glimpsed movement. She walked a few paces forward to the edge of the forest and stared ahead.

'Sirinya, what is it?' Narong called from the car.

Through the trees floated the sound of axes chopping, of trees crashing to the ground, of something heavy being dragged along the forest floor. She was bewildered for a moment, then she heard some words she had heard before; 'Tokkyuu, Speedo,' being screamed angrily, and a stream of Japanese expletives following. The jungle was thick here, but a few yards ahead she could just make out shadowy figures hacking away at roots, teams of half-naked men dragging tree trunks along with ropes.

She felt the blood drain from her face. She turned back to the

53

car. 'It's more of those prisoners,' she said. 'They're working down there. They seem to be clearing the jungle.'

'That must be for the railway,' he said casually. 'That's what they're here for. They must be getting on with it.'

She closed her eyes and swallowed, trying to rid herself of the fear and revulsion of what was happening all around her. She remembered Chalong's words to the Japanese soldiers that first day, 'Now I know you are joking ... That is impossible. It's dense jungle and a mountain range of limestone and granite all the way, it will never happen.'

She turned back to Narong, weak with shock. 'Those poor, poor men,' she whispered.

6

Narong drove home in silence. All the way back to the town Sirinya stared out at the river and thought about the prisoners. How malnourished and ill they looked, how they were dressed in rags, and how their captors brutalised and beat them. Her own problems – her boredom at being confined to the shophouse, her longing for her home village, her difficulties with Narong – all faded into insignificance beside the dreadful plight of those men. She wondered if there was something she could do to relieve their suffering. Would she be able to smuggle them some food? There looked to be hundreds of them, perhaps thousands. She sighed. It was hopeless. Even if she could take them a few pieces of fruit, it would not be a fraction of what they needed.

Narong turned the car into Saeng Chuto Road and drew up outside Chalong's shop. He switched off the engine and turned to her.

'I'm sorry for the way I behaved back there, Siri,' he began, a pleading look in his eyes. 'It was wrong of me. I don't know what I was thinking.'

She stared at him. She had all but forgotten his bitter outbursts, the terrifying drive along the river.

'Don't worry about it. Forget it,' she said absently, reaching for the door handle.

'Will I see you again?' he asked.

'I'm not sure.'

She got out and walked towards the front door without saying goodbye. She could feel Narong's wounded gaze on her back all the way but she didn't turn round. As she let herself inside she heard the engine start up and the car move away along the street.

The shop was closed and the shutters down. There was no sign of Malee or Piak. She went up the stairs. The door to the apartment was locked. She put her ear to the wood. There were murmured voices coming from inside. She knocked firmly three times and the voices fell silent. After a few moments she heard Chalong's voice.

'Who is it?'

'It's me, Sirinya.'

She heard the bolt being pulled back and Chalong opened the door. She stepped inside. Around the table in the middle of the room six or seven men were seated. They all turned to look at her. There was a bottle of Thai whisky on the table and they each had tumblers in front of them. She noticed Somsak on the far side of the table, and recognised a few members of the town council, the headmaster of the school, the local doctor. In the middle of the table a map was spread out.

'Go upstairs please, Siri,' said Chalong in a firm voice. 'Your aunt and Malee are up there. We won't be long.'

She wanted to ask what was happening. Why the locked door, the air of secrecy? But it was clear that her Uncle was in no mood for questions. She remained silent and turned back towards the stairs.

Piak and Malee sat together in Piak's bedroom. The wireless on the dressing table was playing Thai folk music. Piak sat in a chair in the corner, sewing. Malee was sprawled on the bed engrossed in a glossy magazine.

'What's happening downstairs?' she asked. Malee shrugged and turned back to her magazine. 'We don't know. Father won't tell us. He just asked us to come up here.'

'Well, Somsak is down there too. Didn't *he* say anything?'

'No. He said it was secret and I wasn't to tell anyone about the meeting.'

Piak put down her sewing. 'It's best if you don't ask, Siri,' she said, with an anxious look. 'Your uncle will tell us what we need to know.'

'I bet it's about the Japanese occupation. Aren't you curious? Don't you want to know?'

Piak shook her head. 'It's best not to ask,' she repeated with pursed lips.

'There are hundreds of prisoners in the area now,' said Sirinya. 'They're building a camp in Uncle's field. And they're clearing the jungle too. Out of town, along the river. Gangs of them. They're clearing a track for the railway they're going to build all the way to Burma. It's dreadful. They're being driven like slaves.'

Piak said nothing, just frowned at Sirinya and picked at her blouse anxiously. Malee didn't look up from her reading.

'Well, don't you care?' Sirinya burst out, 'I can't believe you can just sit by and ignore it. It's happening right here in our hometown.'

'How do you know they're clearing the jungle?' asked Malee.

'Narong drove me out there. He wanted to drive all the way to Bangkok but I refused to go.'

'I thought you weren't going to see him anymore,' said Malee, closing her magazine and sitting up, finally showing some interest in what Sirinya had to say.

'I'm not. It doesn't matter anyway. What's important is the prisoners. We should try to do something for them.'

'Oh, Siri. When will you learn,' said Piak. 'These things are bigger than us. You can't solve all the world's problems.'

'I know that, but I can't just stand by.'

'Sometimes there are things that happen that are out of our control. You have to accept that.'

'I'll speak to Uncle about it. He'll know what to do.'

Impatiently she crossed the room to the front window and looked down at the street below. The headmaster was just emerging from the front door. He hurried away from the shop and down the road furtively. From where she stood she could see the pale bald patch on the top of his head. She wondered where the others had got to, and realised that they must have left the building by the back door.

The door to the room opened and Chalong stood there. He looked gravely at the three of them, then came and sat on a stool beside Piak.

'Sirinya, please could you leave the room for a moment. I have something to say to Malee.'

Malee looked up in surprise.

'Why, Father?' she said, but Sirinya walked to the door quickly. She knew better than to challenge her uncle.

She waited in her own room restlessly. She lay on the bed and tried to read, but the words on the page of her book slid past her eyes. She put it down and wandered to the window, staring out at the street below. She glanced over at the Kempeitai's house. There was a truck parked in front and she watched some officers get out of it and walk towards the shophouse. Two others emerged and they all bowed to each other elaborately before going on their way. She was about to turn away from the window when she saw something that made her grip the windowsill and her mouth drop open in surprise.

'What the …?'.

A young woman, dressed in a tight-fitting black dress and high-heeled shoes was walking quickly with tiny steps along the pavement.

When she drew level with the Kempeitai's house she turned towards it and tottered up to the door. Malee couldn't be sure, but it looked suspiciously like Ratana, a girl she and Malee had been at school with. The girl went up the front steps and rang the bell. Almost instantly the door opened and a soldier appeared in the doorway. He took the girl's hand and pulled her into the house. Sirinya stared as the door slammed. She could hardly believe what she'd just seen. A Thai woman fraternising with Japanese soldiers! Could it have been Ratana? She hoped not. She knew the family was poor. The father had died when Ratana was young and the mother ran a laundry. Ratana had always been precocious, making eyes at the boys from an early age, flaunting her well-developed figure in the schoolyard. Sirinya could imagine why she'd gone to the house, but she didn't want to think about it. Not now, at least.

She heard Malee run to the next bedroom and slam the door. After a few minutes, she went out and tapped on the door. There was no answer. She could hear Malee's sobs coming from inside the room. She opened the door quietly and went over to sit on the bed beside her cousin.

'What's the matter? What did you father say?'

Malee looked at her with tears in eyes that were already red from crying.

'It's Somsak. He has to go away.'

'Away? But where to?'

'I don't know, that's just it. Father won't say exactly. He just said it was in the north of the country, near the Burmese border.'

'Why, Malee? Did he say why?'

'He told me some things, but I can't tell you, Siri. He swore me to secrecy. I am not to breathe a word. Not to anyone.'

Sirinya swallowed. She felt stung, excluded. They were a family, and although Malee was their daughter, Piak and Chalong had been like parents to Sirinya while she had stayed in their house. They had shared everything and had had no secrets before. She could not understand it. It was not like Chalong to behave like this.

'But he will come back won't he? He won't be going for ever, surely?'

'I don't know. He might not. Something dreadful could happen to him ...'

Malee flung herself down again and resumed her sobbing. Sirinya stroked her hair and tried to comfort her as best she could. After a time Malee's sobs subsided and her breathing became even. She seemed to have cried herself to sleep.

Sirinya crept out of the room and went downstairs to the living room. Her uncle sat at the table, frowning with concentration, poring over the map, smoking a cheroot.

'Sirinya!' he said, beckoning her to come and sit beside him.

'Uncle. Malee says that Somsak has to go away. Is it true?'

'It's true my child,' he said.

'Can you tell me why? I wouldn't tell anyone, I promise.'

He took his cigarette out of his mouth and placed it on the ashtray.

'Listen to me,' he said, looking into her eyes. 'I'm going to tell you this once, then I'm not going to mention it again if I can help it,' he said. 'Can I trust you to keep a secret, Siri?'

She nodded.

'A man came to see me earlier today,' Chalong continued. 'He's a contact of mine from Bangkok. He told me about two resistance movements working underground against the Japanese. There's the V Organisation, who are trying to help prisoners, and there's also the Free Thai Movement. Thailand needs to stand up against the occupation, and those of us who want to fight for our freedom must do what we can to help. They want volunteers to watch the Japanese – report on their movements and the activities of troops. Others will be actively engaged in sabotage, mainly in the north where the Japanese are stationing troops. That's where Somsak comes in.'

Sirinya stared at him. 'What do you mean?'

'I mean he has to go away from here, to a camp in the jungle up in the north of the country. He's going to train with the guerrillas.'

'Poor Malee,' murmured Sirinya.

'She was very upset. And I understand that, but I told her. I said, you must put your own wishes aside my dear. There is a war on. He is young and strong and he wants to fight. The country needs men like him. I'm afraid she blames me, Sirinya. But I told her as gently as I could that it's not just me. It is Somsak himself. He wants to go. I'm sure he'll tell her the same thing himself.'

'Uncle, do you know about the prisoners?' said Sirinya.

He nodded. 'I know that there are thousands of them being brought here, that many of them are ill or malnourished, and they are being put to work to build this railway. It's a crazy idea.'

'They are being driven like slaves,' said Sirinya. 'Isn't there something we can do to help them, Uncle? Couldn't I try to take some food to the camp?'

He shook his head emphatically.

'That would be very dangerous. Please don't do that, Siri. You could be risking your life and risking exposing the movement.'

'But Uncle ...'

He held up his hand. 'I will think about it. I'm sure there will be something we can do. I agree with what you say. We can't just sit by and let this happen right on our doorstep. Just give me a little time to think.'

7

The next day Sirinya sat on the bank of the river, a few yards away from where Malee was saying a tearful goodbye to Somsak. Malee had asked her to come along so that she wouldn't have to walk home alone after he had left. When they'd arrived, Malee had rushed to Somsak and he'd taken her in his arms. Sirinya had felt awkward and walked away from where they stood.

Chalong had told them that Somsak was due to board a rice barge that was going upriver. When the barge had cleared Japanese occupied territory, Somsak was going to be met by guerrillas to be taken to his camp overland. The journey could take days as the transport would have to stick to back roads.

Sirinya wandered along the bank. She thought about Somsak, and how the three of them had been friends since childhood. His father was a carpenter and ran a workshop near to Chalong's own shop. When he left school, Somsak had joined his father as an apprentice, working alongside him, learning the trade. He was skilled with his hands, and even at school his creative talent shone. He had an instinctive eye for detail and was able to paint and carve and sculpt far better than any of his peers.

He was a gentle boy with a generous heart and a dreamy smile. He'd been in love with Malee since schooldays, and her vivacious, outgoing nature seemed the perfect complement to his personality.

Sirinya glanced back at them and could feel the pain of their parting. They were clinging to each other and Malee was sobbing.

A few minutes later a sturdy little tugboat rounded the bend in the river. A convoy of lumbering black rice barges followed in its wake. The tugboat drew up alongside the bank, and one of the crew jumped ashore with a rope. Sirinya watched as Somsak gave Malee a final hug before scrambling down the bank and leaping on board. Malee came to stand beside Sirinya and the two of them watched in silence as the tugboat cast off from the bank, pulled out into the current and began its long journey upriver. Somsak stood on the deck of the little boat and waved. Sirinya stood beside Malee and waved too until her right arm ached, and the tugboat with its long convoy of ungainly barges got smaller and smaller and finally disappeared from view.

'Oh, Siri, how will I bear it?' cried Malee, turning to her. Sirinya put her arms around her cousin and held her tight.

'It won't be for ever. He'll come back soon.'

'It *could* be for ever. What he's going to do is really dangerous. He might never come back. Oh, Siri. We were going to be married next month!'

'But you will be married. Please don't worry, Malee. He'll come back and you will have your wedding. Come on. Let's go home.'

She put her arm around her cousin's shoulders and they began to retrace their steps along the riverbank and back through the town towards home.

They were halfway along Chaokunen Road when Malee stopped, staring at something ahead of her. Colour drained from her face.

'Look at that!' she said, her eyes fixed ahead.

Sirinya followed her gaze. Malee's eyes were fixed on an open-air café. It was a cut above most of the food stalls, selling fresh coffee and cookies. The chairs and tables were painted metal rather than the usual rough wood. The place was deserted apart from two customers sitting together at one of the tables. One was a Japanese officer, a member of the Kempeitai, judging by his white armband, and the other was a young woman. She was dressed in a close-fitting red dress with a low neckline and she was leaning forward and speaking intimately with the officer.

'It's Ratana, isn't it?' Malee said. 'What on earth is she doing? Why is she with a Jap soldier? And why is she all dressed up like that?'

'I saw her the other day from the bedroom window,' Sirinya replied. 'She was going to the Kempeitai house. I had my suspicions that it was her then, and I'm almost sure it is now.'

'Why didn't you tell me?'

'You've been preoccupied with other things, Malee. I didn't want to trouble you.'

They drew parallel with the café, and as they walked past, the woman lifted her head and glanced in their direction. As she turned her face towards them they knew it was Ratana. The same arched eyebrows, fiercely plucked, the distinctive high cheekbones. She was very heavily made up, with scarlet lipstick and dark eye makeup. She looked far older than her twenty years. She must have recognised them because when she caught sight of them her smile froze and she quickly turned away. But as Malee walked past she carried on staring at Ratana and shaking her head.

They walked a few paces along the road and Malee stopped again.

'I'm going to go back and talk to her, Siri. I'm going to say how appalled I am with her behaviour. How can she, when the rest of us are doing what we can to resist the Japanese occupation?'

'You mustn't do that,' warned Sirinya, gripping Malee's arm.

'Think of the consequences! It could risk exposing your father and Somsak and the whole of the movement. Please don't ...'

'Perhaps you're right. But I'll find a way of speaking to her one day, of letting her know how I feel about what she is doing.'

'That might not be a good idea either,' said Sirinya. 'Don't do anything hasty, please.'

They walked home in silence, but every so often, Malee would stop and shake her head.

'I just can't believe it,' she muttered from time to time. Sirinya murmured agreement, but she couldn't help feeling glad that the shock of seeing Ratana with the Japanese officer had provided a useful distraction from Malee's own misery.

As they entered the building, the apartment door at the top of the stairs flew open and two Kempeitai officers clattered down the steps, pushing the girls aside as they swept out through the front door. Sirinya and Malee stared after the two men as they crossed the road to their headquarters.

'What's going on?' Malee, near to tears again rushed upstairs and burst into the apartment. Sirinya followed up the steps more slowly.

'Father, what were those Japs doing here? Malee shouted. Sirinya hung back and stood in the doorway.

Chalong held up his hand. 'Don't worry, my child. All is well.'

'But why were you talking to them? When you know where Somsak is going. On today of all days.'

'Calm down, Malee. Please stop. They came to put a proposal to me. They want me to supply vegetables to the camps. It might sound unbearable at first, but it could actually be to our advantage. It could open up a way for us to help out.'

It is still dark in the tiny attic room as Sirinya wakes suddenly. It takes a moment to fight her way to the surface, free herself from the grip of those long-submerged memories. She is momentarily confused, afraid even, but as her eyes adjust, the shape of the old familiar room, illuminated by the glow from the street lights, comes into view and she remembers where she is.

Rubbing her eyes she pushes the mosquito net aside and slips out of bed. She stretches and yawns. Jetlag is playing tricks with her body clock. The house is still quiet. She remembers that years ago, each morning before dawn she would awake in this room to the sounds of the early morning deliveries of fruit and vegetables being unloaded from the bullock carts which had brought them up from the barges on the river. She remembers the clatter of the wooden crates, the shouts and cries of the coolies. She realises that it must be very early, because it is still quiet outside.

She takes a cushion from the window seat and places it on the floor in the middle of the room. She sits down on it, still in her pyjamas, and tries to fold her legs into the lotus position. Her knees are stiff and uncooperative, so she settles for a half-lotus. She closes her eyes and thinks about what the monk said yesterday. She needs to return to the eightfold path, find right understanding, free herself from harmful thoughts. It is not just about what he said to her though, it is what she herself craves. That inner peace that once she took for granted, that feeling of calm, being at one with all around. It has eluded her for more than twenty years and she needs to find it again.

She closes her eyes and tries to empty her mind. Of the memories that have been haunting and troubling her all night, of the recurring thought niggling away at the back of her mind that she needs to find Ratana.

She tries to focus on her breathing, concentrate on her body, centre herself. But her mind, unpractised and untamed, is unused to any type of discipline. It will not stay empty for more than a few seconds at a time. Thoughts and ideas flit in and out like restless flies.

After ten minutes or so she senses it is getting light. It is stuffy in the room, despite the whirring fan. She hears the whine of a mosquito buzzing around on the ceiling. Then comes the roar of an engine coming up the road, getting closer and closer and finally stopping in front of the building with a creak of brakes. She opens her eyes. That's it. There's no point even trying to concentrate. She might as well give up for now.

She sighs and gets to her feet. At the same time the door opens and Malee stands there, framed by the light in the passage. She is fully clothed and holding a tray.

'I've brought you some tea,' she says smiling. She comes into the room and sets it down on the bedside table. 'I hope you slept well, Siri. I wasn't sure if you'd be awake. I have to go down and supervise the deliveries now.'

Sirinya smiles. 'Just like the old days.'

'Not quite. It all comes by lorry from Bangkok now. The bullock carts are things of the past.'

'Of course.'

'Why don't you take your time? Go back to bed and drink your tea, and have a shower when you're ready. I'll come up in about half an hour and we can have some breakfast in the kitchen.'

Sirinya showers in the new bathroom along the corridor, remembering how they used to wash from a rainwater butt in a concrete cubicle in the backyard. She dresses quickly, returns to the bedroom and watches out of the window as Malee supervises the unloading of countless boxes full of produce. Malee is in full command of the team of men, some are the crew from the lorry, some work in the shop. She walks around pointing and gesticulating, giving orders with calm precision as dozens of boxes are unloaded from the lorry and piled on the stalls in front of the shop.

It's been her whole life, Sirinya thinks. How confident she looks. How different my own life has been from hers, how much further I've travelled. But we are both back here now, and which of us has lived the better life? Which one of us is the most content?

She thinks back to her time in England. How she had arrived in 1945 on the cargo ship with Johnny, and how his family had been polite but incredulous when he introduced her to them, openly staring at her as if she were a creature from another planet. His younger sister, June, had even reached out with an awed expression to touch the glossy black hair which tumbled down Sirinya's back.

She remembers the first painful meal with the family. How they all sat stiffly around a wooden dining table in the front room of their cramped terraced house in the suburbs of south London. Johnny's mother, a thin woman with grey hair and nervous grey eyes, fussed around in a floral apron, plying Sirinya with food as if she came from a land stricken with famine. The father chomped his way steadily through his meal and hardly looked up from the *Daily Mail* that was spread out on the table beside his plate.

It was Johnny who was the thin one, the one who had lost half his bodyweight working on the railway, whose eyes stood out in his gaunt face. He was the one who deserved their sympathy. But to her astonishment the family hardly mentioned his condition, lowering their eyes instead of staring at him, being careful not to allude to it, not to make a fuss. Sirinya toyed with the food, an unappetising, greasy shoulder of pork swimming in tasteless gravy, leathery roast potatoes and over-boiled cabbage.

'We've still got rationing, you see,' explained Johnny's mother, watching Sirinya with anxious eyes as she picked at the meat.

'Johnny, does she understand?'

'Yes, she understands, Mother,' said Johnny patiently.

Sirinya forced herself to eat the unfamiliar fare so as not to appear rude, and wondered if she would ever get used to it. Beside the vibrant, explosive tastes of her homeland, this food had virtually no taste at all.

It is odd looking back, but the years seem to have telescoped and shrunk away and all that remains in her mind are a few memorable incidents. The rest of the time, the long years during which life went on in the same tedious rhythm year after year, have simply melted from her memory.

She and Johnny had been married by the captain on the ship, a simple ceremony out on the open deck witnessed by two of Johnny's fellow servicemen as the ship ploughed on across the shimmering Indian Ocean towards the setting sun. Johnny was keen for them to be married before they arrived in England. But when they did arrive, his mother insisted that they should also have a church service to bless their vows.

She remembers shivering in a long white dress at the altar in that cold stone building, unheated even in the depths of winter, wondering how this strange religion, with its inexplicable rituals, cold music, and forbidding formality could ever warm the hearts of its followers. She glanced behind her at the family in the front pew, wearing their best hats and coats, and saw no joy in their faces. She felt a pang of homesickness for the Buddha, for the chanting of the monks, the discordant clang of the prayer bells, the smell of incense and candles, and the all-embracing warmth of the temple.

She and Johnny lived in the back bedroom of his parents' house for several months until his back-pay came through from the army. It was a tense time. She was still suffering from the traumas the war years had heaped upon her, and so was he. Each was afraid of upsetting the other, and they skirted around each others' pain like tomcats before a fight. Except that there were no fights. Not in twenty-five years. Their marriage was as smooth and calm and featureless as the wide ocean they had crossed to get to that cold island.

She was so very grateful to him though, and her gratitude manifested itself through action. Through doing everything she could to make his life comfortable. Before he awoke in the mornings she would be down in the kitchen making him tea and toast. Throughout the day she would prepare snacks and drinks for him as well as help his mother prepare the family meals. When he went out she would tidy and clean their small room.

'You spoil him,' said his mother watching her first attempt at baking biscuits. 'It can't be good for him.'

When the army pay from all those years Johnny had been a prisoner finally came, Sirinya was secretly relieved to be able to move to a small flat above a launderette a few streets away from the family home. Johnny enrolled in a teacher training course at the local college, so he was out all day at lectures. In the evenings he took a job in a local pub to make their money go further.

It was during those first few months that Sirinya experienced homesickness for the first time in her life. She was alone for long hours at a stretch and the time dragged. It was usually only mid-morning by the time she had finished her housework and prepared the vegetables for the evening meal. She would sit alone, listening to the radio and staring out of the window. She longed for the hubbub of the streets she had once known; the cries of vendors and hawkers, the shrill horns of motorbikes and tuk-tuks. She even longed for the noise and bustle of Bangkok, the city that never sleeps and that she had been so keen to leave behind.

Even when she looked out of the window all she would see would be occasional anonymous pedestrians hurrying past on the pavement below, huddled into their coats and hats. Cars and lorries sped past on the main road. It dawned on her that the British led closed, indoor lives. It was because of the climate, she realised that, and she couldn't blame them. The bitter chill of winter even permeated the flat itself. Who'd have thought there could be frost on the *inside* of the windows in the mornings, or that you'd be able to see your breath in white clouds in the room before the gas fire was lit?

Involuntarily she reaches out and touches the glass of the bedroom window upstairs in the shophouse. It is cool, but the touch of it brings her back from her memories. She realises that she has been daydreaming and that Malee will be waiting. She brushes her hair in the mirror and hurries down to the kitchenette where Malee is already at work preparing a full Thai breakfast. Delicious smells of frying ginger and garlic waft from the stove.

'What are you making?'

'Khao tom and sticky rice.'

'Mmm I haven't tasted that for years!'

'Didn't you cook Thai food when you were in England?'

'I tried sometimes, but it was so difficult to get the ingredients … I learned to cook their food instead. It's what Johnny liked.'

She watches Malee frying the strips of pork in a wok over the gas flame, moving the pan expertly, quickly with her left hand, turning the meat in the ginger and oil with a spatula in her right hand. The sticky rice bubbles away in a saucepan. The smell of rice cooking is as evocative as the temple bells. Johnny hated rice because of his years of eating it in the prison camps. He asked her never to cook it, so she never did. Now she realises how much she has missed it, how the smell rising from the stove is the smell of home, the smell of comfort.

'Go and sit down at the table and I'll bring it over to you.'

Sirinya goes over to the low table and sits before it on a floor cushion; within moments Malee sets two bowls of rice on the table. They contain strips of pork and poached eggs mixed in amongst the rice. Sirinya holds the bowl up to her nose and breathes in the familiar smell.

'Let's eat it and then go down to the temple. Phraa Wicharong told you to go every day, didn't he?'

'Alright, I'm happy to go down there. But I'm not really sure it's going to help me, Malee. Nothing's going to help me except finding Ratana.'

Malee's face clouds over. 'You're not still on about that are you? I thought what Phraa said to you dissuaded you from doing that.'

'I know he's right and I know what I should do. But Malee, I came here for a purpose, I've been thinking about it for years, planning it. I can't just let it drop that easily.'

'So, you need to learn to meditate again. It is hard work, Siri. Don't you remember?'

She nods. She does remember the daily trips to the temple, the hours of meditation, of silent contemplation, the struggle to follow the path, to control her mind. And as a child and young woman she had worked hard at it, and achieved the sort of inner peace she now longs for. But it all slipped away from her over the years through lack of practice. She wonders now if she will ever find her way back to that path.

'I will do it, Malee. I want to do it so desperately. But the problem is, I can't truly settle back to it until I find her. I'll have to go back to Bangkok soon, Malee. Don't look like that. It will only be for a couple of days. I need to find out if she did go there. And if she did I need to track her down.'

8

The first time Chalong took supplies of vegetables into Chungkai camp, Sirinya and Malee helped him load the lorry. It was an army truck with a hooped tarpaulin cover, loaned to him by the Japanese as part of the deal he had signed to supply the camps near to Kanchanaburi. He had spent two days the previous week in Bangkok arranging for additional supplies to be sent each day by road to supplement those that already came by river barge. He was vague and secretive about his trip when he returned, and Sirinya guessed he had also been to see his contacts in the Resistance while he was there.

That day they'd all been working since dawn in the relative cool of the early morning, filling huge wicker baskets with potatoes, kale, onions and cabbages, and heaving them one by one onto the back of the lorry. The two boys who worked in the shop had laboured alongside Malee, Sirinya and Chalong, and by the time they'd finished, Sirinya's bones and muscles were aching with the effort of lifting and stretching, her clothes were soaked in sweat.

When it was done, Sirinya said to Chalong, 'Can we come with you, Uncle?'

She had not asked before, and had guessed that he would not want them to go with him into the camp. Now he turned and looked at her, wiping sweat from his brow with the back of his hand.

'No, Siri. I'll take one of the boys.'

'But please, Uncle. I'd like to see what it's like inside the camp.'

'No, Sirinya. It is no place for a girl. Jip can come with me.'

'But you'll need help unloading. You and Jip can't do it on your own.'

'The prisoners will help. It's all arranged. The Japs won't let me take more than one person into the camp, Siri,' and when she opened her mouth to protest he said gruffly, 'I said no!'

She turned away disappointed, but she knew not to press him further. She and Malee watched as he jumped up inside the cab with Jip beside him and set off down Saeng Chuto road in a cloud of exhaust smoke.

They went inside the shop and began their morning duties. Time dragged. There were fewer customers than usual. Sirinya wondered if they were put off by Chalong's new association with the Japanese, or perhaps because the occupation meant they had less money to spend than before. Those who did come appeared nervous, reluctant to chat, keen to make their purchases and be on their way.

After several long hours the dark green cab of the lorry appeared once again at the end of the road. At the sound of the engine, Sirinya and Malee rushed out to greet Chalong. The lorry drew up in front of the shophouse, but Chalong didn't immediately jump down from the cab. Sirinya exchanged worried glances with Malee. Malee went round to the driver's door.

'What's wrong, Father?' Sirinya heard her say.

Chalong opened the door and got down slowly.

'What is it?' asked Malee, 'where's the boy?'

'Oh ... he rushed off home as soon as we reached the outskirts of town.'

'What happened?'

He shook his head and kept his face turned away from the girls. 'It's alright. Let's go inside,' he muttered.

Piak came running from the front door and put her arms around her husband in a protective gesture.

'Come on upstairs, Chalong. I've made some fried rice for your lunch.'

The girls followed them up the steps and into the apartment in silence. Chalong sat down at the table, held his head in his hands for a few moments, then turned to look at them. Sirinya saw his expression clearly for the first time. On his face was a look of utter bewilderment, his eyes appeared sunken, stunned, as if he had witnessed something inexplicable. Sirinya realised that he was in shock.

'What happened, Father?' Malee repeated.

'Nothing really,' he said slowly. 'We went into the camp. Some of the prisoners helped us to unload the truck, then we came back. Nothing happened.'

'But what did you see? What happened in the camp? Why do you look like that?'

Piak stepped in. 'Leave your father alone, Malee. Can't you see he's tired? Stop bothering him with questions. Now wash your hands and sit down at the table. Let us eat.'

'No, my dear. She has a right to ask,' said Chalong, 'Let me tell you what I saw. Then you will know why I want to do what we can to help those poor souls.'

'We drove into the camp and the guards waved at us to drive across a wide open space – a sort of parade ground – and park up in front of a low bamboo hut thatched with palm leaves. They said it was the store. All the huts were like that, though. There must be ten of them built in a row along the river. There are no proper buildings. They are just atap huts, built from what the prisoners must have found in the forest. Bamboo and palm leaves. I dread to think what will happen to them when it rains.

'We got down from the lorry and looked around. It is mud and bare earth everywhere you look. Across on the other side of the ground we spotted a few men digging a great long trench. From the stench of it I guessed that it must be their latrine. That is all they have for hundreds of men. Those men digging it looked half-starved. They were bone-thin, some of them and they had virtually no clothes. Just dirty rags. Some of them only wore loin cloths and worked barefoot in the filth.

We started unloading the lorry and a couple of prisoners came out of the store to help us.

'"Most men out working on railway. Just sick men left here in daytime. Not fit to work," the guard said, pointing at the two men with contempt. They were as thin as the men digging the trench, and one of them looked very pale and weak. The other one had a great tropical ulcer suppurating on his leg and could barely walk. They avoided looking at us. I wanted to speak to them, to tell them that we are ready and willing to help them, that there is an underground network working for them, but if they stopped unloading the lorry or paused for breath, even for a moment, one of the guards would come up and give them a thump or a prod with a cane or bayonet. So there was no chance to speak, or even make proper eye contact. I even thought the guard might start on me with his vicious stick.

'We finished unloading and turned to get back in the lorry. As we did so there was a commotion on the other side of the ground, we heard shouting and screaming. We turned to look and saw three guards beating up one of the prisoners. That man looked more senior than the others, he was older, and at least had the remnants of a uniform on. The guards were yelling at him in Japanese, beating him with sticks and lengths of wire and when he doubled up and went down the savages all set upon him at once, kicking him again and again.

'The guards who had been watching over us were standing there staring across at what was happening. One of the soldiers who had been unloading leaned towards me and whispered, "That's the camp doctor. He refused to supply sick men to work on the railway this morning. They do that to him most days."

'I was astonished, and opened my mouth to tell the man that we could help, but the guard turned back towards us and started shouting at me and Jip to get into the lorry. He was shaking his stick at the man who had spoken to us. I started the engine as quickly as I could and roared off towards the gates. Jip was sitting beside me shaking. He's only a youngster, you know. He's never seen anything like that in his life before. He didn't speak all the way back to town and as soon as we got near to his road he jumped down and scuttled off. I don't suppose we'll see him here again for a long time.'

'But that's dreadful, Uncle. Truly dreadful. We must do something,' said Sirinya, tears in her eyes.

'Yes my child, we must. And that is why I agreed to take the contract as you know. To give me a chance to get close, to see what the Japs are doing in those camps and to see if we can do anything to help the prisoners. But it isn't going to be easy. I'll try to think of a way of contacting them, letting them know that we can help.'

'Now, come on, let us eat,' said Piak, setting bowls of fried rice on the table.

They began to eat in silence, each with their own thoughts and concerns about the prisoners, and of the danger they could be in themselves if they took the next step towards helping them.

'Oh, by the way,' said Chalong, pausing between mouthfuls, 'I think we need someone else to help out in the shop now that we have the deliveries to the camps and all the extra stock to cope with. Especially now that Jip seems to have deserted us.'

'I could do that,' said Piak quickly.

'No, no my darling. You are not strong. You need to conserve your strength, and besides, we need you to look after us here. No I was thinking about Kitima. Siri, do you think she would come down from the village to help out for a few months?'

Sirinya thought about her mother, strong and capable and good humoured. It would be wonderful to have her here.

'She might be prepared to come,' she said, 'but Grandmother needs her help with the crops.'

'It's coming into the rainy season, there won't be so much work to do up there in the hills now. Do you think you could make the journey tomorrow and ask her? I'm sure she will understand if you explain what's happening here.'

Sirinya thought again about her mother's open face, her ready smile, her gentle brown eyes. Through all these weeks of trauma since the Japanese had come to Kanchanaburi she had missed her mother's comforting presence, the firm enveloping embrace that seemed to make all her troubles and anxieties melt away.

'Of course,' she said smiling. 'I'll go tomorrow, Uncle. I'm sure she'll come if she can.'

So the next day she found herself bouncing around on the back of an open-backed truck, squeezed in between an old woman nursing a basket of young chicks and a labourer chain-smoking cheroots. She had done this journey countless times before but it felt different this time. The passengers were subdued. Instead of their usual chatter and banter, the they kept their heads down, and lowered their eyes as they passed Japanese soldiers strutting with guns and bayonets on the streets.

As the truck left the town behind and sped on along the river valley and towards the hills, the atmosphere changed. People began to relax, to lift their heads, to smile and exchange the odd word or two. A light drizzle began as the truck began to climb into the hills. Sirinya pulled on her waterproof as there was no cover on the truck. The other passengers did the same with barely a break in their conversations. They were used to the rain. It was part of life here.

The road rose steadily through the thick jungle. Raindrops dripped from the teak trees and from the creepers that overhung the road, but as they approached the crossroads where the trail to Sirinya's grandmother's village began, the rain had eased and the clouds were beginning to clear.

She stood where the truck dropped her and watched the tailgate until it had disappeared out of sight around a bend, belching black smoke as it went. Then with a sigh she heaved the bag of fruit she had brought for her grandmother onto her shoulder and turned onto the narrow trail, which wound its way through the forest and into the hills. It was slippery underfoot and soon her flimsy sandals were coated with mud. It normally took a couple of hours to get to the village from the road, but in these conditions she knew that it would take far longer.

The trail was encroached by sharp branches and overhanging creepers. Water dripped from the undergrowth. She pushed through and soon her clothes were soaked with moisture. She had no fear of the jungle, she had grown up with the knowledge that the walls of greenery that hid these buried paths were seething with life. She was not afraid either of the outsized insects that flitted around, sometimes settling on her for a few seconds. She was used to the sawing and hammering of the crickets, so loud at times that it sounded like mechanical tools.

The path underfoot ran like a torrent in places, but after a while the sun began to glint through the foliage, the rain stopped and clouds of steam rose from the undergrowth.

For the first few kilometres the path followed the course of a brook, which ran along the bottom of a steep valley. Then it began to rise upstream beside fast-flowing currents and rushing waterfalls. She trudged steadily on and found herself out of breath as she neared the crest of a rise and stopped to rest beside a teak tree, her heart pumping, sweat running down her face, clothes clinging to her damp body.

The hammering and sawing of the crickets was louder than ever here, but mingled with it was another sound. She lifted her head and listened. It sounded unfamiliar, louder and sharper. As if real hammers and tools were at work here in the heart of the jungle. Then she heard a sound that made her hair stand on end. It was human voices. The guttural shouts of guards that she had heard before.

As if in a trance she moved forward a few paces. Then she stopped dead. Only a few yards ahead of her the ground fell away and a precipice opened up cutting through the jungle like a great open wound. Inside the wound was a sight that made her jaw drop open, a seething, churning scene of constant movement eating away at the flesh of the earth. Dozens of half-naked bodies moved simultaneously, wielding hammers and pickaxes, lifting them high and bringing them down on the top of great spikes held in the rock by stooping men. Bodies glistened with sweat, wet hair plastered to their heads, ribs protruding, arms and legs as thin as twigs.

Japanese guards strutted up and down the cutting, canes held behind their backs, pausing sometimes to bring them down on the shoulders of a man who had paused to stretch or breathe. Sirinya stared transfixed. She found herself searching the faces, and realised that she was trying to catch sight of the boy she had seen a few weeks before on the jungle trail, with whom she had exchanged a glance. It had only lasted a few seconds, but in those seconds she felt she had seen into his soul; a connection had been made. She did not quite understand it, but she knew it was important.

She stood staring, gripping a tree for support. He was nowhere to be seen. She knew she would recognise him again even amongst all these men.

One of the guards lifted his head to look up and she moved back behind the teak tree. She was shivering all over despite the steamy heat. She stood for a few moments out of sight taking deep breaths, trying to calm herself, before slowly turning and carrying on up the trail. It would only be another kilometre or so before the jungle thinned out and she would see the familiar group of wooden huts thatched with palm leaves and where the village children would rush to greet her, to ask for fruit and take her hand chattering with excitement. She walked slowly now on trembling legs, head bowed. She was unaware of the vibrant scenery around her, only seeing the horror of the cutting with its army of stick-thin workers, with their visible ribs, hollow cheeks and eyes full of despair.

9

Sirinya shoulders her way through the crowded compartment as the Bangkok train pulls out of Kanchanaburi station. She finds a seat next to a frail old woman who pulls a hessian sack bulging with fresh mangoes onto her lap to make room for Sirinya to sit down. The sweet smell of the ripe fruit takes Sirinya straight back to Chalong's shop and the old days. With an effort she resists the tug of the past. She glances around the carriage, half expecting to see the man she'd met on the way here, but there is no sign of him, just a throng of locals with their luggage, their boxes of goods, baskets of livestock, their babies and children. She closes her eyes in resignation. She had not expected to be making the return journey to the capital so soon.

Her mind wanders back to the awkward conversation she'd had with Malee this morning before she left.

'You're not leaving already are you, Siri?' Malee asked, finding Sirinya fully dressed and packing when she brought in the morning tea. 'You've only just arrived.'

'I'm not leaving, Malee. I'm just going back to Bangkok for a little while. We discussed it yesterday.'

Malee sighed heavily and set the tea tray on the bedside table.

'Well, I thought you hadn't decided about that yet. And in any case, I didn't realise you meant to go so soon.'

'I need to find Ratana as soon as I can. I can't settle to anything while it's praying on my mind. I can't make any decisions.'

'But how on earth will you find her, Siri? No one here is in touch with her any more. She could be anywhere. You have absolutely no idea where she'll be living.'

'Oh, I've got a shrewd idea where she might be,' Sirinya said quietly. 'Do you mind if I take the photograph with me? The one on the chest in the living room?'

'What? The one of us all on the day we left school? How on earth will that help you? We were fourteen, fifteen when that was taken. She won't look the same now. None of us do.'

'She had such a distinctive face, didn't she? High cheekbones and big eyes. She can't have changed that much. I'm sure someone will remember her.'

'Well, I suppose you can take it if you like, but I'm not sure it will help you.'

'It will be a start at least. Thank you so much, Malee. I'll take good care of it.'

'When will you be back? Assuming that you mean to come back to Kanchanaburi, that is?'

'Of course. Of course I'll be back. I just need to put this to rest. I'll only be a day or two at the most.'

Malee shrugged, gave her a doubting look and left her to her packing.

But as Sirinya came down to the kitchen, Malee handed her some sweet cookies wrapped in greaseproof paper.

'Here, take these for the journey,' she said. 'If you must go. I think you're making a mistake, but you know that. Do come back soon, Sirinya. Now you're here again I don't want to let you go.'

The two of them hugged for a moment then Malee turned away, but Sirinya saw there were tears in her cousin's eyes.

'Dear, sweet Malee,' she breathes now thinking of her cousin. She takes a nibble at the sweet cookie, and as it melts in her mouth she closes her eyes, willing the journey to be over soon.

At Thonburi station she catches a bus across the Chao Phraya river on the Krungthep Bridge into the city. Although it is still well before rush hour, the ramshackle vehicle is packed and stifling. Sirinya finds a seat beside an open window. But the air that comes through it is no cooler than the air inside the bus, and reeks of diesel and exhaust fumes. Her clothes soon stick to her body and her hair is damp with perspiration. The bus inches forward through the traffic-choked streets. She stares out at the densely packed lines of vehicles. Cars, motorbikes, taxis and tuk-tuks sit belting out fumes between the shabby buildings, whose façades are blackened by pollution. Here, as everywhere in Bangkok, food stalls line the road, customers sit inches from the moving traffic eating at low plastic tables oblivious to the fumes and the noise.

The city has been transformed in the last twenty-five years. She stares out, wide-eyed, at the teeming pavements. The sights and sounds are overwhelming. She remembers the streets as they were in the 1940s; wide open spaces lined with trees. Hawkers would trot along the pavement, baskets bouncing from poles on their shoulders. Bicycles and cycle-rickshaws were the main traffic then, with some bullock carts and the odd motor car. Now the place is a pulsating modern metropolis where the petrol engine is king.

She has to change buses in Silom road. She gets down from the first bus and stands sweating on the pavement, dazed by her surroundings, allowing herself to be jostled and shoved aside by passers-by; shoppers in a hurry, office workers on their lunch break. The bus to New Petchburi Road soon appears. It is an equally beaten, decaying vehicle, painted an indeterminate rusty colour, all its body parts moving and vibrating to the rhythm of the engine. It edges along Silom towards Rachadamri Road and she stares out at the thronging crowds. She realises that in her mind the city has stayed the same as it was the day she had left in 1945. She has failed to factor in that this place will have changed like everywhere else. That it has been engulfed by the modern world.

As she reflects on how mistaken she has been, something takes her attention amongst the bustling throng. It is a group of western men. They stand out from the crowd: pale aliens in the sea of brown faces, a head taller than everyone else. Each walks proudly with a pretty Thai girl on his arm, and the thing about them that sends a chill down Sirinya's spine is the fact that they are all wearing identical khaki uniforms. They are soldiers, she realises with a jolt. She cranes her neck to take a closer look as the bus crawls past. She has never seen western soldiers who are not wasted and bone-thin before.

In New Petchburi Road she gets off the bus and heads towards a nondescript side street, or soi, halfway down the busy row of go-go bars and strip clubs. It is narrow and dark, as it always was. The buildings shut out the light of the sky, but it is quiet here, away from the main drag of New Petchburi. She is not sure what is guiding her; why some inner force is propelling her towards the very place she vowed she would never go to again.

At the end of the soi she stops. It is still there. The Golden Key Hotel. With a feeling of trepidation she steps off the heat of the pavement, through the swing glass doors and into the airconditioned building. The lobby is bare, with a brown linoleum floor and orange wallpaper with a modern pattern of random gold circles. This is different too. She remembers pale peeling paint and a marble tiled floor.

The Chinese man behind the desk is bent with age. His brown tunic is shiny with wear. As he lifts his grey head and peers at her through the opaque lenses of glasses with thick black frames, the shadow of a memory crosses her mind. Is it possible that he has been here, minding this desk, day in day out down all these years? This unexpected bolt from the past makes her pause. She feels dizzy. She grasps the Formica desk with both hands for support.

'I'd like a single room please. How much will that be?' she asks in a halting voice in English, not sure why her mother tongue has momentarily deserted her. He stares at her, and answers in Thai.

'The hotel is very full, madam. But I might be able to squeeze you in on the third floor. Single room two hundred baht per night.' His voice is a thin croak. He consults a grubby ledger, then potters to a board behind the desk to collect a key. He hands it to her with a frail hand. 'Third floor. Room 304. I'll ask the porter to take your luggage.'

'No need. I only have a small bag,' she says.

'There is no lift, madam, I'm afraid.'

'I know,' she whispers and turns away from the desk.

As she starts towards the stairs, she hears shouts and commotion outside and a group of western soldiers burst through the entrance and fill the hallway. Their voices are loud and insistent. She recognises American accents. Sirinya shrinks back into the shadows behind the stairs. The men are young, hardly more than boys. Their heads are shaved and their faces sunburnt. They exude energy and pent-up aggression. She suddenly realises why they are here. These are U.S. soldiers fighting in Vietnam. They must be in Bangkok for a few days' leave. R&R as it is known. She thinks about the flickering images from the six o'clock news back in England. The shocking sights of bombed-out villages, of children running screaming from napalm, of choppers hovering over mountainous jungle. One of the young men notices her and stands aside politely, motioning her forward.

'After you, Ma'am,' he says. They all stop and wait for her to go up the staircase before them. As she walks up, she can hear their boots on the steps behind her. She is stunned to find soldiers from a new conflict here in this city, in this country. And again it comes home to her that her mind has been rooted in the past, her thoughts focused on that other brutal war as if the world has not moved on, as if it would never make the same mistake again. How wrong she has been.

She turns onto the third floor and the boots of the soldiers clatter on up the stairs. She hears them walking along the corridor on the floor above, turning keys in locks, slamming doors. And then silence. She realises she has never before seen soldiers so fit and full of life.

Sirinya lets herself into the room and stands still for a moment. The fan has been turned off and it is unbearably hot in here. Flies buzz about around the light fittings. The room is large and sparsely furnished, with the same ubiquitous brown lino on the floor. In the corner is a tiny shower room. She glances in at the bright pink tiles and cracked avocado-coloured lavatory. The basin tap drips rusty water cutting a groove in the porcelain. She wrinkles her nose at the pungent smell of drains. In the room there are two saggy narrow beds with veneer headboards and dark green candlewick covers. The walls are painted beige.

She drops her bag on one of the beds and switches on the fan. She crosses to the window, pushes back the thin curtains and opens it. It gives out onto a narrow passage behind the hotel, even narrower than the one at the front of the building. She leans out and listens to the sounds of the city floating on the air from beyond the roofs opposite. A constant hum of engines, put-putting of tuk-tuks and tooting of horns.

She can feel the thump of disco music from the go-go bars in the main road and she thinks again of Ratana, remembering why she is here. She watches a pack of soi dogs down in the alleyway rummaging in the overflowing bins behind the hotel, snapping and snarling over a chicken carcase. A group of monks pick their way through the rubbish, past the dogs and on down the soi, their robes a splash of saffron lighting up the dark alleyway. At the end between the buildings she glimpses a flash of gold. There must be a temple down there. A haven of peace and beauty in the midst of all this ugliness. Perhaps the changes are only superficial after all? The old heart of the city she once knew still beats strong and hard.

Sirinya sits down heavily on the bed and feels the cut of the wire frame beneath the thin mattress in her thighs. Suddenly she feels vulnerable. Tired and uncertain. The sight of the American soldiers has unsettled her. Perhaps she shouldn't have come? Not to this place at least. Not to this hotel that holds so many memories. And in spite of her resolve not to dwell on those days, being here in this place brings it all flooding back.

This was the hotel that Johnny brought her to when she was on her knees at the end of the war. He had tracked her down and found her when he'd been released from the camp by the Allies. She remembers her astonishment when he'd walked into the bar where she was working as a cleaner. She'd been mopping a table in a corner of the gloomy room, her face pinched with the pain of her aching back, the rumble of hunger in her stomach. The bar had not yet opened for the evening. She'd picked up a couple of dirty glasses to take back to the kitchen and turned around.

He'd appeared from nowhere, standing in front of her like a vision from a bizarre dream. At first she couldn't place who he was, out of context like that. He was as thin as he'd been in the camps. His cheeks were still hollow and his eyes stood out from his face. What she found most strange, though, was that he was wearing clothes instead of a loin cloth. She'd never seen him properly dressed before. He was dressed in a brand new army uniform. He was so skinny that the shirt hung off his shoulders and the trousers bagged at the knees. She stared at him, opening and closing her mouth stupidly. Finally she found her voice.

'Johnny ...what on earth are you doing here?'

'I came to find you. Your uncle said you'd come to Bangkok and that you hadn't been in touch for a very long time. I've been searching for you for weeks.'

'I've moved around quite a bit.'

'I gathered that.'

'There was no need for you to waste time looking for me. Don't you need to go home? Back to your own country. The war is over now.'

'I just wanted to see if you were alright. If you needed anything.'

'That's kind of you but it's not your concern,' she'd said looking away. He must know that things were not alright. By the look on her face, the tattered clothes she was wearing, how her body was skin and bone. He cleared his throat.

'After what happened. I've thought a lot about you. It must have been so dreadful for you, Sirinya ...I just wanted to make sure you were coping.'

'I'm coping fine,' she said, biting her nail, a hard edge to her voice. 'It's all in the past now. I want to forget.'

The owner of the bar loomed behind Johnny. A huge Chinese man, he waddled rather than walked, his face oily with sweat in the stuffy atmosphere.

'What are you doing, girl?' he spoke harshly to her in Thai, clicking his fat fingers. 'Get on with your work. Stop wasting time. I will speak to this customer.'

Her stomach tightened and she shrank back from him instinctively. Her hands were shaking. She walked towards the bar with the glasses. She could hear the owner speaking to Johnny in wheedling terms. She heard Johnny raise his voice in response.

'No thank you. I don't want a girl. I'm here to talk to Sirinya. I knew her during the war.'

'She is meant to be working this evening, sir, but if you want to take her you can. You'll have to pay a bar fine, though.'

Sirinya put the glasses down and clenched her fists, her face aflame with embarrassment.

'Bar fine? I don't pay for women.'

'If you want to take her out you have to pay. A thousand baht. She meant to be working. It will cost me money.'

She watched, tears of humiliation in her eyes as Johnny handed some notes over to the man. Then he turned to her.

'Come on, Sirinya, let's get out of this place.'

She didn't bother to go into the back room to collect her belongings. She knew the other girls were there making up and preparing for the evening, gossiping and laughing. She didn't want them to see that she was being bought too, just like most of them were every day, and by a farang too. She kept her eyes on the floor as Johnny ushered her out of the bar and into the stifling heat of the darkening street.

'Come on. I'll take you to my hotel.'

She stopped walking and turned to him with pleading eyes.

'Oh, I don't mean …. I'll pay for a separate room. Of course I will,' he said 'Come on, let's get a tuk-tuk. You look as though you're pretty well exhausted.'

On the main road they hailed a tuk-tuk which took them straight to the hotel, careering through the early evening traffic, blasting its horn. As she stared out at the buildings flashing past that day, she had a feeling that this would mark a turning point in her life. That she would never go back to the bar or anywhere else like it. She turned to Johnny and smiled for the first time since she'd seen him that day. He smiled back, showing uneven teeth, decayed from his ordeal in the camps, and he gripped her hand on the seat of the swaying vehicle.

10

The light of the day is fading fast as Sirinya leaves the Golden Key Hotel. The old man on reception is sitting watching a Thai soap opera on a portable TV, and he nods to her absently as she leaves her room key on the desk. She walks down the soi towards New Petchburi Road. She is carrying her clothes from this morning in a plastic bag and she and drops them off at a small laundry halfway along the soi. Forgetting the sweat and grime of this city, she had only packed one change of clothes to bring from Kanchanaburi. Leaving the laundry she walks towards the main road. She feels better for a rest, a shower (even though it was only a cold trickle), a change of clothes and some jasmine tea, which she made in her room and drank from a cracked cup. The fragrant liquid revived her flagging spirits.

In her handbag she carries the small bamboo-framed photograph of herself, Malee and Ratana. It was taken that sunny morning in 1937, the day they all left the small municipal secondary school after a prize-giving ceremony. They were holding their certificates up proudly and grinning at the camera. Yesterday she'd been very sure that the photograph would help her track down Ratana, but now in this huge metropolis heaving with strangers, she is less certain. She clutches her bag nervously as she emerges from the soi and turns onto the New Petchburi Road.

The sky is dark now and the street lit up with lights from shops and bars and a thousand flashing signs. The pavement is crowded with groups of young American GIs. There are few women about, and the ones that are out on the street at this hour are bar girls, tottering along in platform shoes and mini-skirts on the arms of the soldiers, having already secured their work for the evening.

Sirinya stands and stares ahead at the bewildering array of neon signs hanging from buildings, announcing the names of strip clubs and girlie bars in vibrant colours. 'Pussy Galore,' 'King's Castle,' 'Cowboy Massage Parlour,' all flash at her, clamouring for her attention. She blinks and shakes her head in bewilderment. This place was full of bars at the end of the war, but it was nothing like this. Back then it catered mainly to Thai men and the occasional foreigner. It had been low key, understated and furtive, not brazenly displaying its wares to the world as it does now. The frenetic energy of the place is overwhelming. The noise is deafening; above the roar of the traffic, western music pumps from every doorway. Taxis and tuk-tuks draw up at the pavement continuously, disgorging yet more groups of young men with their bulging wallets and appetites for beer and lust.

Many of the bars lining the street have plate-glass windows like shop fronts. As Sirinya wanders past, she stops and stares into the first one. Inside, in front of ruched black velvet curtains sit a crowd of girls on tiered seating. They look as if they are posing for a school photograph. They are all heavily made up and dressed in low-cut tops, tiny skirts and high platform shoes. They seem impossibly young. Each wears a large number pinned to her chest. Sirinya walks on slowly, thinking of how vulnerable those girls look, how far they must have come from their simple villages and small provincial towns. At the next window a group of GIs are loudly discussing the girls on display, laughing and pushing one other, egging each other on to go in and place their order.

At the next bar, a wizened old man holds up a list of the live shows, written in chalk as if it were a restaurant menu: 'strip show, woman do pussy ping pong, woman fire darts from pussy, live sex show on stage'. She avoids catching his eye and moves away. Through the door she glimpses a group of slender girls dancing on top of a bar, naked but for tiny bikini pants and high-heeled shoes. '*Give me just a little more time,*' warbles the disembodied voice of the singer that they are dancing to.

She takes a deep breath and plunges inside the next doorway. Here is as good a place to start her search as any. The girls behind the bar are working hard, pulling pints for GIs who stand shoulder to shoulder and three deep. Sirinya pauses behind the crowd for a moment, breathing in the air, rank with stale alcohol and sweat. Her eyes smart from the cigarette smoke. As she waits and watches for an opportunity to move forward, she is jostled and shoved by the men as they push past her with their pints making for the tables. She looks for a gap between the bodies; lacking the courage to push her way between them to speak to the bar girls.

Finally she gives up and leaves. Perhaps somewhere else it will be easier? At the Rabbit-Hop bar next door, waitresses dressed in bunny-girl uniforms ferry the drinks to customers sitting at tables. A line of girls behind the bar pour and mix drinks, working quickly and efficiently, their faces glistening with sweat. Sirinya leans on the bar. One of them glances in her direction. 'Can I help you, madam?' asks the girl. 'If you'd like a drink please sit down at one of the tables and a waitress will take your order.'

Sirinya seizes her chance. 'Do you know this woman?' She shoves the photograph toward the girl who peers at it intently, narrowing her eyes, lowering false eyelashes. She shakes her head and gives the photograph to her friend. It is passed around the bar.

'She is older now,' says Sirinya. She has to shout to make them hear above the music. 'She is about my age.'

All the girls examine the photograph for a few seconds and one by one shake their heads, quickly turning back to their work and their chatter.

It is the same story at the next five bars along the strip. The same crowds and thumping music, the same mild curiosity from the girls, drawn to something out of the ordinary which might break the monotony of the evening. But it is quickly replaced by indifference as they realise they don't recognise the girl in the photo. They shrug and turn their attention back to their work. At one bar a waitress tells Sirinya to speak to the owner. She points out an overweight Chinese man, with long greasy hair, sitting at a table in the corner tucking into a plate piled high with food. Sirinya's heart freezes when she catches sight of him, he reminds her so much of another bar owner from long ago, but she takes a deep breath and suppresses the image. She approaches him, explains that she is looking for an old friend and shows him the photograph. He pushes back his hair, screws up his eyes to look at it, but shakes his head and quickly turns back to his meal.

It is after ten o'clock when Sirinya decides she can't face another bar this evening. She makes her way through the press of people back to the hotel, her spirits low. She feels dazed, shattered; as if her body and mind have been assaulted from every angle. All she wants to do is to lie down and sleep, to find some peace away from the noise and clamour of this sordid place. The street is even busier now, the crowds are even thicker and more rowdy than when she began her search a few hours before.

The hotel is quiet as she enters. The aged receptionist is slumped asleep on the counter, the television still flickering. Wearily she climbs the stairs to her room, takes off her skirt and blouse and lies down on the bed under the whizzing fan, exhausted and reeling from the experience of the evening. Her ears ring from the music. How will she face doing the same thing tomorrow at another set of identical and equally sleazy places? How can she put herself through it? Is it even worth it?

She already has the answer to that question. She knows she will never rest until she has answers. Her mind goes back to the terrible day that changed her life forever. That day in 1943 when she stood on the Bamboo Road beside the river, waiting feverishly with joy and hope in her heart for the sound of his footsteps, for his head to appear between the thickets of bamboo along the track. Her hope was mingled with fear and trepidation.

She waited on the same spot, on a bend in the track where the river laps the bank, from sunrise until sunset. Through that whole day she sat hidden in the bamboo thicket watching the sun mark the passing of the hours as it moved across the sky. Gradually, as time passed and there was no sign of anyone walking towards her between the thickets of bamboo, the dreadful realisation of what must have happened dawned on her, and her whole world collapsed. All the joy and hope of the morning gradually slipped from her and was replaced with horror and bitter disbelief. Ever since that day she knows that she has been searching; striving to find that girl again. The girl she once was. She knows that if she doesn't find Ratana she will never find that long-lost girl inside. Her life will forever be plagued with bitterness and the desire for revenge.

She slips into an uneasy sleep. She dreams that she is being carried against her will by invisible hands towards a closed wooden door. It is the front door of a house. She is fighting, kicking and screaming, but no matter how hard she shouts, no sound will come out of her mouth. No one can hear her. The hands carrying her are gripping her bare arms hard, nails digging into her flesh, bruising her skin. They propel her nearer and nearer the door, and just as she thinks she is going to be slammed against it, it opens soundlessly inwards and she is carried through the doorway and into the house, powerless to stop. Now she is in a narrow hall painted white with doors opening off it. She doesn't know why but she is terrified of what might be behind those doors, sensing something horrifying inside; some evil force. She tries to back away, but the hands still drag her on. One of the doors opens and the hands shove her inside. She keeps her eyes tightly closed, not daring to open them and look at what might be in the room. Someone is shouting at her, telling her to open her eyes and take a look, but she cannot bring herself to. She wakes up with a strangled shout.

She is sitting up in bed, her breath coming in gulps, sweat pouring off her body. It is still dark outside, a pale glow from the street lamps lighting up the buildings opposite the hotel. She glances at her watch. It is only midnight. She has been asleep for less than an hour. The memory of the dream leaves an imprint on her mind so dreadful that she is afraid to go back to sleep.

There are voices in the soi outside, then the thump of several pairs of boots on the stairs accompanied by the clack-clack of high heels and the high, hysterical laugh of a woman. The GIs have selected from the display in the window and are bringing home their purchases. Sirinya lies down again and covers her head with the thin pillow in an effort to block out the sounds, block out the memories, but still they return.

11

As she had predicted, when Sirinya emerged from the jungle path into the village clearing that day in 1942, a group of small children playing in the dirt between the stilted houses looked up from their game and seeing her approach ran towards her in high excitement. They surrounded her, chanting her name, grabbing her legs, seizing her hands. Laughing, she handed one of the older girls some oranges to share around. The children scurried off after the girl, shouting and laughing.

Smiling to herself she walked on along the dirt track that wound its way between the cluster of wooden huts, greeting her neighbours as they came out on their porches to wai to her and say hello. A buffalo tethered to a fence turned and stared at her from under long lashes. Chickens and pigs grubbed at the earth under the houses. The village dogs came out to investigate, sniffing at her sarong, wagging their tails and barking. They accompanied her through the village to her grandmother's house on the far side of the settlement, where the land began to drop away towards the rice terraces.

As she neared the house, she caught sight of Kitima working on the porch, sitting cross-legged on the boards, head bowed as she peeled vegetables.

'Mother!'

Kitima lifted her head and shaded her eyes, peering into the dipping sun. Her face cleared as she saw her daughter. She scrambled to her feet and despite her bulky frame was down the ladder in seconds. She ran to Sirinya and enveloped her in her soft earthy embrace. Sirinya closed her eyes and swallowed tears as she breathed in her mother's familiar scent: a mixture of garlic, lemongrass and wood smoke, the comforting smells of childhood.

'What a surprise, my darling!' said Kitima, holding her at arm's length and beaming into her eyes, 'Go on up. I'll make you some tea. Grandmother is resting.' Sirinya climbed the ladder to the porch while her mother made tea over the cooking fire in front of the house.

'How is Grandma?' asked Sirinya as Kitima came up the ladder with the tea. Kitima settled herself down on a cushion and gave Sirinya a sideways look. Then she leaned forward and said in a low voice, with a twinkle in her eye, 'Oh, you know how she is. Forever harping on about her aching bones and ailments, but as tough as old boots. I really believe that she'll out-live us all.'

Sirinya laughed and stretched herself out. It felt good to be home.

'How are things at Chalong's shop? I've been worried, what with all those Japanese soldiers around.'

'Oh, Mother, it is dreadful in the town. Truly dreadful. Since the occupation ...'

Kitima leaned over, took Sirinya's hands and looked earnestly into her eyes. 'It *is* awful, my darling. I had no idea they would come to this part of the country, but they have even come into our quiet little corner. Here in our beloved Tenasserim Hills, ripping up the forest, cutting through the mountains. Using white men as their slaves. It is truly shocking.'

'I saw it on the walk up from the road. That huge cutting in the forest. I couldn't believe my eyes, Mother. Those poor men, beaten and starved like that.'

Kitima nodded. 'They go on all night with lamps and fires you know. Some of the men from the village went down to give them food a couple of times last week. They hid in the trees and handed bananas and mangoes to a group of men tipping rubble over the side. But last time they went down one of the guards spotted them. They had to run for their lives. Word has it that the prisoners they gave the fruit to were beaten, Siri, judging from the screams and shouts they heard as they ran away.'

Kitima broke off and stared ahead, her usually merry eyes stilled and troubled. Sirinya reached out and took her hand. 'Do people think they will come to the village? The soldiers?'

'They might come but we're not so worried now. We've decided to keep away from that place. Keep ourselves to ourselves. We have no choice if we want to keep our skins.' She shivered, patted Sirinya's hand and smiled into her eyes. 'But what about you, my darling? Tell me about what is happening in the town. It must be far worse there.'

So Sirinya told her. All about the thousands of prisoners being driven through the jungle, about the makeshift camps being thrown up along the river out of bamboo and palm leaves, about the scenes in the jungle she had witnessed with Narong, about the Kempeitai evicting Chalong's neighbour and commandeering the house opposite, about the atmosphere of oppression and fear in the town.

'When they first arrived they came to the house with guns and sticks and forced Uncle to sell them his patch of land across the river. And then they came back, a few weeks later, and made him promise to supply the prison camps with vegetables.'

'Supply the camps? Kitima stared at her. 'So he's working for the Japanese? Chalong? I can't believe it.'

Sirinya glanced around to check there was no one close by. She leaned forward and whispered, 'He has his reasons, Mother. He's part of some organisation. He won't tell us all the details, but he's working against the occupation. He's got contacts in Bangkok. Supplying the camps is part of that. He's going to take extra food in, to help the prisoners. He's already been into some of the camps.'

'Sounds very dangerous,' said Kitima doubtfully, pouring the water from the boiling kettle into a cracked china teacup.

'He wants you to come down to town and help out, Mother.'

Kitima stopped pouring and stared at her daughter. She swallowed and put the kettle down.

'Me? Why me?'

'He needs you to help out in the shop because he's out a lot making deliveries. It's too much for Malee and me. And one of the boys ran away the first time they went to the camp.'

There was a silence. Then Kitima said in a quiet voice, 'Is that why you came?'

Sirinya nodded and looked down at the wooden boards, ashamed. She knew she had not been back enough to visit over the past year.

Kitima bit her lip and smiled quickly, as if suppressing disappointment. 'I thought there must be some reason, Siri. Not that I blame you for not coming here more often. You're young. It is quiet here. Life is simple; boring I suppose for people of your age. I felt the same when I was young like you. Always itching to be away. But one day I stopped feeling that way and realised I didn't need anything more than this. That there really isn't anything more that the world has to offer. One day perhaps you'll understand.'

Sirinya leaned forward and gripped her mother's hand, looking into her eyes, 'But I do understand, Mother. I do understand. It's just that at the moment I'm needed down there. You know that.'

'Of course. Of course I do. Now drink your tea,' Kitima said, handing her a cup.

'So will you come back with me?'

'I don't know, Siri. Let me think about it. You'll stay with us for a couple of days won't you?'

Again Sirinya looked away, shamefaced.

'I can't stay too long, Mother. Uncle is already struggling.'

'Well, perhaps I could come for a short while. But I don't want to be away from your grandmother for very long.'

'But you just said she's as tough as old boots, Mother.'

'That's true. But she's not getting any younger, Siri. She can cope on her own from day to day, but when the rice ripens in the paddies and it's harvest time I'll need to come back. She can't do that on her own.'

'Of course. I understand.'

'Understand what?'

It was Grandmother's voice, hard and high. She stood in the doorway, bony fingers gripping the bamboo frame on either side. Startled, Sirinya scrambled to her feet and bowed deeply to the old lady, bringing her hands up together to touch her nose, in a respectful wai.

'How are you, Yai?' Sirinya asked looking up at her grandmother. The old woman's arms and legs were even more thin and wizened than she remembered, her nut-brown skin shiny and taut from years in the rice fields, her pure white hair flowing past her shoulders. She wore a simple black sarong tucked around her chest. Her feet were bare.

'Not so good, not so good,' the old lady croaked. 'My health fails. It is my age. If you ventured up into these hills more often to visit you would know that, my girl.' Yai pursed her lips, moving forward and dropping into a squat beside Kitima. 'Is that food ready yet, Daughter?'

'Not quite. I need to stoke the fire up, Mother. It will be another half hour or so. Now don't be hard on Siri, you know it isn't easy for her to come up here. Especially now the Japanese soldiers are in town.'

Yai turned her head away contemptuously and spat a thin stream of betel juice over the rail of the hut.

'And why does she come now, eh?' Yai asked, rocking back and forth on her haunches, 'Not just to see us I'll bet. She wants something from us, Kiti. It is always the same.'

'Hush, Mother. Don't speak like that, please. Siri is a good girl. A dutiful daughter. You know that.'

'Hmm. If you say so. So, you were saying something, when I came out … what is there to understand? You two are cooking something up together. And I don't just mean the hotpot.' The old woman chuckled at her own joke, displaying broken teeth, stained red from years of chewing betel nut.

Sirinya glanced at her mother who drew herself up and looked at Yai.

'Chalong needs me to go down and help out in the shop, Mother,' she said in a steady voice. 'It will only be for a short while.'

'So I was right. She does want something. She wants to spirit you away from me. Why does Chalong need you? He has Siri and Malee, and Piak and all his other workers.'

'He has some extra work on, Yai,' said Sirinya. 'The business is expanding. He has to be away a lot, organising supplies.'

Yai turned her beady gaze to Sirinya. 'I wouldn't have thought that business would be expanding, not now of all times. Unless, of course he's in with the Japs.'

'Hush, Mother,' hissed Kitima. 'Don't speak like that. Not here.'

The old woman twisted her mouth into a pout and folded

her arms.

'And what about your duties here, Daughter? What about the harvest?'

'It's not harvest time yet. The fields are planted. There's little to do until the end of the rains. You know that, Mother.'

Yai changed tack. 'You know I'm not well, Kitima. It will fall to other people's children to fetch my water, look after the hens. And what would happen if I had a fall? Who would look after me then?'

'You are strong, Mother. Stronger than many people half your age. And everyone here in the village is happy to help out. You know that. Your friend, Pensri, and her family are always willing to lend a hand and keep you company. I will be back in good time to help you with the rice. I promise. Look, Mother. Siri has brought us some papaya and mangoes.'

Yai took a mango from the bag Sirinya held out to her. She held it up, sniffed it and squeezed it with expert fingers. Her face relaxed a little. 'Nice fruit. Thank you for that, Granddaughter.'

'I won't be away long, Mother,' said Kitima, 'and I'll be earning money. Perhaps we'll be able to buy that boar you've been wanting, when we next go to market.'

'A daughter's place is at her mother's side,' insisted Yai, her arms still tightly folded, her narrow body stiff with disapproval.

'Come, Mother. You're not going to stop me going are you?'

'I cannot stop you. I didn't even try to stop you before, my girl, when you were young and stupid and look what happened then. Marrying a man from the town. From outside our community. No wonder he upped and left. What would he want with a peasant girl?'

'Stop it, Mother,' said Kitima, blushing. Sirinya looked away to spare her mother's feelings. The subject of Sirinya's father had always been shrouded in rumours and shifting half-truths. Sirinya had heard several different versions from people in the village as she grew up. Kitima had simply told her that he had left to find work in Bangkok and never returned. Sirinya had picked up from others that Kitima had met him in Kanchanaburi after Piak had married Chalong. He was an itinerant labourer from Bangkok, working briefly in the paper factory in the town. Kitima had fallen for him and they had returned to the village to be married in the nearby temple. They had left the village and travelled together, finding work in various small towns on the trade route towards Burma. But Kitima had returned alone less than a year later, contrite and heavily pregnant with Sirinya. The story went that he had abandoned her to return to Bangkok with a bar girl from Nam Tok. But it hadn't mattered to Sirinya, she had grown up loved and cared for alongside the rest of the village children.

'Mother, this is quite different,' Kitima said now, recovering her poise. 'I promise, nothing will happen. I'll be back for the rice harvest. I've said so. Now I need to build up the fire for supper.'

Yai rose stiffly and shuffled back across the platform to the doorway of the hut. She turned and stared at Kitima. 'I have a bad feeling about this, Kitima,' she said, raising her voice. 'A very bad feeling. But I know neither of you will listen to an old woman, so I'll keep my own counsel and say no more.' She turned and shuffled through the opening.

'Take no notice of her, Mother. She's just trying to make us feel guilty,' whispered Sirinya, after the hut had stopped wobbling and they were sure that Yai was lying down on her mat in the sleeping quarters in the far corner. But although Kitima shrugged and smiled, Sirinya knew that she was troubled by Yai's words.

Later, as they ate their meal with rice on the veranda of the hut, to the flickering light of the paraffin lamp, Kitima was uncharacteristically quiet, and several times Sirinya noticed her mother's attention wander and her eyes take on a troubled look.

In the morning, they were up before dawn as the village cocks were crowing under the wooden houses. They sat out on the veranda again, sipping herb tea and eating fresh mangoes. Yai had got up with them, but refused any food. Instead she sat in silence sipping tea and watching them eat. Kitima had gathered all the belongings she would need for the trek to the road in a cloth she wound around her waist to carry. They finished their breakfast as the sun rose over the village, and the villagers were emerging from their houses to feed their animals and hens, or setting off with tools to tend their crops.

'We have to leave now,' said Kitima firmly, getting to her feet. 'Say goodbye, Mother. I promise I will make the journey back in a few weeks to see how you are.'

Yai got to her feet and stood in front of Kitima. 'If you go now, we will not see each other again, Daughter.'

'Don't say such things, Mother. We are both in good health. Please don't be gloomy.'

Yai reached out and squeezed Kitima's shoulder and looked into her eyes.

'You have been a good daughter to me, Kiti, and I thank you.'

'Mother!'

Yai held up a bony hand. 'Don't scold me my child. Just remember my words and try to avoid danger.'

Sirinya would never forget that walk back through the village between the bamboo houses. Other villagers waved and shouted greetings to them as they passed. Each time she turned to look back at Yai's house, though, she saw the old woman still there at the top of her steps, standing stock still, staring at them, her shock of hair white against the bamboo wall of her house.

12

As the truck bumped and rattled through the outskirts of Kanchanaburi in the fading light of the early evening, Sirinya felt Kitima stiffen and sit up straight on the bench beside her. Like some of the other passengers who had travelled down from the hills with them, Kitima was reacting to her first sight of Japanese soldiers patrolling the pavements. Sauntering along in their khaki uniforms, they glowered at pedestrians, rifles slung casually over their shoulders.

'What are they doing, Siri?' Kitima muttered. The other passengers averted their eyes, pretending not to hear the question.

'They patrol the streets looking for anyone who might be working against them. They sometimes stop people and check them at random. They're looking for weapons, subversive material.'

Kitima grew pale and pursed her lips. She said nothing but Sirinya could tell she was deeply troubled.

'They mostly leave people alone, though, Ma,' she said trying to make light of the situation.

They had been travelling most of the day. First the long walk from the village in the building heat of the morning, down the winding jungle path, through the forest hills to the dusty road. Kitima was fit and strong. She covered the ground quickly, with a long loose stride, walking ahead of Sirinya, batting insects aside with a home-made raffia swatter. Occasionally she called over her shoulder, her voice bubbling with laughter, 'Am I going too fast for you, Daughter? Just say, and I'll slow down.'

Sirinya refused to admit she was struggling to keep up. But her mother did slow her pace as they drew close to the cutting. As on the previous day when Sirinya had made the walk in the opposite direction the sound of rhythmic tapping and hammering could be heard through the undergrowth above the hum and whine of jungle insects.

'Let's keep to the path, Ma,' said Sirinya, remembering the story of the villagers who had had to flee from the guards.

'No, Siri. I need to see what's happening here for myself. I only have what you and the men from the village have told me. You can stay here and wait for me if you like.'

With that she stepped off the path and began to push through the undergrowth.

'Be careful, Ma,' Sirinya said, but the vines and creepers had already closed around Kitima.

Sirinya stood on the path, her heart thumping, willing the minutes to pass. It seemed as though she stood there alone for an eternity in the cloying heat, her body moist with sweat, the sound of jungle creatures competing with the hammering from the cutting. Just when she was starting to panic, to worry that something had happened and Kitima wouldn't return, there was more rustling from within the jungle screen and Kitima emerged from the undergrowth.

'What happened,?' asked Sirinya, seeing her mother's usually cheerful face pale, her eyes troubled.

'Come on,' Kitima muttered, not meeting Sirinya's gaze. 'We'd better hurry now, or we'll miss the afternoon truck.' She set off quickly down the hill without a backward glance.

Sirinya followed her and they walked in silence for half an hour or so. Then Sirinya noticed that the cloth that Kitima had wrapped around her waist for her belongings sagged and flapped.

'What happened to the fruit you were bringing for the truck journey?' she shouted. Kitima turned.

'Oh I left it under a tree at the cutting.'

'What? You mean you went right down there?' Sirinya hurried to catch up with Kitima, she was panting now, sweat trickling down her face.

'I was very quick, Siri. No one would have noticed me. The guards were all at the other end. I checked where they were first.'

'Do you think the prisoners will find it?'

'Oh yes. I left it under one of the ladders they were using to reach the higher rocks. It was right at the end and wasn't being used. But they'll go back there to get it and then they'll find the fruit.'

'Do you think anyone saw you?'

'I said not. Now stop belly-aching and let's get on.'

Because of that earlier show of bravado, Sirinya was surprised now that they were in the town that Kitima was perturbed by the sight of Japanese soldiers on the streets. By the time the truck dropped them off at the end of Saeng Chuto road, though, she had recovered her composure; colour had returned to her cheeks and she looked around again with her beady observant gaze. As they walked past the Kempeitai house, with two armoured trucks drawn up outside, the drivers leaning on the vehicles smoking, Sirinya noticed her mother's step falter momentarily before she recovered herself and moved on. Piak and Malee came running from the shop, and as the four of them greeted each other with hugs and kisses, all talking at once, the soldiers, and all they represented, were forgotten for those few precious moments.

* * *

Kitima took to the work in the shop with her usual energetic vigour, rising early each morning to walk down to the riverside before dawn to help unload the fruit and vegetables from the barges onto the waiting bullock carts. Then throughout the day she would work beside Malee and Sirinya to unload the carts, re-load produce onto the delivery lorry, and deal with the regular customers in the shop. Sirinya would watch her out of the corner of her eye as they worked, and smile secretly, happy to have Kitima here beside her, proud that her mother had the strength and energy that equalled that of any man.

Within a few weeks, Chalong was supplying all the camps within fifty kilometres of the town. He was hardly at home; he would set off just after dawn with the shop boy beside him in the cab, returning only for fresh supplies once or twice during the daytime. He would often not get home from his last trip until long after dark. His only day off was a Sunday, but that meant that on Saturday, double the amount of supplies had to be sent into the camps.

'You need to slow down, Husband,' said Piak one evening as he sat at the table in the apartment, struggling to keep his eyes open long enough to eat his tom yung gung. 'You never let yourself rest. You'll kill yourself with all this work.'

Kitima was eating her meal. She laid down her spoon and paused, waiting for Chalong's response. Sirinya and Malee, washing dishes at the sink in the corner of the room, glanced at each other. They were used to the all too frequent bickering that had developed between Piak and Chalong lately.

'If I don't do it, the prisoners won't have vegetables,' Chalong said. 'You should see them, Piak. I can't let them down. It's a lifeline to them. Their only one.'

Piak tutted. 'Someone else could easily do it, Husband. There are dozens of merchants within a few kilometres of here who would jump at the chance to supply those camps.'

'But they wouldn't be prepared to help like I do.'

Piak gave him a long, troubled look and shook her head slowly. 'I can't understand why you take such risks. You'd be better off avoiding danger. Only bad can possibly come of it. Think of your family, Chalong. What would we do if anything happened to you?'

Chalong took her hand and looked into her eyes, 'Please don't speak like that, Piak. Nothing will happen to me. I'm very careful, but I need to help. '

'But Husband,' she pleaded, 'Surely there's no need to put your life in danger as you do.'

He looked away. There was a tense silence. Everyone knew what she was referring to.

One day, a few days after Kitima had arrived, he'd brought home a letter that had been passed to him by one of the prisoners who unloaded the truck at Chungkai camp. It had been screwed up and slipped to him covertly. He had pulled the truck off the road to look at it on the way back, but it was written in English and he needed help. That evening, Sirinya and Malee sat together at the kitchen table, smoothed the letter out in front of them and translated it into Thai word by word. They wrote nothing down, and when they had finished, they burned the letter on the wood stove they used to cook the family meals.

Dear Khun Chalong,

I am the Medical Officer in Chungkai camp. I know I am taking a risk writing this to you, but I have met you on your deliveries to the camp and believe you to be an honourable and honest man. I feel confident that you will not let this letter reach Japanese hands. You have seen with your own eyes the condition of men in the camps. They are being worked too hard, they do not have enough food and are vulnerable to illness. They are often beaten by the guards. We have no medicines here and desperately need quinine, emetine and disinfectant. Men are dying in the hospital hut in the camp from malaria and dysentery every day. Others have tropical ulcers and need iodine and antiseptic.

If you are able to help, please bring these things into the camp hidden at the bottom of the vegetable baskets. We unload them into the stores ourselves now as you know, and can ensure anything you are able to bring in is not discovered. We can pay you with watches and other valuables. If this succeeds and we are able to try again, next time we will pay in advance, but this time we need to establish contact and to obtain these medicines urgently.

With sincere gratitude and hope,
Medical Officer, Colonel P Scott

On his next Sunday off, Chalong had risen early to drive to Bangkok in the truck and hadn't returned until after midnight. He had shaken Sirinya and Malee awake, told them to follow him down to the street and not to make a sound. With his flashlight he showed them a stash of medicines, hidden in boxes wedged between the cab and the back of the truck. Together, under the cover of darkness, they took the boxes inside the shop and hid them behind the empty vegetable baskets. The following morning, for the first time, they slipped packets of medicines discreetly into baskets of potatoes, cabbages, onions and kale, hiding them under the vegetables, ensuring that they could not be seen on an inspection of the surface.

That first time, Sirinya had watched Chalong set off for his delivery round with dread in her heart. She could hardly bear to say goodbye, so strong was the feeling that he might be discovered, that he might not return to them. She stood beside Malee watching the tail lights of the lorry disappear down the road, her fingers intertwined tightly with her cousin's for reassurance. All morning as the hours crawled by the feeling persisted, and she, Malee and Kitima worked together in tense silence until the familiar rumble of the engine outside the shop had told them that Chalong was back from his first round of camps nearest to the town, including Chungkai. They hurried out to the truck as usual. The boy jumped down from the cab and scurried round the back to unload the empty baskets. Chalong got down from the drivers' side, a broad smile on his face.

'Don't look so worried, ladies. Everything went smoothly,' he said. 'Everything was fine. In fact the prisoners unloading paid me handsomely with watches and jewellery. I have them here in my pocket. Now I just need to find someone I can trust to sell these to so that I can buy more medicine.'

He had been back to Bangkok twice since then, on each of his Sundays off since that first time. Each time he returned with more medicines for the camps. This time they hid them upstairs in the apartment under their beds, and sent them into the camps in dribs and drabs, agreeing amongst themselves that would be the safest way to avoid detection.

Now Chalong looked at Piak with understanding in his gaze. 'Buddha teaches us to love and care for everyone, Piak, especially those who are in need. I am only following the teachings.'

She sat down at the table beside him, her face twisted with anxiety. 'But I am afraid, Husband. You are putting us all in danger. Who are these people helping you in Bangkok? It could be a trap. You haven't said anything about where you go to get the medicines. Who helps you pawn the jewellery to get the money? I need to know.'

'The less you know the better, my dear. But if you are really worried, I'll tell you. I am dealing with people I know I can trust.

They are an organised group, mostly British civilians, interned in the city, but fairly free to go about as they please. They call themselves the V Organisation. They know about what is happening in the camps and they want to help. I take them the letters asking for medicines, and they get what is needed for me to bring back here.'

'What about payment? Surely they can't pay for the medicines with broken watches and old jewellery?'

'Other friends are helping with that. Some here in the town, some in the city.'

'Other friends?'

'Yes, Piak. You know who I mean. They've been helping ever since the Japanese first came to town. The headmaster, the doctor, that whole group. We all want to do what we can to work against the Japanese.'

'So they know what you're doing? With the medicines?'

'Of course. They are our friends. In times like these, you have to know who your friends are and to trust them. Piak, believe me, the men in those camps are in real need. If you went there and saw them you'd know.'

Piak drew her hand away and shook her head.

'Come and sit down. All of you. I need to ask you all something,' said Chalong. Glancing at Malee, Sirinya dried her hands, and Malee put the plates away. They both came to sit at the table. The women sat there in silence, watching Chalong, waiting for him to speak. He took a deep breath and, staring down at his hands he said, 'I've been asked to take something else into one of the camps.'

'Something else? What? What do you mean? Not medicine?' asked Piak.

Chalong put his fingers to his lips. 'Keep your voice down, please. I've been asked to take a radio receiver in. It is so the prisoners can hear what is happening in the outside world, it will help them get by, help them to survive to know how the war is progressing.'

'Who asked you to do that?'

'Our friends in the V Organisation in Bangkok.'

'You frighten me, Husband. Is there no end to the risks you're prepared to take?'

'Sister,' interrupted Kitima, turning and laying a hand on Piak's arm. 'Please don't be so worried. What Chalong is doing is a good thing. He is trying to help those poor men. They are starving in those camps, driven like slaves, dying of disease and malnutrition every day. I saw some of them at the cutting near our village. They are only young. Some of them only the same age as Malee and Sirinya here. They are somebody's sons too.'

There was silence around the table. From the flickering light of the gas lamp, Sirinya took in the expressions on their faces. Chalong watched the others now, his eyes moving from face to face, a questioning look in them. Kitima was looking back at him earnestly, her kindly face serious for once. Malee looked down at the table, biting her lip, and Piak sat next to her husband frowning, picking at the buttons of her blouse, her body taut with anxiety.

'What do we need to do, Uncle? How are we going to do it.' Sirinya asked.

'I have an idea how to go about it. I'm going to collect the parts next time I go down to Bangkok. I can hide them in the lorry somewhere, either in the petrol tank, or inside the exhaust. There is a man in Bangkok who can do that for me. But we need a way of getting them into the camp. And I thought two of you might help with that.'

'What about the baskets?' asked Kitima. 'Why not just hide them under the cabbages like you do with the medicines?'

'It's too risky to do that. We're lucky that the baskets have never been searched. But if they were, the Japs might be prepared to tolerate medicines. After all, we're just trying to help sick people. They would take a different view of a radio. That's something different altogether.'

'Go on, Chalong. I'll help in any way I can,' said Kitima.

'You'll need to be brave. It won't be easy. And if we're discovered ...'

Piak began to weep silently, covering her face with her hands.

'We know the risks, Chalong. Go on.'

'I thought that one way might be for one of you to come into the camp with me on a delivery and ... and well, to hide the parts under your sarong. I can't do that. They won't fit inside my trousers, and if I suddenly came dressed differently, suspicions might be raised.'

'I'll do that father,' said Malee suddenly, looking up for the first time.

'You will not, my girl. You will not. I forbid it,' Piak got up from the table, still weeping and ran out of the room slamming the door. Her footsteps pounded on the stairs, running up to the top floor, then came the sound of another door slamming.

'We'll do it. Sirinya and me. Won't we Siri?' said Kitima. 'You mustn't worry your mother, Malee. She is not strong. You must stay here and be with her.'

'But I want to help.'

'That would be the best way you could help, my dear,' said Kitima softly. 'Now Sirinya. You'll do it, won't you, my girl?'

Sirinya smiled at her mother with tears in her eyes.

'Of course, Ma. Of course I'll do it,' she whispered, but already her stomach churned and her head felt dizzy with terror at the thought of the incredible risks they would be taking.

13

On her third morning in Bangkok, Sirinya leaves the Golden Key hotel early and makes for a food stall at the other end of the soi. She has her established routine now. She has taken almost all her meals here since she arrived. The stallholder, Tip, recognising her, looks up from chopping vegetables to wai to her with a wide smile. He already knows her eating preferences and much of her life story.

She takes a seat at a stainless steel table and asks him for fried rice with prawns. While he fries the fresh food up in a wok over an open flame, she stares out at the main road. In the dark of the evenings the place at least holds a certain sleazy glamour, but now in the clear light of the morning it looks shabby and dirty. The street is almost deserted, empty beer cans, cigarette packets and food scraps litter the pavements. A couple of garbage-pickers in conical hats, faces shrouded in masks, work with spiked sticks and baskets, clearing the mess away. The bars are closed, steel shutters covering the windows, neon signs switched off. A small group of western men shamble past, unsteady from a night of excess.

Tip brings the food, placing the plastic bowls on the table in front of Sirinya, 'You look tired today, madam,' he said. 'You still search for your friend?'

She smiles wanly and nods. Her bones feel heavy and her mind exhausted. For three nights now she has continued her frustrating search of the bars along the seemingly endless New Petchburi strip, repeating the same words over and over, passing the faded school photograph to countless bar girls and mamasans to stare at, only to have the same blank-eyed response time and time again. Having exhausted the main road on the second night, she spent the last evening visiting even sleazier establishments in the side roads, or sois, where the girls are thinner, their skin sallow and blemished, their eyes desperate. By day she has continued her search, revisiting places she had been to the previous evening, to see if different staff were on the day shift, and if any of them recognised Ratana.

'Where you go looking today, madam?' Tip asks now, hovering beside her.

'Oh, I'm going to give myself a break from searching today, I'm going to look for a present for my cousin back in Kanchanaburi.'

He smiles again, displaying broken teeth.

'That is nice. What type of gift would she like?'

'I'm sure she would like some good silk for a new outfit. It is difficult to buy, and expensive where she lives.'

'Oh, then you must go down to Chinatown. Best silk is found there. I can recommend a merchant I know in Boripat road. Small street off Yaowarat. He's my cousin. I have his card somewhere.' He rummages in his apron pockets and produces a small worn business card and hands it to her.

She glances at it. 'I can't read this, Tip,' she says laughing. 'It's in Chinese.'

'Turn it over. Other side English.' As she does so, the fragment of a memory surfaces. Where did she see something similar recently?

'You take tuk-tuk. Give card to driver. He take you there.'

'I'm not a tourist, Tip,' she says, laughing again. 'I'll take the bus like everyone else.'

Two businessmen on the next table call for the bill and Tip shuffles over to serve them. Sirinya watches him clear the table as they leave.

'You want newspaper?' he calls over to her, holding one up. 'Customers leave it behind.'

'Thank you. I'll take it with me.' She places coins on the table, takes the copy of the *Bangkok Messenger* from Tip and puts it in her shoulder bag. Thanking him she walks to the bus stop on New Petchburi Road.

Like all buses in Bangkok, this one is stifling and crowded. It crawls through the early-morning traffic and Sirinya leans out of the open window to avoid suffocation. She watches office workers hurrying past on the pavement as the bus inches forward, cooking in the heat of the morning. It takes over half an hour to reach the end of the New Petchburi Road, and as it enters Chinatown the streets begin to narrow and the atmosphere changes. It is even busier here, frenetic. Gold traders, Chinese banks and pawn shops dominate, their premises hung with neon signs bearing Chinese characters. It has hardly changed since the war.

She gets off the bus halfway down Yaowarat Road and consults her map. Realising she has got down one stop too early she begins to walk west towards Boripat. Glancing at the shops as she walks, she realises she is passing a coffin maker. Raw pine coffins are piled up on the pavement and the sounds of sawing and hammering echo from within. She looks away quickly and walks on in the direction of Boripat. But this is the coffin-making district, and each shop along this part of the road is the same. She shudders, a feeling of deep foreboding creeping over her, reminiscent of the dream she'd had on the first night in the Golden Key. She quickens her pace, looks straight ahead and is clear of the coffin district after a few minutes, but the feeling persists. Despite the rising temperature, a chill permeates her bones.

Up ahead, the gates to a Chinese temple open off the pavement between two shops. She pauses and glances through the bars. Across a courtyard stands a temple building with a red Chinese pagoda-style roof, the statue of a painted dragon playing with a pearl on its crest. A procession of monks with shaven heads, dressed in saffron robes, cross the courtyard and move towards a side building. Each holds a small brass bowl. They walk slowly with grave dignity.

Still shaken by the sight of the coffins, Sirinya feels the lure of the temple. She crosses the courtyard, takes off her shoes and goes up the steps, the marble pleasantly cool under her hot feet.

Inside the temple building the air is filled with the smell of incense. A golden statue of Buddha draped in saffron robes dominates the cavernous hall. It sits high on a plinth in the lotus position. On its face, a pensive gaze of infinite calm. A few silent worshippers kneel before it, heads bowed in reverence, lighting candles and incense sticks to place on the altar. From an inner sanctum comes the sound of chanting. She puts some coins down on a counter, takes up a few sticks of incense and lights them carefully from the candle burning there. Then, taking her place beside the other worshippers, she kneels. After a few minutes, peace and calm begin to displace the panic and disquiet she has been feeling since she arrived in Bangkok, and which the coffin shops intensified.

She kneels there for a long time, letting the atmosphere seep into her, stilling her body, settling her mind. She remembers the monk's words, and tries to empty her mind of all thoughts, but images of the past keep surfacing. She tries her best to banish them, but they return time and again.

At last she gives up, gets to her feet and wanders out onto the street, frustrated, now even firmer in the belief that she needs to redouble her efforts to find Ratana. When she has done that, perhaps then she will be able to meditate properly, to rejoin the eightfold path and find peace in her own heart?

Boripat Road is not far away, and, from the address and tiny printed map on the business card she quickly finds the little shop. The proprietor greets her politely, ushers her to a seat and brings her tea. She shows him the business card and mentions that Tip sent her. She then spends a pleasing half-hour discussing silk with the man, allowing him to use his salesman's patter one her, to show her skein after skein of silk as smooth as cream. He pulls each bolt out extravagantly, letting the material flow to the floor, filling the little shop with a kaleidoscope of luxurious colours. She finally selects a turquoise rough silk and orders five metres.

'I will pack it up and send it to your hotel by motorbike,' the merchant says as she hands him the money. She waits as he expertly slices through the delicate material with huge scissors. As she watches suddenly the material reminds her of the dress Narong bought her before the war. It strikes her that that dress was that exact shade of blue. Is that why she chose it today, she wonders, an unconscious concession to the pull of the past?

She thanks the man and leaves the shop, and as she walks away she wonders what happened to that dress. Did she ever actually wear it? She remembers the over-eager look on Narong's face as he watched her open the package and hold it up to her body. But she doesn't want to remember Narong. She squeezes her eyes together, trying to erase the image.

It is still early and she has no desire to go back to New Petchburi Road. She walks aimlessly for ten minutes along Boripat, crosses the canal south of Wat Saket, Temple of the Golden Mount, and continues along Mau Chat Road. She walks on and on, deeper into the quarter. The streets become narrow alleys impassable to traffic, and she finds herself in the bustling heart of Chinatown. She turns down a side alley between stalls selling pots and pans, and wanders on, enjoying the sensation of being overwhelmed by the sights, sounds and smells of this bustling place.

The shops here are tiny, stacked high with goods, crammed into small rooms opening onto the alley, selling everything from shoes to water pipes. People press and push their way through, traders bring wares on hand trolleys, hollering at pedestrians to move aside. She passes fruit stalls and meat stalls, stalls loaded with glistening fresh fish, and live ones swimming around in tanks. She passes barbers and cobblers and merchants of every description. After a few more streets, she comes across a food stall that sells drinks. Hot and thirsty, she sits down at a table and orders a pot of green tea. As she waits she watches the endless crowd coming and going. A road sign on the building opposite shows that she is in Jarowee Road. It feels vaguely familiar. Where has she heard that name before? Did she know this place when she was in Bangkok at the end of the war? She used to come to Chinatown sometimes for a bowl of the cheapest noodles in town when she only had a few ticals for food, but she doesn't remember any particular street name from that time.

Remembering the newspaper Tip gave her earlier she pulls it out of her bag while she waits for the tea. She flicks through the pages of the *Bangkok Messenger*, reading slowly. She is not used to Thai script nowadays and she has to peer at the letters and decipher each word carefully. She reads of fluctuations in the price of rice, and floods in the southern provinces. On the third page a story accompanied by a fuzzy photograph takes her interest.

'*Bar brawl in Patpong*,' screams the headline. '*Western men out drinking in the newly established night spots of Patpong Road off Silom clashed with locals last night. A fight broke out in the small hours which ended in one westerner being stabbed in the stomach and taken to hospital, four arrests and all bars in the vicinity being closed down for the rest of the night.*'

The article goes on to say that there has been a rash of new bars opening up in Patpong Road catering to foreign journalists and photographers here to report the American war in Vietnam. The area was normally less rowdy than New Petchburi, but last night had been the exception. A fight had broken out between a group of foreigners over an unpaid bill.

Above the story is a fuzzy photograph of two white men being led away by Thai police in handcuffs, heads bowed, while a group of bewildered bystanders looks on.

'Good morning!' says a male voice next to her.

She starts and looks up, momentarily confused. She stares, the face is familiar, but for a moment she cannot place it. And then she realises. It is the man she met on the train to Kanchanaburi on her first day back in the country. She feels a flush creeping up her face from the base of her neck. He is watching her, smiling.

'So it *is* you!' he says, 'I thought it was, but I wasn't sure.'

Sirinya opens her mouth and closes it again.

'What are you doing in Chinatown?' he asks, his eyes amused.

She draws herself up, making an effort to recover her composure. She gets to her feet, puts her hands together in a wai and inclines her head.

'I was in Boripat Road, buying some silk for my cousin.'

'Please. Do sit down. No need to get up for me. Perhaps I could join you? I'm on my way back from the bank. My shop is just over there,' he waves his hand in the direction of one sign amongst a forest of signs. The one he points to bears a painting of three gold rings intertwined.

'I could do with a tea and a bowl of pork noodles,' he says, 'This is the best stall around. Are you hungry?'

'No, it's not long since I had breakfast.'

The stallholder approaches, and the man orders in fluent Mandarin.

'I didn't realise you were Chinese,' Sirinya says, surprised.

'No, no. I think I told you on the train. I come from Nam Tok. Born and raised there. But I had an uncle who came down to Bangkok for work. I lived with him for a time on and off during the war. Afterwards he found me work with an import-export merchant in Chinatown. I've been here more or less ever since. I picked up the language, had to really, or I wouldn't have survived.'

The food came and he tucked into it, expertly, with chopsticks.

'And what brings you back to the city?' he asks.

Sirinya sighs. 'Oh, It's a very long story.'

He smiles. 'Well I have plenty of time … please, tell me.'

'I've come here looking for someone. Someone I knew during the war. She used to be a friend, but …'

The man glances up from his noodles. His eyes are gentle, kindly. 'Go on?'

'Oh, I'm not sure you'd want to know. I don't even know your name.'

'I'm sure you do! I gave you my card. Don't you remember?'

Of course. That was the card that she had in her mind that was printed in different languages.

'I'm teasing of course. I don't expect you to remember. My name is Kasem. Kasem Suttichart.'

'Sirinya. Sirinya Foster.'

'So, you were saying? About your friend?'

'She's not my friend now. Far from it. We were at school together long ago. I need to see her now. It's a big part of the reason I came back to Thailand.'

'Why? Why after all this time?'

'I can't tell you. All I can say is that it is she did something dreadful. Something unforgivable.'

He falls silent. She looks down and stirs the green tea in the pot. She feels his eyes on her face. She has told no one of her suspicions about Ratana. She has only hinted at it to Malee. None of the friends she made over the years in England knew or understood anything of what had happened during the war here, apart from Johnny. And she couldn't have told him. He wouldn't have wanted to know.

It's all in the past, Siri. In another time and another country, he would have said, patting her hand. There's nothing to be done about it now, my darling, it's best to just let sleeping dogs lie.

But looking back into Kasem's eyes now, she wonders if there is a chance that if she confides in this man he might be prepared to listen and take her seriously. He might not dismiss what she says, or tell her to put it behind her. He is Thai after all. He must have been in Nam Tok during the war years and know something of what had happened, what it had been like for the locals when the Japanese army came to cut down the jungle and drive their railway through the mountains.

'Well, if you need to tell anyone, I am happy to listen,' he says.

She shakes her head, her courage failing her. 'I'm sorry. I can't talk about it right now.'

'Have you been looking for her for long? Do you know where she lives?'

'No, but I've been looking for the past few days in New Petchburi.'

'Why on earth?'

'I thought she'd be there. I assumed ...'

He drops his eyes. 'Oh, I see.' He says, his smile gone.

She shrugs. 'I'll carry on looking this evening, but I've almost given up hope.'

'Look, how about coming to my shop for a while. I've just got a few things so sort out there, then perhaps we could go somewhere together – to Lumpini park perhaps? You look as though you need a break from your search.'

'Oh, I don't know ...' it was a tempting offer. She had felt so alone, especially since coming to Bangkok. So alone and afraid, haunted by memories. It might be nice to spend some time with someone else.

'Come on,' he persists. 'I will treat you to dinner too, if you'll let me? There is a wonderful seafood restaurant on the edge of the park. How about that?'

'Alright,' she says at last. 'That is very kind of you.'

Kasem pays the bill and guides her across the alley to his shop. In the window row upon row of gold rings and chains are on display. Inside, two Chinese men sit opposite each other at a table, bargaining over a tray of rings. They look up momentarily to nod to Kasem as he enters.

'Take a seat,' said Kasem, and she sits down on a sofa just inside the doorway. It is pleasantly cool in here, she feels the chill of the air-conditioning on her face.

'Would you like a drink? I have to pop upstairs to the office for a moment. I'll be less than five minutes.'

'I'm fine thank you. I'll just wait here.'

He disappears behind a curtain and she hears his footsteps on a narrow staircase. She watches the two men deep in conversation. They too are speaking Mandarin.

She pulls out the *Bangkok Messenger* and turns back to the article she'd been reading when Kasem greeted her. She scans it again and looks back at the blurred photograph. She is about to turn the page when something about it catches her eye. The crowd watching the men being led away by police is made up of Thai people; a couple of men and several bar girls dressed in the ubiquitous uniform of high heels and micro skirts. Between two girls stands an older woman, stouter and shorter, but no less painted. Sirinya's heartbeat quickens as she holds the photograph up to the window and looks again. Could it be? Could it be? She is almost sure it is. There are the high cheekbones, the striking eyes, but it is impossible to say for sure.

She puts the paper down, her thoughts scattering in all directions. She must go to Patpong straightaway with the photograph from the newspaper. It should be easy to find Ratana now. Her hands trembling she pulls her city map out of her bag and spreads it out on her lap, her eyes scanning the streets, searching for Patpong. It is not a district she knows or has heard of. She glances back at the article … it is off Silom Road, she reads. She peers at the map intently, and her eyes light on a sidestreet halfway up Silom Road, Patpong Road.

She hears Kasem's footsteps on the stairs. She looks up at him.

'Are you alright?' he asks, frowning, 'You look as though you've seen a ghost.'

14

Sirinya was running down the dark alleyway in the rain. Her sandals slap-slapping through the puddles. Every few steps she tripped and stumbled on the uneven surface of the dirt road. She was running so fast her heart hammered and her breath came in shallow gulps that hurt her throat. The strap of the cloth bag she carried chafed her shoulder and the bag itself swung awkwardly against her, the corners of the little boxes inside it digging into her ribs. Reaching the end of the narrow lane she stopped, pausing for breath. A sob escaped from her as she leaned forward, panting, her hair dripping onto her skirt. Her clothes were soaked through and clung to her skin.

Was she far enough away from the shop now? She strained her ears for voices or sounds which might give her a clue as to what was happening, but there was nothing but the sound of the rain falling, the chatter of tropical night insects and the occasional dog barking in the next street.

It had all happened so quickly. She'd been asleep in bed up in the small room under the eaves, Malee across the room in the other bed. They were awoken suddenly by urgent banging on the shop door on the ground floor. The beam from a flashlight danced on the sloping ceiling, casting strange dancing shadows across the room. Shaking and confused, Sirinya got out of bed. Malee was sitting up, holding the sheet to her chest. Her face was pale in the flashlight. Sirinya crept to the window and, concealing herself behind the curtain, strained to see what was going on in the street. She gasped. A Japanese truck was pulled up onto the pavement directly beneath the window.

The bedroom door opened and Chalong stood there. His hair was dishevelled, his shirt buttoned unevenly.

'It's the Kempeitai,' he said. His voice was steady and his face calm, but Sirinya noticed beads of sweat on his brow.

'I'll go down and see what they want,' he said. 'Now I need you two girls to go into the back storeroom downstairs and take what's left of the medicines out of the boxes. Put them into bags and take them as far away from here as you can. Hide them somewhere. The Japs must have had a tip-off.'

Sirinya looked at Malee. Malee was swallowing, the whites of her eyes wide with fear. She said nothing.

There was more hammering and thumping from the ground floor. Then a shout. 'Open up. Kempeitai!'

'I have to go now. Quickly, please. Follow me down as soon as you can. I'll try to keep them talking.'

With trembling hands the girls dragged on their clothes. Then they crept down the two flights of wooden stairs to the ground floor. As they reached the first landing they heard the sounds of Chalong drawing back the bolts and opening the front door. When they reached the bottom, they could see Chalong's back in the passage and the military caps of two Kempeitai officers in front of him.

'Chalong Wisitsak?' one of the officers was saying. 'You have the contract to supply the camp at Chungkai?'

'Yes, indeed, sir. How can I help you?'

'Come on, Malee, keep close to the wall and they won't see us,' Sirinya whispered.

They needed to cross the passage and cover the few paces along it to the door of the shop without being seen. There wasn't time to think about what might happen if one of the officers noticed them. Sirinya pressed her back to the wall and slid silently along it. She hardly dared breathe. Malee was beside her and Sirinya could feel the heat on her cousin's trembling arm. In seconds they were opposite the closed door. Sirinya took the plunge, stepped forward into the passage and pushed the door open. It squeaked as she knew it would, but within a second they were both inside the shop. Sirinya closed the door as quietly as she could and they stood in the darkness, hearts beating fast.

They hurried through to the storeroom at the back of the shop and shut themselves in. The only light was from the moon slanting through the window high up in the wall. They only had seconds. They each grabbed a bag made of sacking normally used to carry fruit, reached for the cardboard boxes of medicines which were stored on shelves behind some packs of cleaning powder. They crammed the packages and boxes of medicines into the bags. They were almost finished when they heard heavy footsteps in the passage, the sound of the first door opening.

'Quick – let's slip out the back way before they come in here,' Sirinya said, barely in control of her voice, as she shoved the last of the packages into her bag and hoisted it onto her shoulder. The back door stuck on its hinges and Malee had to kick the bottom for it to open. Then they were out in the moonlit yard.

'We should split up and go in opposite directions. We'll be less noticeable that way.'

'But Siri …'

'You go towards the river. I'll head out of town the other way.'

The rain came suddenly, just after they'd parted. Perhaps it was a good thing, perhaps it would hide the sounds of their footsteps, mean that the Japanese officers would want to get back to their quarters and out of the rain quickly.

Now Sirinya stood at the end of the alley, wondering which way to turn. She knew it would be better to avoid the main road, so she turned left, walking quickly westwards, towards the road where the paper factory stood on the edge of the town. Where had Malee got to? Would she panic and do something stupid? Sirinya hoped fervently Malee was coping, that she hadn't been spotted.

Footsteps crunched on the road behind her and Sirinya panicked. She noticed a rickety gate in the alley next to her. She pushed it aside and went through it into a cramped backyard. Chickens fluttered down from a roost behind her and a pig grunted a foot or two from where she stood. She pressed herself against the broken fence. The footsteps came closer and stopped beside the open gate. Sirinya held her breath. Her mouth was dry and she swallowed a sob of terror.

Then, whoever it was stepped inside the yard. Sirinya did not dare turn round. Was it possible that the darkness would hide her?

'Sirinya is that you?' A female voice.

She span round. Even in the darkness Sirinya could see who it was. Ratana stood in front of her. Her curls flattened by the rain. The moonlight glinted on the heavy beads around her neck and on her patent stiletto shoes. She stepped forward and brought her face close up to Sirinya's.

'What on earth are you doing here in the middle of the night?' Ratana asked with a puzzled laugh.

Sirinya suddenly felt giddy with relief, as if she was about to be sick. She took a deep breath to suppress the nausea.

'I could ask the same of you,' she said weakly. Jumbled thoughts crowded her mind. What about Ratana's connection with the Kempeitai? Could she possibly be trusted? Perhaps the Kempeitai had asked Ratana to follow her?

'I'm going to see a friend,' said Ratana, a defiant edge to her voice. 'I should have brought an umbrella, I know, but I left it somewhere. I'll look an absolute fright when I get there.'

Sirinya opened and shut her mouth. What could she say? Ratana was so brazen. Everyone knew she slept with Japanese officers, that they bought her clothes and jewellery and lavished money on her. Her mother had stopped taking in laundry and even she wore expensive clothes and spent her time drinking in bars and cafés.

'So?' said Ratana. 'What are *you* doing out here in the middle of the night. Don't tell me you're going to see a *friend* yourself?' there was a sneer in her voice. 'And what on earth is that you're carrying?'

'Leave me alone,' said Sirinya, instinctively drawing the bag closer to her chest. 'I have to make a delivery.'

'What, at this hour?' Ratana snorted. 'That sounds very odd. So why did you hide?'

'I ... I was afraid. I wasn't sure who was behind me.'

Ratana looked Sirinya up and down and shifted on her heels. 'Well, honestly! Anyway, I have to go. I can't stop here chatting to you in this filthy place.' She took a step towards the gate then turned back. 'But you're right to be afraid, Siri. I'd watch out if I were you. It's not safe for you to be out at this hour.'

Then she turned and hurried off.

Sirinya waited in the yard, listening. What did Ratana mean, Sirinya was right to be afraid? The rain dripped down her neck from a broken gutter. She waited there, shivering, until she was sure Ratana would be out of sight. Then she left the yard and carried on along the narrow lane. She walked for a long time, until she had cleared the town and was walking between paddy fields, and plantations of tapioca and coconut palms. She walked until the rain had stopped and the pale dawn began to lighten the sky above the hills. The clammy air was warm but her damp clothes clung to her body and she shivered with cold.

The track began to rise as it left the flat valley and wound upwards into the hills. Still Sirinya carried on. It was getting light now. She passed a few rice farmers on their way to their fields, carrying hoes and rakes, dressed in dark clothes and conical hats. They stared at her as they passed, but she smiled and nodded to them. She knew now where she was going.

The cave temples were natural limestone formations deep in the forest. There were dozens of them in the hillside; only the large inner ones were used as places of worship. Sirinya turned off the track and made her way through the undergrowth to one of the further disused caves. She and Malee used to come here as children to play. There was one cave on the edge of the escarpment where they would sit and picnic and play games. She still remembered how to get to it.

Entering the warm, dank interior that smelt of musty earth and dead leaves reminded her of those carefree times. She crossed to the back of the cave and stumbled over a pile of stones with some candles on top which someone must have been using as a makeshift shrine. A couple of bats swooped past her squeaking.

The shelf in the back of the cave she remembered from childhood was still there. Sirinya pushed the bag of medicines to the back of the shelf and piled stones up in front of them to hide them from view. Then, exhausted, she sat down on the damp floor of the cave and closed her eyes.

When she awoke shafts of bright sunlight were filtering through the leaves of the trees at the mouth of the cave. She scrambled to her feet. She hadn't intended to fall asleep. Judging by the position of the sun it must be almost midday. She must get back to the shop as soon as she could. What had the Kempeitai done to the place? Had they hurt Chalong? Had they been up and searched the apartment? What about Kitima and Piak?

Her body was stiff and her mouth parched. Rubbing her eyes and smoothing down her damp crumpled sarong she left the cave and made her way back to the main path. Instead of heading straight back down the mountain towards the town she turned in the opposite direction and continued upwards for a short way towards the steps that led down to the little valley where the main cave temple was. There was a spring near the top of the hill bubbling up between the rocks, and when she reached it she bent and drank the cool water from cupped hands. Then she splashed it on her face and arms. She felt instantly refreshed, but the dread and fear of what might have happened back at the shop remained with her. She turned to go back down the mountain, and over the rocks she caught sight of the clearing down below, in front of the cave temple. She could even see inside the great cave itself that was lit with hundreds of flickering candles. The gold statue of the Buddha gleamed in the gloomy interior, and in front of it, a group of monks clad in saffron robes sat meditating. They were perfectly still, their chanting floated up to her on the air. The scene exuded a deep serenity and calm.

As she turned away, it struck her that until recently she'd taken for granted the peace and calm that Buddhism taught, that had been part of her daily life, second nature to her, but lately that had left her. She now felt constantly fearful, suspicious of people around her. How had that happened? She started to walk slowly down the track through the trees clenching her fists, bitterness against the Japanese and their railway and the suffering they had brought to the area threatening to overwhelm her.

She moved quickly back through the forest down the hillside. Hunger gnawed at her stomach, she needed to get home. She started to run. Without the rough straps of the bag dragging against her shoulder it was a lot easier than on the way up, even though the sun was now high in the sky. Soon she reached the wider track that ran between the flooded rice fields. The workers, up to their thighs in water, straightened up and stopped their work to watch her as she hurried past.

Soon she was entering the town again and instead of retracing her steps through the back alleys she decided to take the quicker route along the main road past the paper factory. The low wooden building was quiet as she walked past on the pavement. All the workers must already be there. The two sentries on the gate dozed in their hut. She walked on, remembering suddenly that the next building along the road was the two story villa where Narong lived with his parents when they were in town. She'd never been invited there, she remembered, even on the days Narong had taken her out in his car.

She walked past the wrought iron gates and glanced inside. What she saw made her heart lurch with shock. Narong's green sports car was parked in the drive, and there was Narong himself, opening the passenger door for a woman. Sirinya stopped and stared. It was a woman in shiny stilettos, a short skirt and a low-cut top. She didn't need to look twice. It was Ratana.

15

All the way back through the streets from Narong's house to Chalong's shop on Saeng Chuto road, Sirinya's worry about the Kempeitai and what they might have done to the family was interrupted with thoughts about Narong. The image of Ratana stooping to get into his green sports car, with a coquettish laugh and a toss of her glossy black curls, kept playing over and over in her mind.

Sirinya was surprised at herself. Why was this troubling her, especially at a time like this? She knew she had no right to expect anything of Narong. After all, it was she who had rejected *him*, had hidden in the storeroom behind the shop when he came calling the last few times. Each time she'd seen his car draw up on the street outside, she'd persuaded Malee to go out and tell him that she wasn't at home, that she was unwell, that she was upstairs resting and couldn't be disturbed. Even so, it came as a shock to know that he could even contemplate spending time with someone like Ratana. He didn't seem the type to pay for a woman. Especially a woman who had known associations with the Kempeitai. He surely had more pride, more self-respect? She shook her head, trying to rid herself of the image. She should forget about it, she knew that much, but she also now knew that she'd been right about him all along. He was not a good person; he was not to be trusted.

It was past midday when she entered the shop. The two boys were busy transferring vegetables from boxes into the baskets that would go on the lorry to the camps. They gave her nervous glances as she passed them and went through to the storeroom. She stood in the doorway, gripping the door frame, and stared into the room. Shelves had been torn down and were scattered on the floor, splintered with nails, screws sticking out at all angles. Boxes and rubbish were strewn around. One of the back windows was broken, shards of glass scattered on the floor amongst the other debris.

Slowly, she mounted the stairs to the apartment on the first floor. Kitima was on her knees with her back to the door sweeping up some sugar spilled on the floor. Piak sat cross-legged on a low cushion under the window, rocking back and forth, her eyes faraway, staring into emptiness. Kitima got to her feet as Sirinya entered. She rushed over, put her arms around Sirinya drawing her into her warm comforting embrace. There were tears in her eyes.

'I'm so glad you're back, Daughter. You can't imagine how worried we've been.

'I'm glad I'm back, Ma. Are you and Auntie alright? Where's Malee?'

'Upstairs, resting. She got back a couple hours ago. I didn't know where you were. I've been worried sick.'

'I'm so sorry, Ma, I had to walk a long way. Where's Uncle? What have they done to him?'

'Nothing. Nothing at all. They ransacked the shop. Then they came up here, pulling out all the drawers, checking under cushions, throwing things off shelves. They even went up and searched the bedrooms, pulling sheets off the beds, throwing our clothes out of the cupboards. Then all of a sudden they stopped. The one in charge ordered Chalong to get on with his daily delivery. So we had to just get dressed and get down to the river to unload the barges as usual.'

'Why did they come? What on earth were they looking for?'

'We've no idea. They didn't say. Your uncle thinks they might have found something, perhaps some medicines in the camp in one of the baskets. He was worried they were setting a trap for him, making him go up to the camp this morning. He had no choice but to go.'

Piak gave a great sob and began moaning from her seat in the corner. 'We won't see him again, Sister,' she wailed, rocking back and forth. 'Whatever will I do without him?'

'You need to be strong, Piak,' said Kitima. 'We all must. Chalong will come back. We don't know that the Japanese know anything about the medicines. Please, Sister, take control of yourself. Why don't you get up and make some tea and food for Sirinya. She looks half starved. Wherever did you go, Siri?'

'Up into the hills. To the caves. I left the packages there. It was the only place I could think of. But when I sat down to rest for a moment, I was so tired I fell asleep. What about Malee?'

'Why don't you go upstairs and talk to her. She hardly spoke when she came in. She was soaked through.'

Up in the bedroom under the eaves, Malee was lying fully clothed on the bed. She sat up as Sirinya entered.

'Oh, Siri. I'm so glad you're safe.' They embraced and Sirinya sat down beside her cousin.

'What did you do with the medicines, Malee? Where did you go?'

'I went down to the river. It was hard to find anywhere to put them. In the end I hid them under some bushes.'

'Are you sure that's safe, Malee? Did anyone see you?'

Malee gave an impatient sigh and looked away. 'Why do you question me, Siri? I wouldn't ask you that question. I trust you. Of course no one saw me.'

'I'm sorry. Of course I trust you. I'm exhausted and worried that's all. When it's safe we'll need to go down there and get them back.'

The sound of the lorry drawing up and coming to a stop in the street below interrupted them. They went to the window and watched Chalong get down from the cab wearily. The boy got down from the other side and hurried into the shop.

Sirinya and Malee rushed downstairs to greet Chalong. Kitima and Piak were in front of them. His face was drawn and tired as he came inside.

'I'm alright. Nothing happened to me,' he said sitting down on a wooden crate on the shop floor. 'I'm just tired, but we need to load the truck for the next delivery. I've still got two more camps to do today.'

'You go and rest, Chalong,' said Kitima. 'We can help the boys load up.'

'Yes, come upstairs, Husband. I've made some food,' said Piak, ushering him towards the stairs.

'Before I do that, I need to say something to all of you. Come into the back room.'

They followed them through to the storeroom and shut the door. His eyes widened as he saw the devastation in daylight for the first time, but he didn't remark on it.

'I'm sure we can trust the boys but I don't want to implicate them any more than they are already. We can't take any more medicines into Chungkai camp. Not for the time being at least. We'll need to find another way of doing that. I've found out why the guards are suspicious. They got me in the guardhouse and questioned me when I got to the camp.'

Piak gripped his arm. 'Did they hurt you, Husband? Tell us what happened?'

'No, they didn't do anything to me, just endless questioning that's all. They know if they do anything to me they'll find it hard to get supplies.'

'So what was it about? Why were they questioning you?'

'Two prisoners escaped from the camp yesterday and they thought I might have helped them. The Kempeitai have already recaptured them. I know who was going to meet those men, but I didn't let on to them – it was Sonchai. He lives in a hamlet down the river. The Japanese take one of the army trucks down there each day to collect rice from the barges. He must have been in contact with one of the prisoners who helps out on those runs. Two men were going to give Sonchai money to take them to Bangkok. But the Japs haven't thought of him yet. Sonchai's left the village now. Fled to Burma. They won't find him, but they're going to execute those two poor men.'

Sirinya stared at him. An image of the prisoners walking through the jungle came into her mind. The face of the young man who'd smiled at her. She found herself hoping fervently that he wasn't one of them.

'How do you know all this, Uncle?'

'I just know. Through my contacts in the organisation. I have my ear to the ground.'

Piak shook her head in dismay and rubbed her husband's arm.

'So it's got nothing to do with us or the medicines,' Chalong went on. 'But the officers told me that tomorrow will be my last delivery into Chungkai camp. They are tightening up on security and will come to the shop here themselves with a truck. They're coming for the first time the day after tomorrow. They'll get the prisoners to help. I can carry on delivering to the other camps up the line, but Chungkai will be different.'

'But, Uncle, that doesn't seem to make sense,' said Sirinya slowly. 'If it was because the prisoners were in contact with Thai people through deliveries, why do they think it would be better for more of them to come out of the camp to collect supplies from here?'

Chalong shook his head. 'They don't know it was Sonchai at all. They can be a bit slow on the uptake at times. They haven't put two and two together yet. They think it might have been me because I chat to the prisoners when we're unloading the truck. They're suspicious, that's all. Because they don't know anything they want to control the process more. They'll send guards here with the prisoners to load up the trucks. They think it will be more secure that way.'

The four women stared at him, digesting this new information.

'I'll have to set off soon, once the truck is loaded up. I'm late delivering to Wan Lung camp as it is. There's something I wanted to tell you all before I go, though. I'll be dropping off the empty baskets when I get back and then driving straight down to Bangkok. I need to collect the radio parts this evening. This is our last chance to get them into Chungkai camp. I'll be back before morning. I'll need you to be ready to help me when I go to the camp tomorrow.'

Fear washed through Sirinya at these words. She felt the colour drain from her face.

'Don't be afraid, Niece. It will all be straightforward, as I said before. They will never suspect you or Kitima.'

Sirinya swallowed and lifted her face to her uncle. He was so brave, she didn't want him to know how afraid she was. 'But won't they wonder why you're bringing us instead of one of the boys?' she faltered.

'I'll say that the boys are clearing up the shop after the Kempeitai's visit. Clearing up and repairing all the damage that was done. That's a good enough excuse. They should feel guilty enough not to ask too many questions. And it will be the last time. They'll just want to get it over and done with.'

Sirinya felt her mother squeeze her hand with her warm palms, calloused and hard from working in the fields.

'It will be fine, Daughter. You'll see. I won't let anything happen to you.'

Sirinya smiled weakly and looked up into Kitima's steady brown eyes. She wished she could feel as confident, but she knew that she must do this.

Later as they watched the truck drive off down the road on its next delivery, crates of vegetables loaded on the back, belching black smoke from the loose exhaust pipe, Sirinya smoothed down her skirt and turned to go inside. Now at last she could go upstairs and rest. But out of the pall of smoke left by the truck as it turned out of the end of the road emerged the dark green sports car. Sirinya, her mind racing, wondered if she had time to get inside before Narong saw her, but the car drew up beside the shop with a blast of the horn before she had time to react.

Narong got out of the driver's seat and shaded his eyes as he peered towards the shop. He looked just the same, cool in his expensive clothes, not a hair out of place. He carried himself as if nothing had happened, nothing had changed in the town these past few months.

'Hey, Sirinya, I'm glad I've caught you,' he said, strolling towards her. She felt Kitima stiffen and draw in a sharp intake of breath beside her.

'I haven't seen you for a long time. You always seem to be out when I call.' His eyes flicked to Kitima, appraising and dismissing her in one sweep.

'This is my mother. Mother, meet Narong.'

Narong was well brought up enough to wai deeply to Kitima, bowing his head forward, bringing his hands together and touching his nose with his thumb.

'Good afternoon,' said Kitima, hostility in her tone. 'I'm pleased to make your acquaintance. But I'm afraid have things to attend to upstairs, if you don't mind, Sirinya.'

'There's no need for you to go, Ma. Narong won't be here long.'

'I'm sure. But I'll see you upstairs. Good day to you, Narong.' With that she bustled off.

Narong smiled. 'Your mother is charming,' he said raising an eyebrow. Sirinya felt the heat of anger rising in her cheeks. How dare he judge Kitima?

'You're right, though. I'm not going to stop long,' he said. 'I just dropped by to let you know that I had a visit from the Japanese commander earlier today. They're going to commandeer the factory. They need the paper to supply the Japanese war effort.'

Sirinya stared at him. 'And you just let them?'

'What choice do I have? They are in charge here, Sirinya. They occupy this country. Even the government has rolled over and let them in. Even your saintly uncle does business with them, after all.'

'Yes, but that's different ...' she bit her lip to stop herself saying more.

'So I just thought I'd let you know. I know your uncle is in touch with ... shall we say people who aren't happy about the occupation.'

She opened her mouth to protest, but shut it again. She felt trapped. What could she say?

'I'm on their side, believe you me, Sirinya. I just wanted to reassure you of that, even though it might not look like that when the Kempeitai come into the factory to take over tomorrow. Whatever happens, please remember that about me.'

He was looking into her eyes. The intensity of his gaze reminded her of the time he'd driven her along beside the river, when he'd lost control. Then the image from this morning resurfaced, his hand holding the door open, Ratana getting into his car.

'Go away, Narong,' she said coldly, 'There's no need for you to come here anymore. You don't need to worry about what I think of you.'

'But I do worry. You know I care for you.'

'Look,' she said, confused, avoiding his eyes, 'I have to go upstairs now. I'm very tired. I need to rest.'

'I'll go if you insist,' he said, turning to leave, 'but remember what I said won't you, Siri? I'm on your side.'

She didn't reply. As she mounted the stairs to the apartment she paused for a second at the sound of his car engine roaring into life, the car tyres skidding on the dirt road as he sped off.

16

It was after dark when Chalong returned from Wan Lung camp. Sirinya was waiting for him, sitting on an upturned crate, alone inside the shophouse as the lorry drew up outside.

'Here, let me help you with those,' she said, stepping out from the shadows as Chalong heaved empty baskets down from the lorry.

'Siri?' he said, turning to her, his voice surprised, 'what are you doing down here in the dark? I thought you'd be resting. You had such a disrupted night.'

'You did too, Uncle, but *you're* still working. I wanted to wait for you.' She reached up into the lorry for a basket and heaved one down.

'There was really no need.'

She waited until he came close to her and said in a whisper, 'I want to come with you to Bangkok.' He stopped and turned towards her. 'You don't need to do that, Siri,' his voice was weary.

'I could keep you company. I'd like to help if I can.'

'But you will be helping, tomorrow morning. In a big way. I can go to Bangkok alone.'

She watched him as he walked past her into the shop carrying a stack of baskets. His shoulders drooped with exhaustion, his face was grey and drained. For the first time ever, he seemed old to Sirinya.

'I could drive some of the way,' she said following him, putting her baskets on the floor. 'I *can* drive you know, Uncle.'

'Yes I know, Siri.' He turned to her with a tired smile in his eyes.

'I taught you myself on the motor-rickshaw.'

'So? Why not let me help tonight. You look worn out, Uncle, you could sleep while I drive the first part of the way. To Ban Pong.'

He paused, looking at her.

'Alright then Siri, if you insist,' he said at last, 'you'd better go upstairs and tell your mother and aunt. Tell them we'll be back around five in the morning.'

* * *

Chalong drove out of the Kanchanaburi, eastwards along the road that ran alongside the river towards Bangkok. As soon as they were clear of the outskirts of the town, he pulled off the road and they changed places.

Sirinya sat in the driver's seat and gripped the enormous steering wheel. Chalong had left the engine running. With a crashing of the gears she pulled onto the road and set off. Driving the lorry felt very strange at first. It was heavy and unwieldy, the spindly gear stick vibrated and wobbled in her hand and there was no way of changing the gears without grinding them. She found it hard to control the worn metal accelerator, and at first whenever she put her foot down, the lorry leapt forwards in jerky bursts of speed.

Heat rose from the engine that roared and spluttered under the bonnet. Sweat ran down into her eyes as she struggled to see over the great steering wheel. Within ten minutes Sirinya's arms ached with the effort of holding the lorry straight on the bumpy road, and her whole body felt numb from the vibrations of the truck. Why ever did she volunteer for this? But she knew the answer. She wanted to be involved, to find out about the secret organisation Chalong was part of, to help with whatever they were doing.

She glanced over at Chalong as they rattled into the village of Tha Meuang. He was already asleep, slumped forward on the bench beside her, snoring gently, his head lolling around on his chest. She changed into a lower gear and slowed the vehicle to a crawl as they passed along the single village street lined with wooden houses. In the weedy beam of the headlights, chickens and ducks scattered from their path on either side. People sitting at food stalls or on their front porches looked up and stared as they lorry went through. They must think we're Japanese soldiers, she thought.

Clear of the village, the jungle closed around them and the bumpy road plunged on in darkness. Sirinya gritted her teeth, stared straight ahead of her, focusing on the two thin streams of light cast by the headlights, and just kept driving. She knew the road, she had been to Bangkok many times with her uncle before, but the lorry was maddeningly slow. Every kilometre, every metre, seemed to take an age to cover. They passed through the small town of Ban Pong after about two hours. She slowed down, contemplating pulling over, but Chalong still slept soundly, so she drove on out of the little town, past the railway sidings where she'd heard the Japanese unloaded the prisoners from the trains from Singapore. It was silent and still tonight, with trucks and engines standing empty in the darkness.

It must have been past ten o'clock when they entered Thonburi on the western outskirts of the city. Chalong stirred and stretched his arms beside her. 'You can pull over now, Siri,' he said yawning. 'I will take over. You can get some rest now.'

She slid over onto the other side of the cab and within a few minutes, despite the vibrations and roar of the engine, had fallen into a fitful sleep. As she dozed she was vaguely aware that they were driving deeper into the city, towards its heart, passing through streets of tall brick buildings, majestic temples with golden roofs, rows of shophouses, warrens of sois or sidestreets lit up and alive with busy street markets even at this hour.

She awoke properly, yawning and stretching as they crossed the river on the great Memorial Bridge. She stared out at the buildings lining the banks, lights from their windows reflecting dancing rays on the water, at the pinpricks of light from barges and boats on the river plying their trade to and from the port of Bangkok. Chalong turned right along the riverbank along a main road lined with shops and food stalls, still busy with trade. Sirinya noticed the name Charoen Krung on a road sign.

The lorry crawled along behind buses and tuk-tuks. A tram trundled past in the other direction. After a few minutes Chalong turned off onto a narrow street lined with three-storey buildings and a few yards down manoeuvred the lorry off the road, through some wrought iron gates. He finally pulled up in a courtyard flanked by tall white buildings on two sides and the back wall of a temple on the other. He switched the engine off.

'Where are we?' she asked.

'This is just a place where it is safe to park. The monks in the temple know my business and won't trouble us.'

'So, are we going to see your friends? The people in the V Organisation you told us about?'

He shook his head.

'They aren't in this part of town. They're further upriver at the university. They're imprisoned there actually.'

'Imprisoned?'

'Yes. All foreign civilians in Bangkok have been interned by the Japanese.'

'But … how do you get to see them if they're interned?'

'They are not kept like the soldiers in the camps near us.

Sometimes they're free to go out and meet people, but it is late so tonight that won't be possible. They have to keep to a curfew.'

'So? What are we going to do? Why have we come here?'

'The wife of one of the leaders lives near here. We will go and see her. She's Thai-Chinese and because she isn't an enemy of the Japanese she hasn't been interned. She's a member of the organisation too. She is expecting me to turn up at some point to collect the radio parts. She only lives a short walk from here. I can't park the lorry near her house, the road is too narrow and it would be conspicuous. Come, Sirinya. Let's go.'

They left the truck and Sirinya followed Chalong back through the gates, down the soi towards the river and then on through twists and turns along a series of narrow streets. She could smell the river on the moist evening air. It was only a block away and the mingled odours of dank river water, open drains and rotting fish were strong here. There were no markets in these streets, and the three-storey shophouses were shuttered and dark. It was eerily quiet, apart from the occasional dog barking in a backyard. But the night-time hum of the great city floated on the air, the honking of horns and trams, the blast of sirens from river boats, the high-pitched engines of tuk-tuks and motorbikes.

Chalong stopped in front of a low wooden door and, quickly checking the street, knocked quietly. It was opened almost instantly but only a few inches. Sirinya heard a brief whispered exchange between Chalong and whoever was inside and then the door was drawn back. A pale face appeared in the opening and a small Chinese lady beckoned her in. As she stepped into the house, Sirinya noticed that the woman was beautifully dressed in a black silk-embroidered gown, her face was white with powder and her black hair done up with knitting needles in traditional style. She smiled and nodded, putting her hands together in welcome.

'This is my niece, Sirinya,' Chalong explained. 'Sirinya, this is Mrs Draper.'

'Call me Lian, please. That is my given name. Come – sit down,' said the woman, in perfect Thai. 'I will make tea. You have had a long journey.'

Sirinya followed Chalong as he sat down cross-legged on a silk floor cushion in front of a small table. Lian disappeared behind a painted screen and they could hear the sounds of her boiling a kettle, the rattling of china. The small room was lit with candles and smelled of incense and of Chinese cooking spices. All around were traditional furnishings and ornaments, silk hangings, porcelain vases. Another painted screen stood in front of the window giving onto the street. Sirinya's eyes were drawn to a heavy teak sideboard on the opposite wall, where in pride of place stood the framed black and white photograph of a white man. He had a tanned face, lined by the sun, a pleasant, open smile and a mop of dark hair.

Lian emerged from the kitchen carrying a tea tray.

'That is my husband, Joe,' she explained, with a shy smile. 'I expect your Uncle has told you about him.'

'Not really,' said Sirinya, glancing at Chalong.

'He is such a good man,' said Lian, her face now serious, kneeling down and pouring tea from a porcelain teapot into tiny cups. 'It is a criminal act for him to be interned by the Japanese. He has done nothing wrong. He is just a British trader working here, engaged in the import-export business. But I have to say he is treated fairly well at the university camp, so are the other farang there. They are allowed out. He can come and see me sometimes. Thanks to your uncle, Joe and his friends know all about what is happening in your district and they all want to do what they can to help the prisoners building the railway. Did you bring a letter this time, Khun Chalong?'

Chalong nodded, fumbled in his pocket and handed her a creased white envelope.

'What's that?' asked Sirinya.

'It is from the British officer in charge of the prisoners in Chungkai camp,' said Chalong. 'One of the men passes letters to me when I take the supplies in. They send news of how many sick men there are, and what they need. If they have news of Japanese troop movements they send that too. I give it to Lian to pass on to the organisation so they can help get hold of the medicines.'

'I pass the information about the camp on to a Swiss man, a friend of my husband's,' said Lian. 'He is not interned and that means he is able to communicate it back to London. We also help the prisoners by sending them money via your uncle. My husband has contacts who give what they can. We can buy medicines, too, and your uncle takes them back to Kanchanaburi and into the camps.'

Sirinya nodded. 'I know about that part,' she said.

Lian opened the letter and fell silent as she read it, her lips moving as she translated the words. Then she looked up and said slowly. 'It says that last week five men died of dysentery in the camp hospital. This week they have thirty men in the camp sick with malaria. They need quinine very badly. They also need iodine for men with tropical ulcers. I have some quinine here already, Khun Chalong, that you can take back. I have no iodine though. I might be able to get some in the morning. I will ask Yosakon if he can do that before you leave.' Then she lowered her voice to a whisper. 'I will go down to his house on the river and let him know you are here in a moment. He will come back here with me with the radio parts. He will also bring his nephew and together they will hide them inside the lorry engine for you.'

'We have to go back straight away, Lian. We can't wait until the morning,' said Chalong. 'There was a raid on my shop last night by the Kempeitai. Some prisoners had tried to escape from Chungkai and they think I might have something to do with it. After tomorrow the Kempeitai are stopping me going into Chungkai camp with supplies. Instead, Japanese guards will come to collect the vegetables from my shop.'

'Then it will be even harder to get the medicines in than before,' Lian said, frowning. 'We'll have to find another way.' She got to her feet. 'Now I must go and fetch Yosakon. I won't be a moment. Please stay here, be comfortable and relax for a moment, drink your tea.'

When she had gone, Sirinya said, 'I didn't know you were bringing letters out of the camp, Uncle. You didn't tell us about that.'

'I didn't want to worry you. There was no need for you to know. The people in the organisation here want to do everything they can to get information about what is happening in the camps back to the British Government. I thought, if I'm taking medicines to them, I could easily bring letters with information back out. It's no more of a risk, really.'

'And what else are you doing that we don't know about?'

'Oh, I cash the odd IOU for the prisoners. They'll pay me back when they can. If I haven't got enough money to give them I ask my friends in the town. Those I can trust. You know who I mean, Siri. Sometimes the prisoners ask me to pawn watches, or jewellery too. I've got them all hidden at home, waiting until they all come out and can get it back.'

'Perhaps that's what the Kempeitai were after last night,' she said, her nerves tingling at the thought of the risks he'd been taking.

'Perhaps ... I'm not sure. They didn't find them anyway.'

'Where did you hide them, Uncle.'

'Out in the backyard, in the chicken coop,' he said with a wry smile. 'I thought they'd be safe there, Siri. And it turns out that they were.'

There was the sound of an engine outside, and Lian reappeared in the doorway with two Thai men. They stood on the threshold, not venturing into the house. From where she sat on the floor, Sirinya could see that one looked middle-aged with greying temples, the other looked little older than Sirinya herself. They nodded a greeting to her, but seemed nervous, keeping their eyes down. They were not introduced. Chalong got up and went to the door.

'Did you bring some sacks of rice to put in the back of the lorry?'

'Of course,' said the older man. 'I brought as many as I could load onto my truck.'

Chalong handed over some notes. 'Come, let's go and get the parts stowed away under the lorry,' he said, stepping out of the house. 'You stay here with Lian, Sirinya. I will come back for you as soon as I can.'

When they had gone, Lian made more tea and brought some sweetmeats to the table for Sirinya. She sat down opposite her.

'Your uncle is a very brave man,' she said.

'I realise that,' said Sirinya.

'He doesn't have to help the prisoners at all. He could just do what most people would do, make as much money from the contracts with the Japanese as he could and turn a blind eye to the suffering.'

'He's not like that, though. That wouldn't be him.'

Lian smiled and chewed on a sweetmeat. 'He's a good man.'

'How did he make contact with you in the first place?' asked Sirinya, 'He hardly speaks about the organisation to us at home.'

'My husband found out there was a Thai underground working

against the occupation when he was first interned all those months ago. Your uncle has been part of that from the start. When the prisoners asked your uncle for medicines, he came straight to us. It would be hard for him to get supplies in Kanchanaburi, the Japs would quickly find out. There are several of us here, we want to help in any way we can, with money, medicines, and anything else we can do.'

'Don't you ever worry that you'll be caught?'

Lian shrugged. 'Sometimes I lie awake imagining Japanese footsteps on the road outside, worrying that they will come and knock on my door, but why would they suspect me? I'm just a Chinese tailor's assistant, living quietly here in my little house in a back street. And besides, there aren't many people like me who can speak both Thai and English. While my husband is interned and suffering himself, I will do what I can to help him and others.'

'It must be hard for you, being separated like that?'

'Of course it is hard. It is very hard. You are young, Sirinya, but when you fall in love you'll understand.'

Sirinya fell silent, thinking of Malee and Somsak, how they'd clung to each other before they parted, all those months ago now, and how Malee read the only letter she'd received from him since he left over and over again, keeping it in an inside pocket of her blouse. How she sometimes heard Malee crying herself to sleep on the opposite side of their attic bedroom. And she thought of Narong, their odd exchange earlier that day, and how the sight of him aroused strange, conflicting emotions inside her. That couldn't possibly be love, could it? No, she had never been in love, she decided.

There was a knock on the door. Lian opened it a crack then pulled it back. The younger Thai man stood on the doorstep.

'I'm afraid I've cut my hand,' he muttered. 'Could I come inside and wash it?'

'Come in, quickly,' said Lian, holding the door open and ushering him in. He was cradling his left hand, which was dripping with blood.

'Sit down there. I'll bathe it for you,' said Lian, going behind the screen to the kitchen. Sirinya smiled at the young man, but he looked away nervously.

'How did you do that?' she asked.

He shrugged and coloured slightly. 'My spanner slipped when I was undoing a panel under the truck. It's so dark under there, I could hardly see a thing. I feel so stupid ...'

She didn't know want to say, he seemed so shy, but fortunately Lian quickly returned with hot water and a cloth. 'I've no idea what to bind it up with,' she said.

'How about this?' said Sirinya, wanting to be useful, holding out a handkerchief from her pocket. 'It's clean.'

'Thank you. That will do very well. Oh, but it looks expensive,' Lian said frowning, looking at the embroidered border, 'Are you sure?'

'Quite sure, thank you,' Sirinya said, biting her lip. It had been a gift from Narong and she had no desire to keep it.

* * *

Charoen Krung Road was quiet as Chalong and Sirinya finally set off on the return journey. The markets had shut down for the night and there were no trams and little traffic about now. Chalong and the old man, Yosakon, had come back to the house when they had finished stowing the radio parts under the truck. Then Yosakon and his nephew had bid them farewell and disappeared in their three-wheeled truck towards their house on the river. Sirinya and Chalong had said goodbye to Lian and set off on their long journey home in the lorry.

'Who is the old Thai man?' asked Sirinya as the lorry moved towards the Memorial bridge.

'He's a general merchant here. He supplies us with some of the vegetables that come upriver on the barges. That's how I know him. He's also a member of the organisation. He was able to get the radio parts for us from somewhere in the city.'

'Are you sure you can trust him?'

Chalong shrugged. 'In times like this you have to trust some people, Siri. And sometimes you have to take risks. He has a grudge against the Japanese because they commandeered a temple in his family village up near Nam Tok. He joined the organisation soon after that.'

Chalong fell silent and manoeuvred the lorry off the main road and onto the slip road that led to the bridge.

'Good God!' he said suddenly, slamming on the breaks. Flashlights shone at the windscreen and a Japanese soldier stood in the road holding up his hand for him to stop. There were four other soldiers behind him. Sirinya's stomach lurched and she suddenly felt weak with fear. A roadblock.

'Turn off the engine,' ordered the guard, approaching the window. Chalong obeyed. 'Get out of the lorry. And your passenger too.'

Sirinya fumbled with the door handle and with shaking legs climbed out of the truck. I mustn't show I'm afraid, she kept thinking as she stood beside Chalong. Her breath was coming in shallow pants.

'Where are you going?' demanded the soldier.

'To Kanchanaburi.'

'Why you drive Japanese Imperial Army lorry. You steal it?'

'No, of course not, sir. I work for the Imperial Japanese Army, supplying prison camps with food.'

'You must bow when you meet officer of Imperial Japanese Army!'

'I'm sorry, sir,' said Chalong, hanging his head in a bow. Sirinya did the same, noticing her skirt quivering as she looked down.

'What is in the lorry?'

'Oh, just some sacks of rice. High quality rice, for the Japanese officers in the camps and the Kempeitai. Not for the prisoners. I came myself to Bangkok especially to get it for them.'

The Japanese guard stared at him for a moment, shining the torch in his face. Then a smile spread across his face and he started laughing.

'You very good man. Very good Thai man indeed.'

Still laughing he went to the back of the lorry and shone his torch inside. Sirinya held her breath. He came back to face them.

'Not many sacks of rice in there,' he said, the smile gone.

'No, sir. As I said, special rice. Especially for the officers at Chungkai camp. Only for them.'

There was a long silence. Sirinya did not dare to look the Japanese soldier in the face. She held her breath, staring down at the road surface. She counted the pieces of gravel between her feet. Then suddenly he started to laugh again.

'Good man!' he said. 'I not delay you. You friend of Japanese officers. You go on your way quickly now.'

Sirinya tried not to look as though she was rushing to get back inside the cab; she did her best to appear normal. Her legs were so weak she had trouble climbing up. She noticed that Chalong was making an effort to look relaxed too. The engine misfired as he started it up, sweat standing out on his brow, and he had to try three times before the lorry finally choked into life. All the time the Japanese officer was standing in front of the cab, smiling a fixed smile. At last they moved forward. He saluted them as they drew level and passed the barriers. They crossed the bridge, leaving the road block far behind them. Sirinya did not speak or look at her uncle's face for a long time, not until the tears of shock and relief had stopped streaming down her cheeks.

17

Just after sunrise the next morning, Sirinya sat between Kitima and Chalong on the front seat of the lorry as it bounced along the dirt road beside the wide river towards Chungkai camp. Her heart was beating fast and she could feel its pulse in her throat, but the vibrations and jolting of the truck were so violent they almost disguised it. She clenched her fists and stared ahead. It had started raining as they left the town, and now it was pouring, the puny windscreen wipers no match for the tropical downpour. Mud smeared the windscreen and obscured the view of river meadows fringed with clumps of bamboo, the lines of coconut palms blown sideways in the wind.

'Will it matter, do you think, Uncle?' she asked, her mouth so dry she could barely form the words.

'Will what matter, Siri?' Chalong cocked his head on one side to hear above the noise of the engine.

'The rain. Will it make a difference?'

'No, Siri, calm down. The rain will just mean that the guards will want to get the lorry unloaded quickly. It usually means they will leave it to the prisoners and stay in the guardhouse and keep dry. It is good for us, I hope.'

She tried to force a smile but she knew her eyes were full of anxiety. The roadblock on the bridge in Bangkok had shaken her nerve, reminded her of what a dangerous game they were playing. She told herself she was just tired, that her exhausted mind was playing tricks on her. She could feel Kitima beside her, a solid, comforting presence, wrapped in a brown sarong and tunic. She too was staring silently ahead.

'Now you know what to do when we get there, don't you?' said Chalong.

'Yes, Uncle. We've been over it lots of times. I know what to do.'

Back at the apartment in the hour or so they'd had to rest between returning from Bangkok and leaving for the camp this morning, while the boys loaded the lorry with vegetables, he had handed Sirinya and Kitima the radio parts: two large black batteries, a long round tubular rheostat and an assortment of wires and other small parts.

'You'll need to find a way of securing these to your bodies, so you can carry them without them showing, but so they'll be easy to release,' he said. 'There should be an opportunity to go inside the quartermaster's store with one of the baskets when there are no guards in there. One of the prisoners will give you a signal. He will say, in English, 'the monsoon is early this year,' and then you must simply drop the parts on the ground. One of the men will be there to pick them up. They will be ready.'

'We understand. Now let Siri and me go upstairs, Chalong,' said Kitima a flush spreading over her cheeks. 'We cannot do this with you in the room.'

Upstairs they worked quickly. First they ripped up an old sheet into strips. Then Malee and Piak had helped them hold each radio part to their thighs and stomachs, and bind it closely with the cotton to their skin. Then they wound sarongs around their waists and pulled loose tunics on over their heads. They worked in silence, barely looking at each other. Sirinya struggled to stay calm. She didn't want to discuss what they were about to do, because the enormity of it overwhelmed her. She was afraid she might lose her nerve, and break down and cry at any moment. She knew though she must stay strong for the others, and for the prisoners she'd be helping if their plan worked.

Now in the cab of the lorry, the batteries dug into the flesh on her thighs. She was so hot with the extra layers that her face was running with sweat and the cotton bound against her skin was wet through.

The rickety gates of the camp came into view. They were made of thick bamboo poles, held together with jungle twine. As they approached, two Japanese guards appeared and dragged the gates back. Chalong drove the truck through the opening and into the camp. Although Sirinya had seen it under construction from across the river when the prisoners had first arrived, she could not suppress a gasp as they entered, shocked at how this place she had loved and spent endless hours playing in throughout her childhood was now ugly and scarred, transformed beyond recognition.

Where buffalo had once lazed in the long grass beside the river, there was now a muddy parade ground, surrounded by a dozen or so long huts made of bamboo and thatched with palm leaves. Although it was still early, the only prisoners in evidence appeared to be three men digging a trench at the far end of the ground, their shoulders hunched against the downpour. They lifted their heads and glanced at the truck as it bumped across the ground through the puddles, but quickly turned back to their work.

Chalong drove the lorry to the far end of the muddy ground, passing a hut on the left which appeared to be better constructed than the others. It even had its own steps and platform. A Japanese soldier stood at the top of the steps, holding a baton under one arm, his chest thrust forward, imperiously surveying the camp.

'That's the commandant of Chungkai camp,' said Chalong.

'Don't stare at him. He's got an evil temper, and I've seen it in action. The prisoners call him the Ripper.'

Sirinya shuddered and turned her gaze away from the guardhouse, but she could tell that the commandant had already noticed her and was hurrying down the steps towards them. Chalong brought the lorry to a standstill in front of another hut, set at right angles to all the others. Another, shorter and squatter Japanese guard and three prisoners emerged. Sirinya tried not to stare at the men. They were probably only a little older then her, but their faces were lined. They were very thin, their ribs visible beneath their sunburnt skin, their hair unkempt. They only wore loincloths despite the heavy rain.

'Wait here for a moment. I will speak to them,' said Chalong, jumping down from the cab, slamming the door.

Sirinya and Kitima waited silently, rain pelting down on the metal roof of the cab. The Ripper strode up and addressed Chalong, who bowed his head.

'Where are your usual workers?'

'They are busy in the shop in town today, sir. There is much to do after the visit of the Kempeitai yesterday. I have brought my niece and sister-in-law. They are strong. They are good workers.'

'We'll see about that. Set them to work. I will watch how they do.'

With a nod of the head, Chalong beckoned Sirinya and Kitima to follow him as he went to the back of the truck to collect the first load of vegetables.

With trembling hands, Sirinya opened the door, climbed down from the cab and walked to the back of the lorry. She could hear Kitima behind her, but she did not dare glance back. The battery dug into her thigh and she had to make an effort to walk normally, her sandals slipping and skidding on the muddy ground. The rheostat felt hard and cool against the skin of her stomach, dragging the bandages down. Under her breath she prayed to Buddha that they would hold. How ever are we going to get away with this, she kept asking herself, keeping her eyes on the churned mud of the parade ground.

At the tailgate of the truck she reached up for a basket of potatoes with both arms. She could feel the eyes of the Japanese soldiers on her. As she took the weight of the basket, it felt even heavier than usual, the bindings restricted her movements. Kitima was doing the same beside her. They did not look at each other. Then two of the prisoners followed them and took down baskets themselves. The third man climbed up onto the back of the truck, waiting to pass down baskets stowed further forward. Sirinya hoisted her basket onto one shoulder and walked towards the hut. This meant walking past the Ripper and the other soldier. Would they expect her to bow? Surely not. Not with a basket. She did not dare glance at them, but as she drew level with them the Ripper barked out, 'When you have finish I have something to discuss with you.'

Was he speaking to her? Her eyes darted sideways, and she realised that he was looking directly at her. She stopped in front of him, knees unsteady, a sick feeling in her stomach, and dropped a shaky curtsey, still balancing the basket on her shoulder. He nodded approval with the flicker of a smile and she moved forward. She was just letting out a breath of relief when he said, 'Stop! All of you, stop. Put baskets down on ground.'

Sirinya obeyed, and either side of her Chalong and Kitima did the same.

'We make search of your baskets. Tomorrow my men go to your shop to collect supplies for this camp. You not come here with supplies. These men are not to be trusted. Two of them have escaped. Another is being punish for it.'

His eyes strayed to the far corner of the ground, then returned to Sirinya. She wondered what was going on in that far corner, what pain and humiliation the poor soldier was going through. A shudder went through her.

Then the Ripper nodded to the other officer, who went over to Chalong's basket, bent down and rummaged around amongst the potatoes. After a few seconds he drew himself up, turned to the Ripper and shook his head. His hands, and the arms of his uniform, already soaked through with rain, were plastered in mud from the potatoes. Next he came to Sirinya's basket. He stood in front of it and his eyes moved down her body for a few seconds longer than necessary. She stared at him in disgust. He smelt of tobacco and sweat. That smell took her back to the day in this same field when it all began, when she and Malee had stood there shivering in bewilderment in front of the Japanese soldiers with their guns and bayonets. This guard bent forward and made a cursory search through Sirinya's basket, the gun on his shoulder dropping forwards as he did so. Then he straightened up, shook his head and moved on towards Kitima.

Sirinya picked up her basket and followed Chalong into the hut. Another prisoner waited there in the gloom, rain dripping through holes in the thatch. He took the basket from her, all the time avoiding her eyes. Like the others he was dressed only in a loincloth, barefoot and painfully thin. It was dark inside the hut and she could hardly see his face. He stowed her basket against the far wall and handed her an empty one from the previous day's delivery. As she turned away, he said quietly, 'the monsoon is early this year.'

She hesitated. It sounded so natural, for a second she wondered if it was the signal, or if he was just passing the time of day. Chalong stood half-blocking the doorway, and beyond him she could see the backs of the two officers. She knew she must act quickly. She put the basket down and fumbled inside her tunic. It was easy to release the rheostat, her sweat had loosened the bandages around her waist. She quickly pulled the metal object free, and dropped it on the floor. Then she put her hands inside the slit in her sarong and began to work the battery loose from her thigh. That was more difficult. The knot Malee had tied was so tight that it had become too small to pull undone easily. She bent down and picked at it furiously with her fingernails, her breath uneven, sweat trickling into her eyes and clouding her vision. The prisoner stood behind her, waiting. He had already miraculously darted forward to pick up the rheostat and hidden it from view. Precious seconds were being lost. Chalong had moved away from the door and now Kitima was standing there with another basket.

'Not two people in that hut!' barked the Ripper. 'First one come out now.'

Sirinya stared helplessly at the prisoner and straightened up. He shook his head. 'Try again in a moment if you can,' he muttered.

She left the hut with the empty basket, took it back to the lorry under the gaze of the two officers and was handed another basket by the prisoner on the back of the lorry, this one full of cabbages. Her heart was pounding now. Would Kitima have the same trouble releasing the radio parts as she had? But as she turned back to the hut Kitima was emerging, and from the easy way she walked Sirinya could tell that her mother had been successful. They passed each other without exchanging a glance. The two prisoners were following Sirinya now, carrying their baskets. Each of them in turn stopped, dropped the basket on the mud and waited for the guard to do his search. She thanked Chalong's foresight for not trying to smuggle medicines into the camp this time.

Should she wait for the signal a second time? Could she trust the other prisoners? Scrambled thoughts crowded her mind. The surroundings had become a blur now. She went inside the hut and put the basket on the ground. The two prisoners were behind her, waiting in the doorway.

'The monsoon is early this year,' said the man again. This time she didn't try to undo the bandage, she put her thumbs inside it and started to push the whole thing down her thigh. It took a couple of tries and then began to move. The two prisoners were waiting behind her in the doorway with their baskets.

'No waiting! Move. Speedo. Quickly now,' came the Ripper's voice.

With supreme effort she managed to push the bandage all the way down her leg and quickly stepped out of it. The prisoner behind her stepped forward and picked up the battery and the bandage. Sirinya turned and left the hut, shaking all over. Emerging into the rain she caught Chalong's eye. He nodded and gave her a brief smile. She smiled back.

'You, girl,' shouted the Ripper. 'Why you smiling? You have nothing to smile about. You very slow worker.'

She stopped, fear coursing through her. Had he noticed anything? 'I …I'm sorry, sir,' she said.

He paused and scrutinised her, his eyes narrowed. She hung her head.

'You move on now,' he said finally. 'But you not good worker. I not choose you now.'

As she moved, trembling, towards the truck, she wondered what he meant. Choose her?

After three or four more trips it was over. The lorry was now full of empty baskets.

The rain was easing off as the Ripper beckoned them towards him.

Chalong, Kitima and Sirinya stood in front of him in a line. What is this all about, thought Sirinya. It must be some sort of trick. Perhaps he knows about the radio; he's just been waiting for his moment.

'I choose you,' said the Ripper, pointing at Kitima, who looked up at him with wide, fearful eyes. 'You are good worker. You are strong and tough. You work hard. You not talk or make trouble.'

'She does not speak English I'm afraid, sir,' said Chalong. 'She won't understand you.'

'That is no matter. I explain to you. You can tell her.'

'What is it you need from us, sir?'

'I will tell you. Before this trouble started, I agreed with British officers that I would let them have a small canteen where soldiers could go when finish work and on days off. It would sell coffee, tea and some food – fruit, eggs and so on. Also tobacco. Men could pay for food with the generous wages Imperial Japanese Army give them for working on the railway. We make profit, but it would be a reward for good work. We are fair with our prisoners, we treat them well.'

He paused and stared at the three of them, he seemed to be waiting for a reaction, but getting none he frowned and went on, 'Now I not do that for them straightaway because of escape prisoners. I make them wait. But in a few days' time we can begin. It will be strictly controlled by Imperial Japanese Army. We will bring in supplies with the vegetables from your store, we will let you know what we need and you must add that into your contract price. But we need somebody to cook and serve. Every day. Someone we can trust. This old woman is the person I choose for that job,' he said nodding and pointing again towards Kitima. 'Now, you explain that to her Mr Chalong.'

Slowly, Chalong turned to Kitima and repeated what the Ripper had said in Thai. Gradually Kitima's face dropped and drained of colour as the words sunk in.

'But, Chalong, what if I don't want to do that?' she asked when he had finished.

Anger was mounting inside Sirinya at the man's arrogance. She wanted to run forward and pummel his chest and scream at him. Why should Kitima have to give up everything and come here every day just because the Ripper had ordered it?

'I don't think there is a choice, Kiti,' said Chalong gently, smiling steadily all the time, keeping his voice even. The Ripper was watching them intently. Kitima stood silently for a few minutes, her face expressionless. Sirinya wondered fleetingly if she would make a scene.

'Would I have to come here every day?' she asked at last.

'That's what he said. I'm sorry Kiti … If I had known this would happen …'

Kitima drew herself up and pursed her lips. 'It is not your fault, Brother-in-law. Speak no more about it. If there is no choice, I'll just have to do it. There's no getting around it is there? We are all controlled by them and their weapons now. When does he want me to start?'

'In a few days' time, Kiti. They will let us know.'

As they drove back along the river road towards the wooden road bridge at Tambon Lat Ya, the rain had stopped and the sky was blue and cloudless. Sirinya stared out at the clumps of tall bamboo that shielded the old Bamboo Road where she and Malee used to walk in days of freedom. Beyond that the river sparkled in the sunlight. Kitima sat between her and Chalong, twisting the end of her sarong in her large brown hands. She was silent for a while, then after a few kilometres she said quietly, 'Whatever will Mother say about this? I promised her that I would go back to the village and see her next week, but I won't be able to go now ... she'll be so worried.'

* * *

The next morning the family rose before dawn as usual and walked down to the river to unload the sacks of vegetables from the barges onto the bullock carts. Then, with a smaller load than normal, Chalong set off for the camps upriver, Wan Lung and Wan Takan. Sirinya waited in the shop with Kitima and the two boys, Manop and Pinit, who loaded the fruit and vegetables into baskets. Malee and Piak were upstairs cleaning and preparing food.

As the sky lightened and the sun began to glint golden rays over the roof of the Kempeitai house, Sirinya heard the sound of a lorry at the end of the road. Peering out she saw a different Japanese army truck approaching. It drew up outside the shop and three Japanese guards jumped down from the cab. She watched them go to the back of the lorry and open the tailgate. From under the tarpaulin three prisoners emerged from the back of the lorry. The first one to get down was older than the others and was dressed in a khaki shirt and shorts. He carried himself with the air of authority. The other two wore only the usual grubby loincloths, but at least had shabby boots on their feet. The Japanese soldiers waited by the lorry and lit cigarettes. The older prisoner came forward and stood in front of Sirinya. He put his hand together in a wai and bowed his head.

'Good morning, madam. I am Colonel Philip Scott, Medical Officer and British Commander at Chungkai camp. If you would show me the stores, I and my two men here will load up the lorry.'

'We can help, sir,' Sirinya replied. 'We are used to it.'

'No need for you to trouble yourselves. I do have something to give you later on, though. Don't change your expression when I say this to you. They won't hear what we are saying, but it is important not to react. I have a letter for our friends in Bangkok. You know who I mean, don't you?'

She nodded and lowered her eyes. 'Of course. I will show you the stores in the storeroom at the back,' she whispered. 'Hand it to me when we go in there and I will hide it and give it to my uncle later.'

'Thank you. We can do that after we've loaded up some of these supplies. Now my two men, Foster and Henderson here will help me load up.'

He went on into the shop and the two prisoners moved forward. As Sirinya lifted her eyes to look at them her heart gave a jolt and she felt colour rushing to her face. The first man had a thatch of unruly hair. She thought she recognised his face, but she couldn't place it immediately. She knew the second man's face in an instant. It was him. The young man she'd seen on the jungle road as the column of soldiers had marched past her and Malee as they stood beside the motor-rickshaw handing out fruit. The man to whom her thoughts had returned again and again over the past few months.

His friend had said his name that day, Charlie, and she'd not forgotten it. As he passed her he looked into her eyes. Those were the eyes had haunted her dreams; brown with flecks of gold. There were the same high cheekbones, but he was even thinner now, his cheeks hollow, sallow beneath the sunburn. And there it was again, that incomprehensible spark of recognition, of connection with him that coursed through her like a bolt of lightning.

18

In the cool gloom of Kasem's shop in Chinatown Sirinya stares up at him. She *has* seen a ghost, right here in the *Bangkok Messenger*.

'Look, she's here,' she says, her finger stabbing the photograph. Kasem frowns and peers at the newspaper and she can see he isn't following.

'Ratana! The girl ... the woman I told you about. She's right here, in the newspaper.'

'Let me look,' he takes it from her and holds it up to the light from the window, reading it closely. 'There aren't any names under the photograph. Are you sure it's her?'

'Quite sure. She's hardly changed since the war. I'd know her anywhere.'

'Shall we go there now then? To Patpong? Or perhaps you'd prefer to go alone?'

She smiles up at him, relieved that he understands that she must go there right now. That now she's seen the photograph she can't spend the day strolling by the river or sitting in Lumpini Park with him, or eating seafood in a restaurant. This is far more pressing.

Then she surprises herself by saying, 'Why don't you come too?'

Perhaps she says this through a sense of guilt that she's letting him down, or perhaps it's something more than that? She senses that he seems to understand her, and it would be good to have someone sympathetic with her after all those depressing nights alone patrolling the strip in New Petchburi.

'I'd be glad to. But the traffic will be bad at this time. It's best to go by motorbike,' he says, holding out his hand. She takes it and gets up from the window seat.

'Come this way.' He beckons her towards the back of the shop and out through a rear entrance into a tiny backyard. The two men at the low table continue their bargaining without a pause. The steamy heat and pungent smell of drains and decay hit her once again. She tries not to wince. A rusting old motorbike stands there in the yard, in front of a stack of old cardboard boxes. Kasem pulls the bike off its stand and, holding it out proudly, he pats the seat for her to get on.

'Does this thing actually work?' she asks, laughing.

'Of course!' he says with mock outrage, as she hitches her skirt up discreetly, lifts her leg over and sits astride the passenger seat.

'It goes like a dream. Please don't be afraid. I go everywhere on it. It's the only way to get about in Bangkok now. I know all the shortcuts. We'll be in Patpong in less than twenty minutes.'

He gets on to the seat in front of her, kicks the engine into life and in a flash they are out through the narrow alley and into the wider soi, dodging between shops and stalls, ducking to avoid over-hanging signs and goods displayed under the awnings of shops. At first Sirinya feels self-conscious hanging onto this stranger, but she is soon gripping his waist hard with both hands, holding on as tightly as she can as they swoop round corners, avoiding pedestrians and men with barrows, and accelerate between market stalls.

Soon they are out of the sidestreets and riding along the main thoroughfare, Yaowarat Road, where cars, buses and trucks crawl along nose to tail belting out smoke and fumes. Kasem weaves the bike expertly between the vehicles and takes a sharp turn into another alleyway, passing the rear wall of a temple, where the back of a golden statue of Buddha is all that can be seen from this angle, flying along between the rear entrances of buildings, where washing hangs and junk is stored. A man looks up from taking a shower in an outdoor bathroom and stares at them as they flash past. At one point the alleyway opens up and they are crossing a courtyard where people sit eating lunch at food stalls. Kasem slows the engine and eases the bike past the diners. Wafts of garlic and lemongrass fill the air.

Then they dive back into another narrow passage and after a few more twists and turns emerge onto a wide road lined with tall buildings.

'This is Silom Road,' he says. 'Patpong is not far now.'

He turns left and accelerates between the lanes of traffic, swooping in front of them at some traffic lights and turning left into a sidestreet. After a few metres he pulls up, stops the motorbike and beams at her as he gets off.

'See, I told you it would be quick. This is Patpong Road. It is all new. All these bars have opened up in the last couple of years, since the American war started in Vietnam.'

She gets down from the bike and smooths down her crumpled skirt. As her thumping heart slows, Sirinya stares down the street. It appears to be a replica of New Petchburi, only the buildings here are newer and less shabby, but here are the same neon signs, the same lurid messages aimed at enticing men looking for cheap beer and sex. It has the same tawdry feel as New Petchburi in the daytime, rubbish is strewn on the road and the lights are switched off. A couple of skinny girls dressed in bunny-girl outfits and towering heels hang around outside a bar called the Queen's Castle. Already their attention is drawn to Kasem. They are looking his way, eyeing him up as a possible punter. Further down the street an open-backed truck is parked and builders are working from wooden scaffolding on the concrete frame of a building.

'Let's look at the picture again,' says Kasem. 'We might be able to see which bar it was taken from.'

Sirinya gets the newspaper out of her shoulder bag and they stare at the photograph of the brawl. The small crowd in the photo is standing in front of a bar, but the printing is blurred and it is difficult to make out the name.

'Can I help you?' They look up and a tall woman with perfect features and long black hair stands in front of them. 'I'm Jemima,' she says. 'I work in a bar down the road here. Are you looking for anything in particular, sir?'

She raises an eyebrow and is looking at Kasem boldly, a smile playing on bright red lips.

'Yes, I am actually,' says Kasem, not meeting her eye directly. 'Do you happen know where this bar is?' He holds the paper out. The woman takes it with a flash of long red fingernails. 'Oh yes, I know this place. It is Carousel Bar. It's is in a sidestreet off Patpong Road. You'll find it along there and to your left. But it is closed up now. The police shut it down after the fight the other night.'

'We're actually looking for this woman. Does she work there?'

The tall girl frowns. 'Are you police?'

'No. She's an old friend of mine,' says Sirinya. 'I need to see her.'

The frown is replaced with a smile and she looks at Sirinya as if noticing her for the first time. 'Oh well, that's different. I do know her. That's Mamasan Jo-Jo.'

'Are you quite sure that's her name?' asks Sirinya.

Jemima shrugs and looks at her from beneath false eyelashes with a pitying smile.

'Of course it's not her name, lady. Nobody uses their real name around here. Do you think I'm actually called Jemima? Jo-Jo is her professional name of course. She runs the Carousel. Lives upstairs there. Everyone in Patpong knows her. But she's gone away now. The whole place is closed up.'

'Do you know where she might have gone?'

'Look, lady, how should I know? I only came to talk to you because I thought your friend wanted what I've got to offer. I'm really something quite special, you know. Now why don't you just go down that road where the bar is and ask around down there. They might know where she's gone.'

With a toss of her long black hair she saunters away on her high heels, swinging her hips, her short skirt topping impossibly long legs.

Sirinya glances at Kasem, who is looking flustered. 'Khatoey,' he mutters under his breath.

Sirinya stares at him. 'Ladyboy?' she whispers intrigued and a little shocked. 'Are you quite sure?'

As they walk down Patpong Road towards the side street Jemima indicated, she blows them a kiss from outside a bar where she is leaning in the doorway. Sirinya takes care not to stare.

The Carousel Bar is a few doors down the side street off the main Patpong drag and 'Jemima' was right, steel shutters are pulled down over the shop front. There is a door next to the shutters, obviously opening onto a staircase to the upstairs rooms. Kasem knocks on it and rings the bell but no one appears.

'Here, let's have a drink in this bar next door,' he says, and they sit down at a table on the street outside a bar called Pussy Go-Go. A young waiter with greasy skin and dyed ginger hair shambles over, looking half asleep. Kasem orders two beers.

'Do you know what happened at the bar next door?' he asks the waiter, whose eyes shift sideways.

'There was a fight there,' the boy says in a bored tone. 'It has closed down. The people have all gone away. Went yesterday.'

'Do you know where they went?'

The waiter shrugs and walks away, wiping his hands on his grubby apron.

'I'm sorry, Sirinya,' says Kasem. 'Let's have a drink here anyway and think about what to do. There must be someone around who can tell us where she's gone.'

'Never mind. It's not your problem, Kasem. ' She suddenly feels defeated. The exhilaration of the motorbike ride has gone now and left her exhausted.

'You didn't tell me why you need to see her so badly.'

She looks away from him, staring at the shuttered bar next door, at the blank windows on the upper floors.

'It's not important,' she says.

'It was important enough to come ten thousand kilometres for.'

'It's waited over twenty-five years. It can wait a little longer.'

'Twenty-five years? So it was something that happened during the war?'

She nods silently. 'And where were you then?' he asks. 'Where were you during the war?'

'In Kanchanaburi. Living with my uncle and his family. We were there when the Japanese brought the prisoners to the region. Some dreadful things happened then, Kasem.'

He nodded. 'I know,' and his face is suddenly serious, the shadows of memories crossing his eyes. She takes his hand on his on the table.

'I'm so sorry, Kasem. How thoughtless of me. You must have suffered too. Where were you during the war?'

'I was living in Nam Tok with my parents at first. Then I came down to Bangkok to get work with my mother's family. I've lived here ever since.'

The beers arrive and Sirinya takes a long sip from the brown bottle. It is a long time since she's sampled the strong sweet taste of Singha. She remembers how sometimes Johnny would persuade her to take a sip of beer from his glass on their occasional visits to the local pub in England, but that always tasted so flat and bitter she had trouble swallowing it. Now she feels the alcohol coursing through her veins, seeping into the muscles in her arms and legs, making them heavy and relaxed.

'Is that when you met your husband? During the war?' he asks.

She nods. 'My uncle was a merchant in Kanchanaburi. He sold fruit and vegetables to the Japanese for the camps on the railway. The prisoners used to come to our shop in Saeng Chuto road to load up. My husband was one of those prisoners.'

'How extraordinary that he stayed on here after the war. I thought the prisoners were all shipped to Japan or other places in the Japanese empire after the railway was finished.'

'Some of them stayed in Kanchanaburi until the end of the war. Some were so sick they couldn't be moved. But I'd left there by then. I came here to Bangkok to work. Johnny came to find me when he was released.' She stops. If she carries on she knows she will start to cry.

'Was your uncle called Chalong?' he asks suddenly. His expression has changed, he is looking at her intently.

'Yes he was. Why do you ask?'

'He was quite well known at that time, that's all. He was quite a hero in the local community, wasn't he?'

She smiles, remembering Chalong, his strength and his kindness. 'Yes. He was such a good man. He helped the prisoners as much as he could. He took risks for them. The whole family did …'

The tears really threaten now. She stops. 'Look, I'd prefer not to talk about that time if you don't mind. There are things that happened then that I'd rather forget. It's a long time ago … another lifetime.'

'Of course. I understand,' he says, taking a sip of beer. 'Well why don't you tell me about your life in England. What was it like there?'

'Cold,' she laughs, relaxing. 'Even in summertime. Cold and grey. I often pined for home, for the colours and the sunshine and the people.'

'What did you do there? Did you have a job?'

So she tells him. It doesn't take long to tell him everything there is to tell about her life in England. She tells him about the early years in the flat in the South London suburb, when she and Johnny were so poor she had to wear her coat inside during the day, not being able to afford to heat the place when Johnny was out at work, and how when Johnny qualified as a teacher they moved to a small town a few miles out of the capital, to a terraced house of their own, where they stayed until he died.

She even tells him how she longed and prayed and waited for a baby, but how each month her hopes were dashed and after a few years she gave up. She tells him about her part-time job in Johnny's school as a kitchen assistant, and how although the other women were kind to her, she never really felt as if she belonged, as if she was one of them. She tells him how they pretended not to be able to pronounce her name, and gave her a new one: Susan. She tells him how the children used to stare at her in the school corridors, and how sometimes she would overhear them calling her 'that chinky'. She tells him how over the years she and Johnny saw less and less of Johnny's family, who seemed to make excuses not to visit, or were too busy with his sister's children. In any case, Johnny preferred to spend time with the friends he had made at the school. She tells him how her life in England had been quiet and unbearably dull, and how she now realises that she had spent her days marking time, waiting for the chance to come home, to finish the things she had left undone when she went.

'How very sad,' says Kasem when she's finished speaking.

'Oh, not sad at all really. Yes, I felt very alone all those years, but it became so normal that I got used to the feeling.' She toys with her beer bottle; it is now warm and she doesn't want to drink the dregs.

'What made you go there in the first place?'

'I needed to get away from here. At the end of the war … things happened.'

'And your husband, he took you away from it all?'

She nods. 'I thought I was escaping but it wasn't an escape. It was a refuge in a way, but I was in limbo all those years. I didn't realise that properly until Johnny died.'

A man emerges from the bar and approaches them from between the empty tables. He is stockily built and swaggers as he walks, muscles bulging under a tight black T-shirt, gold chains jangle around his neck.

'I hear you are asking about the next-door bar,' he says standing in front of the table, legs apart, arms folded. 'Are you police? Journalists?'

Kasem looks up at him. 'No, my friend here is an old friend of the woman who runs the Carousel. She came here to look her up.'

'Well Jo-Jo's gone away. Did a flit last night. I own that building and she's gone without paying her rent. If you find her tell her Nong needs to see her.' He clicks his fingers in the direction of his bar, 'Two more Singha beers here, please,' he yells.

'Thank you. We'll tell her if we see her, but we've no idea where to look,' said Sirinya.

'You might try Pattaya. Lots of bars are opening up there now. She's been talking about going there for a while.'

'Pattaya? Where's that?'

'Along the coast, used to be a little fishing village until American soldiers started going there on leave from the war. Now new bars and clubs are opening up every day. People think they're going to make their fortune.'

The waiter comes out bringing the beers the owner ordered.

'Don't forget,' says the man. 'Tell her I need to see her. Enjoy your beers.' And he leaves as abruptly as he arrives, retreating into the gloom of the bar.

'I don't know what to do now,' says Sirinya. 'I'm not sure I can face starting all over again looking in another place. I really thought we'd find her here.'

'Would you like me to take you there?' asks Kasem. 'To Pattaya?'

'Not on that boneshaker of a bike!' Sirinya says laughing, taking a sip from the new bottle.

'My friend has a taxi. He lets me borrow it sometimes. We could go tomorrow.'

'Perhaps ...I'm not quite sure.' Sirinya hesitates. This is a tempting offer, but it all feels too quick. She hardly knows this man and already she has told him far more about herself and her life than feels comfortable. She doesn't want to feel she owes him anything.

'Of course. I understand,' Kasem says, smiling into her eyes. 'Just let me know if you need my help.' They carry on sipping their beer and chatting, and the afternoon draws on. A few groups of westerners arrive and sit at other tables. These men don't look like soldiers, they are older, dressed casually. Some of them speak English, but Sirinya notices French and German spoken too.

'You were telling me about your husband,' says Kasem. 'Before that man came out. About how he took you away from here.'

She nods. 'He did. And I was very grateful to him for that.'

'He must have loved you very much.'

'Yes, he did, poor Johnny,' she takes another sip of beer. 'And I loved him too of course.'

'But?' asks Kasem, looking into her eyes.

'But?'

'It's just that it sounded as if it wasn't the whole story.'

Was it that obvious? Perhaps the unaccustomed alcohol has loosened her reserve. She looks at him.

'But his friend was the one I really loved,' she says, then stops herself and gasps. The words have been spoken. She stares at Kasem, open-mouthed. She has never admitted this out loud before, not to anyone, especially not to Johnny, although he knew of course.

'His friend? Another prisoner?'

'Yes.' The word is barely audible.

She pushes her chair back and stands up suddenly. 'Let's go now, shall we? I've had quite enough beer. I'll decide what to do about Ratana tomorrow. You've been very kind, but I've already taken up far too much of your day.'

19

Sirinya laid the colonel's letter out on the table in the apartment. The whole family were seated around waiting for her to begin, their faces grave and expectant in the flickering lamplight. With long pauses while she struggled to find the right words, and some false starts, she began to translate:

My Dear Khun Chalong,

Thank you again for the recent supplies of medicines and equipment you sent into the camp, and for all the IOUs you have cashed so generously. Thank you also for the other equipment your family so bravely brought in yesterday. In time, that will prove very useful and be a true boost to morale.

The medicines have been most helpful in reducing the suffering of our soldiers and the number of deaths in the camp from dysentery. We are still in great need of quinine as malaria is on the rise again and supplies of iodine are running low too for the treatment of septic ulcers. In addition, if you are able to get hold of any cat gut, that is very useful for operations. We also need chloroform for anaesthetics.

Japanese vigilance in the camp is high again now because of a recent escape attempt as you know. We have even had visits from the Kempeitai this week. As you are not yourselves bringing in the vegetables now it is too risky to attempt to smuggle medical supplies in that way. However, we officers here have thought of an alternative possibility, but it would depend upon further bravery and sacrifice on your part, which we have hardly a right to expect.

The boundaries on two sides of our camp are patrolled by Japanese guards at regular intervals, the other is the river, as you know. On the third side a moat runs alongside the camp, separating it from the rice paddies beyond. The guards do not patrol that section of the boundary for some reason, just as they don't patrol the river. We think it could be one way of getting medicines into the camp, if you had someone who was prepared to swim across under cover of darkness. As mentioned, we know this is asking more than we have any right to ask of you. However, if by any chance you are agreeable to this plan, please ask your family to let us know tomorrow morning and we will place our own sentries beside the moat on the evening you choose between 8pm and 11pm to receive the supplies.

Information requested by the organisation in Bangkok is as follows: 5 deaths from dengue fever yesterday, 3 from typhoid, 5 from dysentery, 3 from septicaemia. Construction on the railway is continuing apace, Chungkai cutting is almost finished, and the bridge at Tamarkan river crossing is well underway with some deaths and many injuries due to the dangerous nature of the operation. We have had no information about Japanese troop movements to pass on at present. Please pass this information on to V in Bangkok when you are able, and thank them most sincerely for their continued support with medical supplies and money. Without it, and yours, many more of our men would already have died.

Sirinya stopped translating and looked round the faces at the table.

'We can do that can't we, Uncle? Swim into the camp with the medicines?'

Chalong's expression was full of regret. He passed his hand over his face. 'I wish I could, Siri, but as you know I can't swim. I've never been able to master it I'm afraid.'

'I could do it father,' said Malee, her face eager in the half-light. 'I'd gladly help.'

'I'll come with you, Malee,' said Sirinya straight away. 'We can go tomorrow evening. First, though we'll need to go and get the medicines back from where we hid them.'

'Please, think about it carefully. It will be dangerous, Daughter,' said Piak, drawing her shawl tight around her throat. 'If you get caught, the Japanese will be sure to shoot you. Maybe worse.'

'Others are doing brave things, Mother. What about Somsak? He is putting his life on the line every day against the Japanese occupation. Let me do this one thing, please. I need to help too,' she turned pleading eyes to her father, who looked at her gravely for a moment, then nodded slowly.

'You can go, Daughter. Thank you for your courage. I only wish I could come with you.'

Piak opened her mouth to protest, but Chalong shot her a warning glance, and she closed it again.

'You will have to cross the river at Tha Maa Kham with the boatman while it is still light, and walk along the Bamboo Road,' he said, 'then you'll need to circle behind the camp to get to the moat. That will take a while so you need to leave plenty of time. You can take the medicines in bags tied around your neck, tucked inside your clothes. Oh and while I think about it, try not to drink the water while you're swimming, it is probably contaminated.'

Piak began to sob gently.

'Sister, please be brave,' said Kitima, leaning forward and putting her hand on Piak's arm. 'You must try to be, for their sakes.

The girls are good swimmers and they will be very careful. They will soon be back home, safe again.'

'Tell the colonel tomorrow morning that you will try tomorrow evening then, if you are happy to,' Chalong said to Sirinya.

That night Sirinya lay awake staring at the eaves of the attic bedroom, lit by the light of the moon, listening to the rasp of the cicadas in the trees outside the window. She was anxious about what the next day would bring, but it wasn't that that was keeping her awake, it was the prisoner she now knew as Charlie. He had clearly recognised her too as he had passed her the first time in the shop. He had stopped, turned towards her and smiled, a wide, generous smile. He'd even put his basket down, put his hands together in a wai and inclined his head to her.

'Sawas dee krub,' he said. 'It was you wasn't it? Who gave us fruit that day we were marched through the jungle?' She nodded, her eyes shining, looking into his. 'Johnny, look who it is!' he said, turning to his friend. His friend smiled and nodded shyly, hanging back.

'I knew it was your face! I can still remember the taste of that orange,' he went on, 'I've only had a few since then, but each time I've tasted one, it's reminded me of the taste of the one you gave me that day. And of you and your great kindness to us.'

Sirinya could hardly reply, her throat was so choked with emotion. She couldn't tell him that she had thought of him too, many times since that day, of how she'd feared that he had fallen ill or died like so many others, or of how overjoyed she was that he was here, standing in front of her now.

'Why don't you have another one now?' she asked instead, picking one out of a crate behind her, to hide her confusion. She handed him the ripe orange, still bearing the dark green stalk and leaf from the tree. 'Oh and here's one for your friend. You can both have one.'

They thanked her and, with the help of the two boys carried on with their work, loading the baskets full of vegetables onto their lorry, under the lax scrutiny of the two guards, who hardly moved from beside the cab. Occasionally one of the guards would step forward, stop one of the prisoners and make a cursory search inside a basket, but generally they seemed more interested in leaning on the wheel hub of the lorry and having a smoke.

Sirinya could not prevent her eyes from following the man, Charlie, as he moved around the shop picking up baskets, swinging them effortlessly onto his bony shoulders. Although he was thin, he was fit and lithe, his skin burnt deep brown from days in the sun. He seemed to bear the work with good humour, sharing jokes and banter with his friend, Johnny.

Was it her imagination or was he glancing at her every so often too? Each time he passed her with a basket, or each time she moved to hand him one, their eyes met, and he smiled at her, little wrinkles appearing in the tanned skin at the corners of his.

Now, lying in bed, she couldn't help hoping that tomorrow morning he would return, that the Japanese wouldn't have replaced him and his friend with different prisoners.

The next morning, after the daily trip to the river to help unload the barges, Sirinya felt the anticipation building. She didn't feel like going upstairs for breakfast, instead she decided to wait in the shop for the lorry to arrive. Her heart beat a little faster as the time grew closer. She waited by the door of the shop, watching the end of the road for the lorry to appear. As she sat there, her eyes wandered over the road to the Kempeitai house. All was quiet there, but two open-backed trucks were drawn up outside, their engines idling, their drivers waiting for officers to emerge to be taken off to their days' work. She shuddered and screwed her eyes shut, trying not to picture what that work might involve.

As she watched, the front door of the Kempeitai house opened, there was a flash of colour and Ratana appeared on the doorstep. She was wearing a bright red dress with a full skirt and high-heeled red sandals. In an exaggerated gesture she blew a kiss to whoever was inside, then flounced away from the house. She turned and walked along the road on the other side to Chalong's shophouse.

As Sirinya watched her, she noticed that two middle-aged women were walking towards Ratana. They were local women she recognised from the bazaar. As Ratana approached, they stopped in front of her and barred her way. Ratana stepped off the pavement and tried to walk round the women but the one on the outside stepped out herself and stood in Ratana's path. Sirinya watched, open mouthed, as the two women started shouting at Ratana, haranguing her. Sirinya couldn't hear their words, but she could see that their faces were distorted in anger. They shook their fists at Ratana and one of them even gave her a push in the chest that sent her toppling backwards. Sirinya was contemplating rushing over to intervene when the familiar sound of the Japanese army lorry made her look the other way.

The lorry came up the road and stopped outside the shop, blocking Ratana and the two women from view. Sirinya waited, watching, holding her breath as the same two Japanese guards got out of the cab and opened up the back of the truck. Would he be there today?

Charlie was the first to leap down, his friend Johnny came next and the colonel followed on behind. Once again, Charlie waied and bowed to Sirinya as he entered the shop, smiling from ear to ear.

Again she felt the colour rise in her cheeks as she looked into his eyes, and again she was sure that his gaze lingered on hers. As the two of them started loading the lorry with the help of the two boys, Sirinya walked to the edge of the pavement beyond the truck to see what had happened. But Ratana and the two women had already disappeared from view; there was no sign of the ugly scene that had just taken place there.

Shrugging, she returned to the shop and supervised the two boys who were handing the baskets to Johnny and Charlie. When they had almost finished, she nodded to the colonel to follow her into the storeroom.

'We read your message,' she said in a low voice. My uncle will pass it on to the organisation when he goes down to Bangkok on Sunday,' she said.

'Thank him from me. He is doing great work,' said the colonel, and she could see from his eyes that his thanks were heartfelt.

'And we can bring the medicines to the camp this evening,' she said. 'Two of us will swim across the moat as you suggested.'

'Are you absolutely sure about that? It could be dangerous.'

She suppressed the nerves in her stomach that threatened to overwhelm her. She swallowed hard and looked up at him.

'Yes, Colonel. We're quite sure.'

The colonel touched her shoulder and looked into her eyes. 'Thank you. You are very brave. I will tell my men to post a sentry there from 8 o'clock.'

The men had stacked the lorry more quickly this time, and as Sirinya emerged from the storeroom Charlie was lingering in the shop with an empty basket. His eyes lifted and he smiled as he saw her.

'Shall I leave this here?' he asked. There was no real need for the question, all the other empty baskets had been stacked in the far corner of the shop.

'I'll take it,' said Sirinya.

'Thank you,' he said, handing it to her and smiling. 'Will you be here tomorrow?' he asked.

She hesitated, suddenly remembering what the evening would bring. 'I ... I hope so,' she said, faltering.

'I hope so too,' he said, looking at her intently. 'Coming here and seeing you these last two days has changed everything for me. Over the past few months, I've sometimes felt like giving up.'

Sirinya didn't know how to reply, she just looked back at him trying not to let the pity she felt at his words show in her eyes.

'Come on Henderson, the Japs'll be getting jittery if we hang about here,' the colonel said emerging from the storeroom.

'Goodbye then, Miss ... I'm afraid I don't know your name,' Charlie said.

'I'm Sirinya. Just call me Sirinya.'

'Goodbye, then ... Sirinya,' Charlie said, smiling at her and looking into her eyes again. Then he turned and walked towards the lorry. As he climbed the ladder at the back and swung his legs over the tailgate he turned back and waved.

Later that morning Sirinya took the motor-rickshaw and rode it out of town on the rough track she had followed on the night of the Kempeitai raid. She rode it through the paddy fields where the workers were weeding, just as they had been on that previous morning. Again they stood up and shaded their eyes to stare at her as she passed. She parked the motor-rickshaw in some bushes at the foot of the hill where the path to the cave temples began. She was careful to conceal it from view. Climbing in the heat of the day was hard work, and by the time she neared the caves her body was pouring with sweat, her clothes clinging to her. She paused where the path forked, and instead of taking the left hand fork to the cave where she'd hidden the medicines, she went forward to the lookout rock.

She gripped the rock, leaned over and looked down into the cave temple. It was quiet today, no monks meditated in front of the Buddha, but the smell of burning candles and incense wafted up to where she stood. On a whim she went back to the path and took the branch that led to the top of the long flight of steps down to the temple.

She entered the temple timidly; she had not worshipped here before and she felt a little self-conscious. She crossed the floor of the cave to the altar, took a stick of incense and lit it from the candles burning there. Then she sat down cross-legged in front of the statue, bowed her head and tried to meditate. She could feel the benign smile of the Buddha penetrate her closed eyes and the calm of his presence still her troubled mind. She sat there for a long while, breathing steadily, emptying her mind of everything; of the danger she could be in this evening, of the risks Chalong was taking, of what might happen if they were caught, of Ratana, of Narong, of the plight of the prisoners, and even of Charlie. She lost track of time, letting the calm and peace of the temple seep through her body and comfort her exhausted mind.

The medicines were still in the back of the cave, where she had left them. As she walked back to the motor-rickshaw with the pack of medicines in her shoulder bag she felt refreshed, filled with renewed vigour that displaced the anxiety she had been feeling about the evening to come. She was now sure that she had the strength to do what she'd agreed to do later, that it was the only right thing to do, and that it was the best way there was to help Charlie and all the men suffering in those camps like him.

Back in Saeng Chuto road, Malee was waiting for her outside the shop. She was frowning, twisting her hands in front of her.

'What's the matter Malee?' asked Sirinya pulling the rickshaw off the road. Malee rushed over to her and grabbed her by both arms.

'They weren't there!'

'Who? Who weren't there?'

'The medicines. I went back to the place I hid them the other night and they'd gone.'

Sirinya stared at her, the implications of what she'd said sinking in.

'Are you sure?'

'Of course. Of course I'm sure. I know where I hid them for goodness' sake.'

'We must go there straight away. Come on. We'll walk. We'll be too conspicuous if we take the motor-rickshaw.'

As they started down the road towards the river, Malee clung on to Sirinya's arm. 'I'm so sorry, Siri. I couldn't have hidden them properly,' she said. 'Someone must have seen me.'

'Don't worry, Malee. It's not your fault. We were in an impossible position that night. We didn't have many choices.'

'What if the Japanese have found them?'

A shiver went through Sirinya, but she managed to sound reassuring as she said, 'That's quite unlikely, let's not even think about that.' She put her arm around her cousin's shoulders.

At the river Malee led her along the bank, towards the north end of town, up the road towards the paper factory. They finally stopped beside a clump of bushes.

'It was here,' she said pointing. 'Under that tall bush right inside the clump. I buried them under some palm leaves. They were really well hidden, believe me.'

They both bent down and peered. The palm leaves were scattered around and there was nothing under the bush, except bare earth.

Sirinya stood up and glanced around. Right opposite them was Narong's house. She shaded her eyes and stared at it. Could anyone have noticed Malee hiding the medicines from one of the upstairs windows? As she looked she thought she saw movement on the front drive and as if to answer her thoughts, the front gate opened and Narong came out and walked towards them. As he crossed the road she saw that he was carrying a familiar white cloth bag.

'These must be yours,' he said holding the bag out.

Sirinya felt the blood draining from her face.

'What are you doing with them?' she asked, trying to sound calm, her mouth dry.

'I was walking past and I noticed something on the ground here a couple of days ago. It had been raining hard and the package seemed to have been washed out from under the bush. So I picked it up. When I realised what it was I was careful to take it away and hide it. There are two Japanese officers living in my house and I need to be careful.'

'Really?' asked Sirinya, alarmed. Where was this leading?

'Yes. They are running the factory for the Japanese war effort now, as you know. I couldn't take any risks by leaving the packages here in the bushes, so I took them and hid them in my garage. I was out in the front drive cleaning my car when I noticed you two searching in the undergrowth. I guessed it must have been you who'd put them there in the first place. Here take them quickly, before the officers come back from the factory. Take them and go home.' He held out the bag for Sirinya to take.

'I can explain, Narong,' said Sirinya.

'No need to explain,' he said. 'I know your uncle is a good man, that he is working against the occupation, and I wish him luck with that.'

Sirinya stared at him.

'How do you know about that?' asked Malee

'More people know than you might think,' he said. 'Believe me, If I had any money I would advance some to his cause, but all my assets are frozen now, I can't take anything out of the factory. I only have enough to eat because the Japanese let me take my meals with them.'

Sirinya looked steadily at him, assessing the situation. Could he really be genuine? She'd never trusted him fully and now he was actually living and working with Japanese officers. Was he setting them some sort of trap with this sudden show of sympathy for the cause, with his admiration for Chalong? On the other hand, why would he lie? If he'd wanted to he could have betrayed them to the Japanese as soon as he discovered it was them who'd hidden the packages.

There was no time to speculate. She and Malee must get the medicines back to the shop safely and prepare themselves for this evening's trip to the other side of the river.

They quickly thanked Narong, and taking the bag from him set off for home. Malee was subdued on the walk back. They were careful to avoid the main roads and only go via the back alleys in case any Japanese soldiers were on patrol. Malee kept her head down and hardly spoke, other than to mutter, 'I'm so sorry, Siri,' every few minutes. Sirinya tried to reassure Malee that she was not to blame, that she had done the best she could that night, but nothing she could say would take that expression of guilt and anguish from

Malee's face.

When they arrived back at the shop, Piak and Kitima were waiting downstairs for them, sitting on an upturned crate. This was unusual.

'What's the matter, Ma?' asked Malee, at the sight of her mother's grave face.

Piak stood up. 'Come here my child,' she said, putting her arms around Malee and drawing her close.

'What is it?'

'Sit down. Sit down please. I have something to tell you.' Her voice broke and she wiped away a tear.

Kitima stood up and shot Sirinya a look. 'Come, Siri. Let's go upstairs.'

'Why?' said Malee, her eyes puzzled. 'She doesn't need to go. Whatever you have to say to me, Siri can hear it.' Her voice was shrill. She sat down on the crate beside her mother. 'Tell me, then.'

Piak twisted the tie of her sarong and began in a low voice, hardly able to look at her daughter.

'Somsak's father was here. He left a few minutes ago. He has had some bad news from the Free Thai Movement, Malee. I'm afraid it is Somsak. He was wounded in skirmish with the Japanese last week and ... and sadly he died, Malee. His father received the letter this morning.'

Malee stared at her mother with wide eyes, as if searching her face for a sign that this wasn't true, then after a few seconds she let out a low moan and fell sobbing into Piak's arms, clenching her fists in the air. Sirinya reached out instinctively and took Kitima's hand. She felt the tears running down her own cheeks.

'Is he sure? Are they quite sure?' sobbed Malee.

Piak nodded and rubbed Malee's shoulders. 'It was gunshot

wounds, Daughter. He died instantly. He did not suffer.'

'Where is he now? I must go to him.'

Piak shook her head. 'How can you go to him, Daughter? He is with the rebels, far to the north of here at a secret hide-out. They have given him a proper funeral at the local temple.'

'Then I must go to his family. I need to be with them. Don't try to stop me!' She stood up, pushed Piak's arms away and ran out of the shop. Sirinya got up to follow her, but felt Kitima's hands gripping her arms.

'Leave her be, Daughter. She needs to do this.'

* * *

Later, Sirinya followed Piak and Kitima upstairs to the apartment where they sat round the table, sipping green tea sorrowfully, saying little. Each nursed her own thoughts about Somsak, his calm, generous nature, his loyal love for Malee.

When Chalong arrived back from Wan Lung camp with the lorry, Piak went down and broke the news to him. He sat for a long time in the corner of the living room, his head in his hands, rocking back and forth in silent grief.

As the light faded, though, they remembered their promise to the prisoners.

'What shall we do? Malee won't be able to come with me now,' said Sirinya. 'She is with Somsak's parents on the other side of town and anyway she's in no fit state to do this.'

'No, you're right. She can't do it now,' said Chalong.

'I can go alone,' said Sirinya.

'That is brave of you, Niece, but it would be safer to go as a pair. You can cover for each other, watch out for one another. We'll just have to tell the prisoners tomorrow that it wasn't possible this evening.'

'No. No we mustn't let them down,' said Sirinya. 'I really don't mind doing it alone. We can't let the Japanese win, Uncle. Somsak died because of them and the occupation. We must carry on doing what we can against them, for his sake.'

Piak put her cup down on the table and stood up.

'I will go with you, Niece,' she said, her voice firm, her eyes shining with determination. 'I am a strong swimmer. Kiti never took to it when we were girls, but I was a natural.'

Sirinya exchanged glances with Kitima.

'Are you sure, Aunt?'

'Quite sure, Siri,' she said firmly. 'It is time I did something to help instead of sitting here, fretting myself stupid. You are right. Somsak was a brave, brave boy. He gave his life to fight this occupation. All we have to do is swim across a stretch of water. Can it really be that hard?'

20

It was just after sunset and pale moonlight flooded the riverbank and shone on the water as Sirinya and Piak reached the boatman's mooring that evening.

'You're lucky I'm still here,' the old man said, stirring himself, stubbing out his cheroot and getting up to hold out a hand to help them on board. Settling himself back down on the bench he cast the boat off and spat a stream of red betel nut juice over the side.

'We were hoping you'd wait for us and bring us back,' said Sirinya. He eyed them suspiciously.

'How long will you be? The Japs don't like me hanging about on the other side too late. Not now they're building that bridge.' He nodded in the direction of the great structure a little upriver. Now they were away from the bank they could see it plainly by the light of the moon. A huge, fragile edifice of bamboo scaffolding, tied together with jungle twine, and inside it the half-built concrete pillars that would one day support a steel railway bridge spanning the great river.

'We'll probably be a couple of hours, that's all. We'd make it worth your while if you did wait.'

He didn't answer, just grumbled a little under his breath as he rowed. Sirinya took a deep breath and tried to stay calm. She had been counting on the old man agreeing to row them back, but she knew she mustn't push him too far. He was well known to be stubborn. Out on the river the temperature was a little cooler, the smell of a thousand evening fires floated on the air.

'What are you going for anyway?' he said at last.

'Visiting relatives, taking them some fruit, that's all,' said Piak a little too quickly, clutching the hessian bag to her. They had taken care to fill the top of each bag with oranges to hide the medicines. The old man was silent.

'The Japs keep a close eye on who comes and goes across the river, you know. They're worried about that camp. Chungkai they call it. They don't want Thai people selling stuff to the prisoners.'

'Really? Well we won't be going anywhere near the camp, don't you worry,' said Sirinya brightly.

As they nudged the bank on the other side, he said. 'Alright then, I'll row you back for fourteen ticals. And mind you aren't any more than two hours. I won't wait longer than that.'

Thanking him, they set off in a straight line until they were out of sight of the riverbank, then doubled back and began to walk downriver towards Chuangkai. They walked in silence, Sirinya taking the lead, Piak following. Soon they were on the old familiar Bamboo Road, walking on the narrow unmade path between great clumps of bamboo which overhung in places and met overhead. The path had been little used since the occupation, and Sirinya found herself having to squeeze through thickets where the bamboo poles had encroached. They had decided not to bring torches, but it was easy to see the path by the light of the full moon in the cloudless sky.

Piak walked more slowly than Sirinya and on several occasions she found herself having to wait for her aunt to catch up.

'I'm sorry, Sirinya, I'm not as young as I once was.'

'I know, Aunt. And your health hasn't been so good lately. You are very good to come.'

'My health is fine, Siri. I'm as strong as a buffalo. It's Chalong and Malee. They want me to be an invalid, you know. They like to look after me. But I won't have it any more. They need me to be strong now.'

Sirinya smiled to herself in the darkness. After twenty minutes or so walking, they neared the edge of the camp. They could hear prisoners bathing, splashing about in the water, the sound of their voices floating up from the river. The light of dozens of gas lamps glowed ahead, and they could see the flickering red glow of a campfire beyond the bamboo fence.

'We need to skirt around the edge,' said Sirinya, as they left the path and crossed the track by which lorries went into and out of the camp. 'We must keep clear of the boundary, or we could be spotted.'

They found a rough path through the undergrowth which followed the line of the camp boundary. Progress was slow and difficult in the darkness. Sirinya went ahead and pushed leaves and branches aside for Piak. Her skirts were continually getting caught on undergrowth, her skin snagged on thorns, her hair pulled by the tendrils of creepers. After half an hour or so of this, when Sirinya was just beginning to wonder whether they would ever be clear of the jungle, they came to another path, which wound its way through a group of wooden houses on the edge of some rice fields. They moved quickly between them, keeping close to the walls, their heads down. Luckily the inhabitants were already inside, probably asleep as they would normally rise at dawn to work in the fields. A couple of dogs barked as they passed through, but they were soon clear of the hamlet and making their way along the high narrow bank that divided the paddies.

'Do you know the way, Siri? Are you sure this is right?' Piak called from behind. Her voice was breathless. Sirinya waited for her to catch up.

'Yes, I think we need to skirt this field all the way to the end, turn left along the far bank and the moat should be over there in the far corner of the paddies, beyond that spinney.'

'Is it much further?'

'Not far now, Aunt, and at least we can walk freely here.'

The flat square shapes of the flooded rice paddies were bathed in moonlight. They walked quickly along the rump of the bank on the narrow path used by day by the rice farmers. Sirinya knew that although the way was easier here, they were very exposed and could probably be spotted from inside the camp.

It took them a good twenty minutes to reach the far corner of the fields. There was a grove of bamboo separating the paddies from the moat. One more hurdle to cross. They squeezed their bodies between the thick bamboo trunks, grazing their arms and legs on the rough wood and brittle leaves, but finally they were through and standing on a bank in front of a stretch of murky water. In the moonlight Sirinya noticed clouds of mosquitoes dancing on the surface.

She peered across to the other side. She could just make out the back walls of a line of bamboo huts above the moat, but there was no sign of anyone on the opposite bank. Panic rose within her. Perhaps the prisoner who was waiting for them had already been discovered, taken away and beaten by the guards? Perhaps even as they stood there, they had been spotted by the Japanese who were lying in wait for them between the huts. She glanced at Piak, who was leaning forward with her hands on her knees, catching her breath.

'Are you alright, Aunt?' she whispered.

Piak nodded and straightened up. 'Where are the men?'

'I'm not sure. Why don't we get ready to swim while we wait for them?'

She rummaged in her hessian bag and pulled out two smaller

bags with string handles. Then she knelt down and divided the packages of medicines between them evenly, handing one bag to Piak. She took off her sarong and blouse and stood there in her chemise and pants.

'Whatever are you doing, Niece?' came Piak's shocked voice.

'I want to keep my clothes dry. It will feel cold enough going home, without having wet clothes too.'

'Well, I'm not taking my clothes off. I always swim in my sarong. There are men over there.'

'They won't see us. It's dark, and we'll be in the water.'

'I think I'll keep my sarong on all the same. I'm surprised at you, Niece.'

'Aunt, this is no time for modesty. No one will notice.'

Piak didn't respond, just stood there stiffly. Sirinya could feel outrage radiating from her, but there was no time to argue. The next moment there was movement on the opposite bank. Sirinya's heart stood still. Had the guards heard them? She peered into the gloom. Two figures appeared from between two huts. She could only see their outlines in the darkness, but she thought she could make out bare legs and loincloths. At least the two men were taller than most Japanese. She breathed a little more easily. Then came a voice.

'Hello? Are you over there?' It was unmistakeably English.

'Yes. We're here,' she replied in a hoarse whisper, relief flooding through her. Now at least she could breathe.

'We're ready for you to swim across,' came the voice. 'Come one at a time. When we see you we'll come down to the edge of the water to collect the packages. There's no need for you to get out on this side. You'll need to be quick.'

'I'll go first, Siri,' said Piak firmly, walking nimbly to the edge of the water, crouching down and easing herself in. Sirinya watched, holding her breath as Piak's head bobbed across the water, ripples radiating out from where she swam. Sirinya's eyes kept wandering to the bank on the opposite side, hoping fervently that no one would appear between the huts. Piak swam quickly and sparely, reaching the opposite bank in a few strokes. There was a flurry of activity as one of the prisoners hurried forward, knelt down and grabbed the bag of medicines from around her neck. Piak turned round and was on her way back.

Shivering, despite the steamy heat of the evening, Sirinya went towards the bank and held a hand out to pull Piak out of the water.

'Hide in the bamboo, Aunt,' she said as Piak, dripping wet stood panting with effort on the bank. Then Sirinya slipped into the water herself. She gasped, the water felt cold. She pushed off and took her first strokes towards the other side. It wasn't far, but the water seemed to stretch ahead of her like an ocean. She swam as quickly as she could, the bag dragging against her stomach, the handle cutting into her neck. Halfway across she remembered a swimming snake she'd once seen on a stretch of water like this and a shudder of revulsion went through her. At the other side she paused by the bank. The moat was too deep to touch the bottom so she trod water as she lifted the dripping bag over her head. Above her loomed two grubby faces, bathed in sweat, anxious eyes standing out from hollow cheeks.

'Thank you. Thank you. You're very brave. Safe return. We must get these to the camp hospital.'

As she turned round and pushed off across the water, she heard the men scramble back up the bank. It wasn't over yet, she knew, but the most difficult part was done. She swam as quickly as she could and soon reached the other side. She had just put her palms on the bank to haul herself out when she heard a fierce whisper from Piak.

'Don't get out Siri. Hide under the water. There is a guard coming.'

Sirinya took a deep breath and dived under the surface, her thoughts scrambling. Where was the guard? Had the prisoners got away safely? Had he seen her swimming? She held her breath as long as she could. She felt unbearable pressure in her chest and the pulse of blood rushing to her head. Her lungs were almost bursting when she broke free of the surface, took another gulp of air and went under again. The next time she came up she felt a hand touch her face. Her heart lurched with fear. She looked up. Piak's face was above her.

'He's gone now,' Piak hissed, her eyes bulging with fear. 'You can get out.'

Sirinya pulled herself out of the water, stumbled into the bamboo thicket and sat down, panting and sobbing.

'What happened? Did he catch them?'

'I don't think so. He came out from the other side after they had gone between those two other huts there,' she said, pointing. 'He just wandered about looking, then he stopped and took a pee into the water. All the time you were there, in the water, he didn't notice. Then he wandered around a bit and went back in the same way.'

Laughter bubbled up inside Sirinya at the absurdity of the situation. She laughed and laughed and Piak laughed too, and hugged her shoulders. They laughed until tears were running down their cheeks and the hysterical laughter became tears of relief.

The return journey was a little easier. At least they knew the way now, and they followed the path they had beaten for themselves on the way there. Even so, it was hard going and they both had scratches and cuts on their arms and faces as they entered the final leg of the journey along the Bamboo Road.

'Do you think he'll have waited?' said Piak, squeezing herself between the poles of a clump of huge bamboo. Her hair was plastered to her head and her clothes were still sodden. Sirinya was glad of her own dry sarong, although she had put it on so quickly that it too was damp from the wetness of her body.

'I hope so. I don't think we've been quite two hours yet.'

As they neared the end of the path the outline of the half-built bridge loomed again in the background, ghostly in the darkness. They could see the boatman there, up ahead. He had a small paraffin lamp on the boat, and the light shone on the water.

They stepped clear of the Bamboo Road, but as they crossed the open grass towards the mooring there was movement in the bushes to their left and someone stepped out in front of them. It was a Japanese guard in full uniform, rifle poised, pointed at them.

'Stop!' he said. He spoke in broken English.

They obeyed and stood shivering in front of him. He poked the rifle towards Sirinya.

'Why you here so late? Where you go?'

She lifted her face and looked him in the eye. His dark eyes were narrow, full of suspicion.

'We have been to visit family. One of them has been unwell. We took fruit,' she said, keeping her voice steady.

'Let me see your bags,' he said, leaning forward clicking his fingers. They handed him the two hessian bags. A few oranges in each still.

'Why you not leave this fruit?' he asked. Sirinya thought quickly.

'They had plenty of oranges. They told us to give it to the boatman as a gift for bringing us.'

The guard grunted. Beside her, Sirinya could feel Piak trembling. He turned his attention to Piak.

'Why you wet?'

Piak glanced at Sirinya, her eyes wide, desperate. She looked near to tears.

'She tripped and fell in the river on the way back. The path was very slippery.' It was all she could think of.

'Really?' he snapped. 'You not go near Chungkai camp, eh?'

'Of course not. Why would we go there?'

'You not ask questions. Chungkai camp very dangerous. Many very bad men there. Not safe for Thai women. You must not go there.'

'Thank you. Of course we wouldn't go there. We have no business there.'

He grunted again, this time grudgingly. 'Imperial Japanese Army is friend to local people. We look after you. You can go on your way now.'

He stepped aside and motioned for them to pass. They hurried to the boat without looking at the guard. The boatman handed them on board and cast off.

As he rowed the boat out into the current he leaned forward to Sirinya and said, 'I told you they didn't like it, didn't I? Those Japs. I told you they don't like people walking about out there late in the evening.'

Sirinya didn't reply, but frowned and glanced at her aunt, slumped in the corner of the boat, shivering with exhaustion and fear.

* * *

Malee lay on her bed listless and silent the next morning, refusing to get up, refusing food. She would not respond to Sirinya or even look at her, turning away angrily to face the wall. She was deep in her own pain-filled world, beyond the reach of any helping hand.

'Give her time, Siri,' said Chalong, scratching his head as he stared down at his daughter. 'She needs time to heal.'

'I will never heal,' murmured Malee, stirring herself and speaking for the first time since she had returned to the shophouse late the previous evening.

Chalong bent down and stroked her hair. 'It feels like that now, Daughter,' he said with tenderness, 'and you're right. Nothing will ever be the same again.'

Chalong turned to Sirinya.

'Leave her be for now, Niece. I know you are tired, but can you face coming down to the river to unload the barges with me and your mother?'

'Of course, Uncle. I'm fine,' she replied although her body was weary, her legs and arms were sore from the cuts and scratches, and her skin itched from multiple mosquito bites which were now swelling in the heat of the morning.

As they left Malee to her sorrow and went downstairs, Chalong said, 'I will stop off at the temple on my way to Wan Lung and ask Phraa Thongphroh to come and meditate with her later. If she had been able to go to poor Somsak's funeral she would have felt differently. Phraa might be able to help her through that.'

Piak was busying herself with breakfast in the kitchen with the sort of vigour Sirinya had not seen in her for several years. There was colour in her cheeks as she brought the food to the table.

'You look hot, Sister,' said Kitima peering at her. 'I hope you aren't going down with fever.'

'Nonsense, I've never felt better,' Piak replied, giving Sirinya a secret smile from behind Kitima's back as she returned to the stove.

After breakfast, they walked down the river as usual to unload the supplies from the barges onto the bullock carts. They were a subdued party. Now the excitement and trauma of the previous evening's mission was over, the impact of Somsak's death had begun to hit home. Sirinya walked between Chalong and Kitima who were both unusually quiet. She couldn't stop thinking about the way he and Malee had clung to each other as they'd parted on the riverbank all those months ago, and how desperately sad it was that they were destined never to meet again.

Sitting beside the driver on the bullock cart as they entered Saeng Chuto road, Sirinya noticed someone waiting outside the shop. As they got closer she saw who it was: it was someone with long black curls wearing a bright red dress. It was Ratana.

Leaving the boys to unload the cart Sirinya went up to her. As she approached she saw that Ratana's face was smeared with mascara. She'd been crying. Surely she didn't know about Somsak?

Ratana rushed up to her.

'Siri, I was wondering if you'd mind selling me some fruit and vegetables?' her eyes were desperate. She had lost weight, her cheekbones were more prominent than before, her dress was baggy.

'Of course I can. Why wouldn't I?'

'I thought … I thought … No one else in this stinking little town will let me in their shop, that's why. They all hate me. I don't have to tell you why. Mother hasn't eaten properly for ages. I have to take food home from my Japanese friends when I can. We have plenty of money now, but we can't spend it.'

'Wait here. I'll give you a bag of vegetables to take home.'

As she was filling a bag with potatoes and cabbages for Ratana inside the storeroom, Kitima appeared in the doorway.

'What are you doing, Daughter?'

'Ratana has come to buy some food, Mother. I thought I would give her some.'

'You mustn't do any such thing! Send her away. She's not welcome here. You know what she does, Sirinya, who she mixes with. She's a snake in the grass. She's not to be trusted.'

'Hush mother, she'll hear you. She's only just outside the front door.'

'I don't care if she does hear me. She needs to know. Tell her to go away. She can get her food somewhere else.'

'But she can't. No one will serve her. We used to be friends at school. Please, Ma, just this once.'

Kitima stood watching her with folded arms. 'You always were soft, Daughter. Too kind for your own good. Let her have them just this once, but tell her she mustn't come back.'

Sirinya went outside and handed the bag of vegetables to Ratana. She opened her mouth to tell her not to come back, but Ratana's face was so full of joy, so transformed by the simple act of kindness that the words froze on Sirinya's lips and she couldn't bring herself to utter them.

'Thank you, Siri. I'll love you for ever!' Ratana said, kissing Sirinya on the cheek. As she turned and walked away with a waft of stale perfume, Sirinya shook her head at her own weakness. What was she doing helping this girl when she knew she was friendly with the Kempeitai? Not only that, she was seeing Narong in secret too.

Later that morning, Sirinya waited for the lorry to turn into the end of the road, her body tingling with anticipation. When it drew up outside she stood in the doorway watching, gripping the doorpost. The two guards jumped down, went to the back of the vehicle and opened the tailgate as usual. The colonel emerged first, then Johnny climbed down. Sirinya waited, but it wasn't Charlie who followed the other two, it was someone new, someone with equally dishevelled appearance, hollow cheeks and skinny legs, but this man was older, his hair was lighter in colour. He didn't move with Charlie's energy. He came towards the shop with his head bowed.

Johnny must have seen the disappointment on her face as he approached. He smiled shyly and said; 'Charlie's ill today, he got sick yesterday when we got back. He's in the camp hospital.' It was the first time he'd ever addressed her directly. He blushed as he spoke and didn't meet her gaze.

Was it so obvious that she'd been waiting for Charlie? That she cared?

'What's wrong with him? Is he going to be alright?' she asked.

Johnny shrugged. 'I hope so. But it's a pretty bad bout of malaria. It's not the first time he's had it.' Sirinya thought of the quinine she'd helped to deliver yesterday, praying that some of it had found its way to Charlie.

One of the guards was coming towards the shop and Johnny moved away from her and went inside to pick up a basket.

'You!' said the guard pointing at Johnny and pushing past Sirinya. 'You not talk to the natives. You get on with work!' For good measure he went up to him and slapped his face several times with the back of his hand. Johnny didn't protest, or even look surprised, just bent back to his task with weary resignation.

'Now, you, Miss! I need to talk to you,' Shock washed through her body. The guards had never addressed her directly before. Had they found out about last night? She glanced at his face. She couldn't be absolutely sure, but she didn't think it was the same guard who'd approached them beside the river.

'This for you.'

He thrust a piece of paper into her hand. It was a list written in

English. It listed various types of fruit, tea, eggs tobacco.

'You collect these for me now. Then you tell old lady she come with us back to the camp. We are ready to open canteen now. We want to start today.'

Sirinya's mouth was dry. All she could do was nod and bow. He watched her through narrowed eyes as she filled an empty basket with the fruit on the list.

'I'll need to go out to another shop get the tobacco,' she said.

'You go tell old woman first. She need to make ready.'

Sirinya went slowly upstairs to the apartment. Kitima was at the table finishing her breakfast, gossiping with Piak. She stopped when she saw Sirinya's face. 'What has happened now, Daughter?'

'They want you to go back with them today to open the canteen, Ma.'

Kitima's face fell. She was quiet for a few moments, digesting the information. Then she got up from the table and dusted the crumbs from her sarong.

'Alright, I'm ready to go. No, don't look like that Siri. I'll be back this evening won't I? I can't stay there. I'll walk along the Bamboo Road to the boatman and come back across the river before sunset.'

21

Kitima left for Chungkai camp with the lorry later that morning, sitting between the stony-faced guards, staring straight ahead of her. Sirinya had hugged her briefly before she set off, but there was little time for a proper farewell.

'Don't fuss, Siri,' Kitima said, patting her back and pulling away. 'Like I said, I'll be back this evening. Please don't worry about me.'

After she'd gone, Sirinya wandered up to the top floor, sat down on the bed beside Malee, and stroked her hair. Malee said nothing, but Sirinya could tell from her irregular breathing that she was awake.

'I'm so sorry, Malee,' was all she could say. Malee just shifted impatiently and turned away towards the wall.

Later that day while Chalong was still out on his rounds Phraa Thongphroh arrived. He came up the narrow stairs, barefooted, holding his saffron robes up so as not to trip. He filled the room with his kind smile and his comforting presence. Piak had cooked him some delicacies and laid them before him on the table.

'I won't eat, thank you Khun Piak,' he said, smiling his thanks to her. 'I will take these back to the temple to share with the other monks, if you'll permit me. Your husband asked me to talk to your daughter, Malee. Is she here?'

'She is resting upstairs, Phraa, but I will fetch her.'

Sirinya waited in the room with the monk while Piak went upstairs. Instead of taking a seat he settled on the floor cross-legged, and turned the beam of his benevolent smile on her.

'I'm so sorry for your loss, my child. You must be grieving too, as well as your cousin. The whole family must. At the moment your loss is only just sinking in. But in order to accept it fully, you will need to experience its pain properly.'

Sirinya felt tears springing to her eyes.

'I know you are doing good work, my child,' he went on. 'And you must carry on with that. It will help you to accept your loss. I know what you are doing has its dangers, but don't give up doing what is right. And don't forget to meditate daily, even if you cannot come to the temple as much as you'd like. You'll find it will help you maintain your strength and your purpose.'

'Of course, Phraa.' How true his words were. She thought of how she'd found peace and strength alone in the cave temple.

Malee appeared in the doorway, her hair lank and unbrushed, her clothes crumpled. There was no light in her face, her eyes were dull. She barely acknowledged the monk's presence. Sirinya left them alone and went upstairs.

Later she heard Phraa Thongphroh in the passage speaking to Piak.

'She has had a great shock and she is grieving. She must be allowed to do that. Give her plenty of time and space. In time she will go through pain but she will learn acceptance, my child. Be patient with her. Come to the temple to make offerings and meditate often. We are always there for you and for your whole family.'

* * *

When Kitima returned from the camp after dark that evening she was walking slowly and her face was grey with exhaustion. She sat in silence for a long time and sipped the soup Piak handed her without saying a word.

'Mother, what's wrong?' Sirinya asked gently sitting down beside her. 'What happened?'

'It's just those poor, poor men, Siri,' she said at last. 'They are so thin and hopeless.' She sighed and shook her head. 'We saw them before, of course, and we see the ones who come here for provisions. They are the healthy ones. When you spend time inside the camp and see all of them together it really hits you. They all look the same, their ribs stand out, their faces are so thin their eyes look huge. Their clothes are ragged and most of them have no shoes. Some of them have dreadful sores on their bodies and legs. Whatever would their mothers say if they could see them?'

'What did you have to do there, Ma?'

'They've built a small hut in one corner of the camp and made a few crude bamboo tables in front of it,' Kitima went on. 'I had to cut up fruit and serve it to them, make tea, fry eggs and sell them tobacco. They were all so grateful, Siri. They had been working all day on that cutting nearby and they were so weary they could barely walk. I couldn't understand a word they said, but I could tell from their faces how happy they were to be able to come and sit down, to drink some tea and smoke and talk.'

Sirinya laid her hand on top of Kitima's, 'At least you are doing something to help them, Ma. To make things better for them,' she said. 'It must make a big difference.'

'Perhaps, Siri, perhaps,' Kitima said.

A new routine established itself. After helping with the morning deliveries from the river barges, Chalong would set off on his rounds of the outer camps, Wantakin and Wan Lung. The army lorry would arrive shortly after that and the three prisoners would load up with the help of the two shop boys. When the lorry left to return to the camp each morning, Kitima would go in it.

Every morning Sirinya stood by the door of the shop and watched the three prisoners get down from the back of the truck. And every day her heart beat a little faster, hoping that this was the day that Charlie would return with them. But every day she was disappointed. She would glance at Johnny hopefully as he entered the shop, but each morning he would shake his head as he passed. She began to worry that one morning that gesture would mean something more sinister; that it would be because there was no hope that Charlie would ever return, that he had given up the fight and she would never see him again. The thought terrified her and kept her awake at night.

On a few occasions she caught Johnny's gaze lingering on her face. If he saw she had noticed he would blush and look away quickly. She never returned his looks and rarely tried to speak to him now. Whenever she'd previously tried to open conversations with him, he'd appeared so confused and self-conscious that she'd decided to spare him the embarrassment.

The colonel was always polite and correct, delivering the letters for the V Organisation every few days, thanking her profusely each time for the help the family was giving. The third man hardly spoke to Sirinya or to the boys. His eyes were furtive and full of fear as he worked and he never seemed to relax. She wondered if he might be thinking that her family was working for the Japanese.

Chalong went to Bangkok that Sunday, this time alone: 'No, Sirinya, there is no need for you to come with me. You've done quite enough. You're needed here, but if Lian and her associates have collected the medicines the colonel wanted, I hope you will be kind enough to repeat your swim tomorrow?'

'Of course, Uncle.'

'Your aunt is set on going with you of course.'

'She was a great help,' Sirinya said, 'but Uncle, you must tell her to put a bathing costume on under her sarong. The wet clothes raised suspicion.'

He smiled and nodded. 'I will do that.'

When he returned from Bangkok late that evening, he had several packs of medicine hidden in a cavity under the lorry. His face was grave as he entered the apartment.

'Sit down, Husband. What has happened?' asked Piak, rushing forward to greet him.

She brought him tea and he settled himself opposite Sirinya at the table.

'Our friends in the V Organisation had a lot of difficulty getting the medicines this time,' he said, 'You remember Yosakon, Sirinya, the rice trader who helped us last time? Well last week his nephew was caught by the guards inside the civilian camp in the University, taking food to the members of the organisation in there. The Japs seem to have tightened things up lately. They are much more vigilant. He's now been interned himself. In solitary confinement. Luckily they haven't linked him to Lian yet, but she is afraid that they will make the connection. She had to go a long way for the medicines this time. She didn't want to use the usual contacts. Old Yosakon was too afraid to help her. He wouldn't even come along to Lian's house with any sacks of rice.'

Sirinya shivered. How long would it be before one of their own family was caught and punished too?

'You weren't stopped on the bridge then?' she asked.

'No, I went a different way this evening.' He seemed preoccupied, lost in his own thoughts.

'Is everything alright, Uncle?' she asked after a few minutes of silence.

'Siri,' he said suddenly, leaning forward, looking into her eyes. 'If anything ever happens to me, if I'm caught like Yosakon's nephew and don't come back, you will carry on the work here for me won't you?'

'Don't speak like that, Uncle' she said. 'We're very careful. That's not going to happen.'

'But if it does, can you give me your word? You're strong, Siri. Strong and capable.'

'Of course, Uncle. You know I would. You have my word.'

It worried her that he had spoken like that. Up to this point he had seemed so fearless, so optimistic. She now noticed weariness in his manner as he set off on his deliveries each day. Kitima too looked tired and reluctant as she set off with the guards to the camp. What was the war and all this hatred and fear doing to this family? She thought of Yai up in the village, watching and waiting for news each day. How worried she must be about Kitima. Sirinya resolved to make the journey as soon as she could to reassure her grandmother that all was well.

These thoughts were going round in her mind as she was stacking the empty baskets from the camp the morning after Chalong returned from Bangkok. There were quick footsteps outside and a customer appeared in the doorway. Sirinya turned round to serve and saw that it was Ratana. Sirinya thought again about Kitima's words. She knew she should turn Ratana away, but she couldn't find it in her heart to do that. We are helping others, so why not help her, she reasoned. After all, Kitima wasn't here and there was no need for her to find out about this.

Ratana was full of confidence this time. She smiled at Sirinya, selecting some carrots and onions. Sirinya weighed them and put them in a bag. 'You're a lifesaver, Siri. What would I do without you? Can I come back in a couple of days?'

In spite of her misgivings, Sirinya nodded. 'Of course,' she murmured.

Later that day there was another unexpected visitor. He came on foot this time. It was just before Sirinya closed the shop, when Chalong was due back from his rounds. It was Narong. He too looked thinner, his hair no longer immaculately styled, his clothes shabby and frayed.

'How are you, Sirinya?' he asked coming into the shop and closing the door behind him. 'I've been meaning to come and check you got back safely with the packages the other day.'

She eyed him sceptically. What did he really want? What was this about?

'Of course,' she replied looking at him steadily. 'Everything was fine.'

'I want you to know that what happened that day will go no further. It is my secret.'

'Thank you,' she said.

'But there is something I came to ask you.'

She looked at him enquiringly. He stepped forward suddenly and grabbed her hand.

'I want to marry you, Sirinya.'

Her eyes widened in surprise, her mouth fell open. His face was close to hers, glistening with sweat. He was breathing heavily.

'But ... why? Why now?' The image of Ratana getting into his car came into her mind. She stared at him, puzzled.

'I love you, Sirinya. I always have. You must know that,' his eyes were pleading now.

She shook her head, easing her hand away. 'I'm sorry, but it's over between us, Narong,' she said gently. 'It was over a long time ago. Surely you know that?'

He grabbed her hand again, and tried to kiss her. She turned her face away and his lips grazed her cheek.

'Please ...' there was desperation in his voice.

'Look, I'm sorry, Narong,' she said. 'You're a good person, I know that, but I can't marry you. I ... I'm sorry, but I just don't feel that way.'

He let her go and took a step back.

'Have it your own way. But I know you'll regret this decision,' he said, turning away and going to the door.

She shut her eyes and waited for the slam, which sure enough came within seconds. She heard his footsteps walking away from the shop, but she didn't open her eyes until she was sure he had gone. When she did, she realised that she was shaking all over.

That evening Sirinya and Piak set off for the camp with the medicines again. Chalong had arranged for a member of the local underground organisation to take them across the river. He had decided it was too risky to use the old boatman. It meant they did not need to go all the way up to the crossing at Tha Maa Kham; instead they met the man downriver from the barge wharf. This time they waited until after dark to cross.

The man was waiting for them in a rowing boat, moored up in the undergrowth. Sirinya nodded to him as they clambered on board. She recognised him as Phichai, a local rice farmer, who sometimes sold river fish in the market. He gave them a gruff greeting, but hardly spoke to them as they crossed the river. It was fast flowing here, and he had to work hard to keep the boat from being swept downriver with the current. Sirinya felt Piak's hand gripping her arm. 'Don't worry, Aunt. He knows what he's doing.'

He dropped them halfway along the Bamboo Road, nudging the boat into a little inlet in the bank, saying that he would wait for them there. That evening the operation went more smoothly than the previous occasion. The route was familiar to them this time and where they had to skirt around the boundary of the camp the undergrowth was still flattened from when they had passed through before. Sirinya found she could hold her nerves in check, and as they emerged from the undergrowth, hurried through the village and began to cross the causeway between the rice paddies, her mind wandered to Narong. She was still in shock from his proposal, not having realised that he still felt for her, or indeed that he ever had. She still didn't trust him. Why had he mentioned the medicines at the beginning of the conversation? She couldn't help worrying now that he would use his knowledge to punish her, even blackmail her.

She put him out of her mind when they arrived beside the moat. She needed to concentrate now. Piak slipped off her sarong to reveal a dark bathing suit, with a prim bodice laced at the throat and tight leggings down to her knees. Two prisoners appeared and signalled to them from the opposite bank. Each swam across and made their drop of medicines flawlessly. There was no interruption from any of the guards this evening.

Chalong was waiting for them in the shop when they got back, his brow was lined and his eyes full of concern. When they had assured him that everything had gone smoothly, he said, 'Come upstairs quickly. It's Kitima. She's not at all well.'

They went up to the top floor where Kitima lay on her bed under the eaves. Sirinya ran to her. She was twisting and turning. Her teeth were clamped shut. She was shivering and covered in sweat, her wet hair stuck to her face. Her eyes were open but she didn't seem to know that Sirinya was there.

'Mother? Mother what's wrong?' Sirinya leaned over her. Kitima uttered a low moan.

Chalong said, 'I'll go down the road and get Doctor Pradchphet. I didn't want to leave her on her own while you were away. Malee is in no fit state to look after her.'

He disappeared. 'Auntie, bring a wet cloth,' said Sirinya, 'I'll try to cool her down.'

Piak disappeared to the kitchen and returned with a bucket of cold water and a hand towel. Sirinya bathed Kitima's face and arms, which only seemed to make her shiver harder. Piak hovered over, her brow furrowed, wringing her hands. The doctor came quickly. He came up the stairs two at a time, carrying an old black leather bag. He had been the family doctor for years, but Sirinya had most recently seen him at Chalong's meeting of the underground, before Somsak left. After taking Kitima's temperature, listening to her heartbeat and giving her a cursory examination, he said, 'It looks like dengue fever. She'll be in a lot of pain. It makes your bones and muscles ache. She'll be like this for two or three days. I'll write a prescription for painkillers. Now make sure she drinks plenty of tea or water and, when the fever has subsided, give her some thin soup.'

'Will she get over it, Doctor?' Sirinya asked, near to tears.

'Almost certainly. She is strong and fit. It might leave her weakened for a while, but she should make a full recovery in time.'

When the doctor had gone Sirinya moved her mattress into Kitima's room. She lay down and tried to sleep, but the sound of Kitima's irregular breathing, her constant writhing and turning, and her long low moans of pain prevented sleep coming. Sirinya thought back over the events of the day; of Ratana, of Narong's surprise proposal, and of the swim across the moat. She thought of Charlie in the camp hospital too, wondering how he was, wondering if she would ever see him again.

It was harder work unloading the barges the next morning without Kitima's help. They had left her in Piak's care, but there seemed to be no change in her condition. Sirinya had been so preoccupied and busy that it was not until she heard the army lorry stop outside that she thought about Charlie again. Would today be the day that he returned?

But again it was the other man who clambered down from the lorry, and again Johnny shook his head as he entered the shop and her spirits sank.

Once all the supplies, including the fruit, eggs and tobacco for the canteen, were stowed on board the lorry, one of the guards approached the shop.

'Where is the old woman?' he asked. 'She is late. Fetch her. She need to come with us as usual.'

'I'm sorry, sir,' said Sirinya, bowing her head respectfully, 'she cannot come today. She is very ill with fever.'

'That not matter. She can come.'

Sirinya shook her head. 'She is very ill, sir. She cannot come. She can't get out of bed. She is going to be ill for some time.'

The guard stared at her, his face reddening. His fists were clenched. 'We need somebody for canteen,' he shouted. 'Imperial Japanese Army making good money from sales. If old woman cannot come then you must come yourself.'

'But ... but I am needed here to look after the shop.'

'That does not matter to Imperial Japanese Army. You can close this shop. We need you to come with us now.'

So she left Saeng Chuto road, sitting in the stifling cab of the army lorry, wedged between two Japanese soldiers, leaving Piak to look after Kitima and Malee, and the two boys in charge of the shop.

Throughout the journey upriver to the road bridge and back down again on the metalled track which ran parallel to the old Bamboo Road, she sat as still as she could despite the lurching and vibrations of the lorry, not wanting her knees to brush up against the knees of the Japanese guards. All the way the two of them shouted and laughed together in Japanese, speaking over her head. She could not tell what they were laughing about, but it made her feel uncomfortable and afraid.

It was raining by the time the lorry splashed into Chungkai camp through the bamboo gates. As she got down from the cab one of the guards grunted at her to follow him. He showed her across the parade ground to the far corner where there was a small hut, set up as a tea stand, just as Kitima had described.

'Officers and recovering sick men can come during day for tea and tobacco and to buy fruit and eggs,' the guard said. 'Later, working men will come back from cutting and they can come too. Prisoners who came to your shop will unload supplies of eggs and fruit and tobacco from lorry. Price list here,' he indicated a blackboard on which someone had listed prices in English.

Inside the hut was a rudimentary kitchen with a stove, a huge kettle, pots and pans and tin plates and cups. Johnny brought the basket with the supplies for the shop from the lorry and put it down inside the hut with a shy smile. She watched him running back towards the quartermaster's store, stooping in the pouring rain.

Not sure what was expected, she began to cut up a mango and put it out on a tin plate. Rain was pelting down on the thinly thatched roof, dripping through in several places. The parade ground was deserted, and there was no sign of any prisoners. After an hour or so the rain cleared and the sun began to shine, steam rose from the ground as it dried.

A group of officers approached the hut. They were all dressed in ragged clothes, but instead of the loin cloths most of the prisoners wore, they each had a shabby shirt and shorts. The first to come was Colonel Scott, who smiled at her and asked for tea for all four of them. She served green tea in metal cups and they sat down at one of the crude tables. One produced a chess set and the four of them were soon absorbed in the game.

A steady stream of men came after that. Most appeared to be suffering from tropical ulcers. They were all pitifully thin, walking on bamboo crutches, their wounds bound with strips of greying cloth. Sirinya was shocked to see that some men had had their lower legs amputated, and quickly averted her eyes. All the men she served with green tea, fruit, tobacco or fried eggs were grateful, thanking her with a wai and smiles, wrinkles appearing in sunburned skin above hollowed cheeks.

Towards the middle of the afternoon during a lull in trade, another group of prisoners arrived. She had worked out that the long hut across the parade ground and directly opposite her hut was the hospital hut. The group came from that direction and they all looked sick, walking slowly, helping each other along, their faces pale and drawn. She watched them emerge from the hospital and walk painfully across the parade ground. As they came closer she peered more closely and her heart skipped a beat. In the middle of the group, supported by two other men shuffled a familiar figure. She was sure it was him. His hair was more dishevelled now, but she would recognise his outline and the way he carried himself anywhere. As he came nearer she realised that he had spotted her too and that he was smiling his huge smile.

'Charlie,' she murmured, unable to tear her eyes away from him.

22

The two prisoners who'd been supporting Charlie as he made his painfully slow progress across the parade ground sat down at one of the bamboo tables. Charlie came forward unsteadily but alone to the makeshift counter where Sirinya stood gazing at him. He stopped in front of her, put his hands together in a wai and bowed his head to meet them. Up close he looked even thinner, she could almost see the bones of his nose and cheeks beneath his skin. He'd been sunburned before but now he just looked sallow and unhealthy.

She'd waited so many days for this moment, but now it had come she found herself tongue tied. She'd not imagined that it would be here that she would see him again, here in this filthy camp amongst all these other men who would be sure to notice if she treated him differently.

She returned Charlie's wai. 'Khun Sirinya,' he said, looking into her eyes, 'I'm so pleased to see you. I've been ill you see, that's why I couldn't come with the lorry for the past week or so.'

'I know,' she said faltering, 'your friend, Johnny, told me … are you better now?'

'Over the worst, but still weak. They thought I might die at one stage.'

'Excuse me lady,' broke in another prisoner, pushing in, leaning in front of Charlie, 'can you 'urry up serving this blighter 'ere? He's not the only one waiting for some grub.'

There was a ripple of laughter from the tables and Sirinya felt a blush creeping up her cheeks. She lowered her eyes. She was unsure of the mood amongst the men; they all appeared good natured and even jovial as they sat sipping their tea, tucking into egg fried rice or smoking, but she knew that could easily change.

'What can I get you?' she asked Charlie in a whisper.

'Tea for three, and a quarter of tobacco, please.'

With trembling hands she poured the tea from the great teapot. She handed the tin cups to him and he said in a low voice, 'I'll try to come and talk to you later, when it's quieter here.'

She nodded and flashed a brief smile at him, then turned her attention to the man who'd complained. She watched Charlie as he took the tea and tobacco and sat back at the table with the two other men. He was there for an hour or so, smoking and playing cards. For that hour Sirinya found it difficult to focus on her tasks. Her eyes kept wandering over to where he sat, and on each occasion her heart surged with joy when she saw that he was looking at her too. He would smile whenever their eyes met, but she would look away quickly, afraid that the other men would notice. That didn't seem to worry Charlie, he appeared to be happy to sit there openly staring in her direction. Before he and his friends left he came up to her once again and said quietly, 'I'll come back at around five. I need to speak to you.'

The afternoon dragged on with groups of officers and sick men arriving at the canteen and staying for a while to eat and drink, chat or play cards or chess. She counted the minutes and the hours as the day wore on. It rained twice; two sudden and intense tropical rainstorms. Each time the men left their tables and took shelter under the thatch of her hut until it passed.

Charlie had been right; there was a lull in trade just before five o'clock. She cleared the tables and as she did so kept glancing across at the hospital hut. Finally he came, alone this time. As she watched him walk slowly towards her she longed to rush across and support him, but she knew she couldn't do that. When he reached her he sat down at one of the tables, panting with the effort, his breath wheezy and short. She wanted to help him, to put her arms around him, to rub his back and comfort him. Instead she brought him a mug of clear tea and set it before him on the bamboo table. He smiled his thanks.

'Why don't you sit down?' he asked. Silently she sat beside him, perched on the edge of the flimsy bench, aware that there could be any number of pairs of eyes trained on them from the surrounding huts. Her heart was pounding but once again she could think of nothing to say.

He cleared his throat and looked at her.

'Sirinya, I just want you to know that words can't describe how happy I am to see you here. When I got ill last week I had a fever for days. All I could think of for the whole time was your face. Your face when you were standing in the jungle handing out fruit that day, your smile each time I came into your shop, the light in your eyes. It kept me going. It's the reason I didn't give up, you know.'

She felt the colour creeping into her cheeks again and bowed her head, letting her hair fall forward. She couldn't look him in the eye. There was a great lump forming in her throat as he spoke and she struggled to hold back the tears.

'So I just wanted to thank you. Thank you for saving my life,' he held his cup up to her.

'I don't know what to say. I've done nothing,' she whispered.

'You've done more than you can ever know. If we never meet

227

again, I'll always remember you as the beautiful Thai girl who helped me to live.'

She was silent, struggling with her emotions, trying to find the courage and the words to respond. In the end she said, 'If you are here tomorrow we *will* meet again. My mother is ill herself. She will get better but it will take time. Until then I must come to the camp each day to run this canteen.'

'Oh, I'm sorry to hear that your mother's ill,' he said with concern in his eyes.

'She will recover, she is strong and she has medicines to help her.'

Charlie sipped the tea and she felt his eyes on her face. 'I need to ask you this, Sirinya,' he said at last, 'Did you ... did you ever think about me while I was ill?'

'Of course. Of course I thought about you,' she said, looking straight into his eyes now, 'I thought of little else.'

He returned her gaze and she caught a glimpse of those tortoiseshell flecks in his pupils and the wrinkles at the corners of his eyes. Then gradually she became aware of the babble of voices coming closer, of the sound of dozens of pairs of feet walking on the bare earth. It was hard to look away from him, but the noise got closer. She looked across the parade ground to see that a column of weary looking men were approaching the canteen. Sweat glistened on their bodies and they were filthy and scarred from the days' work on the cutting. Reluctantly she left Charlie and was back behind the counter before the first wave of prisoners descended.

For the next hour she made tea, fried rice and eggs and chopped fruit and took money with barely a pause for breath. There was a constant press of men in front of the stall. She wondered why they were coming here and not to the cookhouse on the other side of the camp and she asked one of the men. 'We'll go for our proper tucker later. This is far better though. It's a real treat to have rice without weevils even if we do have to pay.'

When the queues died down and she had a chance to look up, she saw that Charlie was no longer seated at the table. She felt a twinge of disappointment. Why hadn't he said goodbye to her? But then glancing across towards the huts she saw him walking slowly back across the parade ground. He had almost reached the hospital hut on the other side when he turned, and seeing her, he waved, before ducking through the entrance and disappearing from view.

At sunset, as she walked along the Bamboo Road towards the wharf at Tha Maa Kham, her thoughts were filled with Charlie and the words he'd said to her. She realised now how afraid she'd been that he might have died these past few days. She thought too about the shocking state of the men, starved and sick, beaten and driven, filthy and dressed in rags. But despite that, she had noticed how even in these toughest of conditions, their friendships, humour and camaraderie shone through.

When she arrived back at the shophouse, exhausted, her mind still filled with thoughts of Charlie, she went straight to the top floor to see Kitima. Her mother stirred and lifted her head as she entered the room. At least Kitima was conscious! Sirinya rushed to the bedside and kissed her mother's cheek. Kitima opened one eye and lifted her hand to touch Sirinya's face. 'You look different, Daughter,' she croaked, 'Better than before. I've been worried about you this past week.'

'You? You've been worried about *me*, Ma?' Sirinya said, laughing with relief.

For the next four days Sirinya made the trip into the camp sitting rigidly between the two guards in the cab of the army lorry. Each morning when she left the shophouse, Kitima was a little stronger. And each day Charlie was a little stronger too. He walked towards the canteen more steadily every time. Each time she looked up to see him approach her heartbeat quickened and the sun seemed a little brighter even in this muddy, desperate place.

Charlie spent hours sitting at the table nearest to the counter, watching Sirinya work, smiling whenever she glanced across at him. She had no idea what the other men thought, but she never heard anyone tease him. Perhaps they didn't notice that he just came to be with her, so absorbed were they all in their daily struggle for survival. Sometimes, if the canteen was empty, she would sit down at the table with him and drink a cup of green tea.

Once she tried to ask him about his home, but his eyes grew serious and he brushed her questions aside. 'I can't think about that now,' he said quietly. 'I might never see home again. I'm here now and today I'm alive and you're sitting in front of me. That's all I can think about. I must live in the moment. It's all that matters now.'

She never asked him again. In contrast, he seemed interested in her life; his eyes lit up when she told him about the shop, about the village in the hills where she grew up, and about her family. He wanted to know even the smallest details. It seemed to help him, and he would listen to her with rapt attention. So she told him as much as she could think of with her limited English. Sometimes when she was telling him an anecdote about Kitima or Yai he would laugh, and the haunted look she had sometimes seen in his eyes since his illness would disappear altogether.

But she didn't have much time to spend talking to him, there were always other customers to serve, plates to wash, food to prepare. And whenever he had been sitting here at one of the canteen tables for any length of time, one of the orderlies from the hospital would come across and fetch him, saying, 'The doc says you need to come and lie down. You'll exhaust yourself sitting here. You need to rest.' Sometimes they would send Johnny across to fetch him. Johnny would always smile his shy smile at Sirinya and hurry Charlie away before she had a chance to speak to him.

On the fourth day, halfway through the afternoon, Charlie had just returned to the hospital hut with one of the orderlies. Sirinya was serving some fruit on tin plates to two men who had arrived on crutches when she sensed sudden tension amongst the prisoners all around her. They had fallen silent, and were looking down at their plates, or staring fixedly at the chess board or cards in front of them. Confused, she looked around for some explanation and saw it striding across the open space towards the canteen. She was gripped with fear. It was the Ripper.

He strode straight up to Sirinya and stopped in front of her. She put the plates of fruit down on the table with shaking hands, inclined her head and did her best to curtsey to him, although she was not sure how to do it properly.

'I know who you are,' he said. Her mouth went dry and she felt the blood drain from her face. What could he mean? Had he found out about the organisation? She kept her eyes fixed on the table and tried to control her trembling limbs.

'Look at me!' he commanded. She lifted her head and looked into his narrow black eyes.

'Yes! I was right. I do know you. You are the girl who came on delivery and you not work hard. Where is old woman? The old woman should be serving here. I not give permission for you to come.'

So it wasn't about the organisation after all. She let out a breath of relief. 'I'm sorry, sir,' she said. 'My mother is ill. She cannot work.'

He put his face close to hers and snorted. 'I hear this all the time from prisoners. Sickness an excuse for no work. Tell her she must come tomorrow, sick or no. I not want to see you here again. You not good for prisoners. You talking too much. You must go. No need to finish here. Pack up and go now. Old woman must come back with lorry tomorrow morning.'

'But sir, she is sick, too sick to work.'

'Sick or not sick, she must come. Or contract with Khun Chalong will be terminate.'

He looked around at the prisoners, staring at their plates or paused midway through games of chess or cards.

'You men. You must all go now. Today canteen finish.'

Sirinya knew enough about how the guards treated the prisoners to be sure that they would not protest. They all got up immediately from the tables and shuffled off towards their quarters without a backward glance.

All she could think of was Charlie. How could she say goodbye to him? Would he know she had to go? Would she ever see him again? As she cleared the table and washed the plates she kept glancing across at the hospital hut to see if he would appear, but the parade ground was deserted. The men clearly knew better than to venture out when the Ripper was at large.

Sirinya took as long as she could tidying the tables and putting away equipment in the kitchen. She knew that if she lingered too long there was a risk that the Ripper would return, but she still managed to string her tasks out for over an hour. Still no one approached. Reluctantly she put the last of the tin cups away, pulled her scarf around her shoulders and set off for the camp entrance in the full glare of the afternoon sun. The guards at the gates dragged them open for her and she walked slowly out of the camp and along the dirt road where the lorries went in and out. Her heart was heavy, and by the time she turned off the track onto the Bamboo Road to take the shortcut along the river, she was close to tears.

The path wound its way over swampy land between patches of jungle towards the river, then it followed the riverbank through thickets of graceful bamboo, some of them so tall that they bent to meet overhead, blocking out the sunlight. The sun was high in the sky and the sound of crickets and the hum of insects was deafening. She walked on slowly, her head bowed, not bothering to control her tears now, letting them stream down her cheeks.

Not far along the path a shadow darkened the ground in front of her. She sensed something moving and looked up, startled. He stood there in front of her blocking the path, his arms folded, smiling at her. She opened her mouth and closed it again.

'I'm sorry if I startled you,' he said.

She brushed the tears from her eyes. 'How did you get out of the camp?'

'It's not that hard to get out, actually. There's a gap in the fence where it goes down to the river. Men get out all the time. Some men get out to trade with the villagers in that hamlet over there. It's getting back in that might be tricky.'

'I didn't know that. I thought the boundaries were patrolled. Why don't prisoners run away?'

'There's no point in that. There's nowhere to go and you're bound to get caught. The Japs know that. They punish anyone they catch who leaves and comes back, they know it happens.'

'Why did you come?'

'Don't you know?' he said stepping closer and smiling into her eyes. 'Aren't you pleased that I did?'

'Of course I'm pleased! All I could think of was that I might not

233

see you again.'

'Me too. That's why I came here as soon as I heard you'd been sent away.'

He put his arms around her and pulled her to him. She rested her head against his chest and they stood there like that for a long time, not speaking, the hum of insects and the babble of the river the only sounds. His chest and his whole body felt desperately thin. She could feel his ribs against her cheek and the arms that held her felt like bare bones. His heart was thudding against her ear and she could smell the sweat and warmth of his body. At last he spoke.

'I've got something for you. That's why I came.'

He let her go and fumbled in a small cloth bag he was carrying round his waist.

'Here it is. What do you think?'

She gasped. He held out a locket, a jade butterfly on a silver chain. It flashed in the shafts of light filtering through the bamboo.

'Where did you get that?'

'I bought it in Singapore before the surrender. I've managed to keep it all these months in the camps. Sometimes I've had to bury it under my sleeping platform.'

'Why didn't you trade it?'

'I was going to, when things got desperate.'

'I can't take it, Charlie. You must save it and trade it for food. I don't need it.'

He took her hand and put the locket into it, closing her fingers around it.

'Take it,' he said. 'You already saved my life. Take it to remember me by.'

She felt the lump rising in her throat again. 'Remember you by? Won't I see you again?'

'The cutting is nearly finished. They'll take us away then. No one knows quite when or where to. I'll come back when the war is over, though. I'll come back and find you.'

Panic rose in her and on an impulse she said, 'Why wait until then? Why don't you come with me now? We could run away somewhere. I could hide you.'

'Sirinya,' he said, grabbing her shoulders and looking into her eyes. 'Please don't say that. You don't know what that would mean. No one has ever escaped from here. The two men who tried to escape were caught by the Japs and shot. Their mate, Tom was almost beaten to death and punished as an example. He was lucky to survive.'

'But they didn't have Thai friends, did they?'

'They must have had some help. But someone betrayed them. If you help me you and your family would be in danger. You mustn't even think about it.'

She fell silent.

'Look,' he said at last. 'I'll try to get back on the delivery round. I'm nearly better now. In a couple of days, I should be fit enough to volunteer for that again.'

She smiled weakly up at him, 'Yes, you must try to do that.'

He put his arms around her again and held her to him. She felt his lips brush the top of her head and she lifted her face and they kissed. It was a desperate, unhappy kiss of despair and longing. She pulled away.

'I need to go, and you should get back before you are missed,' she said, unable to bear the parting, wanting to get it over with. Then tearing herself away from him she fled down the path in the direction of Tha Maa Kham. She didn't look back and she didn't stop until she was so out of breath that she could run no further.

* * *

The next morning, Kitima got up, dressed and departed with the Japanese Army lorry to the camp. The others had begged her not to go.

'You're too sick, Ma,' pleaded Sirinya, 'Please stay at home and rest for another couple of days at least.'

'Nonsense, Daughter, I'm quite recovered now. I will go. The prisoners need that extra food, especially the sick men. And we don't want to anger the Japanese soldiers, raise their suspicions.'

Sirinya wished she hadn't told the rest of the family that the Ripper had threatened to terminate Chalong's contract. That threat had made Kitima even more stubbornly determined to go back into the camp. Sirinya watched her climb into the cab. Kitima had lost weight; she no longer filled out her long dark dress, her cheeks were no longer full and rosy.

That evening, when she arrived back at the shophouse, Kitima was walking unsteadily, her face was grey with exhaustion. Sirinya went to help her but Kitima brushed her aside. She dragged herself up the stairs to the apartment and fell asleep on a mat on the floor, refusing the soup Piak brought for her. Sirinya and Piak exchanged worried looks.

The second day was the same. Despite protests, Kitima was up and waiting for the lorry when it arrived. She sat on an upturned crate in the shop and watched the prisoners and the shop boys load up.

'Mother, please don't go today. You look so pale,' said Sirinya as the lorry was almost fully loaded.

'I must go, Daughter. There is no choice,' Kitima said smiling and patting Sirinya's hand. 'I am strong, you know. The prisoners need me. I'm only doing what anyone would do.'

Sirinya stood on the pavement and watched Kitima struggle up the lorry steps. Johnny stopped beside her for a second on his way back to the truck.

'She's a brave lady, your mother,' he said quietly.

'Yes, she is. I worry about her.'

'Charlie asked me to let you know,' he said, 'he will be coming with us tomorrow. Walt is strong enough to work back on the cutting now and Charlie's going to replace him on the lorry.'

Sirinya's heart missed a beat. 'Thank you,' she breathed, her fingers automatically touching the jade butterfly round her neck. So they would meet again after all.

She spent the rest of the day veering between euphoria at the prospect of seeing Charlie again, and concern for Kitima. Perhaps her mother was right though, and the worry was misplaced? She had been ill before but had always bounced back quickly. Back in the village there was no time for sickness; Kitima had always needed to be out working in the fields, tending to the animals before she was properly recovered.

Sirinya's concern turned to anxiety when darkness fell and Kitima hadn't returned. She sat in the window of the living room looking down into the street, watching for any sign of her mother. Piak was cooking the evening meal in the kitchen. Chalong had returned from his deliveries and was in the backyard taking a shower. Malee sat at the table, sewing. She had stopped spending her days in bed over the past few days and although she was still pale and quiet, Sirinya sensed that she was gradually recovering from her grief.

'Should I go and look for her, Aunt? She should be home by now.'

'Give her a few more minutes, Siri, it is only just after sunset.

She might have had to wait for the boatman to bring her across.'

As Sirinya watched the street there was sudden movement on the pavement and four Kempeitai officers approached the shop. There was a hammering on the door. The three women exchanged anxious looks. 'It's the Japanese,' said Sirinya. 'Shall I go?'

Piak nodded, her eyes wide with fear.

Sirinya began down the stairs, but before she could reach the bottom the door flew open and the soldiers burst through into the passageway. The first one came up to her and grabbed her arm.

'You! You come with us. We need to talk to you.' She recognised him as the guard who had questioned her when she and Piak had crossed the river with the boatman.

'Why? I've done nothing.'

'You will see. We need to ask you questions.' He dragged her forwards, out through the front door. He said something over his shoulder to the other men, and she could hear their footsteps clattering up the stairs and Piak's squeals as they entered the apartment.

Another guard took her other arm and they dragged her across the road towards the Kempeitai house. As they drew her on, she resisted more strongly, struggling against them, screaming, 'why are you taking me? I've done nothing wrong! Please, let me go!'

They took no notice of her yells, she tried kicking their legs, but that made no difference either, they just forced her forward. Their hands gripped her bare arms hard, nails digging into her flesh, bruising her skin. They propelled her nearer and nearer to the house, in through the front door and into a narrow passageway with doors opening off it.

The man on her right kicked open a door and they shoved her into a darkened room.

'This is what happens if you betray Imperial Japanese Army,' he said roughly and slammed the door.

'We talk to you soon.'

She collapsed on the floor sobbing, shaking all over, her arms and legs throbbing from where the guards had dragged and kicked her. She knelt there for several minutes before she realised there was someone else in the room. Light from the street filtered through a high window which had been barred from the outside. She could just make out a figure on the other side of the room. She crawled towards it. She realised that someone had been tied to a chair with rope, their head sagging forward on their chest. Sirinya reached out a trembling hand and touched the face. She drew it away quickly with a stifled scream. Her hand was wet and sticky with blood. But then she forced herself to put her hands back onto the face and she felt again. She traced the shape of the thick eyebrows, the forehead, the smooth hair. She could hardly breathe, fear and dread surged in her chest, blocking her windpipe. Then the head lifted a little.

'Daughter. Is that you?' the figure whispered.

23

'Mother! It *is* you,' Sirinya sobbed, flinging her arms around Kitima and hugging her tightly, 'Why are you here? What happened to you?'

Kitima didn't respond, but Sirinya could feel her mother's chest rising and falling beneath her own. She was clearly struggling for breath.

'Here, let me untie you.' Sirinya began pulling at the ropes, looking to find a way of loosening them. Kitima grunted and shifted in the chair, trying to resist.

'Please don't do that, Siri. They will punish you,' she whispered.

'I don't care. You need to breathe.' With shaking fingers Sirinya traced the length of string that was bound tightly around Kitima's chest and stomach, desperately trying to find a knot to untie, but before she could, the door of the room was flung open. The light from the passage lit up the silhouette of the Kempeitai officer in the doorway.

'You must untie my mother!' Sirinya shouted. 'She is innocent. She has done nothing. She can't breathe like that. She is very ill.'

The guard ran forward and grabbed Sirinya by both arms, trying to lift her up, to prise her away from Kitima.

'You have seen her now,' he said roughly as she struggled against him. 'That is what happen to those who betray Imperial Japanese Army. You come with me. We talk to you now.'

'No! I won't leave her,' she said, tightening her fingers around the back of Kitima's chair. She was no match for the strength of the soldier, though, and he dragged her off, her nails dragging and breaking on the wood.

She screamed and fought as he hauled her across the floor.

'Be brave, Daughter,' Kitima said as the guard dragged Sirinya into the passage and slammed the door. He manhandled her along the bare floor of the passage and into a smaller room in the back of the house. In her state of terror, Sirinya hardly registered her surroundings. This place felt more like a cupboard than a room. Bare walls were lit by a single bulb dangling from the ceiling. It smelt foul; of sweat and urine and of death. The guard forced her to sit on the only piece of furniture, a wooden chair in the middle of the room. A second guard appeared in the doorway with a length of rope. He knelt and bound the rope around Sirinya's ankles, tying them tightly to the legs of the chair. Then he stood up, looped the rope around her waist and tied her down to the seat. All the time she was struggling and squirming.

'That's too tight,' she said. 'It's cutting into me.'

'You stay still. You not move and it not hurt,' said the first guard. 'I need to ask you some question. If you not co-operate it take longer.'

He nodded to the other guard, who disappeared down the hallway. The officer stood still in front of Sirinya, looming over her, staring down at her. She refused to look up at him, instead fixed her eyes on his knees in his worn khaki trousers. She was struggling to stay calm, to resist the urge to panic and scream out. The other guard was coming back. As he approached she realised he was carrying something. Her heart began to beat faster and her palms to sweat as she made out the shape of the object he held in his hand. The truth of what they knew began to dawn on her. With a grim smile he held it up for her to see. It glinted in the stark light. She stared up at it and though she tried not to react, her eyes widened involuntarily. It was the capacitor from the radio that she'd smuggled into the camp under her sarong all those weeks ago.

'You know what this is, don't you?'

She shook her head and frowned as if confused.

'We find in one of the huts in the camp today. We find illegal radio there. This is radio part. You know that, don't you?'

She shook her head vehemently. 'No. I don't know what it is. I know nothing about radios.'

He bent down and put his face near to hers. She could smell decay on his foul breath. She turned her face away, but he grabbed her by the chin with rough fingers and turned her face back towards him, pinching her skin.

'Look at me. You know what this is. You and your mother brought this into canteen, didn't you?'

'Of course not,' she said, with a shiver of relief. If they thought it had come into the camp through the canteen, they must have no evidence at all to link the radio to her and Kitima.

'British prisoners tell us. We question them today. British officers at the camp. Your good friends. They are to be punish severely. They tell us that *you* bring in radio.'

With an effort of will she lifted her chin and looked straight into his eyes.

'That's just not true and you know it,' she said. 'The men could not have told you that because it never happened. You need someone to blame so you've picked on us.'

His eyes narrowed. 'The men did tell us. It must be you. You are the only people who come into camp. If you confess though, we treat you well.' He leaned forward and slipped his hand through the rope that tied her to the chair and twisted it, digging into her thighs, restricting the blood in her legs. She could feel his knuckles against her flesh. She held her breath and resisted the urge to cry out.

She was already in pain, her arms and legs bruised from being dragged across the street. How could she bear any more? Panic rose in her. She thought of Kitima, her face bloody, half conscious. How could they do that to her? The surge of anger she felt gave her courage.

'I'm not going to confess because there is nothing to confess,' she said gritting her teeth. 'However you treat me.'

He let go and straightened up, then paced around in front of her, putting his hands on his hips.

'I see you at the river a few days ago,' he said. Her heart beat sped up. Where was this leading? Had they found out about the medicines too? 'You say you have relative nearby. But you not have relative there.'

She hesitated. Did he really know that? She only had seconds to decide, but she took a chance.

'Of course we do,' she said with scorn in her voice looking straight at him again. 'My great aunt lives in the village by the rice fields. You can take me there and I'll introduce her to you.'

'That not possible,' he said. 'Because it is not true. That day you went into Chungkai camp didn't you?'

'Of course not. Why would we do that?'

'You bring radio parts.'

'But you just said they came in with the canteen.'

'You not contradict me,' he shouted, his face reddening. Suddenly he bent forward and slapped her cheek making her cry out. She turned her face away and he grabbed her chin again and forced her to face him.

'We know it you. You and old woman. If you confess and tell

me who help you, I not harm you. It was the old man wasn't it. Man with contract for camps. The man they call Khun Chalong?'

'Nobody helped me because I've done nothing. Please. Let me go. Let my mother go. She is very sick.'

'You can go when we have information about radio.'

'Please,' she said, tears threatening now. 'You can keep me here, but let her go. She is not strong. She has been ill.'

'She should not have betrayed Imperial Japanese Army. Then she not be in trouble.'

Sirinya felt beaten down by his questions. They went on and on, round and round, going over the same ground, returning to the starting point repeatedly, getting nowhere. Whenever she tried staying silent, refusing to answer him he slapped her cheek or her head. She felt dizzy and weak. The walls of the room seemed to fade into a blur and all she could see was the man's face full of hate, his cruel mouth repeating the same questions, his eyes hard and unyielding. The smell of his breath when he leaned forward to shout at her made her gag, vomit flooding into her mouth. She lost track of how long it went on.

After what seemed like hours he changed tack abruptly. He leaned forward, his hands on his knees and smiled for the first time.

'Your uncle visit Bangkok often doesn't he? What does he do there?'

Fresh chills of fear and dread coursed through her. She had no idea what to say. She opened and shut her mouth, finally she said in a weak voice, 'He goes there to get rice sometimes.'

'Long way to go for rice. He not supply rice to camps. Other supplier from village downriver does that.'

'Look, he gets good rice especially for the Kempeitai. You know that. He brings it across to this house for you. You eat it every day.'

The man said nothing in response, and in the silence of the room Sirinya could hear crickets outside the window. It reminded her that life was going on outside the walls of this hot stinking room. She longed to be outside, to be able to move freely, to breathe fresh air.

'We ask him these questions too you know,' said the officer leaning forward, his face close to hers. 'We search his house now, and we question him. If he say something different there will be problem for you and for him.'

Then his eyes shifted away from hers and looked down at her neck. With a swift movement of his hands he grabbed the locket Charlie had given her and yanked it off her, snapping the delicate clasp. Then he closed his fist around it, with a malicious smile.

He left the room slamming the door shut. She was alone. She could not move in the chair and the heat in the room was stifling, but it was a relief that her tormentor had gone. Thoughts raced around her mind. Would Kitima be alright? What about Chalong and the others? How would they bear up to questioning? Would Piak be strong enough to resist them if they got hold of her?

Her mouth was dry and her tongue felt swollen. She had not had a drink for hours. Her face stung from the slapping and her arms and legs throbbed from the bruises the guards had inflicted. Her frantic thoughts about her family gradually became jumbled and confused and melded into one. At last an uneasy sleep came over her and her head slumped forward on her chest.

* * *

She was woken by the sound of the door opening and two Kempeitai bursting in. She had not seen these men before; they looked younger, more junior than the man who had questioned her. Her head had been lolling on one side and as she straightened it a pain spread down her neck and across her shoulders. She realised with shame that she'd wet herself and that she'd been dribbling. The two men untied the ropes around her legs and body with rough hands, and pulled her to her feet. Then without a word to her they propelled her forward, out of the room, along the passage and out through the front door. It was early morning and outside in the street a few stallholders and food vendors were already setting up. A couple of them glanced in her direction then looked away quickly.

'Where is my mother?' she said to the soldiers, but they did not answer.

Once she was out on the step the soldiers took their hands off her and she heard the door slam behind her. She turned back to the door and hammered on it with her fists.

'Where is my mother? Please ...' She sunk to her knees on the step sobbing, frantic with concern for Kitima. Had she made it through the night? Had the brutal officer with the hard eyes questioned her again? Had her fever returned?

She pounded on the door for a long time, but no one came. Then she sunk down on the step wondering how she could get back in to see Kitima. After a few minutes, though, the door opened again and Kitima was there, in the doorway. She was propped up between the two officers, her head slumped forward, her body sagging as if she could barely support her own weight. The two men manhandled her out of the front door. She took one unsteady step forward then sunk down onto the step. The shock of seeing her in the daylight hit Sirinya like a hammer blow. Blood oozed from a gash on her forehead and one eye was so swollen it would not open. There were purple bruises on her cheekbones.

'What have they done to you?' Sirinya breathed, putting her

arms around her mother, her own wounds and discomfort forgotten. She knew she must somehow get Kitima home as quickly as she could, but she couldn't do that alone. She stood up. She would have to fetch Chalong to help her.

'Ma. Wait here I'll be back soon, I promise.'

She started down the path, but then stopped, thinking again. It might be foolish to ask Chalong to come here, for the Kempeitai to see him and perhaps take him into the house for questioning too. Instead she approached the nearest stallholder. He was busy chopping chicken on a board next to his food stall, his head bent to his task. She knew this man, she sometimes stopped at his stall to buy noodle soup from him. He was small and nervous, with hair greying at the temples. As she approached he was forced to look at her. He laid his knife down and wiped his hands on his apron.

'You want help?' he said, in a reluctant tone. 'Of course. I'll come. You take one arm, I'll take the other.'

* * *

They made a bed for Kitima on the floor in the storeroom behind the shop. For the first few hours Sirinya ignored her own pain and sat on the concrete floor beside Kitima bathing her mother's wounds, rubbing tiger balm into her bruises, forcing her to take sips of tea. Kitima was only half-conscious. All the time Sirinya talked to her in a soothing voice, trying to ease her suffering, urging her to be strong.

Piak had broken down when she came downstairs and saw the pair of them for the first time, staggering into the shop with the help of the old man from the street stall. She had rushed to them sobbing, clinging to them. Chalong had put his arms around them and cried too. Now Piak and Chalong hovered over Kitima, twisting their hands, their faces grey and haggard.

'I'm so sorry, Sirinya,' Chalong kept saying. 'This is all my doing. If I hadn't got involved, this would never have happened.'

'Don't speak like that, Uncle,' Sirinya said through her tears. 'You were only trying to do good. We were all involved together. We knew the risks. Nobody forced us. You mustn't blame yourself for the brutality of the Kempeitai.'

The shop and the apartment had once again been pulled apart by the Kempeitai. Sirinya sat on the floor amongst splintered crates and boxes. Broken baskets and squashed fruit were strewn about, windows had been smashed, shattered glass covered the floor.

'Did they question you too?' Sirinya asked Chalong. He nodded, and closed his eyes as if wanting to banish the memory. 'Did they beat you, Uncle?'

'A few slaps about the face. Nothing compared what they did to you and your mother. Thank the goodness of Buddha they spared your aunt and cousin, though.'

'They found the radio in the camp you know. They were trying to get us to confess to bringing it in through the canteen.'

'I know. I told them none of us knew anything about it, but they weren't satisfied. I'm afraid they might come back, Siri.'

Sirinya looked up at him in alarm. 'Really? But they've no evidence.'

'That doesn't seem to bother them.'

'What about the contract to supply the camps?' she asked, remembering suddenly.

'I told them that if you or Kitima were hurt I would stop supplying the camps straight away. And look at you. Look at your poor mother.'

'Maybe that's why they let us go this morning,' she said. 'But you must carry on, Uncle. What about the medicines you're taking in to all the other camps. You're doing so much good. You can't stop now.'

Chalong sat down on a broken crate and put his head in his hands. 'I don't know, Siri. We live under constant threat of discovery, of exposing ourselves to beatings and maybe worse. Look what I've put you through. Is it really worth it?'

'Of course it's worth it, Uncle,' she replied without hesitating, 'look at the lives you're saving. People you're helping. One day the war will be over and all this will stop. Then people will realise what good you have done.'

'I don't want people to realise, Siri,' he said quietly. 'I just want to help those poor prisoners.'

'I know, Uncle. That's not what I meant really. I meant that if some men go home because of your help, it will all be worth what we have done, the small risks we have taken.'

Piak stepped forward. 'Sirinya. You must go out into the backyard and bathe, then upstairs to rest and recover. I will look after Kitima for a few hours. Please. You look dreadful. Go and lie down. I'll get you something to eat while you rest.'

* * *

For four days Kitima lay on the mat in the back room while the family tidied and mended and repaired the shattered shophouse around her. Sirinya recovered quickly from her own physical wounds, but the she could not banish the nightmare of those hours in that stinking room from her mind. Each time she closed her eyes, she could smell the stench of that place. The face of the Kempeitai officer would dance in front of her, she would feel the ropes cutting into her ankles and her thighs. She would relive the terror of being bound to that hard chair under the bare light bulb, anticipating the pain they might inflict on her.

At night she lay down on a mat beside her mother who tossed and turned on her own mat, burning up with fever, groaning, and muttering incomprehensible snatches of sentences. Sirinya's own mind would be suspended in that half-world between sleep and wakefulness, imagining what might have happened to her there in the Kempeitai house, fearing what might happen to Kitima now.

No one came from Chungkai camp for supplies for two days, and Chalong made no deliveries to the outer camps either. Even so, each morning Chalong, Malee and the two boys went down to the river to collect their orders from the boats; the supplies had already made their journey and Chalong couldn't let down his suppliers. The shop began to fill up with stocks of fruit and vegetables. Sirinya wondered how long they would be able to go on like that. But on the afternoon of the third day a Japanese officer arrived from Chungkai on a motorbike to speak to Chalong. They were shut upstairs in the living room for over an hour. When the man had gone Chalong called Piak, Malee and Sirinya into the room.

'We will start again tomorrow. The lorry will come in the morning to take a load to Chungkai. The Japanese have given me an assurance that they will not question anyone from the family again. I think we've now managed to convince them that it was impossible for us to have helped with the radio.'

'But do you believe them, Husband?' asked Piak. 'They have no conscience, no humanity. Why would they keep to their word about this?'

'I don't really believe them, no. We'll need to be even more vigilant than before. If you don't want to take medicines in any more just say so and we can stop right now.'

Sirinya stared at him. 'Uncle, you cannot mean that! The only reason to carry on supplying the camps at all after what we've been through is because what we are doing helps the prisoners. Otherwise we would be just working for the Japanese, taking their filthy money. How could you carry on and profit from the contract with that on your conscience?'

He patted her hand and smiled for the first time since the Kempeitai's visit. 'I'm glad you see it that way, Siri. I just wanted to make sure that you didn't mind carrying on taking risks. After all you've been through, and the dreadful things they did to you and Kitima. But what about you, my darling?' he asked turning to Piak.

'You don't need to ask me, Husband,' Piak said with tears in her eyes. 'We will carry on. We won't let them beat us.'

'And you, Daughter?'

Malee looked at her father, pale but determined. 'We need to keep going, Father. Somsak gave his life for this. We can't just give up.'

The army lorry arrived from Chungkai just after dawn the next morning. Sirinya stood in the doorway gripping the doorpost, holding her breath. Would he be here this time? With her eyes trained on the back of the lorry, she expected to see Colonel Scott jump down, but the first man to emerge was a slighter, older man with silver grey hair. She knew instantly it was not Scott, but from his demeanour and clothes she could tell that he was an officer. Next to jump down was Johnny. By now she recognised the shape of his body and the way he moved. She was relieved to see him, but her eyes skated past him. There was then a pause before the third man got down. When he finally emerged her heart surged with emotion. It was Charlie. He stood for a moment behind the lorry and stared at the building, and seeing her his face lit up in a smile.

This time the guards were taking no chances. They walked behind the three prisoners with their bayonets drawn, prodding Johnny and Charlie forward. Sirinya realised that this time there would be no opportunity for any conversation between them, no possibility of exchanging lingering looks. She drew back from the doorway and lowered her head, but her eyes still searched for Charlie's, and when he walked past, prodded on by the guard, his eyes locked onto hers and in that brief second they exchanged a look filled with infinite longing and despair.

She stood back and watched as the three of them loaded the truck, helped by the shop boys. She wondered where Colonel Scott was. Why hadn't he come? She realised with dread in her heart that he must have been one of those punished about the radio. Then her mind started spinning with possibilities. If he had been tortured had they pushed him to the point where gave information away about the organisation? How would the organisation go on without him? Would the new officer pass her a letter? He had not even looked at her, and it occurred to her that he might know nothing about the arrangement they'd had with Colonel Scott.

She wondered too how she would ever get to speak to Charlie again if this was to be the new routine. The men worked solidly and quickly, barely looking up, barely exchanging a word. If any of them spoke, one of the guards would snarl at them, saying, 'You work. You no talk,' and prod at their bare skin with the tip of a bayonet.

The lorry was loaded more quickly than usual. With a heavy heart, Sirinya watched the men walk away from the shop. She saw Johnny and the officer climb on board, but then the officer turned, leaned out of the back of the truck and handed something to Charlie. It was a pile of empty baskets stacked together, left over from the last delivery. She watched as Charlie took them and turned to the guard, seeking permission. The guard gave a brief nod and stood back beside the lorry, motionless, his eyes fixed on Charlie as he walked back to the shop.

'I have something for you,' he whispered to Sirinya as he brushed past her in the doorway. I'll drop it on the floor.'

As he bent to put the baskets down in the corner of the shop, something dropped from his loincloth.

'It's for you. Pick it up when I've gone,' he said quietly.

It was a small piece of paper, folded tightly. She was careful not to stare at it, instead she turned her head towards the lorry. 'Goodbye,' he said under his breath as he left the shop.

She stood and watched the lorry move off down Saeng Chuto road in a cloud of exhaust smoke. When she was quite sure it was out of sight she went inside and picked the piece of paper up from the floor. She unfolded it quickly with clumsy fingers. It was a letter, written in pencil, barely legible.

My Dearest Sirinya,

This is the only way I can communicate with you. The Japs won't allow us to speak to you or any of your family now, not since they found the radio in the camp. We heard a rumour that you and your mother were questioned by the Kempeitai. I have been desperate with worry about you, did they hurt you? Were you harmed? I cannot bear the thought of those brutes laying a finger on you. And your poor mother, so good and kind. I hope they didn't hurt her either. It makes me sick with anger.

Colonel Scott and three other men were taken in for questioning and two of them have not returned. The colonel was so badly beaten he is still in the hospital hut, and we don't know if he will survive.

The other officers asked me to write and let you know that we urgently need new supplies of quinine, morphine and iodine for the hospital if you are able to obtain any. However, they fully understand if you no longer want to take the risks you've been taking, for which they thank you profusely. They also asked me to pass on the message that since Colonel Scott last wrote, ten men have died, some of malaria and some of dysentery, and some of malnutrition, in the hospital hut.

While I'm writing I also want to let you know that in about a weeks' time I'm going to be sent further north to another section of the railway. It is just my unit that is going and I'll have to leave my mate Johnny behind. They need reinforcements up there. Conditions are so bad that many men have died. There are rumours of a cholera outbreak too. The doctor tried to argue that I was too weak to go and wouldn't survive the conditions up the line, but the Ripper wouldn't listen to reason. No one in my unit can stay behind.

So my days here are numbered, Sirinya. If I do manage to survive until the end of this dreadful war I will come back to find you. I think about you day and night. Your lovely face lights my dreams and keeps me going in this dismal and brutal place.

I was hoping that we could meet to say goodbye where the bamboos grow beside the river, but at present there is a clampdown on security, the fences are patrolled constantly and there is no chance of getting out. I don't know if that will be lifted before I leave so I can't promise to say goodbye in person.

Please tear this up as soon as you have read it. There might be a way of your writing to me. If you are able to slip a letter inside the basket-work of the first load filled with cabbages in the shop on the next delivery, I will make sure I pick it up myself, and slip the letter inside my Jap-Happy as I walk back to the truck. But if you think *that is too risky, I will understand.*

You will be in my thoughts until we meet again, my dearest Sirinya,

Your ever loving, Charlie.

With tears in her eyes she tore the letter into tiny shreds and stuffed them in the pocket of her apron. She would take them into the backyard and wash them down the drain once she had checked on Kitima. She couldn't bear the thought that Charlie was to be taken up-country to endure even harsher conditions, to be driven until he dropped through weakness and exhaustion. How would he survive such an ordeal? How would she survive here without him?

With these thoughts turning in her mind she walked through to the storeroom. As soon as she entered she sensed there was something desperately wrong. There was a dreadful stillness and quiet in the room; no movement from Kitima's corner, no sound of her stirring or breathing. With a cry Sirinya ran across the room and knelt beside Kitima, flinging her arms around her, shaking her still body frantically.

'Mother, wake up! Wake up! Don't leave me,' she sobbed. But even as she said the words she knew they were pointless. She knew that Kitima was gone from her and that she would never again bask in the warmth of her mother's smile, or feel the comfort of Kitima's ample embrace.

24

It was mid-afternoon by the time Sirinya reached the outskirts of the village. Her back and legs ached from the long walk up the hill through the jungle, and her heart was heavy with grief. As usual the village children rushed out to greet her, dancing around her, chanting her name. The village dogs bounded up too and barked at her with wagging tails. This time she had no fruit to give the children. When they saw the pain on her face, her eyes red with crying and her cheeks stained with tears, they stopped shouting at her, backed away with confused frowns, and went back to playing under their houses.

It had torn her heart to leave Kitima. Even though she knew she could do nothing for her mother, that she was gone forever, her natural instinct would have been to stay there beside her mother's body, stroking her smooth brow, holding her hand as the warmth of her lifeblood slipped away.

Chalong and Piak had heard Sirinya's cries from the apartment and had rushed down to find her there on the storeroom floor, clinging to Kitima, crying uncontrollably. They had lifted her gently up, off her mother's body, and onto a chair. All three of them sat there beside Kitima in stunned silence, broken only by their sobbing. Chalong kept repeating over and over again, 'I'm so, so sorry. This is all because of me.'

'Please don't say that, Uncle,' Sirinya replied weakly, but the fight had gone from her.

After a while Piak said, 'What about Yai? We have to tell her straight away. We must bring her down from the village. She must be with Kitima.'

'You're right. She should be here. I will go and break the news to her and bring her back,' said Chalong.

'No, no. I must go,' said Sirinya With a shudder she remembered Yai's chilling prediction, shouted from her porch, as Sirinya and Kitima had left the village all those weeks ago.

'Are you sure?' asked Chalong, 'Don't you want to stay here with … with your mother?'

'I will stay with Kitima, Husband,' interrupted Piak. 'I will go upstairs and break the news to Malee in a moment. I will ask her to go down to the temple and fetch Phraa Thongphroh. He will chant for Kitima, and he will help us with the hand-washing ceremony; guide us through these dreadful times.'

'I will take you as far as the end of the road, Siri,' said Chalong. 'And I'll wait in the lorry for you and Yai to come back. I'd gladly walk up to the village with you if you need me to.'

'No, Uncle, I need to go alone, if you don't mind waiting. It will be a few hours. I'll need time to break the news to her. And you know Yai is not strong these days. She walks very slowly.'

Now Sirinya walked between the wooden houses in the full heat of the noonday sun. She was grateful that it was too hot for the villagers to be outside, they would be resting in their houses in the shade. She walked slowly, dreading what was to come, what she must do and Yai's reaction to the news.

As last Yai's house came into view. Sirinya noticed her grandmother's four brown chickens and her black cockerel with the red plume pecking around in front of the steps. As she drew closer she realised with a start that there was a still figure standing on the porch. She knew straight away it was Yai. She was gripping the wooden rail with one hand, shading her eyes with the other. She appeared to be waiting for somebody, peering intently down the track. When Sirinya got closer, Yai's body went rigid and she yelled out, as if terrified, 'It is you, Granddaughter, isn't it?'

'Yes. It's me, Sirinya. I thought you'd be resting.'

She reached the bottom of the steps and looked up at Yai and gasped at what she saw. Yai's cheeks were even more sunken than before, her blood-shot eyes stood out from her face and were staring down at Sirinya, filled with terror. She was thinner than Sirinya had ever seen her, her arms, blackened by the sun, looked like the bones of a skeleton, decaying with age.

'Can I come up, Yai?' Sirinya said, her voice quivering, afraid of the look in the old woman's eyes.

'I know what you're going to say,' Yai wailed, crumpling forward onto the rail, gasping for breath. 'I know what you're going to tell me.'

Sirinya leapt up the steps and caught Yai as she fell backwards. She was shocked at how light the old woman was - as light as a tiny bird - all bones and stretched, leathery skin. The two of them collapsed on to the porch. Sirinya gave into her emotions and let her tears fall, but the animal sounds that came from Yai were howls of grief and despair.

'I knew it. I knew it would happen,' Yai shouted hoarsely, spit flying from her mouth, 'I told you, didn't I, before you left, that if she went with you I would never see her again? But she wouldn't listen to me. Neither would you. She defied me. And look what has happened to her.'

* * *

The sun was beginning to dip behind the hills as the two of them made their slow and painful progress down through the jungle towards the road. Yai gripped Sirinya's arm tightly with sharp fingers, digging into her skin. She was frail and walked slowly, slipping and stumbling as she went. Sirinya remembered the way Kitima strode ahead of her the last time she had descended through the jungle, turning round and laughing over her shoulder. Again the tears fell as she felt the pain of her loss. As they passed near the railway cutting Sirinya noticed the sound of a hundred hammers ringing out as they chipped away at the limestone rock. She realised that she must have been oblivious to everything around her on the way up. She had not even heard them then. Now, the sound made her think of Charlie wielding a hammer at that other cutting at Chungkai down in the Khwae valley, sweat pouring from his thin body, his jaw clenched.

Chalong was waiting for them beside the lorry where the path met the rough road.

'What is that vehicle?' Yai demanded to know when she saw him. Sirinya exchanged looks with Chalong.

'Uncle uses it to deliver vegetables to the camps,' she explained. Yai pursed her lips and lifted her head up. 'It is not a Japanese vehicle is it? I will not travel in a Jap lorry. I would rather walk.'

Again Chalong and Sirinya looked at each other. 'No, Yai,' said Chalong slowly, his eyes on the road. 'The lorry is leased to me. You don't need to worry about that. Please, let me help you up.'

Yai sat bolt upright for the entire journey. They travelled in silence. Yai had hardly spoken about Kitima all the way down from the village. She had not even asked Sirinya how Kitima died or when. She seemed to know all that she needed to. As they crossed the river on the road bridge at Tambon Lat Ya, she turned to Sirinya and broke her silence.

'When this is over, when the funeral is done, you will come back with me to the village, Sirinya.' It was not a question.

'I'm sorry, Yai, but I am needed at the shop,' Sirinya said gently. 'Uncle needs me.'

Yai grunted. 'He needed my daughter too. But *I* need you now Sirinya, my girl. I need you to come back to the village and help me. The rice will be ready to harvest soon and I have nobody to help me now. Not now my daughter has been taken from me.'

Sirinya did not know how to respond. She glanced at Chalong who was staring fixedly ahead, eyes on the road, driving in silence.

As they entered the town, they passed two Japanese soldiers on patrol along the road by the river, rifles with bayonets slung over their shoulders. Yai leaned out of the lorry and as the lorry drew parallel with them spat at them through the open window. They turned and stared.

'Grandmother, there is no point ...'

'They killed my daughter. And they will kill you too if you stay, Siri.'

* * *

Yai clung to Piak when she first saw her, crying in great dry shrieks. Piak put her arms around Yai, patted her back and tried to sooth her. Eventually the crying subsided. 'Where is Malee?' Yai asked after a time, looking around.

'I am here, Grandmother,' Malee stepped forward. Sirinya looked at her, surprised. Malee had washed her hair, dressed in clean clothes. She looked so different now from the fresh-faced girl she had been before Somsak's death; she was noticeably thinner, her face was pale and her eyes puffy. Yai embraced her and held her for a long time. 'What has happened to you, Granddaughter? What has happened to all of us?'

The boys had carried Kitima's body upstairs to the apartment and she lay in the living room on a platform made out of vegetable crates and covered with a cloth. Her body was shrouded from neck to toe with a white sheet, but her right hand was draped over the sheet, and her head was exposed. Sirinya went to her and stared down at Kitima's still face. Despite the wound on her forehead she looked peaceful in death, serene even. 'Mother,' she breathed and the reality that Kitima was gone came back afresh.

Later that evening they performed the bathing rites for Kitima. Phraa Thongphroh came, bringing scented water with him from the temple. Everyone in the family approached Kitima's body in turn and poured a few drops of scented water over her hand. When it was Sirinya's turn, she took the gold jug the monk handed her and closed her eyes, tears oozing from them. She knew what she had to do; according to tradition, she must ask her mother for forgiveness for any wrongs she had done to her.

'Forgive me, Mother,' she said. 'Please forgive me. I was not a good daughter to you. I was away from you for a long time. I brought you here and I caused your death .... Please, please forgive me ...' She poured a little scented water from the jug onto Kitima's hand, then backed away. She felt the monk's cool hands on her arms.

'Don't blame yourself my child. Your mother was only doing what she thought right,' he said.

When it was Yai's turn to pour water and ask Kitima's soul for forgiveness, she clung to Kitima's stiff hand shaking and crying.

'Forgive me, Daughter. Forgive me,' she said in a high shrill voice, 'for I made you work too hard for me. I drove you away from the village - it was because of me you went. Please ...' she collapsed on the floor sobbing, dropping the jug, spilling the scented water.

After the ceremony they prepared Kitima's body for her funeral. Phraa Thongphroh placed a gold coin in her mouth, bound holy thread around her wrists and ankles. He put her hands together and placed a lotus flower between them and some sticks of incense, which he lit. Soon, the scent of incense filled the room and Kitima's body was shrouded in sweet-smelling smoke.

In the morning, Chalong rose early as usual to go down to the river to collect supplies from the barges.

'I'm sorry I have to do this today of all days, Siri,' said Chalong, hanging his head. 'But the boys would not be able to manage on their own.'

She watched him from her bedroom window as he walked slowly down the road in the grey light of dawn. Then she crept downstairs to the living room sit beside Kitima's body, to wait with her until the monks returned to perform their chanting for the day.

The room was still and quiet, and as she sat breathing in the sweet smell of incense, she tried to still her mind and focus her thoughts on Kitima. She thought about her mother's cheerful and optimistic nature, about the way she had embraced life with courage, about her constant warmth and her abundant generosity. Sirinya tried to quell the anger that threatened to rise up inside her against the Japanese. But try as she might, the pain and the bitterness kept returning, forcing out everything else in her mind dispelling all the positive thoughts, all the gratitude she had been trying to feel for her mother's love and life. Within a few minutes of sitting down she was clenching her fists, and her jaw, and her body was rigid with anger and hatred.

'Forgive me, Mother,' she breathed. There was a sound in the doorway and she turned to see Yai.

'I will sit with her, Siri, until the monks come, if you are finding it hard.'

Sirinya looked up at Yai whose face was twisted in pain. Sirinya moved to sit beside the window. Yai sat down beside the body and began rocking back and forth, moaning gently to herself. After a time she turned to Siri and said, 'You will come back to the village with me when I go, won't you Siri? Just for a little while, please?'

When Sirinya didn't respond, Yai went on, 'You don't have to stay forever, Siri. But I am frail. I have lost my only daughter. I need you with me for the time being. If only for a month or two.'

Sirinya looked out of the window. People were up and about now, setting up their stalls, opening up their houses. The bullock cart was coming up the road with Chalong sitting beside the driver on the front bench. Her eyes wandered across the road at the Kempeitai house. At that moment the front door opened and the officer who had questioned her emerged. She would recognise him anywhere. She watched him strut down the front path, his baton under his arm, spring on board the truck, while the driver held the door open for him. He settled himself down on the seat, his nose in the air. The engine roared into life.

'I'm sorry, Yai, I have to go outside,' she said on an impulse. She flew down the stairs, out of the shop and across the road. She stepped out into the road and in front of the truck, which was accelerating forward. The driver slammed on the brakes and the truck squealed to a halt centimetres from her.

'You're a murderer!' she yelled, banging the bonnet with her fist. My mother is dead because of you! She died yesterday and her body is upstairs in our house. You killed her in cold blood!'

'I know nothing about this, I have nothing to say to you. Go away,' said the officer, his eyes narrowed. He barked something in

Japanese at the driver.

'Why don't you admit it and say sorry?' Sirinya yelled, her face hot, sweat pouring from her body. 'She died because you beat her up in your filthy house. If it wasn't for you, she'd be alive now.'

'If you don't leave me alone I will be forced to take you in and lock you up,' said the officer. 'Now get off my car and let me go. I won't forget this. Be very careful from now on.'

She felt a sharp pain in her back and realised the driver was now behind her, with his rifle drawn. The bayonet was sticking into her.

'Now go home, or you will pay for this,' barked the officer.

Tears streaming down her face, she walked numbly back across the road to the shophouse, her head hanging. The bullock cart had stopped outside the shop and Chalong and the cart driver were watching her. She could feel the eyes of everyone in the street upon her. People had stopped what they were doing, come out of houses and shops to see what all the shouting was about. Even the bullocks had turned their heads towards her and were watching her with their doe eyes.

She hurried past the bullock cart towards the shop.

'Siri, wait,' Chalong jumped down from the cart and ran to her. 'Come here my child,' he said, holding out his arms. He held her to him.

'I'm so angry, Uncle.' she sobbed.

'I know. Come, let's go inside,' he said putting his arm around her shoulders and guiding her towards the shop.

'I'm sorry. I know I shouldn't have done that. If you are to carry on helping the prisoners, it is dangerous for me to anger the Kempeitai.'

'You are right to be angry. It was because of them that your mother died. We are all angry. Who wouldn't be? If you say the word

I will stop working for them. I can stop today if you want me to.'

'No … no, Uncle. You must carry on. Without your help many more prisoners will die. There is no choice.'

'If I do carry on, I think you should take a break. Take time to grieve for Kitima properly. Why don't you go back to the village with Yai for a few days after the funeral? It would be good for both of you. You need to get right away from here for a time.'

'I know Yai wants me to, Uncle. She keeps asking me to. But you need me here. Who would help in the shop? Who would swim across the moat with the medicines?'

What she couldn't tell her uncle was that she needed to be here to be near Charlie until he was taken away. There might at least be a chance of seeing him, of speaking to him before he went. If she went away with Yai she might never see him again. How could she bear that? The thought filled her with panic. In her grief she needed to be near him more than ever.

'Malee is much stronger now,' said Chalong. 'She can help out. And she's a good swimmer. She and Piak can take the medicines. They could go together.'

There were footsteps on the stairs and Yai's spindly feet and legs appeared. She walked unsteadily down and when she reached the bottom step she said, 'I heard what you were saying. Chalong is right, Sirinya. You need to get away from here and I need you. So let's hear no more about it. In two days' time, after the funeral, you will come with me back to the village.'

Sirinya felt trapped. 'I don't know,' she said. 'I'll think about it.'

She went upstairs leaving Yai and Chalong staring after her. She entered the apartment, where Piak and Malee were sitting in meditation beside Kitima's body alongside the four monks clad in saffron robes, their shaved heads bowed. Incense filled the room and the sound of low chanting blotted out the noise from the street. She took her place on the floor beside Malee and settled herself into the lotus position. She closed her eyes and tried to let the chanting still her mind, allow peace to enter her soul. It worked for a while, but soon her mind returned to her dilemma.

She knew she should take Chalong's advice and go with Yai to the village. What excuse could she make if they insisted? But how could she go and leave while Charlie was still here? She needed to speak to him, to tell him what he meant to her before he left. She needed to get him to reassure her that he would return to her one day. What if he were to die up the line without really knowing that she felt that way? The thought was unbearable, but she couldn't let it go. It went round and round in her mind.

The chanting of the monks seemed to reinforce her terrors, to elevate them into a nightmare trance. After a while the seed of an idea appeared in her mind. Perhaps there was a way to help Charlie after all? A way to ensure that he wasn't sent to an almost certain death, and a way to be with him. The seed only took a couple of seconds to start growing in her mind, and once it had started, it grew quickly, taking over all other thoughts, as rampant and strong and all-pervasive as the great thickets of bamboo by the river.

She got up, bowed to the monks and left the room. She went back downstairs to where Chalong and the boys were loading the baskets and Yai sat on an upturned box watching them.

She said, 'Uncle, Yai, I've made a decision.' Chalong stopped working and looked at her.

'Go on, Niece,' he said

'I will go back to the village and help with the rice harvest. But there is something I'd like your help with if I do ...'

25

Later, Sirinya went up to her room on the top floor, rummaged in a drawer and found a pencil and paper. It didn't seem possible that only a day had passed since she had read Charlie's letter to her. How much had changed in those twenty-four hours. Things had felt bad then, but how much worse she felt now. She leaned on the windowsill and wrote. She wrote quickly. The lorry would be here soon and she must hide the letter in the wickerwork of the basket of cabbages before it arrived.

My Dearest Charlie

If I could speak to you I would, but there is no other way of telling you this. My mother is dead. She died yesterday morning of fever brought on by her brutal treatment by the Kempeitai. I need to go away from here. After mother's funeral I will go to my grandmother's village in the hills.

I want you to come with me, Charlie. It is safe there. The villagers are our friends. I cannot bear the thought of you being transported up into the hills to work on the railway in even worse conditions. You must escape before it is too late. I have spoken to my grandmother and she has agreed to hide you in the pig pen under her house for a few days while I help her with the harvest. If you think it safer, though, you could hide somewhere in the jungle nearby. When the harvest is over we could try to make it through the hills to Burma together. We can hide there in the area controlled by the hill tribes.

It is not too far and I know how to survive. I know the jungle paths from my childhood. You would have a chance of getting through with me by your side.

I know security in the camp is tight now, but in a day or two when things ease up, you could slip out of the camp just like you did before. I will meet you where we met before on the Bamboo Road. I know it could be risky, but it is the one way we could be together. I can't let them take you up the line. It is too dangerous for you there. As you say, many men have already died. This is your chance of freedom.

Please think about this, Charlie, for my sake and for your own. I know it is dangerous for me to write you like this, so please destroy this. If you agree to this plan, drop me a note just as you did before.

While I am writing I must also pass a message from my uncle to the British officers. He will visit the V Organisation in Bangkok next Sunday and communicate the information in your letter to them. We should be able to send the medicines they requested into the camp in the usual way on Monday evening.

I will wait for your letter, and hope fervently that you will agree to my plan,

Your ever loving,

Sirinya

She folded it quickly and hurried down the stairs to the shop. Chalong was out on the road with the shop boys loading supplies onto his truck for delivery to the outer camps. She noticed him glance at her with anxious eyes.

Sirinya waited until Chalong had set off. The boys were outside on the pavement, waiting for the lorry to arrive from Chungkai. She could see the smoke from their cigarettes. She made her way to the front of the shop, moved between the loaded baskets and quickly found the first one filled with cabbages. Her heart pounded as she slipped the note inside the wickerwork near the rim of the basket and settled a cabbage over it. As she turned round a chill went through her. Yai was sitting in the doorway of the storeroom on a box, watching with her beady eyes.

'So you've decided to go ahead with your crazy plan then?' said Yai. Sirinya stopped.

'You agreed, Grandmother,' she said, trying to keep the frustration from her voice. 'You said that it would be alright. We discussed it with Uncle.'

'Because I was afraid you wouldn't come back to the village otherwise. Sirinya, please think carefully about what you are about to do. Hiding an escaped prisoner could get us all killed. Me, you, and the whole village too.'

'Please, Grandmother. I know what I'm doing. No one knows where you live. The Japanese think our relatives live a village along the river near Chungkai. They have no way of connecting me to your village. The Kempeitai don't even know it exists.'

Yai was silent, rocking back and forth, her hands around her bony knees, working her mouth. At last with a great sigh she said, 'Alright, Sirinya. Have it your own way. I don't want to lose a granddaughter as well as a daughter, I will not stand in your way.'

'Thank you. I know how hard it is for you, Grandmother. I know what a sacrifice it is for you and I'm very grateful for that.'

'So, tell me your plan again? You would like me to go back to the village as soon as Kitima's funeral is over. Is that what you said?'

'Yes, Grandmother,' Sirinya said, relieved. 'Uncle will take you back in the lorry. I will follow you on foot as soon as it is possible for Charlie to get away. I don't know what day that will be, but it will be soon.'

Yai was silent for a few moments, rocking back and forth on her box.

'He might not want to do it, your British soldier. Have you thought of that?' she said in a sharp voice, her head tilted on one side.

Sirinya hung her head. 'He might not, but I hope he will.'

There was the sound of movement in the shop. Sirinya had not heard the lorry coming, perhaps the boys had finished their cigarettes and come inside to wait. She looked around in surprise. Ratana stood in the doorway. She was holding a bunch of lotus flowers. She was dressed simply in a dark sarong and pale silk blouse. She wore little makeup and her hair was up, done in the Thai style. She stepped forward, and put her hands together in a wai to Sirinya, then she turned and performed the deepest and most respectful wai to Yai

'I am so sorry for your loss,' she said. 'I have brought these flowers for Kitima. Could I see her and pay my respects?'

'Of course,' said Sirinya. 'Go on upstairs, please. The monks are there performing the chanting. Malee and Aunt are there too. You can join them.'

Ratana turned towards the stairs and Sirinya said, 'And Ratana. Thank you. Thank you for coming.'

Ratana smiled, bowed slightly and went on up the stairs.

When the lorry came Sirinya stood back beside the wall of the shop, watching, holding her breath, hoping against hope that Charlie would be there. She had not given too much thought what might happen to the letter if he wasn't.

The guards went to the back of the lorry and barked orders to the prisoners. First Johnny got down, then the colonel. Sirinya had the sudden urge to rush to the basket and retrieve the letter, but at this stage that would be risky too. She held her nerve and Charlie appeared from the back of the truck. Her heart leapt and heat flooded her cheeks.

The three men came towards the shop, the guards behind them, bayonets drawn. Johnny smiled shyly and lowered his eyes as he saw her, the colonel nodded politely, and Charlie's face lit up in a broad smile. He held her gaze for a split second as he walked past. She raised one eyebrow and inclined her head slightly. He made for the first basket loaded with cabbages. With a thumping heart, she watched him pick it up, and as he did so he passed his hand quickly around inside. After a second he swung the basket onto his shoulders and made for the lorry. Sirinya was barely able to watch him. As he walked she saw his right hand fumbled briefly with his Jap-Happy, as if hitching it up around his hip bones. She breathed again. He had got the letter.

* * *

Dawn was breaking as she clambered out of the rowing boat and thanked Phichai for taking her. He had barely acknowledged her presence as he had rowed her across the river, making her lie down in the bottom of the boat. Now he nodded a brief goodbye. He seemed anxious to push off, to get back to his rice fields and put some distance between them.

It was four days after she'd slipped the letter into the basket of cabbages, three days since her mother's funeral, and three days too since Charlie had dropped another tightly folded letter on the floor of the shop. She had opened it with trepidation, and nerves and excitement raced through her veins as she read it. He had written that he agreed to her plan, that is was his only chance to get away and to survive, that he would come with her as soon as patrols of the camp boundaries had relaxed.

She pushed her way through the swampy reeds on the bank and then through the great clumps of bamboo. Finally she was through them and out on the Bamboo Road. She turned left along the riverbank and walked in the direction of Chungkai. It didn't take long to find the spot where Charlie had stepped out onto the path in front of her three long weeks ago. Her hand went automatically to her throat to feel for the cool jade butterfly, and she felt the familiar disappointment when she remembered that of course it was not there.

She found a small clearing between two clumps of bamboo just off the path, took her spare sarong from her bag, spread it out and sat down on it. She had brought enough water and food in her pack for the day's walk to the village. Without a vehicle to take her and Charlie, and because they would need to walk on remote footpaths hidden from view, the journey would take until well after nightfall.

Charlie's last letter, the one he had dropped on the floor of the shop the day before had said that he would slip out of the camp straight after roll call in the morning.

'*This should give us at least twenty-four hours before there is any chance of discovery. I've spoken to Colonel Bell and he and the other officers have agreed to say I'm in the hospital hut, sick. But they won't be able to keep that up for more than a couple of days. By that time though, we will be well on our way.*'

She pictured herself with him now, making their way through the jungle together, trekking side by side through the hills towards the Burmese border.

Sirinya sat quietly, as the sun rose slowly in the sky and the world around her gradually awoke. She strained her ears for any sounds from the camp just along the river, but here she was not close enough. All she could hear was the rush of the water, the familiar voice of the Khwae, the chatter of the crickets in the bamboo and the call of the jungle birds. Her heart, already full of sadness from the loss of Kitima and the emotion of the funeral, was now heavier still after saying goodbye to Malee, Piak and Chalong. They had clung to her, and kissed her with tears in their eyes as she set off from the back door of the shop this morning. Words had been inadequate to convey what they were all feeling, but their anguished looks had spoken of their love, of their fears for her and their wishes that she would be safe. As she tore herself from them and slipped down the back alley towards the river she felt a deep emptiness she had never known in her life before.

Sirinya thought of Kitima's funeral, and wiped away a tear. She remembered how the house had been filled with mourners who had come to pay their respects to Kitima. They had all joined the family and the monks as they followed the coffin on its procession through the streets of the town and down to the temple beside the river. The dreadful moment had finally come when she had thrown her sandalwood flower onto the pile of wood shavings beneath the coffin and Phraa Thongphroh lit the pile with a taper. She had hardly been able to watch the fire. Through her tears she had said a final good bye to Kitima as the flames leapt around the coffin, 'Thank you, Mother, for everything you've done for me. For your love and your support, and for giving me life and strength.'

Although Kitima had gone from the world Sirinya could still feel her presence beside her, hear her voice inside her head. 'You're with me now, aren't you, Mother?' she whispered into the silence. And in her head she heard the familiar warm voice, 'Of course I'm here, Siri. Do you think I'd leave you when you need me most? Now be careful and be strong. You are a born survivor, but the risks you are taking today will test that to the limit.'

It shouldn't be long now before she heard his footsteps. She stood up and stretched, her knees were stiff. She walked a little way along the path, half expecting him to appear around the next bend, but all was still and silent. There was no breeze, no rustling of leaves; the huge bamboos that lined the path were poised motionless as if they were watching her, as if they were waiting too.

It must be after roll call now. She returned to her clearing and took a sip of water from her can. Charlie would be here soon she told herself. She imagined how he would take her in his arms, how they would embrace quickly before they began their long walk along the river and through the jungle. Time passed slowly and there was no sound of footsteps, no rustling of bamboo. Once or twice she heard boats chug past on the river, the lapping of water against the banks, the shouts of fishermen. After a few hours her stomach began to grumble. She got out the tin of fried rice that Piak had packed for her this morning and took off the lid. But the smell that rose from it made her feel nauseous. She replaced the lid and slipped it back into her bag. How could she eat without sharing it with him?

For a long time she sat there waiting for the sound of his footsteps, for his head to appear between the thickets of bamboo. She watched the sun mark the passing of the hours as it moved across the sky. Gradually, as the hours passed, the hopes of the morning began to slip away from her. Shivers of fear and dread went through her as she allowed herself to contemplate what might have happened to Charlie. Had he been discovered slipping out of the camp? He had assured her that it was safe to slip out now, that the men were allowed to go down to the river to bathe, that the guards no longer patrolled the boundary. Could it be that he'd decided he could not go through with it after all? She shook her head silently, swallowing back the tears. She could not believe that. But wherever was he then? Why hadn't he come?

As the sun began to drop behind the trees she stood up and dusted herself down. Her thoughts were scrambled. She was panicking, not thinking clearly but she knew there was no point staying here. The longer she stayed the more danger she could be in.

Should she give up and go back to the shophouse? She remembered her uncle's parting words: 'Sirinya, promise me you'll come back here if things go wrong. If anything happens ...'

'I can't do that, Uncle. It might bring danger on you and the family. It would be better if I just disappeared,' she had said, not seriously believing that she would ever have to face that choice.

'No, Siri. You mustn't consider that. Please come back here if you are in trouble.'

Tears blinding her eyes she stumbled along the Bamboo Road towards the crossing at Tha Maa Kham. Her legs felt weak and her body exhausted. The path seemed longer than ever before. The old boat keeper might look at her suspiciously, ask her awkward questions but she had no choice. She would have to ask him to take her.

As she neared the end of the path, where it met the road beside the crossing, the great steel railway bridge loomed up in front of her. It was almost finished now, and only one section of it had bamboo scaffolding around the pillars. She was about to step out onto the road when she heard voices. She stopped and listened, her mouth dry. They were Japanese voices. She moved closer, taking care to keep hidden by the undergrowth.

Her heart froze at what she saw. A group of Thai men, villagers and farmers were lined up against a fence near the bridge. Japanese soldiers were standing in front of them with bayonets. She held her breath and listened. What she heard chilled her to the core.

'You know prisoner who plan escape, don't you?' barked one of the soldiers, an officer. 'He had a Thai contact. You know who it is and you must tell us. You live next to camp. It must be someone in your village.'

There were muffled protests and denials from the Thais. Sirinya watched paralysed. What if these innocent men were hurt? It would be her fault. Should she step forward? Should she admit her involvement and save these men? She knew it would be the right thing to do, but she couldn't bring herself to step out of the undergrowth. Instead she waited and watched, trembling in fear, her heart thumping. The officers paced in front of the men, asking the same questions again and again, sometimes prodding the men with bayonets, sometimes yelling at them. The questioning went on and on, getting nowhere.

But as it began to grow dark, the officer suddenly stopped his questioning. He barked at the men ' I know now it is not you. You can go now. Go!'

The men looked at each other, relief and amazement on their faces. Then they fled along the road, back towards their village, their footsteps scuffling on the dusty road.

Sirinya knew she must get away quickly. There was only one way to run. She turned around and rushed back along the Bamboo Road. She knew she was not safe here; the Japanese were bound to discover the path and search the length of it before too long. She ran blindly, branches and leaves brushing against her face, bamboo canes barring her way, tripping her up, tearing at her clothes. Her breath was coming in gulps and sobs. She spotted a narrower path that branched off the main one running beside the river. She turned off the Bamboo Road and plunged onto the narrow path, walking away from the river into the jungle. She walked for several kilometres, taking branch after branch of the maze of little paths, losing track of where she was.

All the time her mind was racing. Where should she go, what should she do? She knew she couldn't go back to the shophouse now. If she stayed away, at least there was a chance that Chalong and the others could say she had run away and they didn't know where she had gone. If Charlie had been caught the Japanese probably knew about her involvement. Should she go on and try to make it to Yai's village? But again came the thought that if she went to the village she might one day be discovered there. That would put Yai and the rest of the village in danger.

It was long into the evening when, sweating and exhausted, she stepped out onto a metalled road. She walked along it for a couple of kilometres slowly and painfully, tears blinding her eyes, not knowing where to go, what do to. After she'd been on the road an hour or so headlights loomed. She heard a throaty engine coming closer and a truck drew level with her. She no longer cared if it was a Japanese truck. They could take her in and beat her to death. She no longer had the will to resist.

The truck stopped and the driver leaned out. He was Thai. His face was friendly He smiled at her. 'Are you alright?' he asked. His voice sounded full of genuine concern. 'Do you need a lift?'

She stared at him. 'There are a lot of Japs about,' he said, 'it might not be safe to be on the road alone.'

'Where are you going?' she asked.

'I'm going to Bangkok. I have to make a delivery,' he said, 'but I can drop you somewhere else along the way if you like.'

Without hesitation she asked, 'Will you take me all the way to Bangkok?'

'Of course, hop in.'

She got up into the front seat beside the driver and they set off into the night. They drove without speaking for a while. The driver didn't ask her any questions and she was grateful for his silence. After a few kilometres she turned to him and asked weakly, 'Do you know why there are so many Japanese soldiers around tonight?'

'Another escape attempt from Chungkai apparently. Just one man this time. The Japs got him though.'

The hairs on her scalp stood on end.

'How do you know that?' her voice shook, she could barely utter the question.

'They've been questioning people in my village. Said they'd caught the prisoner and he'd already been executed. Beheaded apparently, poor fellow. With one of their samurai swords.'

She couldn't reply. The horror of the man's words hit home to her and she was shaking from head to foot, shaking and sobbing, tears flowing down her cheeks. But even in her despair she knew she shouldn't let the man see her distress. Anyone could give her away to the Japanese, even this kindly driver. To stop her sobs she bit her lip so hard she could taste the blood.

The man shook his head and clicked his tongue against his teeth. 'Dreadful isn't it? They are a brutal bunch.'

26

Sirinya stares out of the car window at the landscape either side of the long straight road. The coastal plane is flat, rice fields and scrubland stretch as far as the eye can see on either side. Occasionally the road passes through a settlement where wooden shops and food stalls have been thrown up dangerously close to the speeding traffic. She glances at Kasem. She has been talking since they left the city behind. She has been telling him about the war, about what happened to her and her family; about the V Organisation, and about Charlie. Kasem has not spoken for a long time. He has been concentrating on the road ahead, letting her talk. She could tell he was listening though, from the way he shook his head at some of the things she described, or exclaimed in disbelief.

She'd telephoned his shop this morning from the hotel, shamefaced at the way she had left him so abruptly in Patpong last night. She spent a restless night, sweating under the ceiling fan as it churned the heavy air, disturbed by the comings and goings of the GIs and their dates on her corridor. She was thinking about the past, and wondering why she'd been so curt with Kasem. He was only trying to be kind to her, after all. Why not take him up on the offer to drive her to Pattaya? She had come this far in her quest to find Ratana, why not see if she had gone to Pattaya there as the bar owner had suggested.

Kasem sounded pleased to hear her voice when she called the number on his business card. He accepted her apology, and quickly agreed to drive her to Pattaya. He collected her from the Golden Key in his friend's battered Datsun taxi within an hour of her call.

'How much further to Pattaya?' she asks now. He clears his throat. 'Oh, another hour or so I suppose. This old car can't go very fast. Would you like to stop for lunch somewhere? The petrol is getting a bit low.'

'Whatever's best for you,' she says, not wanting to impose on him any more than she has already.

He pulls up at a roadside fuel-stop, where a skinny boy pumps petrol into the car by hand. They leave the car beside the pump and walk a few paces to a food stall. It is sheltered from the road. They both order tom yum gung and iced tea.

As they sit sipping their drinks waiting for the soup to arrive, Kasem says, looking into her eyes, his brow furrowed, 'Your story is shocking, Sirinya. Things happened back then that it's hard to forget. I understand now why you need to see Ratana. But ... I was wondering, when you were telling me what happened, do you think seeing her will really make any difference?'

She stiffens, 'Of course it will make a difference. How can you doubt that? I need to confront her, to tell her that I know she betrayed us. That she is responsible for Charlie's death. She needs to know.'

'Are you sure you've thought it through properly? '

'Of course. She overheard me talking to Yai when she came to pay respects to my mother's body. She must have heard me talking about my plan to meet Charlie. It makes me so angry even talking about it. How can she have done that? How can she have come to the funeral, pretended to care for us when all the time she was a traitor, betraying us to her lovers, those Kempeitai murderers.'

'Have you ever considered that it might not have been Ratana?' he asks gently, 'that it could have been someone else in the camp who betrayed Charlie? He must have told people what he was planning. You said that he told the officers, after all.'

She turns to him her eyes full of angry tears, 'Don't you think I've thought of everything? I've been thinking about it for twenty-five years. The prisoners wouldn't have betrayed their own comrades, what would have been in it for them?'

He shakes his head, 'I'm not sure. I'm just thinking about what might have happened. If it was Ratana, why didn't she tell them that you and Charlie were planning to meet on the Bamboo Road? If she had told them that, they would surely have come looking for you too.'

Sirinya shrugs. 'Maybe she thought the people in the town would turn against her if she betrayed a Thai. She was unpopular enough already for consorting with the Japs.' She looks into his eyes, he looks unconvinced.

'I don't know, Kasem,' she says impatiently, 'I haven't got all the answers. I just know I need to see her, to satisfy myself that I have confronted her. I need to do it for Charlie's sake.'

They are silent for a while. Sirinya watches a group of tiny children playing catch on a piece of waste-ground behind the row of tin huts. They squeal with laughter, their bare chests covered in dirt.

'I just think you should be careful. I know you think you're sure, but, well, when our mind starts running away with an idea, sometimes we don't think very clearly.'

'Think clearly? I have thought clearly,' she says, irritated. 'I've had all the time in the world to think about it.'

The soup arrives, and Kasem eats hungrily, but Sirinya turns the steaming liquid over with her spoon. She has no appetite now.

'I don't expect you to understand,' she says. 'You couldn't if you haven't been through what I've been through.'

He pauses before taking another mouthful and looks up at her.

'No, I suppose you're right.'

'Why did you offer to drive me if you don't think it's the right thing to do?'

'I just want to help you, Sirinya. When I met you on the train, you seemed a little lost, and when I saw you again in Chinatown yesterday, you seemed alone there too. You had no one to help you.'

She swallows a lump in her throat and stifles the urge to tell him that she doesn't need his pity, that she can manage alone. It would be difficult though, she reasons, if he left her here to find her own way to Pattaya.

They leave the fuel-stop and drive eastwards in silence. It takes less than an hour and the road runs close to the sea for the last few kilometres. The surface is poor, potholed and unmade in places and Kasem has to drive slowly. Sirinya leans out of the car window, gazes out across the Bay of Bangkok and breathes in the sea breeze on the warm air. How beautiful the ocean is here; bright blue and shimmering in the sun. It is so different from the heaving grey waters she remembers from days out in Brighton, where the sea sucked on a pebble beach and seagulls wheeled and cawed mournfully above.

They draw into the town, a long strip of concrete buildings along the seafront, spreading untidily back from the sea in a chaotic jumble of tracks and half-built structures. Building work is going on everywhere around. Bars and guesthouses are being thrown up hastily. Everyone here is cashing in on the need for American servicemen to let off steam on their breaks from the frontline in Vietnam.

Kasem drives slowly along the length of the strip and right out to where the buildings peter out on the other side. Sirinya stares out of the window in dismay. In places it resembles the New Petchburi

Road, or Patpong. Strip clubs and girlie bars vie for attention with their flashing neon signs and brash exteriors. Young girls dressed in bikinis hang around on the pavement, shouting boldly at passers-by. Most of the customers appear to be young western men, hanging about in groups, dressed in shorts and T-shirts, their close-cropped hair showing they are off-duty soldiers. In between the bars though, Sirinya can see that this place was until quite recently a simple Thai fishing village. Opposite the buildings, beyond the line of thatched beach umbrellas, long-tailed boats are pulled up on the white sand, fisherman selling their catch straight from the boats. The new buildings are interspersed with fishermen's huts and old wooden houses.

'How am I ever going to find her here?' Sirinya says.

'Let's check into one of the guesthouses and ask around,' says Kasem.

He drives up and down the strip again a couple of times, and they settle on a small guesthouse opposite the beach that looks clean and cheap. Once they have checked in and left their bags, they wander along the road, past shops, bars and cafés. It is late afternoon now and getting busier, Sirinya finds herself dodging people on the pavement. Rickshaws, and songthaews line the beachfront, motorbikes roar past on the road.

Each time they pass a bar, the girls call to Kasem. 'You so handsome, you want to join us? We give you good time.'

Sirinya steals a glance at Kasem. He doesn't look in the least bit perturbed, he just carries on, smiling calmly, nodding a polite hello to everyone who tries to get his attention.

'This is hopeless,' Sirinya says after a while. 'It's busier than Patpong here. How will we ever find her?'

'Be patient, Sirinya. We will find a way. Let's stop for a drink at this bar here, see what we can find out.'

They step off the pavement into an open-air bar, and sit up on high barstools. Kasem orders two beers and chats to the barman, a young man with bulging muscles.

'Where would I go if I wanted to set up a business here?' he asks. The barman shrugs. 'What sort of business?'

'A girlie bar.'

'Everyone asks the same question. You need to find somewhere to rent, or a vacant lot where you can build. It's expensive though. I can put you in touch with someone who might be able to help you,' he says, polishing glasses with a cloth.

'It's not for me. My friend here is looking for someone we think might have come here a few days ago to set up in business.'

'Like I said, everyone is at it,' he shrugs. 'What's her name?'

'We think she goes by the name of Jo-Jo. Here's a picture of her.'

Kasem pushed the *Bangkok Messenger* across the bar and the barman peers at it.

'Never seen her, I'm afraid. You're not cops are you?'

'Of course not,' says Sirinya. 'She's a friend from a long time ago.'

The barman shrugs and turns to serve another customer.

'Come on,' says Kasem, 'Drink up. If she's here, we're bound to find someone who has seen her. There aren't that many bars here, it's not like Bangkok. Let's go to the next one along.'

To Sirinya it feels just like the recent nights she spent in New Petchburi road, going from bar to bar with the old school photograph of Ratana. The task is daunting, only this time she doesn't feel quite so self-conscious or so alone.

'I don't think I can possibly drink a beer at every place we go to,' she says to Kasem as they clamber onto barstools at the next bar.

He smiles, 'I don't think I can either! Why don't you have a fruit juice or a soda?'

They have been to four or five places, when they sit down at another girlie bar. Scantily dressed girls hang about around the entrance. The man behind the bar eyes the picture and says, 'I think I know her. She might have been in here yesterday asking for work. She's not called Jo-Jo though. I remember that much.'

'Do you remember her name?'

The barman shouts over his shoulder and a girl appears. He pushes the newspaper towards her. 'Remember her? She came yesterday looking for a job. Did she tell you her name?'

The girl shook her head, 'No, I'm afraid not.'

'So you didn't offer her work, then?' asks Kasem.

'No. She didn't seem quite right for us,' said the man

'Why was that?'

'She was drunk for one thing,' said the barman. 'For another thing we're looking for young women. As young as possible. And to tell you the truth she looked like trouble.'

'Do you happen to know where she is staying?'

The barman shakes his head. 'We wouldn't have taken her address if we didn't want to offer her work. Why don't you try asking in the rest of the bars along here? If she came in here, she probably went into them all.'

They spend the next two hours going from bar to bar, as the sun goes down, streaking the sea and sky all shades of red and orange, and the thumping music is ramped up louder and louder. Again Sirinya thinks of her recent trips around New Petchburi. She thinks how young the girls look who drape themselves around the foreign soldiers, plying them with drinks and flattery. With a shudder she remembers those months at the end of the war that she herself spent working in backstreet bars in Bangkok.

In the last bar along the strip, the woman behind the bar looks closely at the picture.

'I remember her, yes. She came in yesterday asking for work.'

'Is she coming back?'

The woman shook her head, pushing the paper back. 'We haven't got anything at the moment.'

'Do you know where she might be staying?'

'She might have left an address in case any work came up. I'll go and check with the boss.'

The woman disappears for a few minutes, then returns with a piece of paper. 'Here we are,' she says, ' ... the Nimbus guesthouse.'

Sirinya has slid off her barstool and is already waiting for Kasem as he pays the bill.

'I know where the Nimbus is,' she says, 'I saw it as we drove into the town. It's that shabby place on the edge of town on the road in. One of the first you come to.'

They take a tuk-tuk along the seafront. It is dark now and the whole place is ablaze with flashing neon signs, their garish colours reflecting in the sea. The Nimbus is above a massage shop in a brand new concrete terrace on the edge of town. Kasem asks the tuk-tuk driver to wait.

'Do you want me to come up with you?' he asks.

Sirinya shakes her head. 'Why don't you go back to our guesthouse? I can make my own way back later.'

'Shall I wait here with the tuk-tuk for a few minutes? She might not be there.'

'Alright,' she says reluctantly, 'Wait here for ten minutes. If I don't come down it means I'm talking to Ratana.'

She finds the entrance which leads to some concrete stairs beside the shop. She climbs to the first floor. The place smells of drains and stale cooking. A grey-haired man watches TV behind the front desk. He seems irritated that he has to tear his attention away from it to speak to her. He stubs out a cigarette and looks at her expectantly. He is sweating, dressed only in a string vest. There is only one sluggish ceiling fan turning above him.

'I'm looking for a friend,' she begins, her voice trembling, aware that in a few minutes, she could be face to face with Ratana. 'I think she is staying here. I've a picture of her.' She shows him the newspaper. The man glances at it and his face clouds over.

'I would think twice about who your friends are,' he says, glaring at her. 'I caught her stealing from my till this morning. She's in the police station now. If you want to take her things to her, be my guest.'

Sirinya stares open-mouthed at him. He picks up a mock leather shopping bag and dumps it on to the counter. The zip is broken and clothes and shoes are spilling out of the top.

'I ... I don't know.'

'I thought you said were her friend. I don't want to see her here again, so if you don't take this stuff, I'm going to throw it away.'

'Alright, I'll take it to her. Where is the police station?'

He gives her directions. As she retreats down the stairs, carrying the bag, she has to press herself against the wall to make way for a young girl coming up, dressed in a mini skirt and towering heels, arm in arm with an American soldier.

Kasem is waiting in the back of the tuk-tuk. She tells him what has happened. 'I'll go to see her on my own, Kasem. You don't need to come with me,' she says.

'I won't hear of it. You can't go to the police station by yourself. It's getting late. Come on, hop in.'

She gets into back of the tuk-tuk and holds Ratana's bag on her lap. She notices the smell of cheap perfume and cigarettes wafting from the bag as they buzz along the seafront, bumping through the ruts and potholes, swerving off the main drag onto a side road. The driver comes to a halt in front of a small single-story concrete building.

The policeman at the desk eyes them with suspicion as Sirinya explains who they have come to see.

'She's the only one in the cells at the moment,' he says. 'She'll be glad to see you.' He takes the bag from Sirinya and gives it a cursory search, holding up a stiletto heeled shoe and examining it, taking out a pink lace nightdress and shaking it. Then he takes the bag and beckons Sirinya to follow him.

'I'll wait here for you,' said Kasem, sitting down on a plastic chair beside the counter. 'Take your time.'

The police station is very small. It still smells of new concrete and plaster. The only cell is down a narrow passage next to the desk. Sirinya follows the policemen, her heart in her mouth. There is no time to think properly, her mind scrambles with nerves. Then the policeman steps through a doorway and the cell is in front of them. It is a cage, floor to ceiling bars lit with harsh striplights. At first she thinks there is nobody in there, then she notices a figure huddled in the opposite corner. She cannot see the person's face, just long untidy hair, tumbling over a shabby red dress. A tremor of anticipation mingled with dread passes through her.

'Stand up. You have a visitor,' barks the officer.

There is movement from the corner and the woman turns her face towards them. Sirinya grasps the bars of the cell to steady herself. It is her. It is Ratana. There is no mistaking the shape of that face. And the eyes, though bloodshot and smudged with black mascara still look the same.

Ratana gets up slowly. She is barefoot, and her dress is torn and smeared with dirt. She approaches the bars. The officer opens the cage door and throws the bag inside. 'Your belongings,' he says. Then he locks the bars again and leaves the room. They are alone.

Ratana peers at Sirinya. Her eyes are sunken, expressionless, her skin is dull and her makeup is smudged around her eyes and down her cheeks. 'Who are you?' she asks, frowning. 'Do I know you?'

'It's me, Ratana. It's Sirinya.'

'Sirinya?' she peers again.

'Yes. From Kanchanaburi. We were at school together.' Her heart is beating hard now. It is difficult to form any words. Her mouth is dry.

There is a long silence. 'Yes. Yes, I remember you. You went away. It's coming back to me now,' her voice is thick and gravelly. She leans forward to look closer. Sirinya smells her rancid breath. 'Why have you come? After all these years? And why here, to this hellhole?'

Anger and emotion threaten to overwhelm Sirinya. She doesn't know where to begin. She swallows hard and draws herself up.

'You betrayed me. That's why I've come,' her voice is shaking. The words sound over-dramatic, echoing against the cell walls.

Ratana frowns. 'Betrayed you? What do you mean?'

'You know what I mean. You betrayed me to the Kempeitai.'

Ratana frowns. 'I don't know what on earth you're talking about.'

'You know very well,' Sirinya says in a low voice trying to keep her temper from surfacing. 'You came to my uncle's shop that day. The day I told my grandmother about my plans to meet my British friend, Charlie. You overheard me telling her and you told your friends, the Kempeitai.'

Sirinya watches Ratana's face. Ratana is still frowning. She shakes her head slowly.

'Of course I didn't. Why would I do that?'

'They were your friends. You did it to get money …'

'The Kempeitai were not my friends!' Ratana says, with sudden force. 'I hated them. I hated myself. I did it for money, yes, but I would never have betrayed you. I would never have betrayed anyone to them.'

'I thought you might deny it. Anyone would. But the whole town knew you were a traitor.'

Ratana purses her lips, her chin puckers as if she is about to cry. She closes her eyes and steadies herself, gripping the bars of the cell with both hands, her knuckles white. Then she opens her eyes.

'Don't I know that? Haven't I paid for it? I tried to rebuild my life after the war. I met someone. We were happy for a few years, but there were people who couldn't forgive me for what I did back then. I got death threats, Sirinya, I got spat at in the street. We were thinking of moving away, then one day it was too late. They burned my house down. My old mother and my husband died in that fire. Don't you think I've paid for what I did during the war?'

Sirinya drops her gaze. 'I know about the fire. I was very sorry to hear that.'

'And here you come accusing me of treachery. When all I was was your friend.'

Sirinya thinks of all the years she has envisaged this moment, the words she would say, the feelings she would experience. She imagined that a great weight would lift from her shoulders, that Ratana would crumble and confess everything. She never imagined this. Panic seizes her. She realises that she must get Ratana to admit to what she did, otherwise she has wasted all these years of bitterness and hatred, all these hours she has spent thinking about it.

'It must have been you,' Sirinya says, raising her voice. 'You were the only one who knew. And you were with the Kempeitai every day. Don't tell me you didn't overhear what I said to Yai that day.'

'I heard you. Of course I heard you. But why would I tell the Japs about that? It was the day I came to pay your mother my last respects. Don't you realise that I was using the Kempeitai, Sirinya, just like your uncle used them. I hated them as much as he did. As much as everyone did. Don't you understand that?'

'So you kept the information to yourself and you didn't tell anyone? I find that hard to believe. You must have told them. It must have been you.'

'Why would I do that? Why would I betray you? I would tell you if I had. I would tell you here and now. My life is finished, Siri. You can see what I've become. I'm too old to sell my body now, so I have to live from hand to mouth. I have to live by selling others if I can, young women who are desirable and wanted by men. But that is precarious too, and dangerous. I had to come here to Pattaya because I owed money in Bangkok. Men were after me for that. They still are. Gangsters, pimps, members of the triads ...'

She leans forward, thrusting her face closer to Sirinya's and as she does so, a chain round her neck swings free from her dress. In a flash she tucks it back inside her neckline, but not before Sirinya has seen it. She gasps. She would recognise it anywhere. It is her very own butterfly. The jade butterfly that Charlie gave her on the Bamboo Road, and which the guard with the hard black eyes had snatched from her at the Kempeitai house.

'Where did you get that from?'

'I've had it since the war. One of the Japs gave it to me. I thought about throwing it away, I didn't want to be reminded of them, of that time, but it's pretty, so I kept it.'

'It was mine! They stole it from round my neck when they took me in to beat me up when they found the radio in the camp.'

Ratana's face falls. 'I had no idea, Siri. Really. You have to believe me. Are you sure it was yours?'

'Of course. I'd know it anywhere. Charlie gave it to me.'

There is a silence. Then Ratana says quietly. 'I'm so sorry, Siri. Do you want it back?'

She takes off the charm and hands it to Sirinya through the bars. Slowly, Sirinya takes it from her. Their hands touch momentarily. 'Thank you,' Sirinya mutters, dropping her gaze. She is confused now. She never imagined that she would accept something from Ratana, but then she never considered that Ratana would have this precious reminder of Charlie. She feels her anger surfacing again at the thought of him, of what he'd suffered. She can't leave it like this, give up on him this easily. How can she let Ratana get away with it? How can she be manipulated like this?

'I still don't believe you, Ratana. And I feel sorry for you. You'll have this on your conscience for ever. You betrayed us. You caused a man's death all those years ago. And now you've got a chance to admit it to me, but you still refuse to do that. Shame on you.'

Ratana looks into her eyes, a pleading look now.

'Siri, I'm so sad that you feel that way. I couldn't believe what happened to your Englishman when we heard the rumours. But I've suffered too. I've suffered ever since for what I did during the war. I did it because we were poor, and because it was easy. But I wasn't evil. I wasn't a bad person. I would never have betrayed you. We were friends once.'

'If you're not going to admit to it, there is no reason for me to stay. But you know that I know. That's what I came to say to you. You ruined my life, just like you ruined your own.'

Sirinya feels defeated, near to tears. Her heart beating fast, she turns towards the door.

'Wait.'

She turns back. Is Ratana finally going to admit what she did?

'Wait. I remember now, I did tell someone. I did tell someone, Siri. But it wasn't a Jap.'

Sirinya frowns. 'Who was it?'

'It was Narong. I remember now. I had forgotten, it is so long ago, but I was in love with him then. He used to take me out in that sports car of his, and he used to pay me to sleep with him sometimes. I thought he could save me. That he could be the answer to my prayers. He was rich, good looking. I saw him as a way out of what I'd got myself into, I suppose. I wanted him to love me, but he wouldn't. He couldn't. He said he'd never marry me because he loved someone else.'

Sirinya hangs her head. 'That someone was you, Siri. You'd rejected him, but he was still waiting for you. When I heard that you were planning to leave, to help a prisoner to escape, I went to his house and I told him. He's the only person I told, Siri, and I told him because I was so desperate for him to marry me. I wanted him to stop loving you, to realise that you were gone, that you loved another man ...'

Sirinya watches Ratana, her eyes wide with shock. She never considered this. Not once. Perhaps Ratana wasn't lying after all. It was beginning to make sense.

'I never thought, Siri, not for one moment that he would tell the Japanese. I thought he was working against them, supporting the resistance in his own way. That he hated them because they'd taken over the factory. If I'd thought …'

Sirinya remembers the medicines hidden by the river, how Narong had gone out of his way to reassure her and Malee that he was on her side. All the time he must have been working for the Kempeitai.

'Where is he now? I need to see him.'

Ratana shrugs. I haven't seen him for years. He sold the factory after the war and went abroad. I think he might be back in the country now, but I've no idea where he is. Someone in the town might know, though.

'I will go back there and find out where he is. I must leave now, Ratana.'

'Do you believe me?'

She hesitates. 'I'm not sure.'

Ratana shrugs. 'You need to let go of your grudges, Siri. A lot of time has passed since then. People do things during wartime they would never do at any other time.'

'I know. Look, I'm sorry to see you like this, Ratana.'

Ratana shrugs. 'It's happened before,' she says.

Sirinya leaves her and goes back along the passage to the front desk. Kasem lifts his face and his eyes light up as he sees her. She approaches the policeman, who is reading a newspaper, feet up on the desk.

'How much is her bail?' she asks.

'Two thousand baht.'

'I will find a bank and bring it to you in the morning.'

She feels Kasem's hand on her back, guiding her, as they leave the police station. 'Are you alright?' he asks.

She nods. 'She was in a terrible state. But it wasn't her who betrayed us to the Kempeitai.'

They climb into the waiting tuk-tuk. 'Wasn't her? Are you sure?'

'Yes, I think so.'

The tuk-tuk roars into life and takes off down the road. She clutches the bar.

'So that's good in a way, isn't it?' he shouts above the engine noise.

'It was someone else. It was Narong.'

Kasem's forehead puckers in a frown, his eyes are full of concern. They are now speeding along the seafront towards their guesthouse.

'Let's stop here.' He taps the driver on his shoulder and asks him to stop. 'We can walk the rest of the way. Come on. Let's walk along the beach.'

It is dark on the beach, lit only by the flashing lights from the bars and clubs which reflect the shapes of palm trees on the sand. Sirinya kicks off her shoes and picks them up to carry. She feels the cool grains of sand between her toes.

'What are you going to do, Sirinya?' he asks gently.

'I'm going to find him of course, and confront him. Let him know what I've found out.'

'Do you really think that's a good idea?'

She stops and stares at him. 'Please don't start that again, Kasem. I need to do this. I have come back to Thailand for this. Nothing is going to stop me now.'

They walk on. 'Don't you think it would be better to forget it? Get on with your life? You're still quite young after all.'

'I need to do this. I don't expect you to understand. No one who wasn't there, who didn't go through what I've been through, would.'

'Perhaps you're right,' he murmurs, staring down at the sand as they walk.

'You haven't told me what happened to you during the war, Kasem. I assumed you were with your family in your village. You must have been aware of what was going on, but the Japs probably didn't bother you that much up there.'

'Shall I tell you what happened to me?' he asks quietly.

Something in his voice makes Sirinya hesitate. Has she been wrong about him?

She hears him take a deep breath. 'I was living in our village, up the line from you, in the hills near Nam Tok. I was twenty when the Japanese invaded the country. My mother had some rice fields and kept a few animals, my father died when I was a child. It was a small community, and there was a temple there, it was the lifeblood of the village.

'Things were reasonably peaceful in the early part of the Japanese occupation. We had heard that a railway was being built from Ban Pong to Burma but no one in the village really knew what that involved.

'One day a group of Japanese soldiers came into the village. They were engineers planning the next phase of the railway. They came roaring in on their lorries and trucks. They went straight to the temple and spoke with the monks. They told them they needed the temple as their headquarters. It was the only building in the area large enough. I remember watching in horror from the porch of our house. Of course the monks resisted, but the soldiers drove them out of the temple with their bayonets and rifles. I'll never forget the humiliation of that day.

'The Japanese took over the temple, and we had to live with them in our midst. The monks had to come and live with the villagers in our houses. We even had to supply the Japanese soldiers with food, which was already scarce.

'My mother was very angry, but there was nothing she could do. We needed more money for food so she sent me down to work with my uncle in Bangkok. He was a rice trader. When he heard about the village temple, he became very bitter about the occupation. He made it his business to find a way of working against the Japanese. Somehow, through his contacts he got in touch with the V Organisation ...'

Sirinya stops walking. 'I'm sorry, Kasem. I had no idea. How thoughtless of me. Here I've been thinking that I was the one who suffered, that nothing had happened to you during the war. Did you help your uncle?'

He nods, then fishes in the pocket of his trousers.

'Does this mean anything to you?'

He is holding up a white cloth, a handkerchief. She takes it and peers at it in the darkness. She can hardly see it, but she can feel that it is trimmed with delicate lace. Her mouth falls open. She takes it, and examines it, her heart beating fast. There it is, she feels it under her fingers, the embroidered 'S'. She has an image of Narong smiling broadly as he gave it to her on her twentieth birthday. It had been folded beautifully, inside an elaborate box.

She remembers Lian, and the pair of them sitting in her tiny living room off the Charoen Krung road that night in 1943, waiting for Chalong to hide the radio parts in the lorry. She remembers the boy, no older than herself, who cut his hand on the lorry, waiting at the door.

'It was you,' she whispers. 'You were Yosakon's nephew.'

27

The lorry driver dropped Sirinya on the edge of Chinatown. It was late evening and the streets were quiet. An empty tram rattled past, the conductor slumped asleep on the platform, and a few rickshaws trundled by touting for trade. She got down from the cab, thanked the driver and stood on the pavement feeling physically drained, her mind numb. She had no idea where to go or what to do. All she was aware of was the pain of Charlie's death and the knowledge that she must disappear, that Bangkok was as good a place for that as any. Above all she knew she must not bring further danger on Chalong and the family.

She felt dazed, bewildered, as she stood and watched the taillights of the truck draw away. She realised it was her last connection with her hometown. When the lights had disappeared round a bend in the road, it was as if the tie had been severed completely. She felt as if her whole world had collapsed, as if she had died that day with Charlie: that the real Sirinya had vanished, and this beaten husk of a woman had stepped out of her empty shell.

She thought about Yai, and her heart contorted with pity. The old woman would be waiting up for her long into the night, leaning on the railings of her porch, peering into the darkness, expecting two figures to appear, walking towards her quickly and quietly between the houses. She knew that eventually, one day, Yai would hear what had happened. Chalong would surely send word when he found out. But until then, she would constantly be watching and waiting.

Sirinya wandered along the main road, past a line of jewellery shops shuttered for night, and turned down a side street which led down towards the Chao Phraya river. She walked aimlessly. She had no idea why she was walking in this direction. She could smell the river as she got closer, see the lights of longtail boats bobbing on the water, hear the sound of the boatmen's voices floating on the night air.

When she reached the riverbank she went down the wooden steps to a jetty and on to a landing stage. She walked across the platform, stood right on the edge of it, and stared out across the dark water. The landing stage moved up and down with the movement of the river, and looking down between her feet she caught glimpses of the murky water through the gaps in the boards. She sat down, slipped off her shoes and dipped her feet in the river. A shiver when through her as the cold penetrated her skin.

Images of Charlie blotted out all other thoughts. Since the truck driver had told her the news at the start of the journey to Bangkok, she had thought of nothing else. Over and over again she pictured Charlie surrounded by Japanese guards shouting and screaming at him, their faces full of hatred. They pushed him to the ground, beat him with sticks and kicked him mercilessly. She imagined his face bruised and bloody, his lips split and his eyes swollen from the beatings. Then she saw him being dragged to a clearing on the edge of the camp, forced to kneel and bend forward, then the flash of a sword in the sun and the sickening chop as the sword come down on his neck. Like the chop and squelch of the butcher's cleaver on the marble slab in the market. She put her hands over her ears, trying to block out the sound, but it was impossible to do that; the sound was in her own head.

How easy it would be to slip into the water here in the darkness and sink beneath the surface. No one knew she was here; no one would see her, or try to stop her, and the great river was running at high tide. She could give herself up to its force. She would not try to swim or struggle, and in no time her body would be swept down on the current and out to sea. What was the point of carrying on without Charlie in the world and without Kitima's love to guide her? She sat there motionless for a long time, overwhelmed by her loss, staring at the glittering black surface. It danced in front of her, beckoned her in. It was so tempting that a couple of times she placed her palms down on the damp boards and eased herself forward. But each time something stopped her, something ingrained deep in her soul. It was something inseparable from her being, that she had learned as a small child. Something that had been reinforced every time she knelt down in the temple before the Buddha to light a candle; every time she had stilled her mind and sought enlightenment in meditation. It came from the teachings of the monks in the temple. Life is suffering, they said, and you need to embrace it and live the suffering. She knew deep down inside that letting the river take her wasn't the answer. She knew that her suffering wouldn't end with her death.

She thought of Phraa Thongphroh, and his words to Malee. 'You need to embrace the pain and experience it, my child.' Gradually she pulled back from the edge of the water and lifted her feet out. She hugged her wet knees, rocked herself back and forth and let her tears fall. She cried for Charlie, for Kitima and for Somsak and for all the prisoners who had died. She cried until her eyes were swollen and her chest ached. She had no concept of how long she was there, but when the tears had finally subsided she took her bag and crawled up the landing stage. She lay down exhausted and wrung out beside the steps from the riverbank down to the jetty. She put her head on her bag and fell into a fitful sleep.

She was awoken by a blast from the horn of a convoy of rice barges moving past on the river. She sat up slowly and rubbing her eyes stared about her. The first rays were piercing the grey sky and on the other side of the river she saw shafts of sun lighting up Wat Arun, the temple of the dawn, making the buildings glitter and shimmer. The sky was streaked with pink and orange and smudged with violet. She felt bathed in its beauty.

Then the events of the previous day came back to her, and her heart ached with the pain of the realisation that the first new day had dawned without Charlie in the world. In a flash she remembered everything; the interminable wait by the river for Charlie, the dawning realisation that he was never going to come, the walk back along the Bamboo Road, the terror of watching the Japanese soldiers question the villagers, and the final devastating blow of Charlie's death delivered by the truck driver.

The jetty steps rattled to the sound of footsteps. People were coming down onto the landing stage now to catch boats and river buses. They stared at Sirinya as they passed, not unkindly but with curiosity. She gathered her bag and got to her feet. Two monks passed and waied to her in greeting, she stood up and waied to them respectfully, bowed her head and moved on. She went up the steps to the riverbank and wandered through Chinatown. Her mind was elsewhere, thinking of Charlie and what he must have suffered. She hardly took in her surroundings as she walked, but she was dimly aware that her stomach ached with hunger and her whole body was weak. She stopped at a food stall and ordered noodle soup, but when it came and she took her first sip from the steaming spoon, she had no sense of taste. With an effort she swallowed the meal.

Then she carried on wandering through the streets towards

Sukhumvit, passing shopkeepers opening up for the morning, hosing down the pavement, setting stock outside. She turned off the main road onto a soi and wandered along it. A little way along were two or three bars. In the window of one there was a sign advertising for staff. She stepped inside the dimly lit room and approached the bar. An older woman, her wrinkled skin covered in heavy make up, her cleavage on display, was polishing glasses.

'I'm looking for a job,' said Sirinya. The woman put down the glass she was drying and peered at her. It was then that Sirinya noticed the two Japanese officers drinking at a corner table. Her blood ran cold. She had to stop herself turning and running away. She clenched her fists and told herself that these officers wouldn't know who she was, and that if she ran it would only draw their attention to her.

'Are you good at cleaning?' asked the woman. 'We need someone to mop the floor and clean the tables.

'Anything,' said Sirinya. 'I'll do anything.'

'You can start today. Where are you living?'

'I'm not sure yet. I need to find somewhere. I've just arrived from up-country.'

'There's a dormitory upstairs. The other girls who work in the bar live there. There is a bunk you could use.'

'That sounds fine. Thank you,' said Sirinya in a flat voice. This would be a good place to be anonymous, she thought, to fade into the background. No one would ever know what she had once been, or what she had done. This way she could lie low, nurse her sorrow, make sure that Chalong and the family didn't come to harm because of her.

The woman showed her up a narrow staircase at the back of the bar. In a shuttered room where the air was hot and stale, she pointed to a slatted shelf in the corner. 'You can stay there. Please be quiet. Other girls still asleep. Come down to start cleaning as soon as you're ready.'

'I'm ready now,' Sirinya said putting her bag down quietly on the bare bunk. On the bed above someone sighed and turned over.

And so it began, her life as a bar worker in the backstreets of Bangkok. The work was not difficult, she was used to physical labour, and it was simple. She had to mop the floor, empty ashtrays, clear the tables and wipe the spills from them. The hours were long and tedious. She worked from eight o'clock in the morning until after midnight with two hours off in the afternoon. The pay was minimal, but three meals were provided in the outdoor kitchen in the yard behind the bar each day and she did not have to look for anywhere to stay. She was glad of the monotony of the work and of the anonymity it afforded her. She gave herself a new name, 'Kanya'. The other girls accepted the story that she told them about her life, which was almost true of course; she said that she came from a village near the Burmese border, and that her parents were dead.

There were three other girls who worked in the bar and lodged in the room above it with her. All three of them came from villages in the Isaan region in the North East of the country. They were all about her age and had already formed strong bonds of friendship. Each tried to be friendly to Sirinya, but without meaning to she distanced them with her solitariness and her preoccupied manner. After a while she noticed that they stopped speaking when she approached, and was sure that they were talking about her, calling her unfriendly. She couldn't blame them, she *was* unfriendly. But she had no room for friendship, no place in her heart for warmth for another human being. Her soul had shrivelled and retreated. She needed time to experience the pain, to grieve properly for Charlie and for Kitima.

The three other girls worked at the bar, taking orders from the tables and serving drinks. The old woman, Wassanna, encouraged them to flatter the customers, to sit down beside them, or on their laps if necessary and tempt them to stay longer, to buy more drinks. Sometimes one of the girls would leave with a customer and return a couple of hours later to hand a sheaf of notes to Wassanna who would peer through her glasses to count it carefully before pocketing a proportion and handing the rest back to the girl. Most of the customers were local businessmen or shopkeepers, but often a group of Japanese soldiers would come in and take over a corner table, drinking shot after shot of whisky, becoming drunker and louder as time wore on.

Sirinya was glad she was just there to clean, and wasn't expected to perform the duties of the other girls. She made sure she kept her head low and maintained her distance when the Japanese soldiers came in, never going anywhere near their table. She could hardly bear to look at them, and found herself sweating and trembling with fear as she listened to them shouting and laughing in their guttural tongue.

When she'd been there a fortnight she wrote to Chalong.

Dear Uncle,

Please forgive me for what I did. I know it was foolish and I will regret it for the rest of my life. I know now that it would have been safer for Charlie to have stayed in the camp. It was my own selfishness that caused me to act as I did. I will never forgive myself for persuading him to escape and for causing his death. I realise too that I brought danger to you and the family, which is why I have not come back. I don't want to bring any more suspicion on you and the organisation.

I have found work in a bar in Bangkok. Please don't try to find me or to persuade me to come home. I need to be alone and to pay for my mistake. Perhaps one day if this war ever ends I'll return, but I cannot promise.

Please let dear Yai know what has happened and tell her that I love her. Please know that I love you, Auntie and Malee too and that I miss you. I hope you are able to carry on your good work for the prisoners without fear now that I'm gone.

Your ever loving,
Sirinya

She stared at the words she had written and wondered how to get the letter to her uncle. She folded it and put it into the envelope she had bought in the local market. At the end of her cleaning shift that day she set off to find a post office. One of the girls had told her there was one on Yaowarat Road. But when she located the building and approached it she realised that two Japanese guards were stationed outside the door, rifles slung over their shoulders. She stopped walking and began to sweat, fear coursing through her. She thought about what would happen if they stopped her and took the letter. She considered going inside and buying stamps and posting the letter elsewhere. Either way, she knew she couldn't walk past them with the letter in her hand. It would risk uncovering her own identity and exposing Chalong and the organisation.

She turned and walked away, feeling the full impact her self-imposed separation from the family. She walked for a while, her head down, hardly registering the bustling surroundings. When she had walked some way she looked up and noticed that she had wandered out of Chinatown along a long wide road. A tram thundered past and she lifted her head to watch it. As it passed, she noticed a road sign on the opposite building; 'Charoen Krung Road'. She had been here before. She remembered the night with Chalong when they came to collect the radio parts. Then another thought occurred to her. Perhaps there might be way of getting the letter to her uncle after all. If she could find Lian's house and deliver the letter to her, Lian would surely be able to pass it on to Chalong. She walked on down the long straight road lined with old three-storey shophouses. She walked for a long time in the steamy heat as the sun beat down on her from overhead. She checked all the sois to her right as she passed, peering down them, checking for the temple where Chalong had parked the lorry. When she came to the turning, she almost missed it, it looked so different in the daylight, but there, a little way off the main road was the red and green roof of a temple. She peered down the narrow street. There was the temple at the back of a courtyard, and the double gates they had driven through that night, only today they were shut.

Turning down the street she walked quickly past the temple and on towards the river. When she reached the row of houses where she remembered Lian's to have been she paused. It was hard to remember which house. She stopped beside two doors, wondering whether to knock, then she recognised it. The door was lower than the others, and she remembered Chalong having to stoop as he entered that night. Feeling apprehensive she knocked on the door and waited. There was no answer so she knocked again.

'Hello? Can I help you?' the voice of a woman came from next door.

'I'm looking for a lady called Lian,' she said. 'She lives here, doesn't she?'

The woman looked troubled. She dropped her gaze and came closer. 'She has gone away,' she whispered. 'She left yesterday. I saw her from my window. She went away in a rickshaw with her luggage. I don't know where she went. Later in the day two Japanese officers came knocking on doors along the street asking about her.'

Sirinya's hear beat faster. 'Thank you. Thank you for telling me.'

Sirinya turned and retraced her steps towards the temple, wondering what had become of Lian. Perhaps she had known there was a risk that the Kempeitai would look for her? She remembered Lian's words that evening: 'Sometimes I lie awake imagining Japanese footsteps on the road outside …' She wondered about Chalong too. Surely he would try to come here one day to collect medicines? Perhaps the Kempeitai had discovered the organisation and would set a trap for him? She needed to warn him.

As she reached the gates of the temple courtyard, she hesitated, remembering the old rice trader Yosakon and his nephew. The nephew had been caught and imprisoned; she knew that much, but perhaps the old man was still there. She paused. Was it safe to go back and talk to him? She turned around and went quickly back along the road past Lian's house and on along the little street towards the river. She didn't know exactly where the old man would be, but she remembered that he had lived further down towards the river. At end of the road steps led to a jetty over the river. She stood on the wall in front of the jetty and saw that it led to a slatted walkway, which in turn led to a row of wooden houses built out on stilts over the river. She stepped off the jetty and walked along the rickety walkway. A woman was beating washing on the wooden platform outside the first house.

'Could you tell me where Yosakon the rice trader lives?' Sirinya asked.

The woman shaded her eyes and peered at her before nodding to the next-door building. A group of flat-bottomed boats were moored up alongside it, jostling against each other on the rise and fall of the water. The walkway to Yosakon's house was slippery and decayed, some of the boards were broken and she had to balance carefully to avoid slipping into the river. She climbed the ladder to the house, knocked on the door and waited. Again there was no answer. She turned to look at the woman beating washing who looked away when she caught her gaze. She peered through a dusty window beside the door. Inside the place looked bare. There was a table and a couple of chairs and a heap of bedding in the corner. She rattled the door handle, but she already knew no one was going to come. She retraced her steps and took the walkway that led to the next-door hut. The woman stared at her.

'Do you know where Yosakon is?'

The woman shrugged. 'I haven't seen him for a long time. I know the soldiers came and took the boy away. He left shortly after that.'

'Do you know where he went?'

'Back to his village I think. He was terrified of the Japs, I know that much. I don't know what he was up to. I don't want to know.'

Sirinya opened her mouth to ask another question, but closed it again. She shouldn't trust anyone.

She wandered back along the road, and when she reached the temple courtyard she opened the gate and went inside. She remembered Chalong's words. 'The monks in the temple know my business.'

She walked tentatively up to the temple building. An old monk, stooped and wrinkled, stood at the top of the steps. Sirinya kicked off her sandals and went up the steps towards him. The monk waied to her.

'Good morning, Phraa, could I ask you something?'

He inclined his head. 'Do you know a man called Chalong?' she asked.

He hesitated momentarily, peered at her closely, then said. 'Of course. Khun Chalong is a very good man.'

'He is my uncle. I am so afraid for him, Phraa,' she said, 'I'm worried that his friends in this road have gone away, and that he will come in the lorry on Sunday and be caught by the Kempeitai.'

'You don't need to worry, my child. Our friends have already communicated with him. He knows that he must go to another place when he next comes to the city.'

'Are you in touch with him, Phraa?'

He shook his head. 'But I am in touch with his friends.'

Sirinya pulled the letter from her bag. 'Could you ask them to give this to him? I don't have any other way of getting it to him.'

'Of course. I'll do my best. Are you expecting a reply?' She hesitated, but the monk when on, 'I will tell him he can leave a note for you and you can collect it here, if you like?'

'Thank you, Phraa,' she said.

'You look troubled, my child. Why not light a candle here, spend some time in the temple to make merit?'

She thought about Wassanna and the bar. She should be back by now, but she felt the pull of the temple, the need to kneel and meditate before the Buddha if only for a short while.

When she returned, Wassanna had already packed her bag and it was standing outside the front door.

'You have let me down, Kanya. You should have been working hours ago. There's your bag. There's no need to return.'

'I can explain ...'

'There is no need to try. I've already hired someone else.'

Sirinya took the small bag of belongings and walked away.

It was not difficult to find another a job, at a larger bar a little way along Sukhumvit. Again, there was a dormitory above for the staff.

'You work tables?' asked the owner, appraising her with narrowed eyes.

'No, I would prefer to just clean.'

'You're a pretty girl. You are wasted pushing a broom. You could make more money than that.'

She shook her head. 'I only want to clean.'

He shrugged. 'Whatever you want.'

She started work straight away. There were more girls here, nine or ten of them, all very young and dressed in skimpy clothes when they worked, all draping themselves over customers and leaving with them to rent a room in a nearby hotel by the hour. She ignored it all and worked hard, all the time thinking of Charlie and what might have been if he hadn't been betrayed. As she emptied ashtrays and tipped the dregs of drinks into a slop bucket and avoided the lascivious stares and the pinches of customers, she pictured herself and Charlie walking through the hills together, through the forests, sleeping by day and walking by night. He could have been free by now, they both could have been. The grief and guilt she had felt at first gradually turned to anger and bitterness. Anger and bitterness at whoever had betrayed them to the Japanese.

After a couple of weeks she wandered back to the temple in the soi off Charoen Krung. She wanted to go there for some peace, some sanctuary, but in the back of her mind she wondered if the monk had news of Chalong. The monk greeted her with a huge smile and a deep wai.

'I have a letter from your uncle,' he said beaming and went into a side room. He returned and handed her a folded sheet of paper. She nodded her thanks to the monk and went outside to read it.

My Dearest Sirinya

I am so sorry that you have decided to leave home. There is no need for you to stay away. There were some visits from the Kempeitai after you left, but that has passed now. Lian has moved to Chinatown to a secret location for safety. Someone in the organisation thought that the Kempeitai might have discovered her work and advised her to find somewhere else to stay. We are still taking medicines into the camps of course and passing information, but the railway is nearly finished now and prisoners are being taken away from the area. We are not sure where they are going, but they are being taken on trains down south again.

I have some very sad new, Sirinya. Yai was found dead in her house a few days after you left. She was very old of course, and died peacefully in her sleep. I went to the village to tell her what had happened to you and the neighbours told me the news. It is a shock of course, but she led a long and full life ...

Sirinya dropped the letter and sank to the floor sobbing. How could she bear this fresh blow? Yai must have died through grief that she, Sirinya, had abandoned her, through fear that she would never come back. How thoughtless she had been. How could she have done that to her grandmother? Like Charlie's death, like Kitima's, she was instantly sure that Yai's death was all her fault.

She felt the monk's hand on her shoulder and turned to him with tears in her eyes.

'Come, child. Come and make an offering with me. We can meditate together.'

She shook her head and swallowed hard. It took some time before she could speak. 'I can't, Phraa,'she whispered. 'I'm sorry, Not now. I just can't.'

In the months that followed Sirinya sunk lower and lower. She had no energy and went about her duties in the bar slowly and listlessly. She barely ate. She knew the other girls were whispering about her and laughing at her. They called her 'Pee' or ghost. Sometimes the owner would pull her aside and say, 'What's wrong with you? You're putting the customers off. You must smile, look happy.' For a while she would try, pretend to smile and to put a spring in her step, but it never lasted more than a few hours. She never went anywhere any more. She stayed inside the bar and went upstairs to lie on her bed and think about the people she had lost. Her skin became sallow and dry.

She found it difficult to sleep, she would like awake for hours, staring into the darkness, listening to the breathing of the other girls, the night-time sounds of the city through the shuttered windows. If sleep ever did come, she would dream of Charlie. It would always be on the Bamboo Road and she would be waiting for him impatiently, watching and praying for him to appear. Eventually her prayers would be answered and he would appear between the canes of bamboo. She would run to him and he would take her in his arms and kiss her. She would wake up to the dreadful realisation that she had been dreaming and that Charlie was never going to appear along the Bamboo Road.

One day she was working in the bar and tripped over the slop bucket that spilled all over the floor. The customers fell silent and everyone turned to look at her. She quickly mopped up the mess, but as she took the bucket to the backyard to empty it, the owner pulled her aside.

'I've given you enough chances, my girl. I want you out of here.

You're a liability.'

She hung her head, knowing it to be true, and went upstairs to pack her things.

She went from bar to bar asking for work, but it was not easy to find this time. There were fewer Japanese soldiers to cater for now, and business was slow. For three nights she slept rough beside the river as she had on the very first night she'd arrived in Bangkok. She wondered then if she should go back to Kanchanaburi, but knew that she couldn't face the family as she was now. She was too ashamed, she needed more time.

On the fourth day she found a bar that needed someone to help out, serving drinks and cleaning. It was owned by a Chinese man with a huge perspiring face and rolls of fat around his belly. He looked at her and at all the other girls who worked there with naked lust in his eyes.

The work was no different here, and again she slept in a large room on the top floor with the other girls. The difference here was that whenever she found herself alone in the storeroom or in the backyard with the owner, he would try to pin her against the wall and touch her breasts. She became adept at dodging his hands, and ducking away from him, but she wondered how long she would be able to avoid him. She knew some of the other girls went with him into the storeroom and let him have his way for thirty baht. But they were girls who sold their bodies to customers every night to make money to send back to their villages. They had little choice, she knew that, and they bore their circumstances with good humour, but she saw a hardness in their eyes that should still have been innocent.

After a few months the owner began to tell her that she too must be willing to go with customers for money. She refused each time he mentioned it, but he became insistent.

'You are a virgin, no? You'll fetch good money. You are a bit older than most, but you still have value.'

'I won't do it,' she said time each time he asked her, and he would bang his fist on the table and shout. 'You will do it or I will turn you out of here. I don't know why I keep you anyway.'

The weeks wore on and he kept reminding her, but for some reason he didn't turn her out. Fewer and fewer Japanese soldiers came into the bar. She heard the customers speaking of a catastrophic American bomb destroying cities in Japan, and then one day everyone was saying that the Japanese had surrendered; they had lost the war.

There were celebrations that night and the bar was filled with Thai men drinking. Sirinya watched but she could feel nothing. Just a deep sadness for everyone she had lost, and a feeling of pointlessness of the loss of all those lives. She felt numb.

'Tonight you will do it for me, won't you?' said the owner, coming up close to her. 'I can get good money for you tonight.'

She turned to him. 'I can't tonight,' she said. 'It is the wrong time for me. You know what I mean.'

He grunted. 'Next week then. You can do it then. You will do it this time, won't you? Otherwise that's the end of it. I've waited long enough for you.'

She nodded wordlessly. Perhaps she would. After all, why did it matter? What did she and her pride and her body matter to anyone anymore?

A few days later, she'd been mopping a table in a corner of the gloomy room, her face pinched with the pain of her aching back, the rumble of hunger in her stomach. The place had not yet opened for the evening. She picked up a couple of dirty glasses to take back to the kitchen and turned around. He had appeared from nowhere, standing in front of her like a vision from a bizarre dream. At first she couldn't place who he was, out of context like that. He was as thin as he'd been in the camps. His cheeks were still hollow and his eyes stood out from his face. What she found most strange, though, was that he was wearing clothes instead of a loin cloth. She had never seen him properly dressed before. He was dressed in a brand new army uniform. He was so skinny that the shirt hung off his shoulders and the trousers bagged at the knees. She stared at him, opening and closing her mouth stupidly. Finally she found her voice.

'Johnny,' she murmured, 'what on earth are you doing here?'

28

Sirinya stands on Pattaya beach in the darkness, listening to the suck and rush of the breakers, a cool breeze on her face. In the light of the moon a scattering of tiny white crabs scuttle along the beach away from her. She still holds the white embroidered handkerchief, peering at it in the darkness, between her fingers she can feel the raised embroidered 'S'.

'I kept it all these years,' Kasem says. 'It reminded me of you. Of your face that night when my uncle and I helped Chalong stow the radio parts in the lorry. Do you remember? I cut my hand and I came back to the house.'

'Of course,' she murmurs. 'I remember. Your hand was bleeding badly and Lian bound it up for you.'

'There was something in your expression that I wanted to make sure I didn't forget. That's why I kept your handkerchief. Your face that night was full of hope and determination, and of kindness. It might sound strange now, but it inspired me.'

'What happened to you?' It is slowly coming back to her. She remembers that Yosakon's nephew was captured and imprisoned, discovered by the Japanese helping the European internees.

'I was caught by the Japs smuggling food to the European civilians interned in the university. I was imprisoned for a while.'

'Lian told my uncle about that. How long were you there?'

'Not too long. A few months, perhaps. Lian and her family helped me to escape one night. I managed to get out disguised as a

Chinese coolie. Lian's brothers had a covered boat waiting on the canal to take me away. I stayed with them, keeping a low profile in Chinatown until the end of the war. They sheltered me and protected me. I owe them everything. After the war they helped me set up in business, loaned me money to buy my shop.'

'That's incredible Kasem … I'm so sorry,' Sirinya says.

'Why? What are you sorry for?'

'For jumping to conclusions before. For not realising that you suffered too. Were you … were you tortured?'

There is a silence, and in the darkness she can sense that Kasem is staring down at the sand. 'I don't want to remember that time in prison,' he says quietly, his voice catching. 'I've put it all behind me. It is in the past, and nothing can change what happened. I've learned to forget, Sirinya. I survived and I have a good life now.'

She doesn't speak for a few minutes, letting this new, stunning information about Kasem sink in. A couple of cars whizz past on the sea front road. She watches the reflection of the moon dance on the dark sea and the silhouette of a fishing boat pass through it. Were these last words aimed at her? Is he judging her, telling her that *she* should put the past behind her and forget too?

'Did you recognise me, on that train to Kanchanaburi a few weeks ago when I first came back to Thailand?' she asks.

'Not then, no. Although I did think there was something vaguely familiar about you. No, it was when I saw you the other day in Chinatown near my shop. You were sitting at that food stall reading a newspaper and you looked up to call the waiter. It hit me then, who you were. I saw it in your face, that expression I remembered.'

'Why didn't you tell me then?'

'I wanted to be sure. It wasn't until you told me your story in the car this morning that I could be absolutely certain.'

They walk in silence now along the beach, each absorbed in their own thoughts about the past.

'So you must know, then, why I need to find out who betrayed me and Charlie. You must understand,' Sirinya says after a while.

'I understand why, of course. But you must know what I think. I think you should try to let it go. Years have passed, there is nothing to be gained by raking it all up now. It was a desperate time. People did desperate things. They did things then that they would never have done in peace time.'

She knows he is right. Didn't she herself do things during those years that she has regretted her whole life? Persuading Charlie to escape, running away to Bangkok to disappear, leaving Yai and the rest of the family to worry about her. She would never have behaved like that if she had lived a normal life, if war and terror hadn't come to their peaceful community, polluting people's lives.

The idea of letting it go fills her with panic. She has been thinking about it for so many years; all those dull years in England her anger sustained her in a way. Besides, this quest is her one link with Charlie. She has come this far. She is so close to achieving what she came back to do, how can she walk away from that now?

'I can't let it drop, Kasem. What Narong did was a crime however long has passed since then. No, I must find him and speak to him. Confront him. I need to do this. I've waited twenty-five years for this. It is so close. I will go back tomorrow and find him.'

They have reached a point on the beach that is parallel to their guesthouse and they turn away from the sea and walk back through a grove of coconut palms to the road. Sirinya slips her sandals back on.

'Well if you must go, will you at least let me drive you back to Kanchanaburi?' Kasem asks.

'That's kind of you, but you've done more than enough to help me, Kasem. I need to find out where Narong is now. He could have moved away. Malee might know. I'll phone in the morning and ask her. If we go back to Bangkok tomorrow, I can catch the train back to Kanchanaburi from there.'

* * *

Early the next morning, after a restless night under a mosquito net in a hot little hut in the guesthouse, Sirinya gets out of bed and dresses quickly. She leaves the guesthouse, glancing towards Kasem's hut. All is quiet and the curtains are still drawn. She walks out onto the road and along the seafront, checking each shop and bar as she passes, until she finds the only bank, housed in a makeshift wooden building. The shutters are down, but she waits at a nearby food stall until she sees the teller arrive to open up the bank. Then she goes into the bank and withdraws several thousand baht from her account.

She flags down a rickshaw and asks the rider to take her to the police station.

The officer at the desk looks up from his magazine as she enters. His face registers surprise. She hands him two thousand baht.

'It is for Ratana's bail,' she explains. 'You can let her go now.'

He stares at Sirinya and shrugs. He takes a writing pad and scribbles a receipt. 'And I'd like her to have this thousand too,' Sirinya says, putting another sheaf of banknotes down on the desk. 'Could you pass it on to her please?'

The policeman takes the rest of the money, turns the page in his notebook to write another receipt. 'Don't you want to see her and give it to her yourself?' he asks as he writes. She shakes her head.

'No thank you. We said all there was to say yesterday. If you could just pass the money on to her please, she might have a chance of paying her debts.'

Back at the guesthouse she uses the telephone at the reception desk to call Malee.

'Siri!' Malee says, delight bubbling up in her voice. 'How are you? I haven't heard from you for days. How are things going in Bangkok? When are you coming back?'

'Today or tomorrow I hope. I'm sorry not to have phoned before, Malee, I've had a lot to do.'

'Did you find Ratana?'

'Yes. I'm in Pattaya. She's living here now.'

'Pattaya?'

'Yes. It's a long story. But it turns out that it wasn't her after all, Malee. I had a long talk with her yesterday and she told me who it was who betrayed us to the Japanese.'

'Really? But you were so sure. Who does she say it was?'

'It was Narong.'

'Narong? Siri that's ridiculous. How can you think that? He hated the Japanese. They took over his factory, you must remember that.'

'It must have been him. I'll tell you everything when I get back, but I need to know where he is now, Malee. Does he still live in the town?'

'No. No, he sold the factory years ago. He married a girl from Bangkok and went to live with her family in the city. I haven't heard from him since he left.'

'Do you know anyone who might know where he is now?'

There is a short silence, then Malee bursts out, 'Why are you doing this, Siri? You're clutching at straws. You were convinced it was Ratana, now Narong. Where will it end?'

'It will end when I find out who betrayed us. Charlie *died*,

Malee. I haven't forgotten that. To me it's as if it happened yesterday. The man I loved was murdered because someone told the Kempeitai about what we were planning.'

'But it could have been someone in the camp,' Malee says, 'Haven't you thought of that? Someone desperate. That sort of thing happened you know. Men were starving. Some of them would have done anything in return for a square meal.'

'But how could it have been one of the prisoners? Charlie only told his officers, and Johnny of course.'

There is a pause. Then the full impact of what she has just said hits Sirinya. Shock waves ripple through her body. 'You're not saying it could have been Johnny, are you?' she manages to say at last, her voice trembling. 'Don't be ridiculous, Malee. He was Charlie's best friend. That has never even crossed my mind. Not for a moment.'

'No, not Johnny, Siri. Of course not, but you don't know who might have overheard him talking about it. You just don't know what went on in the camps.'

'But don't you remember how oddly Narong acted when the Japanese took over his factory? He kept insisting he had no choice, trying to reassure us that he was on our side. It was almost as if he was protesting too much. But what if he was just telling us lies and he working with them all along? I never trusted him. There was something about him.'

'But Siri, don't you remember the time that he found the medicines under the bushes? He kept them secret from the Japs. If he'd wanted to betray us, that would have been the ideal opportunity.'

'I know. It doesn't seem to make sense. I need to talk to him, Malee. Is there any way you can find out where he is?'

'I suppose I could ask the old lady who used to clean his house in the old days if she is still in touch with him. She is very frail now, but I know where she lives.'

'Could you possibly do that today for me? I'll call you again when I get back to Bangkok. If you have an address for him and he still lives in Bangkok, I could go straight to see him before I come back to Kanchanaburi.'

'I can try. I'll go round when I've finished with the deliveries. But I can't guarantee that she'll know. I'll see what I can do though. Why don't you call me this afternoon?'

* * *

Sirinya and Kasem hardly speak on the drive back to Bangkok. She stares out of the car window at the flat countryside, mulling over what the trip to Pattaya has revealed to her. Those few minutes with Ratana tore down illusions that she'd harboured all these years, illusions and grudges that fuelled her, sustained her throughout those long empty days abroad. These were all dissipated in a few short minutes, but to her surprise she has had no difficulty in letting go of the idea that Ratana betrayed her. Perhaps she never really wanted to believe it after all.

It is astonishing too that Kasem is the shy boy she met fleetingly that night back in 1943. She bites her nail in guilt as she thinks about how dismissive of him she was. He must have taken as many risks as she did during the war. She wonders what he suffered at the hands of the Kempeitai. Was he beaten like she was? Did he suffer even worse violence and humiliation? She knows she cannot ask him to speak about it, nor would she want to. His silence and reticence on the beach yesterday evening spoke volumes.

'Shall I drop you at your hotel?' Kasem asks as they enter the city.

'If you don't mind,' she says. 'I'll call Malee from there. She might have found out where I can find Narong.'

'You could always phone her from my office, you know.'

She mulls this over. There is no real need to go back to the Golden Key. She brought her bag and her one change of clothes to Pattaya and settled the hotel bill before she left. But there is something else making her want to go back there. She senses Kasem's disapproval about her contacting Narong. She would prefer to do that alone.

'No. No it's fine thank you. I'll go back to the hotel. I'll need to sort out a room for tonight. I don't suppose I'll be able to see Narong today even if Malee has managed to find out where he lives.'

Kasem drives her through the heart of the city, along Sukhumvit Road where the lines of traffic crawl along in a shimmering pollution haze. She gazes out at the shops and office blocks, wondering where the alleyway is where Wassanna gave her work at that first bar that fateful day in 1943. The place is transformed though, new buildings line the pavement, and it is impossible to see what might have been there before all the crumbling shophouses were pulled down. The old soi with its squalid line of bars and brothels could well have been completely built over.

When they finally reach New Petchburi they pass large groups of American soldiers already out for the evening, loitering around the windows of the girlie bars. The bars are open, flashing their neon signs, and girls in their platform shoes and mini-skirts stand outside blowing kisses at customers. Kasem pulls into the side street where the Golden Key is and pulls up in front of the hotel.

'Thank you, Kasem. Thank you so much for taking me,' Sirinya says gathering her belongings. 'It meant a lot to me.'

'It is nothing. I only wish you'd let me take you back to Kanchanaburi.'

'It's fine, thank you. I'm more than happy to go on the train. You've done so much. I've taken up quite enough of your time.'

He gets out of the driver's seat and comes around to her side to open the door.

'Will you at least let me know what happens?' he asks, an anxious look on his face, 'What you're going to do? I'll worry about you.'

'Of course. I'll call you. There is really no need to worry.'

She stands on the pavement and watches as Kasem drives off in the battered taxi, then she turns and walks into the hotel lobby. The old man still sits behind the desk watching the television as if he has not moved since she left a day ago. Sirinya signs in and he hands her another giant metal room key. She asks to use the telephone and he nods to the one on the desk beside him. She frowns. She would really like some privacy, and for the television to be turned down, but there is no chance of either of those things. Sighing, she dials Malee's number and to her relief the old man turns his attention back to the television.

Malee answers after a couple of short rings.

'Did you go and see the old lady?' Sirinya asks immediately.

'I did. She is very frail and old Siri. I had trouble getting any sense out of her.'

'Is she still in touch with Narong?'

There is a short silence. 'Not any more, Siri,' Malee says quietly. 'When I asked about Narong she got very tearful. I couldn't understand what she was saying at first, she seemed so distressed she wasn't making any sense. But after a while I understood what she said. Narong died a couple of years ago I'm afraid. Lung cancer, apparently. It is such a shame, Siri. He had two children.'

Sirinya's knees go weak with shock and she sits down heavily on a hard chair beside the reception desk. She is aware that her hands are shaking. The old man flicks his attention away from the television momentarily to glance at her vacantly, his eyebrows raised.

'I can't believe it,' she says at last, her mouth dry. 'Are you absolutely sure, Malee?'

'I'm just repeating what the old lady told me. It's tragic isn't it?'

'He was only a few years older than us. Fifty at the most ... I can't believe it.'

'So now that's an end to it, Siri,' Malee says gently. 'You do know that don't you?'

'It doesn't mean it wasn't him Malee,' Sirinya says, 'Just because he's dead. That makes no difference.'

'But it does mean you won't be able to find out for sure, and you'll just have to find a way to put it behind you.'

'Perhaps ...'

'Why don't you come on home? Get the next train? We hardly had time to talk when you were here before. Let's spend some time together. I miss you, Siri.'

'Of course. I miss you too. I'll come in the morning. There are no more trains today. I'll see you tomorrow, Malee.'

'And will you stay this time? Properly I mean?'

'Yes, Malee,' Sirinya say, realising her eyes are wet with tears. 'This time I'll stay.'

* * *

At first light the next morning, Sirinya stands beside her small suitcase on the platform at Thonburi station. She is waiting for the early train. The city is already awake. She can feel its heartbeat, sense its raw energy. The air is filled with the shrill blasts of horns and the hum of a million engines. In the distance, through the shimmering pollution haze, she sees the glow of lights from traffic crawling along a flyover.

She shifts in the heat. Despite the hour, sweat is already running down the inside of her blouse, but she is used to it now. She thinks about the last time she made this journey, only a few short days ago, and how different things are now, how her homecoming has revealed truths to her about the past and about the present.

She glances at the other travellers waiting on the platform, people returning to their villages from the capital, with bulging packages and bags, baskets of fruit, cages of day-old chicks, buckets of live fish. This time she feels she truly belongs amongst them; part of the crowd, not an outsider any more as she did the last time she made this journey.

Her heart beats a little faster as the old blue and white diesel train creaks into the station. She turns and scans the passengers against not quite understanding why. But then she stops and checks herself. She realises she is looking for Kasem, but of course he is not going to be on the train today. She spoke to him last night after she had finished speaking to Malee. She told him the news about Narong's death.

'I'm sorry to hear that,' he said after a pause. 'Does it mean that you might try to put it all behind you now, though? Move on with your life?'

'I'm not sure, Kasem. I'm not sure I can ever do that.'

'You must, Sirinya. If you don't you'll forever be in limbo, you know, thinking about the past. You'll forever be waiting on that Bamboo Road.'

She swallows, suppressing the tears that threatened. Perhaps he was right.

'I need to get back home,' she says. 'I need to see Malee and I'll spend time at the temple. That might help me come to terms with it all.'

The train comes to a halt beside the platform with a squeak of brakes and Sirinya climbs on and takes her place in third class carriage beside the window. As it rattles through the outskirts on the city past canals, rice paddies, houses built over the water, she stares out at the familiar scenery and begins to feel a calm descend on her. A deep peaceful calm, such as she had not felt for decades.

29

'There's someone to see you in the shop, Siri,' Malee's voice calls up the stairs.

Sirinya glances at her watch. 'He's early,' she mutters to herself and checks her face in the mirror. Then she takes her handbag and sunglasses from the sideboard and makes her way downstairs.

She's been back in Saeng Chuto road for two months now, and this is the first time she'll have seen Kasem since her return, although they have spoken on the phone several times. He telephoned yesterday to say he's borrowing his friend's taxi again and is going to drive up to visit his mother up in Nam Tok instead of taking the train, and does Sirinya want to come with him?

'Perhaps,' she said, tentatively, 'but don't you want to see your mother on your own? You surely don't want to be bothered with company?'

'Not at all. She'd love to meet you. I've told her all about you.'

This alarmed Sirinya. 'I'm not sure,' she said trying to think of an excuse. 'It's quite a long drive,' she said weakly. He laughed and she felt a little guilty that he'd seen through her words.

'We could always stop off on the way,' he said, 'Find a roadside food stall for lunch.'

She hesitated, then an idea came to her. 'Would you mind very much taking a bit of a detour on the way?'

'Of course not. Where would you like to go?'

'It would be good to go back to my old village in the hills. I haven't been there since 1943. It would be interesting to see it. Malee and I have been meaning to get up there, ever since I came back, but we haven't found the time to get round to it yet. I believe there's a single-track road up to the village now.'

Now she reaches the bottom of the stairs and enters the shop. Kasem is standing with his back to her looking out at the street. He turns when he hears her step he comes forward and puts his hands together in a wai, smiling broadly at her.

'Malee, this is Kasem,' she says. 'Kasem, meet Malee, my cousin.'

Malee smiles warmly, 'It is wonderful to meet you, Kasem. Sirinya has told me so much about you,' she says, making a wai. Kasem wais back and bows his head, 'likewise, Malee. It is very nice to meet you too,' then turning to Sirinya he says, 'And how are you, Sirinya? You look so well! So much better than you did in Bangkok.'

'Thank you. That's all down to Malee, and being back home again,' she smiles, thinking how, over the weeks that she has been back at the shophouse, her life has been transformed. She easily slipped into the old routines of the business, getting up early each morning to help Malee with the deliveries, working in the shop to serve fruit and vegetables each day, chatting with customers, taking up old friendships and making new ones amongst the young people. The time has flown by, and she has almost managed to put all thoughts of Narong out of her mind. She has virtually accepted now that she will never know for sure whether he betrayed her and Charlie to the Japanese.

Sometimes, though, she still has dreadful dreams; dreams of the war, of Charlie, his face bloodied and battered, lying on the bare earth in the middle of a scrum of guards being kicked and beaten with sticks. She finds herself sitting bolt upright, sweating, angry with herself for not being able to forget. But her regular trips to the temple, her conversations with the monks and her daily meditations have helped her to cope with her memories. She has mastered the art of meditation and mindfulness again, and for most of the time now she feels settled, at peace. She feels almost as good as she felt as a teenager before the war.

Kasem drives out of town, across the bridge at Tambon Lat Ya and heads east across the river valley towards the Tenasserim hills. They chat easily and the time passes quickly. Sirinya tells Kasem about Malee and the shop, about old acquaintances in the town she's met since her return. She asks what he's been doing and Kasem tells her about how business is booming; many GIs have been into his shop to buy jewellery for their Thai girlfriends, or to take home to America.

'If that dreadful war in Vietnam ever ends,' she murmurs, staring out at the emerald green rice paddies flashing past.

The road begins to rise and zigzag through the hills. After an hour or so they reach the crossroads where in the war years the songthaew used to stop and drop her at the start of the path that wound up through the jungle to the village.

'It's here,' she says and Kasem turns the car onto the single-track road which winds its way up the valley through the thick teak forest. At first the surface is good, but as the road climbs higher it becomes rutted and bumpy where the surface has been worn away by the monsoon, and the engine roars and the wheels spin as Kasem drops a gear and coaxes the old car on. They continue on like that for a couple of kilometres, but eventually the tarmac peters out altogether and the road becomes too muddy for the tyres to gain any grip. Kasem pulls the car half off the track and parks it under the trees.

'Is it far to walk from here?' he asks.

'Not far. I used to walk all the way up from the main road

without any trouble at all.'

'Shall we go then? Or would you prefer to go alone?'

'No, you come with me. I don't even know if anyone will be there who will remember me.'

They get out of the car and start to walk up the track between the green walls of jungle on either side. It is hot and steamy and soon they are both perspiring heavily.

'What happened to your grandmother's land?' he asks.

'Uncle sold it to one of the villagers and sent me the money. By that time I was already in England with Johnny. It was hardly worth anything, but it was useful to the man who bought it. Someone else will have taken over the house. That's how things work in the village. But then you know that, Kasem.'

After half an hour or so the trees begin to thin out and the wooden walls and atap roofs of the village are visible through the vegetation. Three yellow dogs bound up to meet them, their tails wagging, and escort them forwards. They walk along the track between the houses. People come out onto their porches to wai and call greetings to the strangers. To Sirinya the place has hardly changed in twenty-five years, except for the occasional radio aerial protruding from the thatch and the odd motorbike parked under the trees in the shade. Still pigs and chickens root around under the houses and the village children smile and wave just as they did when Sirinya was young. But now there are few faces she recognises.

They walk on and at last Yai's old wooden house comes into view on the far edge of the settlement. Sirinya's heart contracts with guilt once again as she sees it, remembering how Yai must have stood on the porch peering into the darkness, waiting for her and Charlie to appear on that fateful night in 1943.

A woman sits peeling vegetables on the porch of Yai's house. She looks up at Sirinya and smiles. They must be about the same age, and Sirinya recognises her as Lamai, the granddaughter of one of the older women, a contemporary of Yai's.

Lamai gets to her feet and wais to Sirinya.

'Good morning Khun Lamai,' Sirinya says. 'Do you remember me? I used to live in this house.'

'Of course. Of course I do. I remember you and your mother and grandmother very well. Come on up, both of you. I'll make tea. Would you like anything to eat?'

'I don't want to put you to any trouble. I just wanted to come and look at the place again. It's got so many memories for me.'

'I'll just get my grandmother. She is resting. She'd love to see you, I'm sure. She often speaks of your grandmother.'

Sirinya glances at Kasem, who nods and smiles encouragement and they both go up the old familiar steps to the wooden porch where they sit down on cushions.

'Sirinya, my dear,' the voice of an old woman croaks from the doorway. She turns in surprise. For a split second the voice reminds her of Yai. She recognises the old woman who stands there smiling, dressed in a red cotton sarong. She is much stouter than Yai, and Sirinya recognises the kindly eyes and the toothless smile of Pensri, one of Yai's oldest friends.

Sirinya bows and wais to the old woman who moves forward and crouches on the porch. Lamai brings tea in pottery cups and a plate of stuffed banana leaves.

'Please, eat,' she smiles, gesturing at the plate.

Pensri sips her tea and begins to speak.

'I knew you would come back one day, my dear. It was only a matter of time. It is understandable why it took you so long. What you must have been through ... no wonder you kept away. No wonder you went halfway across the world to escape.'

Sirinya drops her eyes to the dusty planks of the porch. She is not sure she wants to speak about this now. This isn't why she came back here. But she can hardly ask the old woman to stop. She must show respect to Pensri owing to her great age. After all she is in Pensri's house, receiving her hospitality.

'Those were dreadful times. Truly terrible times,' the old woman goes on, shaking her head. 'Things happened then ...'

'Hush, Grandmother,' says Lamai, 'Sirinya didn't come back to talk about those times.' Sirinya catches the warning look that Lamai shoots at the old woman, but the old woman lifts her chin and carries on.

'I hope you have forgiven your grandmother for what she did back then. She did it out of love for you, to protect you, you know. She didn't know anyone would die. And it killed her, didn't it? When she realised what she had done, she just lay down in her house; this house, and gave up on life. It was only a short time afterwards. But she knew she couldn't carry on after that. She lost the will to live.'

Bolts of shock course through Sirinya's body. What is the old woman saying? Sirinya's brain is refusing to process the words, her surroundings become a bur, everything around her slows down.

'I don't understand ...'

'You must try to understand why she did it, my dear. Yai only went to talk to the Kempeitai because she wanted to protect you, Siri. To stop you leaving her, to stop you putting yourself in danger. She didn't tell them who you were, but she knew the name of the man you were going to meet. She told them what he was planning so they would stop him leaving the camp and you would come back to the village and stay with her. She was desperate. She did it out of love for you Siri, and because she had lost your mother. She didn't want to lose you too. She couldn't bear the thought of it.'

'This can't be true ...' Sirinya murmurs. She is dimly aware of Kasem's hand reaching out for hers. She takes his and grips it, hanging onto it like a lifeline. Everything else around her feels as though it is spinning out of control.

'Don't you know?' the old woman persists. 'Surely you knew about it? I thought that must be why you ran away. Never came back.'

Sirinya shakes her head, tears blinding her eyes.

'But I've been waiting all these years so I can explain it to you,' the old woman goes on. 'Yai asked me to do that for her before she died. She wanted you to forgive her. I remember being with her when she heard the news that they had executed that poor young man. She just crumbled and fell apart. She went into the house here, lay down and never got up again.'

Sirinya puts down the tea, slopping it on the boards of the porch and gets to her feet.

'I'm sorry, but I think I should go now,' her voice is shaking.

Lamai gets up too. 'Please. Please don't be angry. My grandmother doesn't know what she is saying. Forgive her.'

'There is no need for forgiveness, please,' says Pensri, leaning forward, looking up into Sirinya's eyes. 'I am just passing on a message from Yai. I've waited a long time to do that. It is Yai she needs to forgive.'

Sirinya walks blindly to the steps and goes down them.

'Please don't go like this,' Lamai's face is a picture of shame and distress. 'You are my guest. Please, won't you stay?'

'I'm sorry. I have to go. Thank you. Thank you for your hospitality.'

Sirinya turns and hurries away from the house. As she walks she hears Kasem's voice thanking Lamai, and his quick footsteps behind her catching her up. He draws parallel to her and they walk silently side by side out of the village, the dogs and children following at a distance, seeming to sense her need to get away. They pass the last wooden houses and reach the start of the track where the jungle begins. They carry on walking in silence. Sirinya stares at the ground, tears blurring her vision. After a few moments she feels Kasem's arm slip around her shoulders and pull her towards him. She doesn't resist and as they walk she moves closer to the reassuring warmth of his body, leaning against him, letting him support her. The great teak trees close around them as they walk and the jungle canopy closes above them, blotting out the sun.

MORE BY ANN BENNETT

In 1943, Thomas Ellis, captured by the Japanese at the fall of Singapore, is a prisoner-of-war on the Death Railway in Thailand. Forty years later, his daughter, Laura, travels from London to Southeast Asia to retrace her father's past and discover the truths he has refused to tell her. In a blend of stirring fiction and heart-wrenching history, Ann Bennett narrates the story of a soldier's strength and survival in the bleakest of times and a daughter's journey of discovery about her father and herself.

Juliet Crosby has lived a reclusive life on her Malayan rubber plantation since the Second World War robbed her of everyone she loved. However, the sudden appearance of a young woman from Indonesia disrupts her lonely existence and stirs up unsettling memories. Juliet is forced to recollect her prewar marriage, her wartime ordeals in Japanese-occupied Singapore and the loss of those she once held dear.

Bamboo Heart, *Bamboo Island* and *Bamboo Road* form a Southeast Asian WWII trilogy of historical fiction that can be read in any order.